Readers are gripped by John Connor

'It'll be the rare reader able to put *A Child's Game* down after a chapter or so . . . the police procedural novel is given the kind of spruce-up it has been in need of for some time' *Daily Express*

'This is a first-rate thriller with a terrific climax'
Sunday Telegraph

'Sharpe is a welcome addition to British fiction's police service' *Observer*

'Top notch . . . meticulous attention to detail and complex characterisation' *Daily Record*

'John Connor's debut novel *Phoenix* starts as just about the most impressively detailed police procedural that I've ever read . . . I have high hopes that this new series will turn out to be something a bit special' *Morning Star*

'Leeds-based barrister John Connor drives his complex tale of secrecy and betrayal along at a cracking pace. Not for the faint-hearted, but highly recommended'
Irish Independent

'He's created a beguilingly complex character, perfectly suited to his taut thrillers' *Daily Mirror*

'A riveting tale, with a thrilling climax' *Yorkshire Post*

John Connor left his job as a barrister to write full time. During the fifteen years of his legal career he prosecuted numerous homicide cases in West Yorkshire and London. He advised the police in numerous proactive drugs and organised crime operations, many involving covert activity. He now lives in Brussels with his wife and two children. His novel *Falling*, a part of the Karen Sharpe series, was shortlisted for the prestigious Portico Prize for Literature.

Also by John Connor

Phoenix
The Playroom
A Child's Game
Falling
Unsafe
The Vanishing
The Ice House

A Child's Game

A Karen Sharpe Thriller

JOHN CONNOR

ORION

First published in Great Britain in 2006
by Orion,
This paperback edition published in 2019
by Orion Fiction,
an imprint of The Orion Publishing Group Ltd
Carmelite House, 50 Victoria Embankment
London EC4Y 0DZ

An Hachette UK Company

1 3 5 7 9 10 8 6 4 2

A CIP catalogue record for this book is
available from the British Library.

ISBN 978 1 4091 8879 7

Typeset at The Spartan Press Ltd,
Lymington, Hants

Printed and bound in Great Britain by Clays Ltd,
Elcograf S.p.A.

MIX
Paper from
responsible sources
FSC® C104740

www.orionbooks.co.uk

For Anna

Very special thanks to Yvette Goulden.

*Thanks again to John Markham, Ray Dance,
Max McLean (West Yorkshire Police).*

*Thanks to Sue Hogg (BBC), Phil Patterson
and Luke Speed (Marjacq Scripts).*

*And thanks again to Rachel Leyshon,
for so many excellent suggestions.*

Friday, 31 December 1999

ONE

Stijn could feel the man shivering. After they had poured the petrol over him the look in his eyes had changed. He had known then that there was no point in trying to shout or struggle. Shouting just meant the gag would be tightened until he choked, and Stijn doubted he had strength left to struggle. Akhtar, the *kaffir* he had been told to use as local help – the man now cursing and swearing from the far corner of the apartment – had beaten the man so badly he might die anyway. Akhtar had used a broken chair leg, lashing out at the man's head and face before Stijn could get it off him.

Stijn had asked him if he could handle violence before they set off. Akhtar had smirked, as if insulted by the question. That was three or four hours before they got here. But within seconds of it starting, Stijn had known he had made a mistake.

He doubted Akhtar had hit anyone in his life. His movements were too full of fright – thrashing around without aiming, anxious to get it over with. Stijn had told him not to cause injuries that would bleed. Yet he had picked up the chair leg and struck the man's head, retching as he did it.

There was a lot of blood coming from a gash at the crest of the man's skull. Some of it was running over Stijn's hand, irritating him. The man was going into shock; his breathing was rapid and shallow, his pulse slowing. Shock alone would kill him, if they left him to it. But that wasn't what he had been told to do.

So now everything reeked of petrol fumes and he would

have to discard all his clothing, scrub down and bathe to eliminate the odour and the evidence. It was a typical *kaffir* thing, he thought, to want the man burned. In this case there was good reason, but he had heard they went for it anyway, regardless of reasons. In Pakistan the favoured form of political violence was pulling people off trains and setting fire to them. He didn't like burning people. The odours were unpleasant. But in South Africa he had smelled worse things in common jails.

As a child he had watched roebuck in the veldt, caught in metal snares, struggling for hours on end, dislocating their bones, tearing apart sinew and muscle as they tried to escape. But when the time came to take them out and kill them they would just lie there, a helplessness in their eyes, completely calm; partly because they were exhausted, partly because they were just animals. Because they had no real conception of death they could reach a point where there was no longer any fear, just the waiting. That was where this man was now. Waiting.

He had been an animal when they had first bound him – something mad, without any capacity for reason or ability to control his fear. It had sickened Stijn to witness the loss of dignity – the pleading and begging, the whimpering as they struck him, calling out someone's name. *Susie* – maybe she was his wife, or his mother. He had read that dying people shouted for their mothers, though he had never seen it before and couldn't imagine doing it himself. But he had hardly known his own mother.

The petrol fumes had put things in perspective. Now the man was just shivering; he knew what was going to happen. To fight was pointless – Stijn had his hand on the back of his neck, a hand so large he could practically close it around the throat. The man had been overpowered even

4

before Akhtar had botched it with the chair leg. Stijn looked down at him. He was small, perhaps half his size and weight, with the same soft, helpless eyes he had seen on the roebuck.

It made Stijn uneasy. Perhaps he should say something to the man – to help him out. But that was impossible. The man was alone now; no one could help him. Besides, it might start him struggling again. Sympathy weakened people. The man stank – of sweat, fear, piss, of blood and desperation, of petrol. He needed putting out of his misery.

'You should have paid your debts,' Stijn said to him, regretting it immediately. The bastard probably couldn't even hear him. He was slumped on a high-backed chair, legs bound tightly at the ankles, hands tied behind his back. The gag was a dishcloth of some sort. Where it was pulled into his mouth there was blood bubbling over it, a bright frothy blood that must have been coming from his lungs. Akhtar had stamped on his chest with both feet, long after he had been capable of doing anything to protect himself.

Stijn looked over to Akhtar, angry with him. He was at the sink, panicking, trying to stop his hand from bleeding. Somehow or other he had cut himself as he struck the man. It would need stitches. Stijn had already told him that, expecting him to just wrap a rag around it and leave it at that. But Akhtar was running water on it, looking for medicines or bandages in the cabinet above the kitchen sinks. He had already pulled the bathroom apart to no avail.

Stijn checked his watch. It was 3.57 a.m.

'We have to go,' he said quietly. 'You've messed around for long enough.'

Akhtar looked over to him, fear in his eyes. 'I am leaving my blood all over this place—'

5

'It's too late to worry about that. We will burn it as we leave. Write the note, like I told you to.'

'Burn the place? But what about him?' Akhtar pointed at the man.

'Write the note,' Stijn said. He had told Akhtar the bare minimum, but the *kaffir* was afraid of him. He would do as he was told.

When the note was in the metal safe in the bedroom closet Stijn told Akhtar to watch the man. Then he walked through the main room of the apartment and opened the sliding doors leading to the narrow balcony. He stood for a moment in the freezing night air, looking out at the city. Intermittent traffic noises mingled with the sounds of drunken youths.

It was a penthouse apartment and they were nine floors up. Below him the place called Leeds lay in an asymmetrical pattern of light. To the north low wedges of darkness cut into it. He guessed they were hills, but the night was too black to be sure. The sky was thick with low cloud, obscuring the moon. The building he was in was one of the highest in the city centre.

He walked to the parapet – about two feet wide – and looked over the edge, feeling the tingling in the backs of his knees which had once signalled a fear of heights. The drop was straight into a narrow alleyway, filled with garbage containers. Not high enough to guarantee death, as he knew from the mistakes of others. People had lived and spoken of it after dropping from almost double this height.

There was a short ladder fixed to the wall beside the sliding doors, leading up onto the flat roof. He climbed it and looked over the top, just to make sure no one was there. Then he went back in.

'Take one,' he said to Akhtar, pointing at the three plastic petrol containers standing by the door. 'You do the office downstairs. I'll do up here. Douse the desks and paperwork. Don't bother with the walls. Lead a line up the back stairwell into the bedroom through there.'

'Is it safe to do this?' Akhtar's voice was high-pitched. Stijn knew he wanted to ask about the man again, but didn't dare.

'Don't light it yet. Just spread it. And be quick – the fumes are noxious.'

He watched until he had disappeared through a doorway leading to a short stairwell, then checked the man. His eyes were closed now, the breathing irregular. He left him, unscrewed a cap from a container and began to lay thick lines of petrol from all the combustible objects in the room back towards the doorway. The floor was expensive parquet and the liquid spread quickly across the varnished surface.

The flat was in a development which Stijn guessed would count for prestigious in this part of the world. In the heart of the city centre, the single tower overlooked a relatively new shopping complex with a glass atrium, through which he could see crowds of young people still busy with alcohol, even at this early hour. The top floors of the block were office space for the financial and legal sectors in the city. He knew because he had checked the place carefully. The flat they were in was connected to one such office on the floor below, but was the only residential letting in the building. It would have come at a price.

Yet there were few items of furniture for Stijn to set alight: an austere leather sofa; a wide-screen TV; the chair he had sat the man on, another he had broken during the struggle, a couple of tables, a wooden double bed in the bedroom – without sheets or quilt – a set of wardrobes

7

containing only the (empty) safe and some old newspapers; on the walls there was just one picture – ironically, a view of Cape Town and Table Mountain at dawn; in the bathroom no toilet roll, soap or toothpaste. There weren't even pot plants or bookshelves.

He finished before Akhtar and took hold of the man by the legs, pulling him off the chair and onto the floor. The back of the head banged sharply off the ground. Stijn dragged him by the feet to the sliding doors, then bent down and took out his clasp knife. He pressed the point gently against the man's throat, getting no response at all. Quickly he cut the plastic ties binding the hands and feet, then sawed through the gag and pulled it from the mouth. He carefully pocketed all three items. The man began to gasp a little, but his eyes were closed now. Stijn took hold of his feet again and dragged him onto the balcony.

The outside air already felt fresh by contrast. As a precaution against the fumes Stijn pulled the sliding door shut behind them. Then he hoisted the man by the shoulders until he was leaning forwards, over the parapet, bent at the waist. He thought he could hear him saying something, but the mouth was too damaged for it to make sense. His arms dangled over the side.

Stijn stepped back, took out his Zippo and lit it. Without pausing he held it to the jacket the man had on, waiting a second for it to catch. It ignited with a percussive rush, like a gas ring lit after being left on, the blue flames flashing momentarily into his face before blazing yellow and orange, so hot Stijn felt his eyebrows singe. He stepped back and watched, fascinated.

The flames spread quickly. They had caught the layers of clothing beneath the jacket and were wriggling through the man's hair before he began to react. As he tried to move Stijn quickly picked up his legs and heaved him forwards. The torso caught on the parapet and Stijn saw the head twist towards him, eyes open. The expression was one of confusion, not pain. Stijn could see him trying to focus even as the flames raced around his head. He opened his mouth, gasping at the air like a goldfish. The flames had caught in his trousers now – within seconds he would be completely engulfed. His arms came to life, flailing at the air around his head. Stijn stepped back and kicked him. The body jerked backwards, tilting over the edge. The hands were still slapping at his burning hair as he went over. There was no attempt to stop the fall, no noise, no screaming. Just one moment he was there, the next he was gone. Where he had been leaning against the parapet he left a small cloud of acrid smoke and a whiff of burned skin.

Stijn didn't look over the side to check. Ducking quickly back through the doors he ran into Akhtar coming in the other direction, terror on his face. He was shouting at him: 'What have you done?'

Stijn walked past him towards the door. 'You started this,' he said. 'These are *your* consequences.'

Akhtar looked paralysed, torn between wanting to go out onto the balcony to verify what he had seen and the urge to run from Stijn.

'We have to get out of here fast,' Stijn said. He checked that the door back down to the office was pulled open, checked the line of petrol that Akhtar had trailed through it. It would be better to set the fire on both floors, but he had no time now. He opened the main door to the room – the one leading to the fire exit and lifts – then took out the Zippo again. In the room the petrol fumes were suffocating. He stepped out into the hallway and called back to Akhtar.

'It's going to get uncomfortable in here. You coming?'

When Akhtar was past him he slid the burning lighter across the floor.

TWO

The alarm clock beside her bed said 4.35 a.m. It took Liz Hodges a few moments to work out why she was looking at it. The knocking sound she could hear wasn't in her dream. Someone was at her front door.

She pulled on a dressing gown and walked to the bedroom window. She lived in a cul-de-sac on the outskirts of Gargrave, just west of Skipton. Gargrave itself had less than two thousand inhabitants and there were only five other houses on her street. It was hard for people to make a mistake about what house they were looking for. She felt nervous as she peered carefully around the side of the heavy felt curtains she had brought with her from London three years ago.

There were two cars parked up on her driveway. One of them wasn't hers. From her position she couldn't see below the porch to her front door, so had no idea who was standing there – or how many there were. But the car pulled up behind her own – blocking it in – contained two rear-seat passengers. They looked male, though the nearest streetlamp was two houses away. She reached for her phone and listened again to the knocking. A gentle, polite tap, nothing urgent or alarming about it. Except the time. She watched lights go on and curtains twitch in the houses of the Armstrongs, directly opposite, and the Byfields, next door but one. She felt slightly reassured.

She had suffered no problems since she had moved to Yorkshire, but she had left a lot of problems behind. It was always possible that one of them would catch up with her one day. The phone was a cordless model with a memory. She skipped down through the numbers until she had the emergency number they had given her when she had first arrived. Below her, on her front path, she saw a male step out of the darkness of her porch and look up to her windows. She kept still.

He appeared to be looking directly at her, though she doubted he could see anything other than a dark gap between the curtain and the wall. Liz thought he looked very definitely official. She exhaled a little. He was wearing a smart trench coat, the collar not turned up and, beneath that, a suit and tie. His shoes looked polished. His face was young, hard.

Suddenly the phone in her hand began to ring. She started slightly, then looked down for the number. It was withheld. She stepped back into the shadows and answered it.

'Miss Hodges?' A quiet male voice.

'Yes. Who is that?'

'Francis Doyle. Do you remember me?'

She tried to think. The name rang bells. She stepped up to the window and peered out again. The first man had been joined by a second. He had his back to her and was speaking into a mobile phone.

'I don't think I do,' she said.

'I brought you up here. Three years ago.'

She recalled now. She smiled slightly, relieved. Of all the people whose hands she had been passed through he had been the most sympathetic. She had needed sympathy.

'Yes,' she said.

'I'm standing outside your house. Are you in?'

She had a moment of relief, quickly replaced by confusion. What were they doing here?

'I'll let you in,' she said.

Doyle had aged. She watched him scrutinizing her from the doorstep. His stockier colleague hung back in the shadows.

'What's the matter?' she asked.

'We're looking for Karen Sharpe.'

She frowned. 'At this time of night?'

'Yes. Is she with you?'

'No. Why would she be?'

'You're a friend of hers.'

'I was. I haven't seen her for over a year. Why are you—'

'Can I come in?'

'Of course.'

She let him walk past her and waited for the other to follow.

'He will stay there,' Doyle said. 'Just shut the door on him. It's OK.'

She led him through to her sitting room. He looked around, listening, as if he might find Sharpe behind one of the sofas.

'When did you last see her?' he asked.

'I don't recall. Has something happened to her?'

He turned to face her. 'I hope not. But she may be in danger. Can I look upstairs?'

She felt herself becoming annoyed. 'Why? Don't you believe me?'

He held his hands up, shrugging. 'I just have to do my job. You know how it is.'

'Well, maybe I should see some ID,' she said. 'It's very late.'

He smiled at her, reaching into his jacket pocket. 'But you know me. You know who I am.'

'I know who you said you were three years ago. I don't

13

know who you are now. I don't even know who you work for.'

He held a strip of plastic in front of her face. 'I still work for the police. For Witness Protection.'

She looked at the ID. It was an ordinary Metropolitan Police warrant card. She nodded. 'OK. Look upstairs. If you have to.'

It didn't take him long. She sat down on the sofa and waited. She had been about to offer him a tea before he had asked to search the place. She heard him opening cupboards and doors, pulling down the ladder to the loft and climbing up.

'It's a nice place you have here,' he said, when he returned. He brushed dust off his coat – a cheap-looking anorak, not like the more expensive thing the man outside was wearing. 'Is everything OK with you?'

'Everything's fine,' she said. 'Is Karen a witness, then? A witness you've lost?'

'Not a witness, no.' He dug around in his wallet and produced a business card. She took it and read 'Sergeant Francis Doyle: Diplomatic Protection Service'. She didn't think it worth querying the two different IDs. She had learnt that three years ago. He was never going to say who he really worked for.

'If you hear from her, give me a call.'

'I already have your number.'

'You have Sutherland's number. Call the one I've given you. It's quicker.'

'So she *is* lost?'

'Lost?' He frowned, as if he didn't understand the word. 'We need to find her quickly. That's all.'

'I thought she was with you lot. I thought that's why she disappeared.'

'Did she disappear?'

She scowled and stood up. 'You know she did. You should have been watching her. She has a child with her. She's your responsibility.'

He looked uncomfortable for a moment. 'I'm just doing what I'm told to do,' he said. 'If she contacts you, call me. Even if she asks you not to. She probably doesn't realize how much danger she's in.'

From the front door she watched the car pull off the driveway and turn around. She waved at Fred Armstrong – still at his upstairs window, watching out for her – letting him know everything was all right, then she went back in to think about it.

DC Karen Sharpe had been her local police contact when she had first arrived here. Karen wasn't from North Yorkshire Police, who covered Gargrave, but from the larger West Yorkshire force, just to the south. North Yorkshire police had been told nothing about Liz.

Karen had befriended her, looked after her. Not as part of her job, but because someone had asked her to, someone from a world she had once been part of. Someone Francis Doyle would know. Karen had understood what Liz had been through because she had endured a similar situation herself. By happy coincidence her daughter, Mairead, had also been in Liz's class at the local school. Or maybe not such a coincidence, since the people Doyle worked for had virtually set up the teaching job in the first place. In those days Karen had lived only five minutes' drive from Gargrave. Through that and other things Liz had got to know Karen well, but not as well as she had thought.

She walked up the stairs to the room she used as a study and sifted through an envelope full of photos. She was wide awake now. She found one of Karen, Mairead, Pete Bains and herself, and checked the date on the back:

January 1998. Time had passed quicker than she thought. It was in fact nearly two years since she had last seen Karen Sharpe. Just over twenty-one months since Karen had so suddenly left them. She looked at the image of them all smiling, together. Karen was bending over slightly, face in profile, saying something to Mairead. She looked worn, but still happy. A tall figure with too-thin limbs and shoulder-length dark hair, almost as tall as Liz herself. She had a pair of jeans on, so her legs were covered, but Liz could remember clearly the still healing gunshot wound to her right thigh. The photo had been taken six months after the shooting, but the injury had still given her trouble. Pete had one arm over Karen's shoulder, the other holding Mairead's hand. Liz was standing a little to the side. She had placed the camera on a rock and taken the picture on a timer.

She selected Pete Bains's mobile number and called it. He answered almost at once.

'Pete?'

'Liz. What's wrong?'

She paused. Things had moved on a little since January 1998. Something was developing between Pete and herself, something intimate and relatively new. She wasn't clear what it should be called, wasn't comfortable with the idea that they were 'together', but there was definitely something starting. She had met him through Karen though, and neither of them could forget that. Around the same time the photo had been taken Karen had sold her house and moved into Pete's place in Bradford. When Karen had walked out on them Liz had lost a friend, but Pete had lost much more than that. Even if he were over Karen, Mairead had been like a daughter to him. Liz had to be sensitive.

'Have you had a visit?' she asked.

'A visit?' Bains sounded confused.

She remembered the time. 'Sorry. It's early. Were you asleep?'

'No. I'm at the Bridewell, still on duty. I've been trying to get away all night. A visit from who?'

'Witness Protection. They just left me. They were asking for Karen.'

'Witness Protection?'

'That's what they said. But they're never who they say they are.' She listened to the silence on the other end. 'They thought I might be hiding her.' Still silence. What would she feel if Karen were with him, if he were to tell her that? 'So I thought maybe—'

'I haven't seen her,' he said, reading her thoughts. 'Have you?'

Despite herself, for a moment she felt relieved. 'No. I'm calling to warn you. They will come to you next, I think.'

'Then I'll tell them the truth. She walked out twenty-one months ago and I've heard nothing from her since. You know that.'

Liz paused, thinking about it. He thought she had called to accuse him. Maybe she had. 'I'm worried about her,' she said finally. 'They say she's in danger—'

'She made choices, Liz. She took her daughter with her. She's not our problem.'

'I know, but—'

'No buts about it. She made a choice. We can't help. We've moved on.'

They both listened to their thoughts for a while. She heard someone calling for Bains.

'I have to go, Liz,' he said. 'I've got a death in. Someone jumped from a fire in a nine-storey block in the city centre. They say he was burning as he fell. I'll try to ring you later.'

17

She nodded silently, trying to ignore the chewed-up morsel of his working world he had innocently dropped into her mind.

'OK?'

'OK,' she said.

'Remember: she's not our problem.'

THREE

Anna Hart dreamed she was floating. She had this kind of dream often. Tonight she was submerged beneath a deep stretch of profound blue ocean. She had no difficulty breathing. She was on her back, skimming through the water, moving without effort, weightless. She wore no clothes, but the water was warm, moving gently around her skin, supporting her. She could hear whale noises in the distance and far, far above her she could see waves rippling the surface. As she turned to slide upwards the water was fractured by bright shafts of sunlight, slanting down towards her. She felt ecstatic.

Something kept pulling at her though – a voice, a noise. Still half asleep, she turned away from it and pulled the quilt above her ears. Too late – she had registered the sound: a telephone was ringing and someone was shaking her shoulders. She opened her eyes. Her eleven-year-old daughter was standing by the side of the bed, holding the phone. She groaned.

Rachel's brow was creased with worry. 'That was the alarm call. It's five o'clock.'

'Alarm call? For what?'

Then she remembered. She sat up. They were in a hotel just west of Leeds/Bradford airport. They had arrived the night before in order to make an early start. She had booked an alarm call for 5 a.m. and the taxi would be here in half an hour.

She pushed herself to the side of the bed, waiting for the sleep to clear from her eyes. Rachel had that intense look that schedules of any sort provoked in her.

'It's all right,' Anna said. 'I'm awake. Stop worrying.' Her daughter was already dressed. 'Did you wash?'

'I showered.'

'And I didn't hear?' Anna rubbed her hands through her own cropped blonde hair. She felt she needed another four hours. 'I don't know whether I can be bothered—'

'Mum! We have to get going now!'

Anna stood up. 'I'm joking, Rachel. Why do you get so panicky?'

'I'm not panicky. I'm excited. I don't want to miss the plane—'

'It's a charter plane. It can't leave without us.'

'Not that one. The one at the other end.'

The other end. The references to their unknown destination had long ago become tiresome. Her daughter had been obsessed with this trip ever since Nick had announced it two weeks ago. Anna herself had shared the excitement originally – at least in some small way (Rachel had been so keen it was difficult not to get excited) – and she could understand why Nick would want to increase Rachel's interest by keeping their final destination secret, but she had long ago ceased to understand why he couldn't tell *her*. She was thirty-nine years old.

As a surprise gift he had specially chartered a Lear jet to fly them direct to Paris, from where they were to board a scheduled flight to a destination he would not disclose, to see in the 'New Millennium'. Anna guessed they would be flying east to get closer to time zones where the Millennium would first arrive, but it was difficult, from what he had given them of the itinerary, to work out where. They had to leave early in order to fly a long distance, she supposed, but it couldn't be too far, otherwise they would miss midnight altogether. Not to the South Sea Islands, for instance.

She wouldn't have chosen this trip for herself. Not at her age, perhaps not even when she had been younger. Nick knew that, of course. He was ten years older than her and it wasn't something he would have chosen either. There was something excessive yet cheap about it – flying thousands of miles just to see in a New Year. Last year they had opted to join a small group of friends at Tiny Chadwick's place in Argyle; a low-key and relaxing affair. But this was a case of putting Rachel first and both Anna and Nick having to make the best of it. The destination would at least be comfortable and tasteful. She consoled herself with the knowledge that other parents had to endure trips to places like Disneyland. At least that sort of thing had never interested Rachel.

Originally Nick should have been with them, and they should have flown out a week earlier. Anna had an opening at her gallery in York on 4 January 2000 so the trip couldn't be prolonged into the New Year, but the week before, including Christmas Day, had been clear. Two key estate sales in Northumberland had messed things up. Because of them, Nick couldn't get away at all. Wherever they were going he was set to arrive separately, flying by different routes, once he had closed the deals in the north.

As she stepped out of the shower Rachel presented her with an ugly-looking cup of instant coffee, made from the facilities left in the room. She could see it was instant because there were small lumps of the stuff floating on top of the puddle of UHT milk muddying the surface.

'You're a star, Rach,' she said, appreciating it nevertheless. She sat down on the edge of the bed and sipped at it.

'Your mobile bleeped as well.' Rachel handed her the phone. 'It's the same message you had six times yesterday.'

Anna took it off her and read the text message on

the screen: '*TIME TO CHANGE YOUR MOBILE. CHANGE YOUR MOBILE URGENTLY.*'

'The mobile company again,' she said.

'The number wasn't Orange. It was withheld.'

'So?'

'So why would they do that if they were just trying to sell you something?'

'You think it's *not* someone trying to sell me something?'

'I don't know, Mum. I just think you should think about it.'

Anna frowned at her, still half asleep.

'Shall I go to the foyer and wait for the cab?' Rachel said.

'What good would that do?'

'In case he arrives and we're not there.'

The cab had been booked at the last minute – something which had also preoccupied Rachel (she had developed a view that last-minute things were all unreliable). They had driven to the hotel in Anna's Range Rover the afternoon before in order to avoid driving in the dark on roads that might well have been icy in the early hours of the morning. Their home – Black Carr Hall, on the outskirts of Reeth in Swaledale – was no more than forty miles from Leeds/Bradford airport, as the crow flies, but the road through Swaledale was poor and treacherous in winter conditions. So much so that they would normally use the airport in Cleveland if they needed to fly anywhere. Nick had insisted Rachel and Anna stay in a hotel near the airport and travel down during daylight hours. Then he had called near to midnight from Newcastle, worried about them driving even the short distance to the airport during the early hours and urging them instead to hire a minicab.

'The hotel might be locked and he might not be able to find us,' Rachel insisted.

'There's someone on reception all night. I checked.'

'If we're not ready he might go.'

'He wouldn't earn much money like that, would he?' Anna said.

'Can't you drink the coffee and get dressed at the same time, Mum? We've only got ten minutes.'

Anna looked at her daughter. The twitchiness over deadlines and schedules was a relatively new development in her life and usually nothing more than curious. She would run ahead to call the lift in Harvey Nichols, for instance, then be visibly agitated at the prospect of the doors closing before her mother had caught up. Or be ready to meet the man they employed to drive her to school at least fifteen minutes ahead of time, each and every morning, but only by omitting to eat breakfast.

But under conditions such as these, the fear of missing something, of not quite being on time, could threaten to upset her so much it would spoil everything. Just last week Nick had managed to wind her up so much about being late for a school concert that she had begun to cry.

'We will make it, Rachel. We've an hour in hand once we get to Paris.'

'But we have to check in.'

'We're in business class. It will be quick. Come over here.' She waited until Rachel was standing in front of her. Anna was tall – just over six feet, without heels. If anything her daughter was going to be taller; she was easily the tallest member of her class at school. Her facial structure was impressive; high cheekbones and thin features that would tend to the bony if she ever lost her appetite.

'Are you excited about this trip?' Anna asked her.

'Of course. I just don't want to—'

'So am I. So trust me and relax. Think about it. Think about what you are worrying about. Will I get you there or not?'

She watched her consider it. She looked intelligent, Anna thought, though the impression might have been triggered by no more than the crease in the centre of her forehead. Nick liked it (he had one too) but Anna thought she frowned too much and had even had her sight tested, just in case. Her eyesight was perfect, the cause being nothing more than concentration. At least she did try to concentrate, Anna told herself. She ran a hand through Rachel's hair. It was thick and at the moment jet-black (she had dyed it three weeks before, without telling Anna she was going to). This morning it was hanging loose and long, pushed back over her ears and reaching almost to the middle of her shoulders.

'Will I get you there?' Anna asked again.

'Well, we missed the train in Amsterdam in June because you slept in longer than—'

Anna smiled. 'I've learned from that mistake though. You gave me so much shit it could never happen again.'

Rachel frowned at her. 'You need to get ready.'

'A kiss?'

Rachel gave her a quick hug and pecked her cheek. As Anna let go of her she could tell her daughter wasn't in the slightest bit reassured.

She dressed quickly in stretchy black Swaine moleskins, soft calfskin Tod's, a plain white T-shirt under a buttermilk suede jacket and a pale cashmere throw. She folded her big mohair winter coat unceremoniously into the Tote. If it were cold in the cab she could put it on. Aside from the coat her clothing wasn't too practical for UK winter conditions, but one of the few things she had managed to get out of Nick was that it would be warmer where they were going.

In the end they arrived at the foyer on time and exactly as the taxi was pulling in to the turning circle outside. The driver looked tired. Anna stood in the freezing early-morning air, trying to wake herself up, as Rachel fussed around with the baggage. The hotel was built on a chalet model, with low buildings hidden in a newly planted birch forest. It was practical, clean and close to the airport. They had only had to put up with it for one night.

The entrance was surrounded by the more mature woodland which led up to the Otley Chevin, about a mile away. She looked at the trees flanking the driveway, dark lines obscuring the view to the country road beyond. Her car would remain parked here until they returned. Anna shivered and listened uneasily to the night silence.

She didn't like darkness. What she craved was light – bright, bruising Mediterranean light and heat, afternoons full of dust and silence, drenched in sunlight. Her taste in art was the same. Though most of the works she exhibited were modern, the styles she really liked were those that fed on the heritage of Corot or Pissarro. Everything came down to light. They had a house in Provence, where the light was just as she wanted it to be, but getting to it was a hassle requiring a good two-week break. She couldn't afford the luxury of that much time off.

Through the branches of the trees the sky was black, filled with low cloud, not a star in sight. The ground was covered with a crisp frost, but so far there was no snow. It was still too early for the birds and when the taxi driver switched off the engine of his Mercedes the silence was almost total. Almost. Anna's breath puffed out in front of her face as her eyes followed the driveway back into the trees and she picked out the source of the noise spoiling the quiet: a faint red glow deep within the trees, probably the brake lights of a parked car on the country road. Evidently they were not the only ones leaving early. She fished around in her pocket for her cigarettes.

'Let's go, Mum! You haven't got time for those filthy things!'

She sighed and put them away. Her daughter would never let her smoke within the confines of the taxi.

The car was too warm inside, the heating on full blast, the windows steamed up. She sat in the back, beside Rachel.

'Sorry to get you up so early,' she said to the driver as he started the engine.

'No problem. I work nights. This my last trip now.' His English was heavily accented. There was a pennant of some sort hanging from the rear-view mirror, with swirls of Arabic script in gold on a green background. He looked about fifty years old, and was dressed in white traditional clothing, with a tight round headcap. His skin was a leathery colour, the beard on his cheeks neatly clipped.

'Where you want to go?' he asked.

'Just to the airport.'

'Manchester airport?'

'No, Leeds/Bradford. I told them that when I booked you. It's only five minutes away.'

She watched his eyes scrutinizing her in the mirror.

'We have an early flight,' she said.

He shrugged and started off. She rubbed her hand across the window to her right, clearing it. As they drove up the driveway she looked for the car she had seen parked up, but it had gone.

'What time is your flight?' he asked her as they turned onto the country road. 'They don't have flights this early.'

'It's a specially chartered flight,' she said.

He shrugged again. 'Don't matter. They're not allowed to take off for another hour at least.'

She looked at her wristwatch. Five thirty-four. The flight was chartered for six. 'This one will,' she said.

'I don't think the airport will be open,' he persisted.

'My daddy has booked the flight specially,' Rachel said. 'The airport will *have* to be open.'

Anna saw the pride in her expression give way to confusion. She reached out a hand and patted her leg, mouthing, '*Don't worry*', then glanced behind.

'What are you looking for?' Rachel asked.

'I saw a car,' she said. 'I was just . . .' Headlights came into view on the road behind. She looked forward and saw that the driver had seen them too. A dry-stone wall and trees slipped past them. In the narrow headlight beams of the taxi the air looked as if it were full of tiny particles of glinting frost. She could see a junction coming up.

She turned back to look at the headlights again. They were catching up too quickly. She could even hear the car's engine now. She was about to make a comment when the driver began to swear. She twisted in her seat again. There was no doubt about it. The car behind was travelling too fast. Either it would have to brake sharply or run in to them. The single-lane road was too narrow for it to pass. As it closed Anna turned away from the head-lights, now too dazzling to look at. Facing forwards she felt a surge of adrenalin in her neck.

'It's going to hit us,' she said to herself, then shouted it out loud, '*It's going to hit us!*' She saw Rachel staring up at her (saw that she was wearing her seatbelt) and yelled the words again: '*It's going to hit us!*' Panic flashed in Rachel's eyes. Anna was reaching out a hand to her when the vehicle struck.

The noise was tremendous, a massive clash of metal on

metal. She saw Rachel snapped forwards against her seatbelt, a thousand tiny pieces of glass erupting over head. She felt the car beginning to spin. The driver was shouting from the front. Rachel began to scream. Behind them she could hear the squealing of brakes, an engine bigger and louder than their own at full revs. The initial impact turned into a grinding sound. The two cars were jammed together, skidding across the road. She felt herself flung to the side, her head banging off the window. She could see the dry-stone wall hurtling towards them.

The taxi hit the wall rear end on, spun through 360 degrees then stopped dead in the middle of the road. Anna's body sprang back against the seat, jerking her head backwards. As she fell forward in the seat she caught a rush of freezing air through the shattered back window. Then silence. She couldn't even hear Rachel breathing.

FOUR

Francis Doyle sat in the warm interior of the Volvo and felt the dread filling his gut. Everything was moving too slowly. No one was taking this seriously enough, not even Sutherland, who had told him Karen Sharpe was AWOL. He thought she was probably back with Pete Bains. But Doyle kept people alive by assuming the worst. They had put out numerous Priority One Recalls and she had failed to respond. That should have meant 'immediate recovery', using all the manpower they had spare.

But Sutherland wouldn't do it. Doyle had argued with him, but got nowhere. Either Sutherland was allowing Sharpe's volatility to cloud his judgement, or something else was going on. He had given Doyle only three men, each of them so clumsy that Doyle couldn't risk letting them loose alone.

Outside the car, one of them – Brian White – was in front of Bains's house, hunched over the locks to the front door. He had been struggling for over ten minutes. Luckily the place was a detached house, well back from the road and screened by trees, with enough room on the gravel driveway to conceal both the cars from neighbours. Doyle had already knocked on both rear and front entrances and decided that Bains wasn't home.

'Why doesn't he just fuckin' kick it?' Kirk asked, sitting beside him in the driver's seat.

Doyle extracted a cigarette from a battered pack, lit it, took a tentative mouthful of fumes and looked at Kirk. Until recently Kirk had been someone he had known only from the car pool at Marylebone, a driver. Sutherland had seen fit to elevate him a little (though only a little) and the move had gone to his head. Kirk's new job entailed (amongst other things) telling Sutherland everything Doyle was doing. Kirk thought that gave him authority. Doyle was thoroughly sick of it.

'Because I told him not to,' Doyle said.

'If she's got any sense she'll hear him and be out the back door.'

Doyle wound his window down and blew smoke into the darkness. 'Robbins is round the back,' he said wearily. 'And Sharpe isn't in there.'

'We don't know that. And even if she isn't, Bains might know where she is.'

Doyle rubbed his hand across his forehead. He could feel the creases there deepening. It was like being with a five-year-old. Kirk wanted to chatter, all the time. Doyle ignored him, took another drag on the cigarette and felt the smoke catch in his throat.

'He could be hiding her somewhere else,' Kirk said. 'They could both know where she is – Liz Hodges and Pete Bains. I reckon there's something going on between the three of them.'

Doyle coughed, then cleared his chest and spat out of the window. 'Is that what you reckon?'

'It's my opinion.'

'And I value it highly, Kirk.' He coughed again, a deeper rasp this time. It wasn't that long since he'd been off work with a chest infection.

'You should give up those things. They're filthy,' Kirk said, a smug smile on his thin lips.

'Just like you did?'

'That's right. Two years ago. Forty a day I was—'

'But you were smart enough to make a choice?'

Kirk turned to stare at him. White finally signalled that

30

he had the front door open. Doyle opened the car door and began to get out. Kirk did the same.

'No. You wait here,' Doyle said.

'Why? It will be quicker if—'

'You wait here. Do as you're told.'

He shut the door on him.

At the front of the house White was messing around with a collapsible cosh.

'It took you long enough,' Doyle said, pushing the door open in front of him.

'Sorry, boss.'

'Follow me – and put that thing away.'

'Sharpe might be dangerous.'

'She's *in* danger, not dangerous. We're here to help her.'

He stepped into Pete Bains's darkened hallway. They should have seen this coming, he thought. Fifteen months earlier, in October 1998, he had warned them about Karen Sharpe, warned Sutherland specifically, when she had failed to call in for two weeks. At the time they had thought she was living in a house in Stainforth, just outside York, along with her then ten-year-old child, Mairead. The placement required her to live there as herself, Karen Sharpe, but by day to run an art gallery in one of the more upmarket streets near the centre. Doyle had checked the house in Stainforth and found it empty and up for rent. When he checked the local school for Mairead Sharpe he discovered she had not returned for the new term. The information had triggered a minor panic.

He switched the hall lights on now and looked at Pete Bains's home. In the silence he could tell already that the place was empty. 'She's not here,' he said, turning back to White. 'You go ahead and check. I'll wait here. Don't touch anything.'

White crept forward, his hand still on the cosh in his coat pocket. Doyle stepped back through the open front door into the porch. In the car Kirk was straining to see what was happening, eager to join in anything that might involve his fists. That was his other specialism. Doyle turned away from him and continued with his cigarette.

Sharpe had surprised him fifteen months before, in more than one way. Sutherland had spoken about her, of course. It was clear he didn't like her, didn't even trust her perhaps, but he held a grudging respect for what she was capable of. So Doyle had been forewarned. Sutherland had told him all about her past. He had even let him have access to the file. But the changes had still taken him off guard.

He had met her maybe four times prior to that day in October 1998 to arrange the rental of the art gallery. The owner of the place had been an ailing widower genuinely keen to give it up. But nothing else about the transaction had been real. Doyle had been called David Morris then (a solicitor from Scotland, friend of the prospective tenant), the funds had come from Her Majesty's Government (one way or another) and Karen Sharpe, the new manager of the place, had been called Anna Hart.

That was her new name. But he had met her as DC Karen Sharpe before that. They had even had lunch together in Bradford. So she knew him. Consequently, he had been expecting her to react when she saw him at the gallery. That was his first surprise. She had looked through the top panel of the glass door, squinted at him, unlocked the door and pulled it open.

'Hello. Please come in. I'm sorry about the locked door, but we were burgled last night.' She had smiled pleasantly and stepped aside for him to enter. Not even the faintest glimmer of recognition.

He had stood rather awkwardly in the gallery space, a converted Victorian town house. Sharpe walked past him towards an ornate, mahogany desk at the rear of the long room; he had watched her with unease. 'Fortunately they only took small change,' she said, her back to him. She looked completely unlike the woman he had first met six months before.

The clothing was all different, of course. She was kitted out in expensive designer gear now – a long, loose-fitting skirt by Lauren, a pastel New and Lingwood shirt, Loboutin shoes with a red heel, some kind of diamond necklace at her throat – a far cry from the ordinary jeans and T-shirts she had worn as a police officer. She looked like a wealthy, pampered housewife who ran a little art gallery for fun.

Her hair was styled to match. Karen Sharpe, Doyle knew, had naturally dark hair, but Anna Hart had short, bleached-blonde hair, dyed perfectly to the very roots, with not a millimetre of her own colour showing through, and cut so as to look stylishly ruffled.

But the clothing and hair were just the tip of it. Almost every aspect of Sharpe had been subtly changed. The woman in front of him had spoken with a different voice – the inflections and accent, the way of trailing off sentences slightly at the end, even the vocabulary – and she had walked with less swing to her hips, more grace and poise in her step. In fact, all her movements were altered, her gestures more gentle, her expressions understated where they had once been emphatic. These were tiny, almost imperceptible differences, but taken together they built a powerful impression of an entirely new personality.

Six months before Karen Sharpe had been edgy, ill at ease and nervous. They hadn't told him what was going on in her life to make her like that, but everything from

33

the deep crease in the centre of her forehead (how had Hart managed to get rid of that?) to the tight-lipped way she had spoken to him, had conveyed an impression of barely restrained anger. Anna Hart, by comparison, looked comfortable, relaxed and calm. It was effective and uncanny. He felt as though he had only just met her. And the look in her eyes was genuine. She was looking at him as owner of the gallery, as Anna Hart.

There had followed a ridiculous exchange about whether or not he wanted to buy a painting. He could scarcely believe it at the time, but she had even looked him up and down, noting the cheap Marks & Spencer suit, the shabby green anorak pulled over it, the scuffed shoes, and he was sure she was trying to assess his worth, judge whether he would have enough money to afford a painting from her gallery.

'I want something for my wife,' he had said. The temptation to play along, to see how far she would go, was overwhelming. 'She complains I never buy her flowers. I thought I might get her a painting with flowers in it.'

'Well, we do have some still life works,' she had replied. 'But I'm not sure they would be what you had in mind. As you can see,' she waved a hand around the walls, 'we tend to concentrate on contemporary styles. They're not very literal.'

Not something he would understand, she had meant.

After that he had dropped it and introduced himself. Surprise number two: his name had meant nothing to her. Or at least that was how it had looked. Normally he was good at telling whether people were lying.

Mentioning Sutherland's name had produced a more promising reaction (a flicker of fear?) but when he had gone ahead and explained that Sutherland had arranged the burglary of the night before, precisely in order to sweep the place clean of listening devices just so that Doyle could speak with her *as herself*, as Karen Sharpe, she had immediately become agitated. Pressing the matter had brought tears to her eyes. She seemed to have forgotten who she was. It was the tip of a psychological iceberg and he wasn't equipped to cope with it. He had the distinct impression that if he were to push things she would break down.

He was almost relieved to hear the gallery door open behind him. A young girl and a man entered, the girl calling out as she came forward, 'We're here, Mum!'

That was his third and greatest surprise, which he had focused on in his report to Sutherland. Sharpe's kid – Mairead – had come in *with* Hanley. *With Nicholas Hanley.* Doyle had struggled not to react. Sharpe had quickly wiped her eyes and ran to meet her daughter, pushing past Doyle, but both the child and Hanley had already picked up that something was wrong. Doyle had volunteered then that he was from the local police, there in connection with the burglary. That had taken the tension out of it.

'Miss Hart got upset thinking about the break-in,' he said to Hanley. 'It's not surprising. Especially considering that so many of your own paintings are hanging here.' That was a slip.

'Do I know you, officer?' Hanley had asked immediately, shaking his hand with a grip that had hurt.

'No, but I know you, sir. I've seen your picture in the local newspaper.' It was the best recovery he could muster. Not bad, since he remembered that Hanley's picture *had* been in a local paper – he'd been showing his paintings at some charity fair.

Hanley then bent his ear at length about local thugs, druggies and hooligans, and all the while Sharpe stood behind him, her eyes firmly fixed on Doyle's. He recognized her expression then, the suppressed anger glinting at him, exactly as he had seen it the first time he had met her.

Within ten minutes Doyle had the picture and he had spelled it out clearly in his report to Sutherland. History (if Sharpe's file was accurate) was repeating itself. Without telling them, she had moved in with Hanley. Worse, her emotions for him seemed genuine. She held his hand in front of Doyle, spoke to him as if he were a lover. Hanley, with some slight embarrassment, had responded in kind. And all the time, standing between them, an arm linked through both of theirs, the kid had looked up at him with a happy, healthy smile.

'They looked like a fucking family, for Christ's sake,' he had said to Sutherland. 'Even the kid has lost sight of it. You have to pull her out of there.'

But Sutherland had only smirked. 'Pull her out? She's doing what she does best. That's why we use her.'

'I saw her. I don't think she knows *who* she is. If you leave her in place she could end up cracking. The same thing will happen as last time.'

'Are you a psychologist now, Doyle?'

He had turned to leave Sutherland's office, angry and confused.

'I know what I'm doing,' Sutherland had called after him. 'You should trust me.'

Doyle had turned back. 'I've already put the report up to psychiatric services.'

'Of course. That's sound procedure, Doyle. Well done.'

But that had changed nothing.

He heard Kirk calling to him from the car. Control had come through. Doyle dropped the cigarette outside Bains's door, stubbed it with his foot and left it. From inside the house he could hear White's feet creaking the boards along the first floor. He walked back to the car.

'Liz Hodges phone?' he asked Kirk, once he had the door closed.

'Yes. She called Bains as soon as we left. I knew she would do it.'

They had put in a request to log all traffic to and from Liz Hodges's numbers, mobile and fixed.

'Where is he?'

'Milgarth police station. We should tell Sutherland. She warned Bains we were coming . . .'

'That hardly matters.'

'. . . Sutherland should know.' There it was again. Sutherland's little spy.

'I don't think so.'

'He asked me to warn him if—'

'I'll tell you when and who you can warn, Kirk.'

'But she tipped Bains off.'

'So fucking what? Did she know where Sharpe was?'

Kirk shook his head.

'I thought not. What about Bains?'

'Nothing.'

'Damn.'

He leaned back in the seat. Kirk was right. He should tell Sutherland now. Why was he reluctant? If she wasn't with Bains it was serious. He could feel it like a weight, the crushing weight of experience; all his years pulling people out, putting them in, pulling them out again. He bit his lip.

'Shit,' he said. 'She's in trouble. I know it.'

FIVE

She reached over to Rachel, closing her hands either side of her face to examine her. Rachel was dazed, but her eyes were open and she was breathing. There was no blood. Anna brushed pieces of glass from her hair.

'Are you hurt?' She unfastened her seatbelt and undid the catch on Rachel's. She needed to get her out. She could hear nothing of the other vehicle now, but it could not have passed them. She knew what had happened. They had been rammed at speed, deliberately. Turning to look through the broken rear window she could see that both cars were positioned across the middle of the road, blocking it.

'Are you OK, Rachel? Tell me if you are OK?'

Rachel nodded. From the front Anna could hear the driver cursing in Urdu. She heard the catch on his door click.

'No,' she shouted. 'Don't get out. Drive on.' But already he was stepping out. She began to panic. 'It wasn't an accident,' she shouted. 'It was deliberate.'

The driver began to shout at someone in broken English. She caught a glimpse of violent movement through his open door and heard him gasp. Inside her bag her hand found her mobile and brought it out.

She reached to open her door but it was opened from the outside before she had the chance. The shape of a man filled the frame, turning a flashlight into her face, then Rachel's. She shielded her eyes from it, trying to make out the features behind it.

'Get out now. Both of you.' The voice was a deep rasp,

like a shouted whisper. In her confusion she couldn't identify the accent. She saw a hand reaching inside to take hold of her and shrank back, cowering so far into the seat that he had to lean into the vehicle to seize hold of her coat. The mobile slipped from her fingers. She began to shout at him, wriggling from his grasp and leaning over Rachel to open the door on her side.

'Go, Rachel!' she whispered. 'Get out and run.' The man stepped back and dropped the torch into the road, then suddenly he was in the vehicle, pushing something against her head.

'Get out. Now. Get out or I'll kill you here!'

His mouth was pushed so close to her she could feel his breath all over her skin. He was holding a gun against her jaw.

'OK. I'll do it,' she said, still trying to find his face. Beside her Rachel wasn't moving. 'Who are you? What do you want?'

His free hand reached up and closed around her throat. 'No questions. Get out now.'

She felt a freezing sensation in the pit of her stomach. It was a car-jack, or a robbery. She tried to recall how much cash they had with them.

'I don't have much money—'

He struck her, holding the gun away and punching at her face in a short deliberate movement. She saw it coming but couldn't move quickly enough. Her head snapped back, eyes clouding. For a second she could hear nothing but ringing in her ears. Then he was screaming at her again: '*Get out! Get out now!*' Rachel began to cry.

'I can't get out!' Anna shouted. 'I can't get out with you standing there.'

He moved backwards, out onto the road again. She looked down at her daughter.

Rachel's eyes focused on her nose, where he had hit her. Anna could taste blood in her mouth.

'I'm frightened, Mummy—'

'Get out of the car. No talking!'

She ignored him, didn't even turn to look at him. 'Remember who you are, Rachel. Remember everything we have ever said about this kind of thing. Remember!'

'Your nose is bleeding—'

'It doesn't matter. Listen to me. Do not be afraid. Do not cry. Do not show him you care—'

'But he has—'

Now! Get out now!

'I'm coming. I'm coming now.'

She got out onto the road, her legs weak. The taxi driver was collapsed against the front of the vehicle, gasping for breath. His eyes caught hers as she turned to help Rachel out. What had happened to him? She had heard no gunshot and she could see no blood. She took Rachel's hand and turned to face the gunman, seeing him properly for the first time in the light thrown up from the taxi's interior. He was short and squat, his face covered with a full balaclava. He looked like a terrorist. Had the accent been Irish?

'What do you want?' Her voice was trembling, betraying her. She wanted to appear unafraid.

'You and the kid get into the car. Now. Any fucking around and I kill you here. You get it?'

Liverpool. He had a Merseyside accent. He was waving the gun towards his own car. The gun was an automatic. She could see it now. An automatic with a silencer. She looked past it, to where his car was stalled in the road, driver's door open, headlights off. It was a Range Rover, the old shape, with bull bars on the front. She couldn't see a mark on it from the collision.

'You get into the driver's seat,' he said. 'I'll be in the back with the kid. Do it now.'

She knew if they got into the car they were lost. 'No,' she said. 'Tell me what you want. I'm not getting into your car.' Her voice was so shaky the words barely came out. She heard him grunt. He was standing about two yards in front of her. She held Rachel's hand tightly and glanced along the road. They were about a mile from the hotel. The road was empty, the night sky black, the air freezing. Rachel was shivering, she hoped with cold, not shock. How long before a car drove along here? She didn't even know where the road led to. The taxi driver had taken a left instead of a right as they came out of the hotel, and she only knew the other way to the airport. Presumably it was a short cut, but all she could see in the surrounding darkness were fields and trees. Her only chance was to delay him for so long that someone drove along and found them. She watched him stepping towards her and waited for it.

'You stupid cow,' he said, pushing the gun against her chest. 'If I kill you here it makes no difference to me.'

'We're not getting in the car.' Her words sounded distant. The noise her heart was making was louder. She watched him pause, his eyes tiny specks of white through the slits in the balaclava. What he wanted was money. She had to remember that and stay calm. There was no reason for it to be anything else. They were wealthy; he had targeted them. It was as simple as that. There was no reason to kill them. 'I have money,' she said, trying to hold his eyes. 'I can give you money—'

His hand caught hold of Rachel's hair, dragging her back towards him. Anna moved to grab her, to stop him, but he swung sideways and struck her shoulder with the butt of the gun, knocking her back. She staggered against the car, feeling for the first time his strength. He was short, but powerful. By the time she recovered he was holding Rachel by the hair, the gun pointed at her face.

'*You want me to kill her? Is that what you fucking want?*'

Rachel started to scream, a high-pitched little girl scream. He yanked on her hair, twisting her head. 'Shut up. Shut the fuck up.' His voice was fraying. He was worried. He looked up and down the road, then back at her. He knew what she was trying to do. He only had a certain amount of time before someone would come.

She began to plead with him. 'Please leave her. Leave her and I'll give you money. I have plenty of cash. We have—'

'This isn't about money! Get in the fucking car.'

There was movement to the side of him. The taxi driver was getting up.

'I can take you to a cash point—'

'I don't want money. Get in the car.'

The taxi driver was standing, trying to say something. The gunman looked towards him.

'Leave the girl alone,' the taxi driver said. His voice was pained, breathless.

'Shut up. Keep out of this.'

'I said leave the girl alone.' She watched him bend over by the door to the Mercedes, then straighten up. He had a short metal bar in his hand.

'Put that down and step back.' The gunman was nervous. He was losing control.

The taxi driver took a step towards him, the bar raised to shoulder height. 'I am not frightened of you,' he said. 'Let go of that girl.'

The gunman moved the gun so that it was pointing straight at him. But already the driver was closing on him. She expected a shot, but instead the gunman stepped

42

away, his hand still tangled in Rachel's hair. *This isn't about money*. Was that what he had said? Suddenly her mind was teeming with confusion. She had to do something. The taxi driver looked strong, angry; but he was no match for a gun. (Unless the gun wasn't even loaded. Maybe everything was a bluff!) The whole thing was unfolding in front of her but she was frozen, helpless. *This isn't about money*. Those were the words. She saw the taxi driver begin to swing the bar. The tip of it crossed the gunman's face, arcing through the air with a hiss. Rachel ducked. The driver didn't pause. He took another step forwards and swung again, using both hands. This time the gunman wasn't quick enough. It struck him above the elbow, knocking his hand away from Rachel's hair. He cried out, a strange rasping noise, caught in the back of his throat. Rachel ran towards Anna immediately. Anna caught hold of her as the driver was stepping forward again. The gun went off.

The noise was like a whip. The driver doubled up at once, collapsing to his knees in the road, then falling forward onto his chest. A strangled noise started to come out of his mouth. Anna pulled Rachel to her, turning her eyes away from it. The gunman tugged the balaclava from his head, revealing a mess of brown hair and a stunned, pock-marked face. He looked about forty years old. He stepped forward and stood above the driver, cheeks quivering, lips tight, saying nothing. The driver curled into a foetal position, his face rigid with pain or shock. Beneath him blood was running onto the road.

'You've shot him,' Anna said. Her voice sounded stupid. She waited for the gunman to react, but he did nothing. He was clutching his arm where the bar had struck it.

As they watched, the driver went into convulsions.

The noise coming out of his mouth turned into a retching sound. There was blood coming out of his mouth, choking him.

'You have to help him,' Anna said. 'You have to get an ambulance.'

She heard the gunman swear softly. In one movement he stooped, pointed the gun at the driver's head and pulled the trigger.

SIX

DS Pete Bains had his mobile phone pressed tightly against his ear. He had walked to the rear of the Fire Service's Command and Control Unit to try to get away from the noise generated by the fire appliances and radio receivers, but he could still barely hear the engaged tone.

He had three numbers for Detective Chief Superintendent Alan White – his home number, his mobile and his pager. As Duty Senior Investigating Officer – SIO – White should have been available at all hours on one of the numbers, but Bains had tried them all repeatedly over the last half-hour with no success.

Bains looked back to where firefighters, burdened with breathing apparatus, were just beginning to emerge from the vestibule of Spencer Tower. The side of the building was alive with blue and red emergency lights, making it look as if there could be a fire behind every window he could see. In fact, the blaze had been confined to the ninth floor.

To be sure of containing it, the Fire Service had brought in six appliances (only two proved necessary) and set up an Incident Control Unit. The block was in the heart of central Leeds overlooking the new entertainment and shopping development called the Light. To fit in the six appliances, an ICU van, five police vehicles and two ambulances, they had cordoned off both Albion Street and Great George Street at junctions further back. Fortunately there was little traffic at six in the morning.

Despite that, small crowds had developed on the Headrow and Great George Street, forcing Bill Chambers (who was Duty Sergeant that night for Leeds City) to use six men for security. Chambers had only been able to scratch up nine men to cover the entire incident. Bains, who was there to cover the body that had fallen from the burning flat, had been able to muster even less. By calling around other divisions he had managed to get a grand total of three detectives. As a precaution, the Duty DCI had already called the death as suspicious, but until an SIO – in this case, White – confirmed the decision Bains was unlikely to get more help.

He stepped over the lines of hose snaking from the appliances to the tower and made his way towards the Incident Commander. The Sector Commander had been briefing him for at least ten minutes. Meanwhile, no one was allowed into the building. Bains checked his watch. It was 5.56 a.m. He still had no idea what he was dealing with. Was it an accident, murder or suicide? He had seen and examined the body already. It wouldn't answer his questions until an expert looked at it. The inside of the tower might do better though.

For not the first time that night he wished bitterly he had not voluntarily changed shifts two weeks ago. If he had stuck to his original working pattern he would have been on leave from 28 December through to Millennium Eve, starting his shift at 8 p.m. on 31st. The entire Force was working Millennium Eve because management had cancelled all leave ten months before when the hysteria about the Y2K bug had got going. That didn't bother Bains – he had nothing planned for the last night of the century and would probably prefer to forget it – but another sergeant had asked him to cover 28 to 30 December two weeks ago. Consequently he had got caught up with an armed robbery from the city centre that had come in just as he was due to go off. That had held him throughout the night, right up to the point where the call for this one came in. The chances now were that he would be working straight through.

He walked round to the front of the van and listened as the Incident Commander gave instructions to his Command Support Officer. Only when he had finished did he speak to Bains.

'It's out,' he said. 'With no serious structural damage. It looks like arson. The office below was doused with some kind of accelerant, probably petrol, but a fire door closed between the floors. Only the flat on floor nine is damaged. It's the only residential unit in the building. Luckily, no casualties – apart from the one you're dealing with. The top floors were empty. Nothing obvious by way of forensics except the possible remains of plastic petrol containers and a Zippo lighter. Our forensic team won't get here until day shift. We've left everything in place, but bear in mind the water damage. There are fumes still on the eighth floor, so we can't let you in there for a while.'

Bains nodded politely. If this turned out to be a murder scene the Fire Service forensic team wouldn't get anywhere near it.

'Can I go into the flat now?' he asked.

'You can.'

Bains thanked him and walked to where a DC called Jodi Hayward was questioning three of the firefighters who had just come out of the building.

'You can go in, Jodi,' he said. 'No structural damage.'

'Good. Thanks, guys.' She turned to Bains. 'You coming up?'

'Not yet. When I'm finished round the back. Take a uniform with you and preserve everything the Water Fairies haven't washed away.'

'OK.'

47

'Take your time and do it properly. We haven't a clue what this is yet.'

He saw the three firefighters looking askance and turned away from them, staring up to the top of the building where a thick pall of black smoke still hung in the air. Behind the noise of the appliance compressors he could hear a sound like rainfall, caused by the flood of water spilling from the roof. There would be similar quantities of water making their way through the inside of the building. It would probably be unusable for weeks, if not months.

When he had arrived the top floor had still been on fire, flames licking over the edge. He had gone down the alleyway to the rear of the building despite the danger of falling debris. He had not been the first on the scene. A security guard from a club on Great George Street had been told about the body there and had run to the scene with a fire extinguisher. He had doused the body, but by that time the man was already dead, probably from the fall rather than the flames.

The victim's back, hairline and face were severely burned, the clothing scorched away and the skin beneath a raw, suppurating mass of black and red. So much so that Bains had been forced to pause, step back and cover his mouth for a while. But much of the clothing was relatively intact and he had managed to find a wallet in an inside pocket, damaged, but not so much as to melt the credit cards. In another pocket he found a scorched British passport. The holder was given as Nicholas Hanley. It hadn't taken long to trace his addresses. He had four. One of them was the flat he had fallen from. He stepped through the gathering puddles of water now and ducked back under the incident tapes blocking the alleyway. It was damp and cold; an unfamiliar odour hung in the air.

The Duty Sergeant, Bill Chambers, was standing with the detective Bains had brought with him from Milgarth – Paul North. They were both staring at the body. There were no emergency lights in the alley, and the night sky was beginning to grey with the first signs of dawn. Bains stood beside them, feeling again the disgust he always felt when looking at dead bodies. It wasn't the injuries that got to him – at least, not only the injuries. He had seen too many mutilated corpses in his ten years of service. Bad burns still made him retch – the way they looked (not very different, in the really bad cases, to a joint of well-roasted beef), the particular smell – but these were merely physical impulses. He could control them. What really ate at him were the thoughts they provoked. There was always something absurd about the dead. Bodies never looked like human beings.

He recalled only too well the first corpse he had seen – a gangland execution. The killers had stunned the victim, then carefully positioned the head against a curb and backed a car over it. When Bains had reached the scene the head had been split into two quite distinct halves, from the crest of the skull down to the beginning of the neck, a division running right through the middle of the face. Once past the physical revulsion Bains had been unable to take his eyes from the thing. It looked not like something that had once been living and breathing, but like a prop from a special effects department.

It had been the same with virtually every body since then. When you extracted whatever gave life, all that was left was inert matter. The indignity of it shocked him every time. A human being was complex. It struggled with thoughts, desires, opinions and hatreds; it had the power of speech. But in the space of seconds it could be reduced to something very simple, a slab of dead meat. It took him by surprise every time.

This one was no different. Lying in a space between an empty skip and a collection of garbage bins, the legs and waist were bent beneath the chest, suggesting that the spine had completely severed just above waist height. There were thin wisps of smoke still curling from the charred outer layers of clothing and hair, but apart from that it looked like some kind of floppy rag doll, collapsed into a heap, bent double, forehead resting on one of the feet.

The bouncer had drenched everything, making it difficult to identify injuries, liquids and marks, but at first examination it seemed as if there was no blood anywhere except the head.

'I'd say his head struck the skip on the way down,' North suggested loudly. 'Hence the wound to the head.'

'No blood on the skip,' Chambers said.

North shrugged. 'Maybe the bouncer washed it off when he sprayed everything.'

'I think he hit the skip,' Chambers offered. 'But with his back. That's what snapped it.'

'And the head wound?' North asked.

'From the ground.'

Bains sighed. 'So what do we say it is?' His voice was muted. Another thing he couldn't help in the presence of the dead.

'What did you say?' North asked.

Bains had to stop himself from asking him to speak quieter. 'What do we say it is?' he repeated. 'A suicide or something major?'

Chambers shrugged. ' "We?" Until White gets here that's your call, Pete, not ours. Are the lab on their way?'

'Yes. And a pathologist.'

'I would wait. What do the witnesses say?'

50

Bains pulled out his notebook. 'Nothing helpful. I only have three at the moment—'

'And the guard,' North added.

'He didn't see the fall. The others saw nothing useful. A "human torch" *falling* from the building, *leaping* from the building, *falling* through space . . . that kind of thing. They didn't see anyone else on the balcony.'

'He came from the balcony, though, not the roof?'

'So they say. But none of them actually saw the moment he fell.'

'Was the guy dead when the bouncer got to him?' Chambers asked.

'He thinks so.'

They were silent for a while, staring at the mutilated shape. Bains wondered whether Chambers or North were feeling anything. They were older than him by a good eight years. Maybe he would end up like that.

'The ID on him is for a Nicholas Hanley,' he said eventually. 'He's a property developer. He has a company which has an office on the eighth floor.' He pointed up the side of Spencer Tower, a metre behind them. 'And a little flat above that. The witnesses say he fell from the flat, and it's the flat that was burning.'

'Are we in there yet?' North asked.

'Yes. Jodi has gone up. There were signs of arson, according to the Water Fairies.'

'Who's doing next of kin?' Chambers asked the question.

Bains smiled grimly. 'We can punt that one. He lives up in Swaledale. I've contacted North Yorks already.'

'Wife and kids?'

Bains shrugged. 'I've no idea. He lives with some-one . . .' He looked for the details in his notebook.

'How did you find all this out so quickly?' Chambers asked.

'I put Chris Greenwood onto it. He's good at that sort of thing.' He found the page. 'Anna Hart,' he said. 'That's her name. So maybe she's not his wife.'

SEVEN

1998. A crisp, clear September day with a cloudless blue sky. They wore their big winter coats and walked up the long lane to the farm, kicking the leaves already fallen from the beech trees. An early frost made the leaves brittle and crunchy, the mud beneath them hard enough not to stick to their boots. Their breath puffed out in front of their faces as they laughed. They were all laughing, but Rachel most of all. Anna could not recall seeing her so happy. Nick told stupid jokes all the way from Swaledale and she laughed so much she couldn't catch her breath. Part of it was the excitement. Nick had a surprise gift for her and she thought (correctly) that she knew what it was. As they left the A658 Rachel realized they were heading for Nick's sister's stables at Calverley. That was enough to guess it.

The riding bug had bitten Rachel suddenly. Her interest in horses had passed from trivial to obsessive in the space of a few months, taking Anna by surprise. The first time Rachel had met Nick he had taken them to a neighbour's stud to see a pair of week-old foals. That had been enough to spark it off. She had wanted her own horse ever since.

There were already seven horses in the stables at Black Carr Hall, Nick's house. Four belonged to Kiki Camitz, the woman Nick had employed to care for his assorted animals. The other three were too old to ride and were usually turned into the upper paddock to pasture. One of them – it had been Nick's favourite fifteen years ago – could hardly walk and cost a fortune in vet's bills each month. Nick was too soft to have it shot.

After they had moved in Rachel had thrown herself into helping Kiki look after her mares, getting up every morning at the crack of dawn, mucking out the stables, brushing them down, clipping them, learning to boil up the smelly preparation of linseed she fed them as a treat each week. In return Kiki let her ride one of them. It was a good horse, mature and well trained, with exactly the kind of temperament Anna thought safe. In addition, Nick took Rachel to stables on the other side of Reeth every Saturday, sometimes staying with her while she took lessons.

But none of this was enough for Rachel. During the school summer holiday, long hours hanging around Kiki gave her other ideas. Kiki had been a professional dressage rider in her youth, before a bad fall had curtailed her ambition. Now she kept less volatile horses, but she could still talk with passion about dressage, and apparently had done just that, hooking Rachel before she had even a clue what the discipline entailed.

'Advanced dressage requires a very particular kind of horse, Mum,' Rachel had told her one night. 'Nothing in Reeth has enough power.'

'*Advanced* dressage?'

'Yes. Not just mucking around on ponies. I want to be a professional.'

'Like Kiki?'

'Yes.'

'Do you have to be that now – at the age of eleven?'

'I'm nearly twelve.'

There was no getting around it. What Rachel yearned for was something dangerous, young and punchy, something she could learn to train herself. Anna knew the shape of the dream – it was beyond the capabilities of an eleven-year-old. She had hoped Nick wouldn't nurture it.

She watched him run ahead with Rachel and almost had to pinch herself. They had been together for less than three months – and he had known Rachel even less than that – yet it felt already as if everything had always been like this. She could hardly remember the time before they had met.

'Are we going too fast, Nick?' she had asked him that morning, as Rachel was getting dressed. 'Aren't you worried?' She had been standing behind him at the time, arms around his waist, hugging herself to his back. It was one month to the day since she and Rachel had moved in to Black Carr Hall.

'If we go much slower I'll be dead,' he had replied, joking, then turning to face her. He was ten years older than her. 'Are *you* worried?'

She had nodded, the fear fluttering in her chest like a bird. 'I've never been this calm,' she said. 'Something will take it away.'

'Don't go over the top,' he said, smiling. 'You've never been this *calm*? As an expression of my effect on your life, isn't that a little exaggerated?'

She smiled back at him. 'You're always calm, Nick. You were born with it. You don't know how important it is.'

'Stay calm, then. Stop worrying. We're not nineteen-year-olds. We've spent a long time filtering out the rubbish. Don't you think we know what we want by now?'

But the fear wouldn't go away. Something would come along, something would happen. It would all be taken from her.

He had bought Rachel a horse – 'to celebrate us living together for one month'. It wasn't to curry favour with Rachel (or Anna). He didn't need to do that. Rachel had been besotted with him in her childish pre-teen way since the first time they had met. Perhaps because he had little experience with children, he had, it seemed, known exactly how to handle her. From day one he had spoken to her as if she were his age, treating her with just the right mixture of interest and distance to make her want him to like her, as if she had been Anna's twin sister, rather than a child. There were times when Anna had caught Rachel almost trying to flirt with him.

She had seen it before, of course. There had been other men and Rachel had latched onto some of them in the same way. Thinking about it brought on pangs of guilt and intensified the fear. It wasn't just herself she had to think of. Every time she messed it up Rachel ended up heartbroken. Her need for a father figure was almost palpable. It didn't take much by way of interest for her to be won over. Responding to generosity wasn't so bad, but worryingly Anna had noticed that she also responded to being kept distant. If she didn't get that out of her system before her teens she would end up throwing herself at boyfriends who could do nothing but hurt her.

Anna knew it all too well. She had been there herself. One of the most depressing things about being a mother was being helpless to stop the unconscious propagation of every trait that had conspired to ruin her own life. She was to blame for everything. There was no getting away from that. Her lifestyle, her inability to settle, her own tastes and history (somehow) had done this to Rachel. Before long she would be calling Nick 'Dad'.

They reached the farm ahead of her and waited at the gates, shouting for her to hurry up. Although the place belonged to Nick's sister, Diana, she wouldn't be there. They had been before – two or three times – and she was never there. Nick didn't get on with her. Anna had pressed him on the exact cause of the problem, but it was something to do with money. Diana spent most of her time in Portugal these days. She had met someone from the polo circuit who lived out there and had, Nick said, 'happily' abandoned her husband and children after twenty years of marriage. Nick didn't approve. He wouldn't come to Calverley if Diana was there.

'You go on,' Anna shouted. The day was too pleasant to run.

They went to hunt out Lisa Beadle, the woman who ran the place in Diana Hanley's absence, and Anna leaned for a moment on a stretch of fencing next to the gateposts, watching them as they moved around the farmyard together, Rachel chattering continuously. When the dogs appeared, Nick held her by the hand and stood slightly in front of her, protectively.

Lisa had organized everything for Nick, from the selection of the horse through to its shipment across the Channel. Anna knew already what it was, and how much he had spent. It had come from a specialist dressage horse dealer in Paris; a Danish warmblood. Rachel had read about them in one of her magazines, Nick had noted the interest. It had set him back nearly £15,000.

As she saw them walking towards the stable block she followed, then, held back by something she couldn't work out, she waited outside the huge arched doors into the building, until she could hear Nick's soft voice talking quietly and Rachel, for once, in complete silence, mute. Then she walked in.

Rachel was crying. Not through being miserable or disappointed, she could tell that at once, but because nothing like this had ever happened to her. They were about halfway down a row of eight boxes and Rachel was standing stock straight in front of the horse that Lisa had led out for her, not touching it, not moving, just standing there with her hands at her side, shoulders shaking quietly.

Beside her Nick looked at a loss for words. Neither of them were aware of Anna behind them.

As she watched, Rachel turned to Nick and held her arms out. He bent down slightly, folded his arms around her and they hugged for a second, parting just as quickly. Then Nick stood back and looked shy, Rachel equally so. It was the first time it had happened.

Anna walked up to them and placed a hand on Rachel's head. 'A very particular kind of horse, I believe,' she said.

'She's called Hilsen,' Lisa Beadle said. The horse was tossing its head now and she was struggling to hold it. 'You won't be able to ride her for a while. You'll have to let Kiki train her first.'

Rachel was still staring at the animal, as if she could hardly believe it was there. 'I will ride her one day,' she muttered. She looked up to Anna. 'She's called Hilsen, Mum,' she said.

Anna glanced at Nick and winked. He was standing beside Lisa, one arm out and leaning on the open half-gate of the horse's box. His face was flushed with embarrassment. Anna could see he had been surprised by Rachel's reaction. He had grown up with money and gifts, never wanting for anything. That had made him careless with money, but also generous. Until now he probably hadn't been close enough to anyone who was so capable of appreciating a gift.

'Thank you, Nick,' Anna said to him.

He took the reins off Lisa and, together with Rachel, led the animal outside. Anna sat down on a stoop and watched them. Lisa lit up a fag and called out instructions, warnings, encouragement.

'They look good together,' Lisa said. 'I don't think I've ever seen old Nick so happy.'

Anna tried to think about it. This was different. Inside

her – inside her chest – it felt different. She wasn't restless. She was happy to be right here, watching them. Something in her had stopped struggling. How had he done that?

He was decent enough to look at. He had most of his hair still, no paunch, a boyish face still full of eagerness despite his age. He was shorter than her, of course – nearly all her exes were. He dressed well enough, as she would have expected from someone his age and class: country gear (cords, Barbour, Guernsey sweater, wellies) or suits. There was nothing, she thought, *wrong* with him. But was that the best she could come up with? If so then why did her heart skip like this as she watched him with Rachel?

Everything had gone wrong in the past because *she* had been different. But she had changed now. She was ready for this, ready to stop. She was just starting to live. Even her relationship with Rachel was better. In the past they had done nothing but fight. But for the last few months it had been perfect; mother and daughter, exactly the way she imagined it should be.

That was why she was so frightened. This wasn't make believe. She had not planned it like this, but it had come along and it was real. If there was one thing she knew for certain that was it. Everything she felt for Nick, everything Rachel felt for him, everything that was happening in their lives was *real*.

EIGHT

The fields looked pink in the early-morning light, covered with a frost almost thick enough to be snow. Michael Kenny couldn't take his eyes off it. The change was startling. From the first suffusion of orange and pink, settling along the rim of the horizon like liquid, to this sudden explosion of light, staining everything, changing white to pink, grey to red, black to purple, hanging in the higher trails of cloud as if something just out of sight had burst, scattering a spectrum of colours. He had never seen anything like it. Directly above him the sky was still bruised black, the night lingering on. But the horizon was alive with colour and sound. He could hear birds singing from the line of bare trees at the end of the field. His eyes caught the pattern made by the branches, clawing the air, the blood-red of the new sun creeping between them. It looked like something from a painting he had seen as a kid, in an art book. Even the sky looked painted. Splashed with crazy random blotches. Like something his daughters would have done three or four years ago and brought home to him from school.

He looked down at his hand, resting on the car door-frame, the cigarette gripped between his shaking fingers. Why was he noticing things like this? Was it some kind of premonition, suddenly to be noticing the world? He had heard stories about people with brain tumours experiencing things more intensely, all their senses tuned up. He could smell the air too, the freshness of it, the traces of frost carried within it, the rich black soil odours lurking beneath.

Every day now for over eight months he had thought he

was going to die. The thought didn't come from nowhere. There was a reason for it, something his body, or his mind, was trying to tell him. His GP had told him he was depressed, or hypochondriac, or neurotic – the same way he put every little physical pain down to a 'virus'. But there was more to it than that.

There was always something wrong with him. Other people weren't like that, not at forty-three. Even little physical problems seemed to linger: a cold that lasted three weeks; nagging joint pains that wouldn't go away. He couldn't go to the toilet without seeing blood in his shit. They had done tests and told him they weren't sure what it was, but meanwhile it wouldn't kill him. What if they were wrong?

Kenny sucked on the cigarette and turned away from the view, filling his lungs, mouth and nasal passages with the foul stink of tobacco. He hated smoking. That *would* kill him, eventually. A long piece of ash dropped from the butt into the lap of his shellsuit. He brushed it away impatiently, clumsily. He could still feel his heart pounding. If he thought about it his head would fill with the images all over again. Everything had gone wrong. And not just today. His whole life had been a fuck-up. He spat bitterly out of the window. How had he ended up here, doing this? Out of the corner of his eye he could see the woman looking at him, watching.

He looked down at the angry swelling developing just above his left elbow. The arm was now so stiff he could barely bend it. He should have shot the cabbie as soon as he picked up the bar. That was the error. But the cabbie wasn't on the ticket. He was just some old Asian duffer, in the wrong place at the wrong time. The girl and the kid were all he was interested in, all he was being paid for. He didn't want to kill bystanders.

The woman was starting to speak again. 'How long are you going—'

'Shut up!' he shouted at her, then looked away immediately. Every time she got a reaction like that, she won. That was what she was trying to do. He was fearful of her already. She did nothing he told her without arguing. The kid was just as bad. They were frightened of the gun, but they didn't think he would use it, not on them. He shifted it so that it was pressing against the kid's leg, where she was sitting beside him on the back seat.

Before he had shot the taxi driver they hadn't thought he would use the gun at all. So the death had served some kind of purpose. It had got them into the car. He could remember the shock on their faces as the body twitched on the ground, the blood puddling around the head. It was so cold there had been steam rising off it. He sucked again on the cigarette and flicked the ash out of the window.

'Can I at least smoke now?' she asked. For the third time.

'No.'

Cigarette butts were DNA traps. He needed to minimize everything that could point back to him. He shouldn't have been smoking himself. Or spitting. But spit would wash away, or dry out. And he could collect his own butts. There was no reason to run around after her though. Soon it wouldn't matter to her whether she'd had a last drag or not. As soon as he got the call he would get them out and do it. There was a small drainage ditch alongside the road. They could lie in that. He would walk up behind them and put one in the back of each head. Quick and easy. They wouldn't even know what was happening.

Beside him, the girl was starting to cry again. Kenny glanced at her. He didn't want to look at her too much. How old was she? Eleven, twelve? The same age as his Sally. The mother was tall, blonde, attractive. Long legs, short, cropped hair that had some kind of tips or highlights, green eyes that looked right through you. He guessed maybe thirty-three years old, and healthy, fit. Hands and skin that had known nothing but leisure. It was the sort of thing he would go for in a magazine. But in the flesh she was a bitch. And an upper-class bitch at that. The way she dressed, the way she spoke, even the way she spoke to him – everything stated her background. She would have nothing but contempt for him. She would know just listening to his accent and looking at his cheap shellsuit, his hairstyle, the way he walked, exactly what kind of overrun, working-class Catholic poverty he had crawled out of. It was stamped all over him like refinement and wealth were stamped all over her. He couldn't even appreciate the scent of the perfume she was wearing. It smelled like oranges to him.

His phone rang. Finally. He placed it against his ear. 'Yeah,' he said.

'Where are you?' Stijn's voice.

'Where we said.' He looked around. The dirt track was still deserted. There were no houses, no people. Flat, barren fields on all sides. It had taken him three days to find this spot. Completely isolated, yet only a couple of miles from the main Harrogate to Skipton road, it was possible people would hear a shot, but they wouldn't get anywhere near the scene until he was well out of it via back roads. He had driven for nearly thirty minutes to get here, to await these instructions.

'Success?' Stijn asked.

He thought about it for a moment. It would be all over

the media before long. 'Not totally,' he said. 'I have them. But there was a cock-up. The driver got hurt.'

Stijn was silent.

'These things happen, Mr Stijn,' he said, trying not to sound afraid. 'It couldn't be helped.' The woman was still watching him from the front seat. He knew the kind. If she got the chance she would try to escape.

'How badly hurt?' Stijn asked.

'Bad enough not to worry about. He won't be saying anything.'

Another pause.

'What's that noise?' Stijn asked.

'The kid crying,' he replied. He looked at her again. 'What's the instructions?' He needed to get it over with.

'Change of plan. I need to see them first.'

'They're the right ones. I checked the photos against their passports.'

'I still need to see them.'

'You don't trust me?'

'I'm sure it *is* them. But things have changed.'

Kenny felt like screaming at the man. He wasn't a kidnapper, he didn't take hostages. Already he was well out of his depth. But Stijn wasn't the kind of person you screamed at. Besides, he was paying. He took a deep breath instead. 'OK. You coming out here?'

'No. I need somewhere more private.'

He waited.

'There's a place I know,' Stijn said eventually. 'Next to a ruined church called Kirkstall Abbey, on the A65, Abbey Road. Do you know it?'

'That's almost in the centre of Leeds. I'm not sure—'

'It's private. I was there yesterday meeting . . . people.'

'But that means I will have to drive her back through Leeds. They might be looking for her by now.'

64

The woman reached her hand between the seats and took hold of the girl's hand. She had tried it once before and he had hit her. His hands were full now. He would hit her when he came off the phone.

'You will have to find a way,' Stijn said, so loudly Kenny was sure the woman could hear. 'It's an abattoir, down by a canal. It's the only property I know up here that's safe.'

Kenny gritted his teeth as Stijn gave him the exact address in his grating South African accent. 'When?' he asked, once he had repeated it to himself.

'As soon as you can.' Stijn cut the line.

She moved her hand before he could strike it, anticipating.

'You were frightened of that man,' she said, before he could speak. He felt the sweat running down his back. How was he to get her through central Leeds? She would try something, for certain.

'That's right,' he said. 'Too frightened of him to screw this up. Wipe your face.'

There was a line of blood running out of her nose, from where he had hit her. She drew the sleeve of her coat across it.

'Not with that,' he said. 'Nothing visible.' Too late. There was blood all over the sleeve now. 'Use the rag I gave you.'

'Can I smoke?' she asked again. She was doing it deliberately.

He sighed. Beside him, the child had at least stopped whimpering. He looked at his watch. Nearly six thirty-five. This should have been over and done with by now. 'Not while you're driving,' he said. 'You can have one when we get there.' A concession. He could feel his guts bloating and twisting even as he said it. He wasn't sure he

65

was going to make it to Leeds without needing the toilet. He could feel the meal he had eaten last night swilling around inside him like water.

His guts had been messed up for over a year now. Nerves made it worse. What had started as mild diarrhoea had quickly turned into something chronic. The doctors had told him he might have something called Crohn's disease. But they were never sure and always wanted to take more blood, stick more cameras up him, do more tests. Meanwhile, he had tried every medication they would give him, but nothing worked. Nothing except Imodium, and he had been so nervous that morning he had left the house without it.

'Get where?' she asked, starting the engine without waiting for him to tell her. It was all a game for her.

'You heard,' he said. 'The A65, Abbey Road.'

She indicated and pulled out.

'Remember what I said,' he said, raising his voice. 'I can't fuck up.'

She showed no sign of having heard him. She was driving carefully, without panic, concentrating on the road. She followed the track he had directed her down on the way in, without questions, as if she had already memorized the route. Without hesitating she turned right onto the two-lane track which led back down to the A59.

'You won't want to go back via the airport road,' she said. Not even a question. 'The police will be there by now. I'll go over Ilkley Moor instead. Then down into Shipley.' Her voice was so calm it made him nauseous. How could she be doing this to him?

'*I can't fuck up!*' he shouted again. 'I'm warning you now. You saw what happened back there on the road. I can do that again, right here in the back, right now.' Still no reaction. 'I have nothing to lose,' he added pathetically.

'I doubt that's true,' she said, then slightly louder, to the child, 'Don't be afraid, Rachel. He won't hurt you. Remember everything I've told you.'

He gritted his teeth. He wanted to lean forward and whack her with the gun, or stop the car, drag her out, and kick her until she couldn't walk. But he needed her to drive. Even the kid was staring at him now.

'Is this some kind of blackmail thing?' the woman asked. She was patronizing him. 'Who are you taking me to see? The "boss"?'

'Shut up,' he muttered. It wasn't worth arguing with her.

'We could solve this another way,' she said.

'Shut up.' His voice sounded desperate. He knew it, but couldn't control it.

'I could give you some—'

'*I said shut the fuck up!*' He lunged forward, temper flaring behind his eyes. He was moving the gun to jam it against her head when a car flashed past on the other side of the road. The kid let out a little scream.

'*Shit!*'

He pulled back, squirming into his seat, and tried to regulate his breath. He was going to hyperventilate if he wasn't careful. He looked back out of the window. Red lights drawing into the distance. Brake lights? Had the driver seen anything? When he turned back he saw her eyes on him again in the rear-view mirror. No expression on her face, no change in her driving.

In his bowels he felt the first contractions starting.

NINE

Bains stood at the open balcony doors and watched the dawn sun bleed into the fading night. He took a long breath of air, savouring the icy wind blowing out of the north. Behind him everything stank of soaked, charred wood, sulphurous artificial fabrics and petrol.

Not two yards away from him he could see a black stain on the ledge from which Nicholas Hanley had apparently thrown himself. He was meant to step forward and look over the edge. That was his job. Not out of idle curiosity, but in case there was evidence to be found, something remaining from Hanley's fall; fibres stuck to the stonework, blood smeared where it shouldn't have been, that sort of thing. But he didn't want to.

He shifted his eyes upwards from the stain and focused into the distance again, watching the new light creep across the grey rooftops of Headingley. At the horizon, faint with haze, he could just see the southernmost ridges of the Dales. That was where he would have liked to have been. There or the Lake District. He allowed himself a little private moment, remembering himself lounging beside a wide, clear rock pool at the bottom of Hell Gill, buzzing insects and rising skylarks singing above the gurgle of the stream, the high summer sun luxurious on his face and bare chest, the towering mass of Bowfell beneath him. Then he stepped forward and looked carefully at the ledge.

Beside the smoke stain there was nothing this side. He leaned further forward, stepping sideways so as not to touch the stain, then peered over the edge. For a moment his legs trembled. He hated high edges, always had. As a child, on a school trip to Clifford's Tower in York, he had once frozen on the top ledge, paralysed with fear. Unable even to stand near the edge he had sunk first to his knees, then, when that didn't work, flat on his belly, gripping the narrow ledge as if the whole tower were moving. They had to lead him back down, all his classmates whooping and laughing at him. He had been there since as an adult. The battlements weren't even that high.

Not this high, for example, nine floors up. It wasn't much, but it was enough to set him off. The feeling that he was spinning slightly was unbearable. He stepped back and took a breath. He had read that a fear of heights was a sublimated desire to fly. He often had flight dreams, of one sort or another, and it was true that even his fear of this ledge couldn't quite disguise a powerful internal urge to vault it. But was that an urge to fly, or merely a desire to conquer the fear?

He stepped forward and looked over again, his feet wide apart. Below him he picked out the shape of Natasha Atkinson, the pathologist he had left with the body, and beside her Paul North, notebook in hand. A third person he guessed to be the police photographer was moving around, setting something up. In front of them all was the crumpled shape of Nicholas Hanley.

He heard someone stepping through the flat towards him and extended his hand backwards to warn them to stop. He could force himself to look over the edge like this, but he couldn't bear someone standing beside or behind him while he was doing it. He brought his eyes up the wall of the building, seeing nothing of interest until he got to within a few inches of the ledge. There he saw smeared black marks, about on a level with the smoke staining on the other side. He stepped closer, ignoring the feeling in his knees, twisting his head to look. It was a smudged streak of blood, he was almost sure of it.

He took a breath and turned round. Just inside the flat, Jodi Hayward was watching him with a slight frown.

'You frightened of heights, sir?' she asked.

He nodded. 'I am.'

She smiled slightly.

'It's not funny,' he said, then: 'Take a look over here. Is this blood? Don't touch anything.'

He made way for her, stepping back inside the flat and looking at the mess made by the fire and the Fire Service. Twisted, unrecognizable objects stood in puddles of black ash and debris; the walls and ceiling were almost totally charred. Everything was still awash with dirty, freezing water. He watched it dripping from the ceiling, as a chunk of plasterboard gave way and fell to the floor.

Hayward came back into the flat. 'Looks like it,' she said. 'What does it mean?'

'Assuming Hanley left it there, that he was bleeding before he fell.'

'Or jumped,' she said. She handed him the evidence bag in her latex-gloved right hand.

'What is it?'

'A suicide note from a safe in the bedroom cupboards.'

He tried to read it through the clear plastic, but couldn't. Behind him he could hear the last two fire-fighters still trampling through the place, contaminating everything.

'What does it say?'

' *"Not worth it. None of it is worth it. Tell Rachel it is not her fault."* '

'That it?'

'Yes. More or less. It's dated and signed by him. Looks like his name, anyway.'

70

'Funny note for someone who set himself on fire and jumped nine floors.'

She frowned at him. Hayward had been a detective for about three months. 'It reads like a normal suicide note,' she said.

'Exactly. Normal suicides take tablets. You have to be crazy to set yourself on fire.'

'You have to be crazy to kill yourself,' she said, with too much confidence.

'I'll assume you've never been there if that's what you think,' he said.

She frowned again. He could see her trying to work him out.

'Maybe catching fire was an accident,' she said. 'Maybe he just meant to torch the flat.'

'And the office,' he added. There were enough odd details to make him suspicious, but speculation was pointless. He needed to know what Natasha Atkinson thought about the corpse. 'Handy having a fireproof safe,' he muttered. Hayward didn't hear.

Atkinson had promised him she would look at the body as soon as she got it to Leeds General. She had guessed that would be at about nine. He checked the time. Nearly seven o'clock.

'Do you know who "Rachel" is?' Hayward asked.

'His kid, I think. We need to get Scenes of Crime up here. Let's seal the place and get back to Milgarth. Find out what Chris has. We can come back to look at the office when they open up the floor below.'

'Is anyone informing next of kin?'

'North Yorkshire constabulary, I hope. Did you try to raise Chief Superintendent White again?'

She raised her hand to her lips. 'Sorry, boss. I forgot to

tell you. The Control Room told me he was at a scene up near the airport. A shooting.'

Chris Greenwood intercepted them in the first-floor corridor at Milgarth.

'You have people waiting for you,' he said to Bains. 'In the DI's office.'

Bains looked past him, through the open door into the CID room. He could see two men pacing about behind the glass partition that served as an office for DI Greg Oxford.

'Is Greg in there?' he asked. He already knew who the visitors would be.

'No. They wouldn't let me in either. Wouldn't say who they were. I'm guessing they're—'

'I know who they are.' He was grateful now that Liz had warned him. 'What have you got for us? Before I go and deal with them.'

Chris Greenwood was someone Bains had worked with before. Short, skinny, bespectacled and bookish, Greenwood looked harmless but had a mixed reputation, the result of a murky disciplinary past involving some kind of sex allegation. The mud had stuck. But Bains's own record sheet was far from pure and he knew exactly what Greenwood was good at – painstaking, tedious research tasks, anything involving computers, video or CCTV.

'What are we calling it?' Greenwood asked, yawning. 'Major or minor?'

'That depends on the PM, SOCO and anything you've got to say now. What have you got to say?'

'The autopsy is at nine,' Hayward said, beside him. She was only half listening, trying to catch a view of the men waiting in the DI's office. 'SOCO will be there within the hour.'

'So what have you got?' Bains asked Greenwood again.

'Not much,' he said. 'From the height and build it could be Hanley—'

'Why wouldn't it be Hanley?'

Greenwood shrugged. 'No idea. I'm just dotting the "i"s. At the moment we don't have ID, not officially. We should have within the hour though. I've tracked down his sister.' He looked at the A4 pad he was holding, removing a stubby pencil from behind his ear and running it down the list of notes he had made. 'She's called Diana Hanley. She was at one of his houses – Black Carr, it's called – when North Yorkshire called there twenty minutes ago—'

'No wife?'

'Anna Hart, you mean?'

'Is she his wife?'

'No. Not according to the sister. They've been together less than eighteen months. She says they had an argument yesterday and Hart and her kid . . .' he searched for the name, '. . . Rachel Hart – she's eleven – Hart and the kid stormed out. Nicholas Hanley went after them, leaving his sister alone in the place. This was about three o'clock yesterday afternoon. She hasn't seen them since.'

'The sister's coming to ID the body?'

'Yes. She's coming to the Bridewell first.'

'Good. Jodi, you get in touch with Natasha Atkinson and warn her we're coming over with a relative.'

'I've also traced his business partner, Imran Akhtar. He works out of the office below the flat that burned. It's a big business with only two partners – Hanley and Akhtar. They sell and buy high-value property.'

'Estate agents,' Hayward said.

'Posh estate agents,' Greenwood corrected her. 'At least Hanley is. He handles the wealthy private clients. Akhtar handles the commercial side. They have an office in York as well. Akhtar lives in Heaton – that's near you, isn't it?' He looked at Bains.

'I don't know him,' Bains said, 'if that's what you mean. There must be a hundred and fifty Imran Akhtars in Bradford.'

'That's not what I meant.' Greenwood stared at him. Bains waited for him to continue. 'Akhtar should be here within the hour. He can ID him as well if you want. Assuming the body is not too burned.'

'Half a face left,' Hayward said.

Greenwood glanced at her, frowning.

'Good,' Bains said. 'See how the sister does first. We may not need Akhtar for ID, but we can talk to him.'

'What have you got from the scene?' Greenwood asked him.

Bains saw the man in the anorak had spotted him and was starting to open the office door. 'A suicide note that looks false,' he said. 'Maybe some blood. I'd better go and see these people.'

'You think it's suspicious?' Greenwood asked.

'Maybe. But I'll wait for the autopsy.' He moved past Greenwood as the man started to walk through the CID room, heading in his direction.

'Pete Bains?' he called out.

Bains nodded, then stopped in the middle of the office, waiting for it.

'Can we speak, please?' the man asked.

'And you are?'

The man scowled at him. 'You know who I am, Bains. Can we speak in private?'

'I'm really busy,' Bains said.

'Doesn't matter.' The man turned and walked back to the office.

Bains knew better than to ignore him.

'I need a coffee,' he said, closing the door behind him and moving over to the coffee machine in the corner. 'I've been on all night,' he explained.

'So have we.' The other one spoke. He wore a more expensive coat, and there was a slight sneer to his features.

'I'm Francis Doyle,' the first one said, voice more pleasant now. 'I'm looking for Karen Sharpe.'

'I haven't seen her,' Bains said, putting a heaped spoon of Greg Oxford's coffee into his filter machine. 'Do you want coffee?'

'No, thanks. When did you last see her?'

Bains realized he would have to get water from the kitchen. He turned to face them. 'Who are you with? Do you have some ID?'

Doyle took out a wallet and passed him a slim strip of plastic, credit card size. 'Of course,' he said. 'We're with SO13.' Bains looked at the card. It was an ordinary Metropolitan Police warrant card. The anti-terrorist branch, he guessed, wouldn't necessarily have advertised their department on their cards, so it might have been true. But Liz had said they claimed they were from Witness Protection. He sighed. 'I last saw her twenty-one months ago,' he said. 'On the twenty-fourth of March nineteen ninety-eight.'

'Has she been in contact since then?'

He shook his head. 'Not a word. Keeping in touch isn't Karen. Why are you looking for her?'

'To help her.'

'Does she need help? We were told she'd gone home to Northern Ireland on a career break, to spend quality time with her kid.' He gave the official police line with more than a hint of sarcasm.

'She's in trouble,' Doyle said. 'We have to find her

quickly.' He bit his fingernail, looking nervous. 'The kid as well,' he added.

Bains stared at him, determined to say nothing, to keep his face expressionless.

'You're not bothered about the kid?' Doyle asked. 'She might get hurt.'

'I haven't heard from either of them.'

'You were close to the kid.'

'I haven't seen them. Nothing you tell me will change that.'

Doyle took a breath, staring at Bains, trying to weigh him up. Bains stared back, his eyes blank. 'I hope you're telling the truth, Bains.'

'Why shouldn't I be?'

'Because she might have told you she doesn't want help.'

'She's not my problem. Go look in my house if you don't believe me.'

'We already have.'

Bains stepped towards him, angry. 'You've been in my house?'

'You just said we could,' the other one said.

'That was now! You had no right—'

'The door was open,' Doyle said.

The other one stood up. He was much taller than Doyle, thick-set. 'We shut it for you,' he said, without a trace of a smile. 'You should be thanking us.'

They both stepped towards the door. Doyle held out a business card.

'If you care about Karen and Mairead, call me if you hear anything from them. Anything. Understand?'

'What does this have to do with terrorism?' Bains asked, restraining himself.

Doyle just looked at him, card still held out. Bains took it.

He watched them until they had left the CID room, then walked to the window to watch them leave the station. They crossed to an illegally parked Volvo. Bains waited until they had driven off before leaning back against the wall and closing his eyes.

In his head he could see Mairead speaking to him the day Karen had left. Tuesday, 24 March 1998. He knew the exact date. He could not forget. She had given no warning, left no message. It had been left to Mairead to write him a note, probably without Karen realizing she was doing it: '*I don't want to do this, Pete. I hope you will be OK.*' From a ten-year-old. He had hated Karen Sharpe then, hated that he had ever set eyes on her. She had done nothing but argue and bicker with her daughter in the entire time they were together, yet she had removed her from his life without a word of explanation.

TEN

It was slipping from her. Everything the three of them had together, everything she had become, she could feel it slipping away. Already the scenes in her head – Nick, Rachel and herself – were like dream images, things that had happened to someone else. What she had feared most was happening again; the past, lurching up from inside her as it always had, threatening to pull to pieces everything she had worked for. She had to fight it. She had to remember who she was.

I am Anna Hart. I am Anna Hart. She repeated it to herself, over and over.

Terror. She could feel it in her body like a static charge, flooding her with so much adrenalin her skin was prickling. He had a gun against her daughter's chest. He had shot the taxi driver in the head. Whatever it was he wanted, whatever was going to happen, she had to keep control. Now wasn't the time to leap to conclusions. The voice rising up through her throat had to be held back. She had no idea what was going on here. Find out what he wanted, find out what was happening. *Then* work out what to do. Meanwhile, she was Anna Hart.

But there was someone else inside her – someone she had spent eighteen months trying to forget. That person wanted to take control *right now*. She wanted to scream at the top of her voice, give in to the fear, thrash out. Above all, thrash out. Get his gun off him, turn it on him, empty the thing into his gut. She had to hold it back. He had the gun on Rachel. He would kill her if she put a foot wrong. *Be Anna Hart*, she thought.

78

But she was dealing with someone Anna Hart had never encountered before. He wasn't from her world, he wasn't like anyone she had ever mixed, met or dealt with. He had bent over in the road and fired the gun at the man's head. If he was capable of doing that he was capable of anything.

She had acted parts before; this was no different. She had to observe, note, assess, plan, think. *Think!* She screamed it silently to herself. *Think!*

A hostage situation. She knew what she was meant to do. Act as if she was not afraid of him. Get him talking, find out about him, tell him about herself. Stop him from thinking of her as a job, an object, something that didn't matter. Humanize herself. Then it would be difficult for him to hurt them.

'You look like you're in pain,' she said. 'Did you get hurt?'

She heard him hiss with disgust, or anger – she couldn't tell. There were beads of sweat running out of his hairline and his hands were shaking. Maybe the killing had affected him. Perhaps if she just kept quiet for long enough he would break down, start crying, give in. But he had stepped up to the taxi driver deliberately, as if he had done it before.

She had heard the voice on the other end of his phone. *Change of plan.* That was what he had said. So what had been the original plan? What if this wasn't a robbery, or a kidnapping? What if the original plan had been to shoot them? *This isn't about money.* She bit down on her lip, pushing the thought from her brain.

Anna Hart had no enemies. She had done nothing wrong, cruel or spiteful in her entire thirty-nine years. She ran a tiny art gallery in York, lived in a house with no near neighbours, looked after her child, kept herself to herself.

The only thing he could want was her money. It didn't matter what he said. It *had* to be about money.

'You look hurt,' she said, trying again. 'Do you need help? If you are hurt we could—'

'*Shut the fuck up! Shut the fuck up!*' He leaned forward between the seats and screamed the words into her ear. She held her breath. She could hear Rachel crying again, more softly this time. The tears were panicking her.

'I'm sorry,' she said. 'I'm only trying to help.'

They were coming down into Addingham. She slowed, watching the rows of houses slipping past. Twenty past seven and few signs of life. No one to see them, no one to hear his ranting. She felt a peculiar sense of unreality. How could all this be happening to her? How could a man be threatening to kill her daughter? How could she have seen someone's head split apart by a bullet? His blood and brains were caked around the bottom of her trousers, yet in this village they were still sleeping behind drawn curtains, getting up, dressing for work.

'Do you want me to drive through Ilkley, or—'

'I'll tell you what I want. Just drive.'

She watched him screwing his face up. He *was* in pain, she was sure of it.

They reached the A65 and he told her to turn right, towards Ilkley. To the east the sky was brightening, the red dawn light passing quickly into Yorkshire grey. A feeling of discomfort rippled up her spine. An alarm bell. She had not been here for nearly eighteen months. She could feel the pressure of buried memories, pushing to get out. She needed to anchor herself, to get a sense of reality. She tried to think back to her childhood, to find something there that would strengthen her. But Anna Hart's existence had been cosseted, privileged, trouble-free. Nothing she had ever done could have prepared her for this.

'Turn here, to the right. Now.'

A back lane, leading up to the moor. No witnesses, no traffic, no police. But what would she do if there were any? Stall the car, open the door, scream for help? Crash it deliberately? Not this time. He had a gun right on her daughter. So long as that threat existed, *nothing* was worth the risk. If he had been beside her, sitting in the front seat, pointing the gun at her instead, things would be different. There would be possibilities. But there was nothing she could do while they were in this car.

She felt like crying. She had become useless, caught in a fairy-tale world of wealth and privilege. Could she even remember what she should be doing in this kind of situation, in *reality*? She moved a hand down to her leg and twisted a lump of her flesh until the pain flashed in her brain. *Wake up!* She had been living a dream, and all the while, out there, this filth had been waiting for her.

She struggled to hold the lump in her throat and forced herself to think it through. She had stood by at the roadside and let the cabbie act alone. Stupid, useless. That had been the time to move. She couldn't let another chance like that pass. If she did not do something he would get her to this place – *somewhere more private*, she had heard – and that would be the end of her. He could not let her go now. She had seen him, her daughter had seen him. They could identify him. He had killed. The first shot had seemed like an accident, the gun just going off as the cabbie had advanced on him. But not the second. He had executed the man because he did not want witnesses.

'Stop here! Stop now!' He was shouting at her again.

'Where?' She was confused. There was desperation in his voice, but they were nowhere near the A65 and there was nowhere to stop. Why did he want to stop here? The road was a single lane, leading up through beech and sycamore trees, a back lane which would eventually bring them over to the back of Rombald's Moor and across to Keighley, or east to Shipley. She looked for a wider space to park, slowing down.

'*Stop now!*' He was between the seats, gun against her head. '*Do as I say!*'

She floored the brake pedal. He lurched forward slightly, off balance. For an instant she thought to grab at the weapon, but he was back too quickly.

'Get out of the car. Follow me. Do exactly what I say.' His face had drained of colour. As he moved back to take hold of Rachel she could see his free hand was touching his stomach. Had the cabbie managed to hit him there? There was no blood on him, nothing she could see that looked like an injury.

She stepped out into the road, watching for cars. Nothing could get past them. The Range Rover was blocking the lane. *What was he doing?* She saw him pulling Rachel out of the other side and ran to stop him, shouting at the top of her voice, 'Leave her! Stop pulling her like that.'

He was dragging her into the trees. She felt her heart bolt. One of his hands was twisted through Rachel's clothing, the other was waving the gun in the air. Rachel had fallen to her knees and was crying out in pain. He was dragging her along behind him.

'What are you doing?' She was struck suddenly, sickeningly, by the thought that he was a sex offender, that what this was about was *sex*, not money, that he was going to rape her daughter. She ran after him, eyes searching for a branch or a stone.

He turned on her suddenly, holding the gun into Rachel's terrified face. 'Shut up and follow. Follow me now or I swear I will kill this kid.' His face was twisted with pain. 'I don't want to do it,' he said. 'I have a daughter of my own. But I will if I have to. Follow me now.'

She stopped. His voice had changed tone. He was pleading with her. Something was wrong with him.

'I'll follow,' she said quickly. 'But whatever you are going to do, don't bring her into it. Leave her alone.'

He bent double suddenly, clutching at his stomach. They were hardly into the tree-line. If anyone drove up now they would see them.

'It has to be here,' he said. He began to pull at the shellsuit he was wearing; undoing zips with one hand, holding Rachel's hair and the gun with the other. His eyes were on Anna.

'What are you going to do?' Her voice was trembling, terrified. She took a step forward. To the right of her she could see a stone about the size of a half brick.

'I have to shit,' he said.

Her thoughts froze. 'What?'

'I have to shit.'

His trousers were around his ankles. Rachel was grimacing, turning away from him. He was leaning against her, trying to squat, hang onto her and still be able to point the gun, all at the same time.

'I have a disease,' he said. 'A problem . . .' His face creased up. He was defecating. She couldn't believe it. She turned her face away, caught between relief and disgust.

'I feel sick, Mummy,' Rachel said.

'Shut up, you little bitch.'

Anna turned back to him, forcing herself to watch.

'Get me some tissue,' he said.

She could smell him now. She brought her sleeve up to her face.

83

'There's tissue in the car, in the glove compartment. Bring me it.'

He tried to point the gun at her, twisting Rachel's head at the same time. She pulled her head away, threatening to unbalance him.

'Stand still! Stand still or you'll suffer.' He wrenched at her hair again, making her shout out.

'Stay still, Rachel,' Anna said.

'Get me the tissue!'

She turned and hurried back to the car. The tissue turned out to be a toilet roll. She picked it up, left the door open and began to walk back towards him, her eyes fixed on the stone. As she approached he was struggling to stand, trousers still around his ankles, looking down at the mess he had made on the ground. His eyes were off her. She dropped the tissue when she was almost in front of him, letting it roll towards him, then stooped quickly to retrieve it. He saw the movement and started to say something. As she came up her hand closed over the stone instead. She swung it up at him.

He saw it coming and flinched, surprise in his eyes. She held it flat in her hand and swung it underarm, up into his chin. His head jerked back and a little grunt came out of his mouth. She stepped forwards and swung it again, sideways. It struck his temple as he toppled backwards, letting go of Rachel.

'Run!' Anna yelled at her. But Rachel was off guard, surprised. She took a step, then paused, looking back. In that second of indecision the gun went off.

The report was muted in the woods. She saw the recoil and a puff of dirt and leaf litter near him. He was flat on his back, arm outstretched. Rachel was out of the line of fire. Anna stepped forward and tried to kick the gun from his hand.

'*Run!*' she yelled again. But Rachel was terrified now, rooted to the spot.

He rolled through the dirt and came up facing her, eyes burning with rage, face red, the gun pointed directly at her chest. She went rigid. He began to curse and swear, struggling to stand up and keep the gun on her.

'You run anywhere and you are fucking dead.'

He dragged at his trousers, pulling them up, face flushed, panting. Anna took a step back, away from him. She had screwed up. A perfect chance. She had hit him, but not hard enough. She had thought he would go down unconscious, be unable to move. She had thought she would be able to get the gun off him. She had expected something more than just knocking him off balance. She felt petrified.

He strode over to Rachel and grabbed her arm.

'You twat!' he yelled. 'You have covered me with shit!' He brought the gun down onto her head, sending her sprawling across the dirt.

ELEVEN

'It wasn't a good relationship.'

Bains nodded, trying to focus on Diana Hanley's words. It was difficult. For four weeks the division had been undergoing 'building works' at Milgarth. As a consequence, all the cells and most of the interview rooms were closed, forcing the staff to process all prisoners and many witnesses in Leeds City Bridewell, a vast subterranean cell complex beneath the magistrates court, at the other end of the Headrow. The Bridewell enjoyed no natural light, low ceilings, narrow corridors and an air supply that was piped and stale. The place was more like a troop ship than a police station. The ventilation and heating system made a continual low-level background hum, like the reverberations of a ship's engines. Even the doorways were built into walls that looked like bulkheads. The place was such a warren of twisting passages and dog legs that Bains could still get lost, after nearly ten years on the Force.

He sat in a tiny, airless interview room and considered what Hanley's sister had so far given him.

'You told my colleagues from North Yorkshire constabulary that your brother and Anna Hart argued yesterday?' he asked.

She dabbed at her eyes with the box of tissues he had given her. He didn't know why. There were no tears. Diana Hanley was clearly still in the first stage of grief, her brain not yet registering the brutal reality of what she had just seen. Refusing advice, she had driven straight to the scene before they had a chance to remove her brother's body to LGI and appropriately present him to her. The sight had thrown her into a state similar to shock, a kind of clinical numbness. Bains guessed it would be some time before she started to cry properly.

'They always argued,' she said. She had a deep voice, with an extravagant public school accent. 'Like I told you, it was a terrible relationship. They should not have been together.'

Bains nodded sympathetically. 'And you were there when they argued yesterday?'

'Yes. She even threw things at him.'

'Could that have injured him?'

'Maybe. I don't know. I tried to keep out of the way. I sat with Rachel while it was going on.'

'Rachel? Their child?'

'*Her* child. I told you already that they were only together for just over a year.'

'Her child, then. Was Nick close to Rachel?'

'He was like a father to her. Rachel was closer to Nick than she was to her mother. Anna hated that, of course. It didn't fit in with her plans.'

'Her plans?'

'Yes. I think she knew what she was doing.'

Bains waited for her to elaborate. She didn't.

'You told me he was depressed,' he continued. 'Was he on any medication for depression?'

She shook her head. 'I don't know. I doubt it. I doubt he even told anyone. We weren't very good at talking in my family.' She looked up at him. 'We English aren't very good at asking for help, you know . . .' She coughed uncomfortably. 'If you see what I mean.'

Bains knew what she *meant*, though she had *said* slightly more. 'We English' was meant to exclude him. He ignored it. 'Has he ever tried to commit suicide before?'

'God no! He was never depressed. She has caused this.'

'In less than eighteen months?'

'Why not? She wanted to make him ill and she did.'

'Why?'

Hanley raised her eyebrows. 'Why do you think?'

Bains shook his head. 'I don't know. Tell me.'

'My brother was a wealthy man, officer. I believe it may have all come down to money, in the end.'

Bains rubbed his temples. The neon tubes in the Bridewell were like emergency lighting from a 1950s naval war movie. They were giving him a headache.

'You don't like Anna Hart, then?' he asked, trying to put the question gently.

She looked up at him. 'Is it *that* obvious?'

Sarcasm. Twenty minutes after identifying her brother's corpse. But he shouldn't hold it against her. Everyone had to deal with grief in their own way. He knew that from bitter personal experience. Some people just got nasty for a while.

'I believe she has killed my brother, Inspector. She drove him to it. She knew what she was doing. She's not a stupid woman.'

He realized he was tired. He had been working for over fifteen hours now without a rest break, almost twenty hours in total. The woman's edginess was bound to get to him.

'She was manipulative, Inspector. You will see that if you ever have the misfortune to meet her.'

'Sergeant,' he said, yawning. 'I'm not an inspector.'

She shrugged. 'That hardly matters.'

'You're sure it was your brother?' he asked again.

She looked away from him. 'I could see enough . . .'

She frowned intensely. She was almost attractive when she frowned. The frown gave some character to a face

88

that, for Bains, was too horsey, too English-upper-class-jodhpurs-and-whips-brigade. Usually when he spoke to Hanley's type they managed to make him seem like a little piece of brown shit, stuck to the bottom of their shoe.

'That mole I pointed out,' she said, sniffling slightly. 'It was very distinctive. It was definitely Nicky.'

He made a note of her reference to the mole. That would have to go into the statement.

'Did he have a GP?'

'I think so. Someone in Harley Street. I'm not sure who.'

'No one local?'

'I doubt it.' She almost sneered the words. No one local would be good enough.

He sat staring at her for a few moments, trying to gather his thoughts. She had given him everything he wanted to close this job now. She had positively identified the body, told a history of possible psychiatric disturbance and even provided a nice little trigger in the form of a difficult relationship. So why was he still bothered?

'Any idea why he would set fire to himself?' he asked, articulating only the most obvious of his doubts.

She looked up at him and for the first time he saw something like real emotion cross her features. What was it though? Not pity, or grief, not shock or even horror. It was *fear* he could see in the back of her eyes. Because she knew as well as he that people like Nick Hanley didn't do that kind of thing. She shook her head.

'OK,' he said. 'I understand how awful all this is.' He folded the sheet of paper on which he had written his notes. 'I'll get a short statement typed up and you can sign it later. I know you'll want to get back to your family now.' She had told him she lived with her husband and two children in 'Chelsea and Cornwall'. She had been visiting to attend to some 'business affairs' when this had happened.

'Will you be staying in Reeth?' he asked. He couldn't recall the name of Hanley's spread up there. 'Or going straight back south?'

'I don't know,' she said. 'I have a place in Calverley – we breed Cleveland Bays there . . .' She looked at him to see if he knew what they might be. He looked back at her, face empty. 'They're an endangered breed,' she explained.

'Of course,' he said. Pigs, sheep, horses? They could be anything so far as he was concerned.

She frowned. 'I usually stay there. She – Anna Hart – didn't like me staying at Black Carr Hall. Not normally . . . I don't know . . . I don't know what I'll do . . . .'

'Well, if you could let us know where you are,' he said. 'Just in case something else comes up.' He stood up. He could just imagine what the place in Calverley was like. Diana Hanley had come to identify the corpse of her brother dressed in a quilted green sleeveless jacket, a scruffy Barbour, tight brown riding breeches and a pair of wellies.

She stood up, running her hand through untidy, brown, shoulder-length hair. She had given her age as forty-four, but her face was smooth and lightly tanned, her hair showing no signs of grey.

'And you have no idea where we can locate Miss Hart?' he asked again.

'None whatsoever. But why would you wish to, Inspector? She walked out on him yesterday. And it's not as if she's kin.'

TWELVE

She drove with tears streaming down her face, trying to control the vehicle but hardly able to keep it in a straight line. He sat in the back with Rachel's head pulled into his lap, his arm locked tightly around her neck, the gun pressed against her temple. If she tried to say anything he shouted obscenities at her and tightened his grip on Rachel's neck until she screamed out. But her cries were muffled, subdued.

The blow had struck Rachel across the back of her head, knocking her off her feet. Anna had run to her immediately, throwing herself onto the ground between the gun and her prostrate body. When she had moved her head to examine her, Rachel's eyes had been open but shocked. She had not lost consciousness, but for all Anna knew he had hit her hard enough to crack her skull. He had tried to pull her away from Rachel by taking hold of her by the hair.

She had started to attack him then, grabbing at the gun, standing to kick and punch him, yelling at him with sheer fright. She felt sick thinking about it. She was useless. She had hit him twice with a stone and failed to damage him. She had moved her arm sloppily, without co-ordination or power, like some pathetic schoolgirl throwing a ball. She had punched and kicked him with all her strength, in a rage, and he wasn't even marked. Nothing she was capable of could stop him. He had punched her four times in quick succession, once in the stomach, taking the wind out of her, three times in the head, so hard she had momentarily blacked out. By the time she was able to stand again he had already put Rachel in the car, locked it and was coming back for her.

Everything stank of his faeces. He couldn't stop cursing her because of it. She tried to stop crying, tried to focus on the road ahead, but her mind was full of blind panic. There had been no blood on Rachel, just an immediate swelling at the crown of her skull, but the blow had been hard. Her brain might be haemorrhaging even now. She needed to get her to a hospital.

'You said you had a daughter,' she shouted. 'Would you do this to her?'

For once he didn't respond with a threat.

'Why are you doing this? She is only eleven years old. Whatever this is about, she is innocent.'

'She is fine,' he said, voice hard. 'I can do worse to her.'

'You don't know that she is fine . . .' She tried to see her.

'Turn around! Concentrate on the road!'

'Sit her here, in the front, so that I can see her—'

'Turn around!'

She heard Rachel groan as he moved backwards, bringing up a foot to kick through the gap between the seats. She turned back to the road quickly, wiping her eyes. They were almost at the other end of Rodley now, on the B6157. She had taken back roads all the way from Baildon, down through Shipley, Calverley and Rodley. She had convinced him it was the best route to avoid Guiseley and the airport area, but the intention had been to drive through as many built-up areas as possible. Could it be true that nobody had seen them? They had passed many cars and several pedestrians. The clock in the dashboard said it was 7.50 a.m. People were leaving their homes to go to work, traffic was building up. The day was dull and grey, the sun still low in the sky. But soon there would be complete daylight.

'She might be injured. You can't tell—'

'So get a move on. The quicker you get us there, the quicker this will be over.'

'Don't you care that you might have hurt a child?'

He didn't reply. She felt guilt gripping her chest. *She* had done this to Rachel. *She* had exposed her to this. There was something evil inside her, something reckless. How could she have introduced her to Nick in the first place? Everything had seemed safe, easy, but there were rules. Nothing was ever how it seemed. She had forgotten the rules and fallen in love with him.

She caught her breath. She was panicking, thinking too fast. He had said it wasn't about money, but if she could work out what was going on, maybe they would find their way out of it, get things back to normal. She had to hold it together.

'Are you OK, Rachel?' she said. 'Can you speak to me, please?' Rachel had said nothing since it had happened. 'She can't even hear me—'

'She can hear.' His voice was tense, angry.

'If she could hear she would—'

'She's playing games. You both are. *Say something to your mother.*' He hissed the words through gritted teeth.

Anna listened. Ahead she could see the crossroads at Kirkstall Road, traffic lights. She needed to turn left onto the A65, Abbey Road.

'If you don't say something I'll whack you so hard—'

'All right. I'll say something.' Rachel's voice was suddenly clear. 'You stink of shit.'

Anna held her breath. At the lights she could see a police car, pulled up and waiting for the change. 'She's only a child,' she said. 'Please don't hurt her for—'

'Shut up!'

She heard a sharp intake of breath from Rachel. What was he doing to her?

'There's a police car,' she said quickly, desperate to distract him. She heard him move, heard Rachel gasp for air, then swear at him. Then he was leaning forward, his head between the seats.

'Where?'

'Straight ahead, at the lights.' She pointed to it.

'Put your fucking hand down! Don't point.' He moved back. 'If you do anything, I'll shoot her through the face.'

'I won't do anything.'

'You better not. I mean it. *I mean it.*' He was panicking again.

She turned left in front of the police car. It was a marked Volvo and there were two occupants in the front, both male, both staring at her. She stared back at them, eyes desperate, but face without expression. Then she was past it. She brought her sleeve up and quickly wiped the trickle of blood from her nose. In the rear-view mirror she saw him turning to look out of the back window, to see if they would follow. Had they seen the blood running from her nose?

She reached up and twisted the mirror so that she could see Rachel. She had done it before and he had told her not to. He was still staring out of the back window, watching for the police. Her eyes found Rachel's, wide open, bright with anger, head held firmly in the crook of his left arm. Anna tried to communicate with her eyes only, tried to tell her that she would be safe, that this would pass. But Rachel just stared at her. He began to turn back. She looked away.

'They're not following,' she said. The ruins of Kirkstall

Abbey passed her on the left, followed by the flat area of parkland leading down to the River Aire and the canal. The road behind her was empty.

'Turn here,' he hissed. 'This is it.'

The sign said 'Abbey Industrial Estate'. There were the names of a few units on a big board, slots where others were still vacant. She turned off and followed a ramp down from the main road towards the river and canal.

'Stop!'

There was a high chain-fence and gates leading into the site. She stopped the car and looked over, trying to memorize the location. There was a group of big, low sheds – long, modern, lightweight construction – then other buildings of older design behind them. Then a bank of tall poplar trees, probably flanking the canal or the river. Behind her Abbey Road passed uphill towards Horsforth, obscured from view by more trees and bushes. To her left, once again screened behind vegetation, were the open parkland and playing fields leading to Kirkstall Abbey. The place was too private. You couldn't see it from the road, the parkland or the river.

'Drive through the gates.'

She felt her heart beginning to pound again. 'Which place is it? There are—'

'Drive through the gates!'

She pulled the Range Rover through and saw a door in the furthest shed begin to open. There was a column of steam or smoke rising into the air behind it from a chimney or flue she couldn't see. The yard in front of her was concrete, dirty, strewn with shreds of bubblewrap and old cardboard boxes. In between parked cars, there were skips placed up against the fronts of some of the sheds, laden with office junk, broken crates and bits of machinery. A tall man stepped out of the doorway to the furthest shed and beckoned her over with his hand. She drove towards him.

'That's him. That's Stijn,' the gunman whispered. 'Do as he says.'

She stopped in front of the shed and the man called Stijn shouted something to someone inside. She turned to look at Rachel. The gunman was no longer holding her. She was rubbing her neck, an irritated look on her face.

'We're almost in the middle of Leeds,' Anna said. 'No one can hurt us here.'

The man outside walked up to her door and opened it.

'Get out,' he said. He had a South African accent. She looked out at him. He was massive, thick with muscle. She looked at his hand, holding the door open. It was a shovel of broken knuckles and heavy, calloused fingers. His head was clean-shaven, top and bottom, showing a skull uneven with bony protrusions, cheeks pitted with old acne scars, a squashed, deviated nose, old scarring around his eyebrows, shredded ears; a rugby player, or a boxer. He was wearing a clean, immaculately pressed suit, a pale blue shirt and matching tie. Even his black leather shoes looked cared for.

She stepped out and the smell of the place rose around her at once – the stink of live animals, cooped and fearful, their ordure, the sickening smell of putrefaction and fresh blood. She retched at once and looked back to see Rachel screwing up her face against it. From somewhere within the shed nearest her she could hear the bellowing of a goat or a cow, a long, desperate, mournful noise, punctuated by the intermittent throb of some kind of machine.

The man beside her smiled, showing a perfect set of gleaming teeth, then reached a hand to the top of her head, closing his fingers around her skull like it was a football, forcing her down to her knees in front of him.

Without saying a word he brought his knee up into her face, slamming her back against the car. She heard her nose crack, felt the blood flowing over her mouth. Rachel started to scream, but the sound was cut short by a brutal thud. Anna tried to stand, to see what was happening, but her legs were useless.

'Get them inside.'

Someone was taking hold of her, under the armpits. Another set of hands in her hair. They were dragging her across the concrete yard. Her vision cleared and she struggled to stand up. She could hear herself shouting, 'I can walk. Leave me. I can walk.'

She stood and looked desperately for Rachel. She was being carried by the gunman. She looked limp in his arms. Beside her the shaved man closed his hand around her jaw and squeezed until she began to shriek with pain. She heard something splitting in her mouth. He pressed his lips up against her ear.

'I don't care about you. I don't care whether you live or die. I will do everything in front of your daughter. I will cut you, beat you, rape you. Then I will do the same to her. Do you understand?'

She tried to speak to him, to tell him that she understood, but he had her jaw in a clamp.

'You will tell me everything I want to know.' He released her. She gasped in pain and brought her hands up to examine her jaw. Immediately he pushed her in the back, knocking her to the ground again.

'Get up and get inside. You said you could walk, so walk.'

She got to her knees and heard him step up behind her, hands wrapping through her hair and slipping off again. It was too short to hold. He kicked at her instead. She scrambled sideways, stood up.

'I'm doing it!' she shouted. Her voice sounded tiny,

pathetic, full of incontinent fear. 'Leave my daughter, please. I will do everything you want.'

She staggered past a pile of broken cages, used to transport chickens or turkeys. There were feathers still stuck to some of the bars. He followed her quickly, pushing her through the door of the shed and pulling it shut behind them. She heard him shout, 'Get the car out of sight. Move it around the back.'

Her eyes adjusted to the flickering strip lighting. The noise of machinery was loud, but she could hear the pathetic wail of frightened animals. They were in an abattoir. She could see a long holding area, with crates and pens, straw and old faeces on the floor. At the end was a wall with several openings; the noise of machinery coming from beyond it. She saw someone, an Asian man, in overalls and wellies walking casually along a line of pens, a dripping hose trailing behind him. She looked for Rachel but the gunman had disappeared with her.

The man called Stijn took her by the arm and pulled her into a corridor. He closed another door behind them and pushed her along to an office created out of flimsy partitions. She stepped through and saw Rachel lying on the floor, the gunman standing above her lighting a cigarette. Rachel's eyes were open and she was hunched into a foetal position, shivering and crying. There was a trickle of blood coming out of her nose. Anna tried to go to her, but Stijn caught her by the arm.

'Stand her up,' he said, speaking to the gunman. Anna noticed for the first time that his voice was high-pitched, out of place in his body. He spoke functionally, without looking at the man, who bent down and pulled Rachel to her feet. Stijn reached over and took the cigarette off him. 'No smoking.' He scrunched it in his hand and dropped it on the floor.

Anna tried to take in where they were, but her eyes couldn't leave Rachel's. What had Stijn done to her in the yard? She was crying uncontrollably. Anna began to move towards her daughter. But before she could get to her Stijn threw something in an underarm movement. She saw it cross the space between them, saw the gunman stepping away to avoid it. Rachel was standing as it hit her. It splashed across her head and face, drenching her in black liquid. She realized what it was as the stench caught in her throat. He had tossed a bucket of blood at her.

Rachel staggered backwards, spluttering, the stuff running into her eyes and down her neck. Anna saw her hands move to wipe it, then she realized what it was and began to vomit. Stijn turned to face Anna, setting the bucket down.

'That's what she's going to look like,' he said. 'But the blood will be hers.'

Anna felt her legs giving way again. She thought she might have wet herself. She leaned a hand out to steady herself, but Stijn caught her by the jaw again, holding her upright at arm's length.

'I have two questions for you,' he said. 'Do you understand?' He waited until she was looking into his eyes. 'I want no lies.'

She tried to tell him she agreed, that she would not lie, but he was holding her too tightly.

'I'll start with the easy one,' he said. 'Where is Nicholas Hanley?'

99

THIRTEEN

Bains was in a makeshift interview room at Milgarth, talking to Imran Akhtar, when Alan White opened the door on them.

'Pete. I need to speak to you.' White glanced at Akhtar, then stepped back out into the corridor and closed the door. He hadn't knocked.

Bains smiled at Akhtar. 'Sorry. If you just wait here a moment.'

In the corridor White started to walk, moving in the direction of the CID office. He was a short man, but he could walk quickly. Bains hurried to keep up with him.

'I've been trying to get you,' Bains said.

'I know. I've been ignoring your calls.' White grinned at him. He was about five years older than Bains with short, tidy black hair and slightly sallow skin. Unlike Bains, his face was clean-shaven, his suit, which looked expensive, neatly pressed. They said he was good, that he got results, but when Bains had spoken to him in the past he had been put off by a rapid alternation between furious concentration and dreamy distraction. They turned into the CID office and White walked straight over to Greg Oxford's office. Jodi Hayward was in there, using the phone. It was nearly eight-thirty and the place was only just beginning to fill up.

'Can we have this office, please?' White said, not bothering to find out who she was or who she was on the phone to. Bains heard her apologizing. She hung up and stood to leave.

'We won't be long,' Bains said to her.

'What's your name?' White asked, suddenly noticing that she was a woman.

'DC Hayward, sir.'

'She's working with me on this suicide,' Bains said.

'You look very young,' White said. 'Younger detectives are refreshing to have around.' She blushed, not sure how to respond. White moved behind the desk to sit down, but she was still in the process of getting up from the chair. Bains watched him lean over her and help pull the chair out for her. He stood just too close for comfort.

'Especially younger women,' he said. 'That perfume you're wearing is gorgeous. It's Happy, isn't it?'

Bains frowned. Hayward turned a brighter shade of pink.

'It is,' she said, standing in front of White now. 'How did you know?'

'I wear it myself,' White said. 'Happy for Men, of course. You can't smell it?' Bains watched in amazement as he leaned his face closer to Hayward, inviting her to sniff him. Hayward looked panic-stricken. She stepped back a pace.

'It's very nice, sir,' she said.

White winked at her. 'Great minds think alike, eh? Will we have the pleasure of your company on bug watch?'

She looked at Bains, as if to ask what planet White was from.

'The Millennium,' White said. 'The Y2K bug. Civil society is going to break down tonight. Remember?'

'Oh,' she smiled nervously. There was a 'Force Disaster Plan' to cope with the predicted effects of all computers crashing on the stroke of midnight.

'Are you working?' White asked, still grinning at her. 'Tonight?'

'Yes.'

Bains could see that she was frightened the question was going to be the prelude to some kind of invitation. 'We're both meant to be off already,' he said. 'We're back on at eight. Everyone is.'

'Shame,' White said, eyes moving quickly up and down her figure as she turned her back on him. 'I was going to get you assigned to my squad. You could have kept me company.'

Bains didn't say anything until she had closed the door and left them.

'She's married,' he said then. What he had wanted to say was something more cautionary. But he knew White well enough. It wasn't worth it.

'Doesn't matter,' White said, sitting down. 'Great tits.'

He looked at Bains as if expecting a response. Bains said nothing.

'Can she think?' White asked.

'She's very good,' Bains replied, still standing. 'Though she hasn't been a detective long.'

'Did you notice her tits?' White asked him.

Bains looked at him. White was himself a married man and Bains knew his wife. Jane White was a detective assigned to domestic violence at Killingbeck. A sharp, practical woman, she had been dealing with male bigotry for nearly ten years. Bains wondered how Alan White ever got along with her. Was it possible that White was a totally different person at home? If he had even dropped a hint to Jane that he spoke about female officers in this way Bains doubted his feet would touch the ground.

'I love women,' White said, fishing something from his briefcase. 'All shapes and sizes. I love them all. I'd shag anything once. Are you a faithful man, Bains?'

'I'm not married.'

'No. Of course not. She's a looker, isn't she?' He slid a

photograph across the table between them. Bains sat down and took it. It was a picture of a woman.

'Who, sir?'

'DC Hayward. That little brunette. You must have difficulty keeping your hands off her.' He looked away from Bains, staring out of the window, dreamily. 'I don't know how a man like you can stay single. Is it a religious thing?'

Bains scowled at him. 'No, sir. It's not.'

'What do you think of that one?' White asked him, pointing to the photo. Bains looked at it again. It looked like a holiday snapshot; a woman in a bikini on a beach. She was tall, with short, cropped blonde hair, a thin figure. The face was angled sharply upwards, looking at something in the sky. Bains thought there was something familiar about her, but with the face angled and in profile he couldn't be sure. 'Who is it?' he asked.

'Gorgeous, isn't she?'

Bains shook his head. White was so persistent it was almost amusing.

'It's Anna Hart,' White said. 'We found that in her luggage.'

'Anna Hart? How did you . . . ? What? What luggage?'

White smiled, pleased that he had surprised him. 'We might be investigating the same thing,' he said. 'I've got a fifty-one-year-old Asian male, shot twice; once in the chest, once in the back of the head. Both close range, the head shot from no more than a foot away, as he was lying on the ground wounded. Looks like a professional hit.'

'Your airport incident?'

'Correct. The man was a taxi driver. He was found lying in the middle of the road beside his cab. A small country lane just to the west of the airport. His cab had been in a collision – rear-end damage. All the doors were left open. In the boot we found four pieces of packed luggage. That photo came from one of them. Documents within another showed the bags belonged to Anna and Rachel Hart. Anna is thirty-nine years old – though fit with it, as you can see from that photo; Rachel is eleven. I'm still trying to get hold of a photo of her. They checked into a hotel not two miles from the scene yesterday afternoon. The guy from hotel reception says they left in a cab just after five-thirty this morning. A few minutes later the cabbie gets popped. I get there at just after six. No sign of Anna or Rachel Hart. I send DC Gainsford up to the address they gave the hotel – some huge baronial spread up in Swaledale – he finds the place empty, but with a North Yorks bobby posted at the front door. Turns out you've been looking for her, too.'

'You think she shot your taxi driver?'

White shrugged. 'Who knows? But we need to find her. Now tell me why you are looking for her.'

Bains told him the main details of Nicholas Hanley's death. 'I've been trying to get you so you could decide what to do with it,' he said, when he had finished.

'You sure it's a suicide?' White asked.

'No. Not at all. I'm waiting for the PM.'

'And you have his business partner back there in the interview room?'

'Yes. He's just given a positive ID over at LGI.'

'And the sister, too?'

'Yes.'

'Didn't you trust her?'

'How do you mean?'

'She ID'd him first. Why not run with that? Why bring in Akhtar?'

Bains shrugged, puzzled himself. 'I'm not sure. To be certain. Maybe I didn't trust her.'

White nodded, as if he understood. 'So are you sure now that it's Hanley?'

'Enough to go with.'

'Did the sister have any photos of him?'

'She said not. Weren't there any in the baggage?'

'No. Just Hart. In the kid's luggage – picture of Mum.'

'You realize there're no flights from Leeds/Bradford at that time of day?'

White feigned surprise. 'Really?'

Bains sat forward in his chair. Before White had arrived he had been tired of the whole thing and waiting to get back to his bed. But he was excited now, trying to work out the connections. 'So what's the call?' he asked.

'Do you know this Imran Akhtar?' White asked.

Bains frowned. 'He's not known. No form. He's a straight-up businessman.'

'I mean do you *personally* know him?'

Bains almost laughed. 'Why? Because he's Asian?'

White smiled, then opened his hands out in front of him. 'Why not? You're Asian, he's Asian. Yes. That's exactly what I meant.'

'I'm a Sikh, he's Muslim. And even not taking that into account—'

'A Sikh? Why no kit?'

'Kit?' Bains was getting angry now.

'Turban, long hair, that kind of thing.'

'I'm not religious. And I don't think it's very—'

White stood up, interrupting him. 'It was a joke, Pete. Where's your sense of humour?'

Bains closed his mouth.

'You go and have a chat with Akhtar, as you were doing, then get yourself up to the incident room at Weetwood for first briefing. We'll need to run these things together.'

'So you'll take it off me?'

'No. You can keep it for now. At least until we get the PM results. I need to think about things. At the moment I can't see a story which would link everything. But there must be one. Bear that in mind when you interview Akhtar.'

'How do you mean?'

'Caution him.'

Bains looked carefully at Akhtar when he sat down opposite him again. He was wearing a charcoal suit, a gold tiepin set with a large diamond, a luxuriously coloured silk tie, black brogues. Smelling faintly of aftershave, hair still wet from the shower, slightly pock-marked face, but clean-shaven. Short, oiled black hair. He certainly looked like a normal businessman. The only thing out of the ordinary was the bandage wrapped around his right hand.

'Sorry about this,' Bains said, 'but to do things properly I'm going to put this tape in the machine and record what we say.' He slotted two tapes into the machine sitting on the table between them.

Akhtar shrugged. 'Whatever. If that's what's normal.'

Bains switched it on and did the introductions: 'DC Bains 4705, in interview room at Milgarth police station with . . .' He held his hand towards Akhtar. 'Could you introduce yourself, sir?'

'Imran Akhtar.'

'OK. You are not under arrest, Mr Akhtar. You are free to leave at any time. You can get a solicitor free of charge at any time. You understand that?'

Akhtar looked puzzled. 'Of course,' he said.

'However, I do have to caution you. You need to know that if you choose to remain here you do not have to say anything, but if you do say anything it will be recorded and anything you say may be used in evidence. It may harm your defence if—'

'Wait a minute—'

Bains held a hand up. 'Let me finish, please. There's a standard wording. It may harm your defence if you do not mention, when questioned, something which you later rely on in court.'

'Defence? Court? What have I done?'

'It's a formality,' Bains said. 'It's called a caution. Did you understand it?'

'Yes. But I came here to help you. Why do I need to be cautioned?'

Bains sat back and toyed with his pen, thinking. Akhtar had already given him a perfectly credible alibi (though at the time he had not even been looking for one), a full account of the business interests of Hanley and himself and a quite clear opinion that Hanley was not the sort of person to set fire to himself. Akhtar said that he had noticed nothing in Hanley's behaviour to suggest he might consider suicide. But it was, he claimed, over three weeks since he had spoken to Hanley.

He heard Akhtar again ask him why he needed to be cautioned. He looked up at him and shrugged. 'Don't worry about it,' he said. 'It's just a formality. What I want to do now is quickly go over everything you've already told me so that we get it onto the tape. That will make it easier for me to write it out in statement form. OK?'

'OK.'

'First though, can I ask you a personal question?'

Akhtar shifted slightly in his seat. 'What kind of personal question?'

'Were you close to Nicholas Hanley?'

The question seemed to surprise him.

'Close to him? What do you mean?'

'Friendly with him.'

'He was a business partner.'

'But there were just two partners in the business?'

'That's right.'

'Will you gain anything from his death?'

Akhtar's features clouded. 'No. I won't. His side of the business will go to who he left it to.'

'In a will?'

'Yes.'

'Do you know where the will would be?'

'In the safe in the office, or at his home. Or with his lawyer. I'm not sure.'

'Have you seen the will?'

'Yes. I was a witness. So I *can't* gain anything.'

Bains didn't know enough law to know whether that was true. 'Is it a complicated will?'

'No. He left everything to his sister.'

Bains was surprised. 'Not to Anna Hart?'

'No.'

'Or Rachel Hart?'

'No. He hardly knew them.'

'I see.' Bains nodded to himself. 'But he was living with them?'

'Yes. But they weren't family.'

Bains looked up at him again. It was the second time in an hour that Anna Hart had been written off because she was not family.

'What happened to your hand?' he asked.

'Sorry?'

'Your hand?' Bains pointed to it. 'It's bandaged. With spots of blood on the bandage. Did you hurt it recently?'

Akhtar started to say something, then stopped himself. 'Why? What has this to do with Hanley's death?'

Bains stared at him for a while. Hanley's sister had been

a drama queen compared to the amount of emotion his business partner was showing.

'You're right,' he said, smiling. 'I'm just being nosy.'

a drama queen compared to the amount of emotion his
business partner was showing.
'You're right,' he said. 'I'm just being nosy.'

FOURTEEN

Stijn didn't wait for her to answer.

'Bring the kid.' The instruction was shouted to the gunman. He pushed his lips into Anna's ear. 'I'll show you what will happen,' he whispered. He closed his hand around the back of her neck and began to push her out of the room. She tried to catch her breath. He was gripping her neck so hard she could feel her brain beginning to throb, the blood supply cut off. She could hear Rachel sobbing behind her.

They walked through another corridor opening onto a yard full of penned sheep, bleating helplessly. Then into an older brick building. She tried to turn to see what was happening to Rachel but he held her neck firmly, keeping her head pointed forward, marching her in front of him at arm's length. She saw a group of three men ahead of her, standing around a machine. They were all Asian, dressed in dark grey overalls. They parted slightly as he approached, fear in their eyes. They knew him already and were frightened of him – they wouldn't help. One of them was an older, bearded man completely in white traditional dress. He had a long knife in his hands, with a very thin blade. Somebody standing beside him was holding something out to him, wrapped in a cloth. She saw the old man's eyes look at her, then down to her side, where she could hear Rachel crying. Stijn said something to the man, angrily, telling him to get on with it, to stop staring. One of the men in overalls bent forward and whispered urgently to him. Something in front of the old man suddenly moved and she saw that it was a sheep's head.

Its eyes were open and it was protruding from inside the machine. The men standing next to her were looking at her with frightened eyes, as if she too was a threat to them.

One of the men nearest the machine pulled a lever and the entire machine hummed with an electric buzz. She saw the sheep tense, then its tongue protrude slightly from between its lips. It was inside a kind of cylinder which began to rotate. The movement turned the sheep so that it was now upside down, tongue lolling out, its neck just in front of the old man in white. He was saying something (praying?) glancing back nervously at Stijn. He reached out and drew the blade across the sheep's throat in a single, clean movement. Blood began to rush out. She heard Rachel beginning to sob again. Beside her Stijn said, 'Hold her head still. Make her watch.'

She could see the sheep quivering. The jets of blood began to lose pressure. Stijn placed his mouth against her ear again. '*We will put the kid in there,*' he hissed. '*Cut her throat and bleed her dry.*' She had no time to react. He pushed her forwards, through the crowd of men and up some metal steps.

'Keep walking,' he said. She could hear that Rachel was still behind her.

They came to a set of wooden doors, leading to a meeting or break room with a long table and chairs.

'You wait in here with the kid,' he shouted back. 'Make sure she can hear. Make her listen.' He pushed Anna through the room to another door. It opened onto a store-room of some kind. There was shelving piled with boxes. She felt dizzy, still disorientated from the blow to her face. He pushed her to her knees and left the door slightly open. She could no longer hear the noise of the machines, but she could still hear Rachel weeping. Stijn stood in front of her.

'Where is Hanley?'

'He's in Newcastle.'

He lashed out at her, striking her face and knocking her flat onto her back. She cried out, then bit her lip, trying to silence herself. He was making Rachel listen.

'Not good enough,' he said. He reached into his mouth with his fingers and twisted at something, easing it away from his jaw. His teeth came away from the gums and he held them up for her to see, smiling. They were dentures. He did the same with the lower jaw, placing both pieces on the shelving next to him.

'I'm preparing myself,' he said. His voice sounded soft, unclear, his gums like an old man's. He began to un-buckle his trousers. 'You're a sexy woman,' he lisped. 'Take off your clothes.'

She began to sob at once, then pushed her fist into her mouth to stop it.

'Take them off, or I will.'

She pushed herself to her knees. 'I swear to you, he's in Newcastle.'

He leaned forward and took hold of her jacket, pushing her back with one hand and dragging at the jacket with the other. She heard it tearing and tried to hang onto it. He punched her, once, in the side of the head. It was like an explosion between her ears. Her limbs turned to jelly, collapsing her to the floor. A capsule of silence snapped shut around her, closing off the world. She was completely without motor control. She could feel herself flopping around the floor like a beached fish as he handled her, twisting her this way and that, removing her clothing. She could say nothing, do nothing, hear nothing. The room was spinning. She could see him taking off his trousers, then pushing her onto her chest, his hand on the back of her head, grinding her face into the flooring. She felt a weight in the centre of her back, driving the air from her lungs, then something pushing her legs apart. She knew that she was screaming, but could not hear it. She tried to control herself, to close her mouth, to stop the panic. She had to keep quiet, for Rachel . . .

FIFTEEN

Michael Kenny could feel his panic increasing by the minute. He sat in the room, holding onto the girl, trying not to focus on what was happening. The door to the storeroom had swung half open, so both he and the kid could hear everything, but Stijn and the woman were out of sight. He was surprised Stijn wasn't doing it in front of them. But then maybe he couldn't, with people watching. With a child watching.

Beside him, the girl had stopped crying and was shivering uncontrollably. He had let her sit on one of the chairs at the table, alongside him. He held onto her now only by the wrist, just in case. She had been a cheeky little bitch back in the car. He had hit her then when he shouldn't have. He knew that. But the pair of them had got to him; he had thought they would get away. Stijn would have killed him if they had escaped.

The woman shouldn't have hit him with the stone. She was playing with all their lives, not thinking of the consequences. He had fallen into his own shit and the smell was still in his nostrils now. His backside was still dirty with it. The blow hadn't hurt the kid. She had still been a lippy little bitch afterwards. And it had been nothing compared to what Stijn had done to her. Kenny had watched him knee her mother in the face. The child had seen it and started screaming at once. Without the slightest hesitation Stijn had punched her, straight into her face, fist clenched. She wasn't so lippy now.

He looked down at her, snivelling and sobbing to herself. The bucket of sheep's blood Stijn had thrown all over her was still streaked across her face, matted into her hair. All her attitude had been a show, a put-on. His own kids were the same. They could give you lip, they could create merry hell, but when you whacked them you saw immediately what they really were: frightened little kiddies, pretending to be grown-ups. This one was terrified now. Every time her mother cried out she flinched. He wondered if she knew what Stijn was doing to her. This wasn't the way any of it should have been done.

The mother was trying to be quiet, to control it. He could tell from the way her sobs got strangled in her throat. Stijn was making a lot of noise. It sounded like he was hitting her at the same time. At one point the woman started to wail uncontrollably, the noise punctuated by sharp exclamations of breath, like he was punching the wind out of her. Stijn started to yell things, but not in English. It was some kind of South African lingo that Kenny didn't know. His voice sounded different, less distinct. Kenny had to stop himself from imagining what was happening behind the wall. Stijn was so massive, so heavy, the woman so skinny. It made him cringe to think of it.

Stijn was getting excited. Kenny had thought he would do it to frighten her, to get out of her what he wanted. But he was enjoying it; he could tell that from the way he was panting. The noises were getting worse. Kenny squeezed the kid's wrist slightly, to get her attention, to distract her. She looked up at him and he saw the total confusion and horror written in her eyes. He felt his chest constrict. No kid should have to hear things like this. The mother was a rich twat, maybe she had something like this coming to her, but that wasn't the kid's fault.

'It's OK,' he said to her, speaking quietly. He didn't

know what to tell her to make it better. 'It will be over soon,' he said. 'Your mum will be OK.'

But it seemed to go on for ever. Kenny squirmed uncomfortably in the seat. He wanted desperately to smoke. Stijn had stopped him before, because he hated the smell. Kenny had forgotten that from the last time he had met him. Did he have long enough now? He put the gun down on the table and found the cigarette packet in his pocket. He heard Stijn begin a long, slow groan. The woman started to shout, but Stijn must have done something to her – hit her, blocked her mouth, nipped her windpipe – because the noise got cut off midway and for a while all Kenny could hear was Stijn, noisily finishing it off.

In the silence that followed he put away the cigarettes. He glanced nervously at the kid. The mother was totally quiet. Had Stijn killed her? Suddenly she began to splutter and gasp. Kenny was relieved. He heard movement and then a rustle of clothing. He picked up the gun.

Stijn appeared in the doorway, drawing a sleeve of his crumpled blue shirt across his mouth, as if he had just taken a long drink of something. His eyes were fixed on the kid. He bared his teeth and clamped them together once.

'Did she get that?' he asked. His legs were bare, covered in dense red hair and as thick as tree trunks. He had kept his socks on. He would have looked ridiculous, but Kenny could see his flaccid cock dangling below the shirt. It looked as if it were covered in blood.

'She heard everything,' Kenny said.

'Good.' Stijn stepped back out of sight again. 'That's just for starters.' Kenny could hear the woman whimpering. Stijn stepped back into sight, pulling his trousers on. He had his mobile phone out. He fastened the buckle on his belt then began to punch in numbers. His fingers were too big and he had to try a few times before he got it right. The phone looked tiny in his hand, like a toy. He held it to his ear, standing in the doorway and looking back down to where the woman must have been lying on the floor.

'Where are you?' he said, speaking into the phone.

Kenny couldn't hear the response.

'Did you find him?'

Stijn began to pace up and down in the storeroom, phone stuck to his ear. The woman was still crying, but more softly now.

'No. She says he is in Newcastle . . . I don't know. I'm not finished with her yet . . .' Kenny could just hear the other voice, but too faint to pick out words. 'What did they ask? It doesn't matter. Stop panicking. Get the stuff I asked you for and bring it to me. Then I can ask her about them. She will know where he is. It's just a matter of time before she tells me. No, not here. Not if they've already seen you.' Stijn stood in one corner, hand on the wall, staring at the floor, considering. 'I'll come to you,' he said finally. 'You say where . . . somewhere safe . . . wait a minute . . .' He turned to Kenny and shouted, 'Remember this,' then listened again to the phone. The person on the other end must have been giving him an address. He repeated it as it was given then turned to Kenny and said, '11a, Clifton Lane, Pudsey. Remember that.'

Kenny tried to memorize it. Beside him the girl started to whisper something to him. He squeezed her wrist again to warn her.

Stijn was still talking on the phone. 'Are the staff here safe? If they're not it will be down to you.'

Kenny looked down at the girl and raised his finger to his lips. The look in her eyes was wild, incomprehensible.

She closed her mouth, but she was staring at him as if she hadn't understood a thing.

'I'll see you in forty minutes,' Stijn said, then cut the line. He walked out of sight and Kenny heard three sharp blows, then movement. Stijn reappeared in the door-way, dragging the woman under the armpits. The girl gave a little squeal of fright. The woman was naked, streaked with blood, trying to hold her legs together. Kenny stood up.

'I can't be bothered with this,' Stijn said, dropping her to the floor. Kenny could see that her eyes were open, but she looked in shock. One of her eyes looked like it was bruising up, and there was blood running from her nose and mouth. He shifted his grip to the child's hand but held her in place.

'I know who you are,' Stijn said, leaning over and speaking to the woman. 'Do you understand? The game is over. I know who you fucking are.' She tried to roll away from him, to curl into a protective ball. 'I'm going to leave you here,' he said, pulling her arms away from her face. 'You think about what has happened and whether you want me to do the same to the brat. When I come back I want to know where Hanley is and I want to know what you know. Do you hear me?' He kicked at her head with the side of his foot.

'*I hear you!*' she screamed. '*I've told you already! I've told you what I know.*'

Stijn straightened up. 'You haven't even started,' he said. 'I don't know who you think is protecting you, but they're not here now. No one can get to you. If I don't have the truth when I get back then I start on the kid.'

He stepped away from her and walked up to Kenny.

'I need to leave for a few hours,' he said. Kenny cursed to himself. 'You watch these two.'

Stijn sniffed and looked down at the soiled shellsuit. 'There's a shower in the next room,' he said. 'Use it before I get back. You stink.'

SIXTEEN

Bains was late for the autopsy, which was a relief. Unlike many other experienced officers he had never learned to regard the progress of a surgical saw through human tissue and bone as anything other than precisely that. The high-pitched whine of the blade and the sights and smells which followed were not something his stomach would tolerate so early in the morning. He waited instead in Natasha Atkinson's consulting room on the third floor of LGI and let Paul North witness the event. North seemed incapable of regarding corpses as anything other than the furniture of the job.

'Sorry I missed it,' he said, as Atkinson and North entered. He finished the coffee her secretary had made him, feeling the caffeine stirring in his empty guts. He had only recently taken up drinking coffee and still found the effects on his stomach unpredictable.

'You will be,' North said. He looked mildly excited.

Atkinson always looked to Bains to be too young to be qualified for what she did. He would have guessed her age as well under thirty. She was dressed in a smart grey trouser suit, her brown hair pulled back into a tight bun. Presumably to keep it out of the bodies. She wore flash, metal-rimmed spectacles and what appeared to be dia-mond earrings. She looked like she was about to chair a business meeting, and not as though she had just cut into a corpse with a saw.

'I haven't finished,' she told him, sitting down behind her desk. 'The body from the airport is just in and I had two on the go already. I'm juggling corpses here.' She smiled at him. 'I can give you some preliminary stuff though.'

He opened his notebook and waited.

'Cause of death might be the fall. If so he would have died shortly after impact. He seems to have landed feet first.'

Bains winced.

'He has what you would call second-degree burns over nearly a third of his body. Smaller areas of third degree. Mainly his back, his head and some of his face. It wouldn't have killed him though. Not under ordinary circumstances. Of course, I don't know what the circumstances were. It is possible for someone to suffer heart failure as a consequence of this kind of trauma.'

'I understand,' Bains said. 'It wouldn't be normal, but you're not sure.'

She smiled at him. 'That's right, officer. I'm not sure. Even more because he has severe head injuries which might or might not have pre-dated the fall. Until I've finished I couldn't really say whether he was dead before he hit the ground. I might never be able to say, in fact.'

Bains wrote it down. He remembered now how infuriatingly cautious she could be.

'I've noted all this already,' North said.

Bains ignored him. 'Go on,' he said to Atkinson.

'Leaving aside the deeper head injuries, he also has other more superficial injuries which might not be attributable to the fall.'

Bains looked up. 'Might not? Is that *probably* not caused by the fall?'

'No. Not probably. *Possibly*. Blunt instrument trauma to his head and body, perhaps. I'm not certain, because there must also be extensive trauma from the fall. Once again, I'll know a little better when I've looked closer, but for now I'd say some marks – I pointed them out to Mr North – look so specific that they might not be caused by the fall.'

'Whereabouts on his body?'

'Large laceration top of skull . . .' She indicated where on her own head.

'Not from the fall?'

'I don't think so. At least, it *looks* too superficial. But then again—'

'Would it have bled?' Bains asked.

'Yes. Copiously, in common with all scalp wounds. Also two sets of what appear to be tramline bruises across his upper arms, three across his right thigh and multiple similar injuries to his chest.'

'Tramlines?' Bains asked, frowning. Each pathologist seemed to have their own slang. 'You mean double lines of bruising?'

'Caused by being struck with a bar or such like. That is the most typical cause, at any rate. There could be other causes.'

Bains wrote it down. It seemed she couldn't give any conclusion without qualifying it.

'But most importantly,' she continued, 'he has ligature injuries to wrists and ankles.'

'He was tied up?'

'And possibly gagged,' North added. Bains raised his eyebrows to Atkinson.

'Possibly gagged,' she confirmed. 'Patterns of bruising around the lips and left cheek consistent with a very tight gag. Possibly.'

Bains nodded, thinking about it. 'But *definitely* tied up?' he asked.

'Yes.'

He waited for the rider. There wasn't one. He nodded

appreciatively. 'That's good,' he said. 'We can work with that.'

She shrugged, as if to say, 'I do my best.' He was almost frightened to ask her for more.

'Can you say *when* he was tied?'

She looked thoughtful. 'Not after he was burned.'

Bains nodded, looking at her. She wasn't joking.

'What about just before he was burned?' he asked.

She twirled an expensive-looking propelling pencil between her long manicured fingers, frowning intensely. Bains waited.

'That would be going too far,' she said at last.

'A day before he was burned?' Bains tried.

She held up her hand. 'I know what you want, officer. Just let me think it through a moment.'

Again he waited.

'I would say . . .' she began, then paused. 'I would estimate that he was *very possibly* tied with hard ligatures within a space of several hours before his death.'

Bains raised his eyebrows. 'Hard ligatures?'

'Not rope or string. Something hard, like wire or plastic, something that cut him, and not in the way that rope burns injure.'

'OK,' Bains said, writing it down. 'But there were no ligatures on him?'

'Not when he got here. And I saw nothing at the scene. But I'm not a scenes of crime officer.'

'You need to tell SOCO about this,' Bains said, turning to North. 'So they know what to look for.'

'I already have,' North said, sounding tetchy.

Bains turned back to Atkinson. 'Is that it?' He tried to sound polite.

'I'm afraid so. That's all I had time to do. Give me to the end of tomorrow for the rest.'

Mobile phone use was prohibited within the hospital, but he rang Alan White at the Weetwood incident room as soon as they were out.

'I'm just out of the preliminary on Hanley,' he said. 'He was tied before he fell.'

White was silent, thinking. 'Anything else?' he asked, eventually.

'Nothing certain. It was Natasha Atkinson. We're lucky she confirmed death.'

White laughed.

'What do we do?' Bains asked, walking towards the Crown Court, where he had left his car.

'Call it a murder,' White said. 'I'll ring command and get it allocated to me. The two must be linked.'

'You still want me at briefing?'

'Yes. You need to stick with it. I'll give you the team looking for Anna Hart. That's the priority now.'

Bains ran a hand across his face. The lack of sleep was beginning to catch up. He wasn't sure he wanted to run a team on a homicide case. Not that White was giving him a choice.

'You're going to the press with the details?' he asked.

'Already done. It should go out on Radio Leeds this morning. I've got pictures of her going into the *Yorkshire Evening Post* and *Telegraph & Argus* for the lunchtime editions. I'm doing the local TV in a couple of hours. I've got the chopper up over the moors, in case she bolted. I've got twenty detectives coming in during the next hour or so. We have to assume she's in danger. She's not the sort of person who would know how to use a gun, let alone execute a taxi driver. You have to find her, Pete. We could end up with a dead kid if you don't.'

Bains felt a momentary sensation of panic. The

immediate movement of responsibility wasn't what he had been expecting.

'I'll do my best,' he said, uncertainly.

'Will that be good enough?' White asked. 'It's your task, so it's down to you now. All eyes will be on you. I'm not sure "doing your best" will be adequate.'

Bains began to stutter something about needing help.

'Relax, Pete,' White said, cutting in. 'I'm joking. It's my responsibility.'

Bains closed his eyes and counted to five. It had been too long a night for this. 'What do you think is going on?' he asked. 'If it's a blackmail attempt I can't see how that would link with killing Hanley.'

'Too soon for firm theories. It's just play it by ear at the moment. Chuck ideas up in the air, see where they fall. Try it.'

Bains blinked, considering the task ahead of him. 'How many men will I have to—'

White interrupted him again. 'I said try it.'

'Try what?'

'Give me a line, a theory. Spin a thought. Share an insight.'

'I'm not sure I know enough about—'

'For fun.'

'I'm sorry, sir?'

'Do it for fun, to humour me. It won't hurt. We're all running around with our heads up our arses up here. No one has a clue really.'

Bains looked down Oxford Place at the traffic building up on the Headrow. White wasn't filling him with confidence. He searched his brain for thoughts, but it wasn't working. He needed food and sleep.

'I have no idea,' he said finally. 'I have no idea how the two could be linked.'

'Me neither,' White said. He sounded completely calm. 'You know what you do when that happens?'

'No.'

'You follow the book.'

'The book?'

'*The ACPO Murder Manual.* That's the difference between me and you. I've been on the SIO course; you haven't. They give you the book on the course. It tells you how to solve a murder. I've got it here. So we should be OK.'

There was a silence as Bains wondered whether he should laugh.

'It's a joke,' White said.

SEVENTEEN

It was prowling inside her, something lethal. She knew it from the terror of nightmares she had suffered since she was a kid, something caged and lurking, a knotted, ugly gargoyle of destructive force, waiting to lash out. And the bastard had set it loose. He had put his dirty, clumsy fingers inside her and snapped the chain. She had to find a way to get the lid back on. She repeated the sentences to herself, over and over again: *She was Anna Hart. She ran a stupid provincial art gallery in York. Nothing about her was violent. She had a daughter she loved* . . .

She turned her head and opened her eyes. Rachel was lying with her head in her lap, arms tight around her waist, sobbing, her hair and face smeared with animal blood. Beside her was the man with the gun, shouting something. She felt the thing twist inside her. She couldn't fight it. Everything she had built around her was about to collapse. She had passed a lifetime trying to fight the anger, to keep it caged. In the last few months she, as Anna Hart, had even forgotten it existed. But these idiots had taken that apart in the space of minutes. The thing was there, awake, injecting her with black energy, blotting out the pain, clawing its way through the back corners of her mind, screaming. She could feel its strength surging through her veins like adrenalin. If she gave in it would flood her, cloud her vision with its filth, drown her in rage.

She turned away from him. She had to find something to hang on to. Something that wouldn't pull her into this hell. She forced herself to remember what she had learned about 'Anna Hart', reciting the facts by rote: *She had led a charmed life. Her parents had doted on her. This feeling was not her. She was Anna Hart. She was calm, balanced, unemotional. Everyone said it about her. Even her best friend – Sue Mostyn-Phillips. Good old jolly Sue . . .* a jealous, suspicious bitch with a sewer of a mind. Sue probably hated her.

She took a mental breath. Anna didn't react like that. She never had. *Her mother had told her that she had been one of the happiest kids she had known. She never had to raise her voice to her once . . .*

That man – Stijn – had said he knew who she was. But she had heard that before. December 1986. She had hung from hooks in the basement of a Manchester pub for three days while men told her they knew who she was, then burned, beat and starved her. But she had held on. Nothing was certain in this game. If you held on for long enough you could convince them of anything. They had suspicions, fears – maybe even information – but they didn't *know*, not for *certain*. And the gap between suspicion and certainty was all she needed to stay alive.

. . . Anna Hart's mother and father were diplomats. She had spent her childhood travelling from one country to another, never settled, always moving. She had seen the world – suffering, grief, poverty – but always from a distance, from behind the tinted windows of the embassy limo . . .

She had won that one in Manchester. She had convinced them they were wrong. She could win this one. To give in meant it was over, pure and simple. The man who had done this to her would not let her go now, not if he *really* knew who she was. If he *really* knew she would probably be dead already. So she had to hold the anger down, remember that she *was* Anna Hart. She had her manners, her clothes, her speech, her memories . . .

. . . *Nick sitting across the table from her in the West Room at Black Carr Hall, a proud smile all over his face. June 1998 – their first 'date' since she had met him at the gallery. He had cooked for her: pheasant in red wine; duchess potatoes; green beans. He had given Mrs Rimmer the night off so they had the place to themselves. Afterwards, talking about herself, strolling across the west lawn in the warm evening sunlight . . .*

The memories were real. She didn't have to invent. This man – Stijn – had wanted to know where Nick was. Which meant – if her cover *was* blown – that it had nothing to do with Nick, which meant there was still hope. She could get back to him, get out of this, pick up where they had left off. She could still be Anna Hart, still be with him. That was something to hang on to. She began to cry again. She had told him where Nick was straight away, without any hesitation. She had betrayed him. Nick had been nothing but gentle to her. He had taken to her daughter as if she were his own. But she had been ready to place him in Stijn's hands just to . . . to what? Not to suffer what had happened anyway? To save Rachel? *Rachel.* That wasn't her daughter's name. But she had to think of her as Rachel, *keep* thinking of her as Rachel . . .

She realized the man with the gun was prodding her with it, his voice getting out of control. She looked up at him, seeing her surroundings for the first time clearly. They were in the meeting room; she remembered it. A long table, dirty windows down one wall, discarded plastic cups on the tables, a kettle on the window sill, a coffee jar, a cheap radio, a single poster on the wall showing a panorama of snow-capped mountains, Arabic writing underneath . . . Probably the staff used the room for breaks. She was lying near the table, on worn linoleum, curled up, holding Rachel to her. The man with the gun was sitting on a chair, leaning forward, speaking to her. She had thought, from the shape of his mouth, that he was shouting, but he wasn't. He was holding something out to her.

She pushed herself into a sitting position and tried to focus on his words.

'You can put these on. You'll be cold. That won't help.'

She looked at what he was holding – an item of clothing, not her own. She looked down at herself, naked, streaked with blood.

'Where are my clothes?' she asked. Her voice sounded weird.

'They're torn, dirty. You don't want them. This is clean.'

She took it off him. It was some kind of grey overall, like she'd seen the Asian workers wearing. She looked around her, wondering absurdly where she could put it on. He pointed to a door in the corner of the room.

'There's a shower through here. You can wash . . .' He looked confused. He was trying to be kind to her, but he still had the gun. 'You can wash and put these on. I'll keep the kid through here.'

She prised Rachel away from her chest. 'I need to wash her first,' she said. 'I need to get this blood off her.' She felt dazed. Nothing seemed real. It felt like she had been kicked between the legs, very hard.

'We can all go,' he said. 'We can all wash.'

She felt a wave of nausea. 'You keep away from us. You've done enough to harm us.' She lifted Rachel's chin.

130

'Are you hurt, darling?' She was shivering. They both were.

'She's OK,' he said. 'I checked her. She's just . . . shocked . . .'

Rachel's lips and nose were still bleeding.

'What did he do to you?' Anna asked.

Rachel shook her head. 'It wasn't him. It was the big one. He punched me.' She started crying again.

Anna tried to check her teeth, to see if they were loose, but her fingers were shaking too much.

'Can you breathe through your nose?'

Rachel nodded.

'She was lucky,' the man said. 'He could have broken it.'

Anna looked up at him. '*You* could have cracked her skull, you fucking arsehole . . .'

He bit his lip and stood up quickly, pacing to the end of the room. Rachel leaned towards her.

'I need the toilet, Mum,' she whispered.

'I'm trying to be reasonable—' the man started.

'So I should thank you?' Anna spat the words at him. 'When's that other bastard coming back?'

He walked to the windows running along the wall behind the table. 'I don't know. He said a couple of hours. You need to give him what he wants. I warned you.'

'He's already taken what he wants.' She ran her hand through her hair and felt her head throbbing. She needed to check herself for injuries, but not now. She couldn't think about any of that, mustn't allow herself the luxury of shock or self-pity. They were still here. Stijn was coming back. She had to get her mind working. She had to do something.

He walked over to a radio and plugged it in. The sound

of some girl band bashing out a pop song blared out of the speaker. He turned the volume down.

'What's your name?' she asked. She tried to keep the hatred out of her voice. He was bent over by the radio, fiddling with the dial, trying to tune it.

'You don't need to know my name,' he said, not looking at her.

'My daughter needs to go to the toilet,' she said.

He found a news station and straightened up, turning towards her.

'You can go one at a time,' he said. He pointed again to the door, using the gun. 'It's through there.'

Anna stood Rachel up, spoke quietly to her. 'Will you be OK by yourself?'

Rachel nodded, then whispered to her, 'Just keep him away.' Then she turned to him and called out, 'Thank you. I'll be quick.' She was learning.

He made no attempt to follow Rachel. He looked as if he was even embarrassed to look at Anna while she was naked. Or perhaps it was the injuries, the blood, shaming him.

On the radio there were two news items about the impending Millennium celebrations at the Dome, in London, then they cut to a reporter at Leeds/Bradford airport. She watched the gunman stiffen, listening. Not many details were given. An Asian taxi driver, a father of three, had been brutally murdered. The police weren't releasing any other details. It was a short report. He was about to turn the radio off when they skipped to the next news item. She heard the words just as Rachel came out of the toilet:

'Property developer Nicholas Hanley is believed to be the man involved in an earlier incident in central Leeds. Police say the body of Mr Hanley, aged forty-nine, has been *positively identified . . .'* She heard Rachel gasp, eyes wide. '*. . . He is believed to have jumped from a burning apartment in Spencer Tower. The police say they are continuing to investigate. The Fire Service now has the fire under control and streets in the vicinity have been re-opened . . .'*

'Did they say Nicholas Hanley?' the man asked.

Rachel was still staring at her. Anna felt her head beginning to spin and sat down on the chair the man had been using.

'*I said, did they say Hanley?*' he shouted.

'*Yes!*' she shouted back. She tried to make sense of the words, but couldn't. They had said Nicholas Hanley. They had given his age. They had said he was dead. But the three things didn't add up for her. Did they mean Nicholas Hanley? *Her* Nicholas Hanley?

'Come here, Rachel,' she said.

Her daughter crossed the room and stood in front of her. Her eyes were red-rimmed, sore, her face devoid of colour. She had tried to wash it, but there was still blood matted through her hair and smeared down one cheek. Her lip was split in at least two places, her nose still bleeding. Her shirt was damp where she had tried to sponge the blood from it.

'Don't listen to it,' Anna said. 'We don't know what it means—'

'They said the body had—'

'We don't know who it is. We don't know anything.' She pulled her to her and hugged her. There was a ringing noise in her ears. The man came over and stood in front of her. He was speaking to her, asking her questions about Hanley. Stijn must have told him nothing. She turned her face from him, burying it in Rachel's hair. Rachel brought her arm up and held onto her head. Anna thought she would really start crying now, but instead Rachel pressed her lips against her ear and whispered, her voice full of excitement, 'There's a knife in the toilet, under the wastebin.'

EIGHTEEN

Elaine Merrington – the SOCO they had given him – called Bains on his mobile as he was on his way down to see Chris Greenwood. She was still at the scene. He updated her with the findings from the preliminary PM.

'Alan White is taking it,' he added. 'We need to treat it as a homicide now. It could be connected to the shooting at the airport. You might want to get the fire people in from the lab.'

'I treat all fatalities as murder until I know otherwise,' she said. 'Do you want an update, or shall I call Alan White?'

He listened. So far she had recovered blood from the external wall just below the balcony, where he had seen the staining, and from the office below the flat. She had lifted a wide range of possible fingerprints, mainly from the office below.

'There were what appears to be dishcloths balled up on the floor by the sinks in the office toilets,' she said. 'Also blood-stained.'

'Not burned?'

'The office was smoke damaged, but not burned,' she said. 'The fire took hold in distinct places in the flat above the office. They tried to burn the office too by leading a trail of accelerant from one floor to the other, but the fire door between the floors seems to have shut. Water was the greater problem as far as traces were concerned. Nevertheless, we found a lot of prints down there and in the connecting passage, plus the blood.'

'The amount of water I saw I'm surprised you got anything. Do you know what the accelerant was?'

'Not certain yet. Smells very strongly like petrol, though. The fire was set in the main room, just inside the doorway. It looks like the accelerant was transported in hard plastic containers. We have one intact from the office and traces of perhaps two others at different sites in the flat. There was a lot of accelerant used. I found a Zippo lighter, possibly used to start things – no prints but possible DNA. Ditto the rags and the blood, obviously. In fact, we will probably get a lot from here, but it will take time and there's no guarantee any of it is from the perpetrator.'

'Did you find any plastic or wire? The pathologist reckons Hanley was tied with something hard; if so it must have been removed before he went over.'

'Nothing. There is broken furniture though. I would say there was a struggle before the blaze was set. I've got fibres from some broken items and from the balcony. I'll let you know as we get more.'

Bains thanked her, pushing open the door to the tiny ground-floor room Chris Greenwood had commandeered to watch videos. Previously it had belonged to the station cleaners and there were still some mops, pails and brushes stacked in one corner.

'I've got five minutes, Chris,' he said, sitting down.

'That's all you'll need.'

Greenwood was sitting in front of a tiny video monitor. Bains pulled up a chair.

'Three cameras in the building,' Greenwood said. 'One on the main door, one in the underground garage, one covering two side exits out the back. Two were in the loop – the main entrance and the car park. The side exits were off, damaged. The fault was reported at nine o'clock yesterday morning.'

'So we can't cover all movement?'

'No. Not from the internal system. I've got nearly all the tapes from the surrounding streets and junctions – eight cameras cover about half the possible exit routes – but that will take a little more time to process.'

'About half the exit routes?'

'Yes. It's not watertight. But let me show you what I have so far.'

Bains watched as he set off a grainy black-and-white tape showing a barely visible underground car park. The camera, Greenwood explained, pointed into the garage and caught all movement in and out via the one external entrance and exit.

'This car is coming in now.' He placed his finger on the screen. 'You can't see it very well, but if you pause it enough you can catch one frame where the plate is visible. It checks back to Hanley . . .'

The camera switched suddenly to a high angle of the main vestibule of the building, from inside, camera pointed out through the doors. Bains could see that it was daylight outside. He checked the time on the bottom-right corner of the image: 15.17. The date was given as 30.12.99.

'It's a time lapse,' Greenwood explained. 'The tape takes four seconds from each of the two cameras in turn.' It switched back to the garage. The car he had shown Bains was just beginning to park.

'The quality is terrible,' Bains said. 'What kind of car is that?'

'An XJ8. A Jag. Admiral red. One of three cars Hanley owns. The other two are Range Rovers.'

The camera switched again to the vestibule. Greenwood fast-forwarded it until they could see a man getting out of the car in the garage. The image was so unclear it was hard to accurately determine his height.

'It's useless,' Bains said. 'Can you even see what he's wearing?'

'I can see that it's dark trousers, dark shoes, some kind of lighter shirt and a jacket—'

'Which matches our corpse. But that doesn't say much.'

'You think there's a doubt as to the ID?'

Bains shook his head. 'No. Not really. I'm just being careful. Can you get any good shots of the face?'

Greenwood shook his head. 'No. But it's Hanley. It's his car and he gets into the building by swiping an ID card which comes back to him. The system times exits and entries and matches them to personnel. The timings here tie up.'

'Does he leave the building?'

'Not in that car. The Jag is still in the garage now. The quality from the vestibule angle is much sharper. If I had a photo of him—'

'I asked Paul North to get you one.'

'— I could check faces to see if he leaves on foot.'

Bains sat back. 'OK. That's good work, Chris.'

'That's not it. Wait.' He pressed the buttons on the remote, skipping the tape forward to a time he had noted on his pad. 'Watch this.'

The image showed the garage again. Bains watched a figure return to the same car. It looked like the same person. The time showed 16.33, same date. Opening the boot, he extracted two light-coloured containers, then set off towards the lifts carrying one in each hand. They looked reasonably heavy.

'They don't look like bags,' Bains said, frowning.

'He comes back for a third,' Greenwood said. 'They look like petrol containers to me.'

NINETEEN

The man was called Kenny. She didn't know whether it was his first or last name. She knew because he had phoned Stijn in front of her, using his mobile. The line must have been unclear because he had to raise his voice and repeat his name. She had tried to stop him calling Stijn, appealing to him, hoping for something human.

'If you tell him about the radio broadcast he will return sooner,' she had said. She must have looked frightened. She felt it.

The man – Kenny – seemed uncertain, but not for long. 'I have to tell him,' he had said, rubbing his forehead. His voice was like someone with throat cancer. 'I'm sorry. I have to. Maybe it will be OK. Maybe all he wanted was to know where this Hanley is.'

The call took only a few seconds. She listened as Kenny told Stijn about Nicholas Hanley being dead. She held on to Rachel as they watched him.

'He already knew,' he said, when the line was cut. He was frowning hard.

She didn't understand it either. She felt like breaking down again, giving in. Stijn was asking her where Nick was, but he knew Nick was dead. It was some kind of nightmare. She wouldn't be able to stop it. She caught the sob in her throat and stood up, holding the overalls he had given her.

'I'll wash, like you said,' she said. She saw Rachel look away from her.

Kenny walked her to the door, opened it and looked in, checking. 'I'll be out here with the kid,' he said. 'Remember that.'

She nodded. 'Your name is Kenny,' she said. 'Thank you, Kenny.'

He appeared uncomfortable. 'You should forget my name,' he said.

She nodded, then looked past him to where Rachel was standing by the table, watching. 'I will be quick, Rachel,' she said. 'If anything happens, shout.'

'Nothing will happen,' he said, and closed the door on her.

She waited to be certain he wasn't coming in, then looked around the room. It was small and narrow – a toilet cubicle and, in front of that, an area tiled off to make an open shower. A chair behind the door, a rusting mirror above a small basin, a paper hand-towel dispenser on the wall, a wastebin outside the toilet, stuffed with used towels. She lifted it and picked up the knife. Had Rachel found it elsewhere and hidden it there? She felt a surge of pride.

It was an ordinary kitchen knife with a serrated edge. She ran her thumb along it. It was blunt. The blade was thin, about six inches long, pointed. She bent it. It was weak, flexible. It wouldn't cut anything and it would break if it struck something solid. But it was all she had. She put it in the back pocket of the overalls.

Then she turned on the shower and washed herself quickly, not even waiting for warm water, not thinking about the puddle of dirty, bloodied water running away at her feet. All she thought about was the knife. Then she rinsed her hair, her face, inside her mouth and, finally, between her legs. There was no soap. She didn't count her injuries, wouldn't think about the pain. She dried herself as best she could on handfuls of coarse, blue paper towels, then put the overalls on. They fitted well enough, but would not be warm outside – if they ever got out. She buttoned them up to the throat and looked at the little cloth badge sewn onto the breast pocket. There was some Arabic writing on it. The pocket at her backside was large, hiding the knife well, but the outline would probably show if she turned her back to him. She would have to be careful.

She opened the door and stepped back into the room. Rachel's eyes caught hers and communication passed silently. She was seated at one end of the table, Kenny was at the other. He stood up as she came out.

'My turn,' he said. She walked over to Rachel, thinking furiously. How was he to shower and keep control of them? He would have to leave them here. That would be her chance. Maybe she wouldn't have to use the knife.

'You have to come with me,' he said, crushing the idea. 'Both of you. I'll keep the gun on the kid and you can wash me.'

She felt her face twitch with disbelief and panic.

'There's no other way,' he said, seeing her expression. 'I stink of shit. That's your fault. I let you wash and change. Now you have to help me.'

She spluttered some words, protesting. At the same time her brain registered the opportunity he was giving them, but she kept the thought away from her face.

'I can't do it any other way,' he said. 'You will run if I leave you.'

'Please,' she said. 'I give you my word. If you leave us here—'

'Don't be stupid.' He took hold of Rachel's arm and began to push her towards the door, gun held lazily at his side.

Anna let her face soften a little. 'Wait,' she said. He paused. 'Do you promise that is all you want?'

He looked offended. 'I'm married,' he said. 'I have two little girls. I'm not like *him*.'

142

He almost sneered the words. She saw him standing above the taxi driver, aiming the gun. She blinked. 'OK,' she said. 'I'll help you. Leave her alone.'

He let go of Rachel. They all walked to the shower room.

With all three of them inside the place felt cramped, claustrophobic. He told her to shut the door. She shut it and stood back against it, feeling the knife pressing against her backside. He told Rachel to stand near to him, then began to strip. He held the gun against Rachel's head. Anna waited to see how he planned to keep the gun on her and get into the shower. All she needed was a few clear seconds.

'Turn the shower on,' he said to her. He stood so that he was facing her, naked, the shellsuit in a crumpled heap on the floor. Rachel was screwing her nose up, smelling him, trying not to look at his body, but Anna saw and smelled nothing. Her brain was racing.

He was weak. He was not like Stijn, as he had said. He had shot the taxi driver, but there had been no relationship there. Already he had spoken too much to them, had given away too much of himself. The situation was not the same. He had two daughters. He felt bad about hitting Rachel, about what Stijn had done. And he had told her all of this.

She stepped over to the shower, onto the wet area of tiling sloping towards the drain. Her eyes were fixed on the gun he had against Rachel's head. If it came to it he would kill again. But he didn't *want* to. And because of that he would make errors. She scrutinized the gun carefully. It was old, large, clumsy, ex-Soviet bloc – probably a Stechkin 9mm, which would give it a twenty-round clip, if he could find that much ammunition for it. At some point he had taken the silencer off it; it hadn't worked well so she was guessing it was some kind of home-made effort. The safety mechanism was obvious – a big selector lever on the left of the slide with three positions, all labelled. 'NP' meant safe. That wasn't something Anna Hart would know; but *she* knew it. She could clearly see the letters, she knew what they meant. He had it set to safe. That was all she needed.

She stepped up to the shower head and moved it. It was attached to a long tube. She turned on the water and let it run away at her feet.

'What do you want me to do?' she asked. Her voice sounded suddenly calm. She looked up and down his body, taking in the details. He was thickset, full of muscle. Short, powerful thighs, a bull neck, hairs coating his upper back and chest, scars across his shoulders. She could see each and every muscle. The bone structure was clear. There was hardly any fat on him. He saw her watching and began to colour.

'I'll keep the gun on the kid.' His voice was edgy, uncertain. 'You . . .' He pointed to the shower. '. . . You wash me . . . quickly . . . with that . . .'

'Wash you where?' She could feel her heart speeding up.

'All over. Just do it. I'll have the gun against her head. If I feel anything wrong I'll kill her.'

She paused, looking into his eyes, telling herself again that the safety was *on*. 'OK. But step back a bit, nearer the thing.'

He stepped towards her, turned sideways now.

'Turn round,' she said. 'I'll do it. You can trust me.'

He was unsure. He had picked up something in her voice, something different. She cursed herself silently, then said, 'You promise you won't try to do anything to—'

144

She saw him relax slightly. 'Start doing it,' he said. 'I don't want anything off you. I just want to be clean.'

She felt the water temperature with her fingers then sprayed it onto his thigh. He was still turned sideways, still watching her, still nervous. His left hand was holding Rachel, but trying to hold her at a distance, so she wouldn't push up against him, wouldn't touch him. He was too anxious that neither of them should get the wrong idea about him. He was under-estimating. But the right hand was still pressing the gun against Rachel's head.

'Turn round,' she said. 'Let's get this over with.'

He turned his back to her, moving slowly, head still twisted so he was watching her. She looked at his backside. It was a mess, caked with his own shit. She had to get him to turn his head.

'You're covered with it,' she said. 'It's all over your backside.' She met his eyes. He averted them at once, shamed, embarrassed, then immediately turned his head away. 'I'll wash it off,' she said.

She switched the shower head to her left hand and turned it onto his lower back. She saw him tense. She counted down quickly from the nape of his neck. The vertebrae were clear, the line of the shoulder blades standing out against the muscle. Because his arms were down, the gap between the edge of the left scapula and the beginning of the spinal column was less than three inches. The ribs were at their thickest right there. If she hit a rib that was it, the blade would break. Her right hand closed around the handle of the knife. She marked the spot in her mind as she stepped up to him. Between the sixth and seventh ribs. She spaced her legs, drew her right arm back behind her head then swung down.

The blow was like a short, downward punch with the side of her hand. Her fist struck the flesh of his back, knocking him forwards. She stepped back, expecting to see the blade broken. She had felt nothing, no resistance. She tried to keep hold of the handle, but as he moved the thing came straight out of her hands.

She stood back, amazed. The blade was buried in his back, the handle jutting out. She had hit him exactly where she had intended. He was staggering forward, falling into Rachel. She heard him take a breath, then start to turn, his legs buckling. She moved forward, trying to close on the gun arm. He was twisting over sideways, falling onto his back, his mouth open in shock, but no noise coming out. His left hand pulled Rachel down with him. She began to scream. As he hit the floor his legs went up in the air and his head struck the wall of the room. He had Rachel pulled across his chest, the gun still against her head.

He began to gasp for breath. She saw his eyes find hers as her hand closed over the gun. His left arm was pinning Rachel to his chest. He started puffing, his chest heaving. His eyes wavered, losing focus. Anna got one hand over the gun, the other around his hand. Rachel was still shrieking. She began to prise his fingers away from the gun. He was holding Rachel against the barrel, pressing the trigger again and again. She couldn't tell whether it was deliberate or a reflex motion.

'The safety is on,' she said, looking into his eyes. 'It's useless.'

He couldn't hear her. He couldn't hear anything. He could do nothing but lie there, staring at her, his face gradually turning blue. She watched his eyes go vague, the strength beginning to leave his fingers. She pulled the gun away from his hand and placed it behind her. Then she moved his arm from Rachel. Rachel wrapped her arms around her and they stood back, the water from the shower sloshing around their feet, spraying over his legs. There was no blood at all.

She stroked her hand through Rachel's hair and waited. He was still trying to breathe, still looking at her. His back began to arch and his face contorted in pain. There was a gargling noise in his throat. She watched his chest jerking. The knife had gone straight through his heart. There was nothing he could do about it. Bubbles of bright, pink frothy blood began to form between his gaping lips.

She waited until his chest was rigid, turning Rachel's head away from him as his limbs began to ripple with involuntary twitches, his arms splayed out, the head twisted back, the eyes wide open on nothing.

'It's OK,' she said to Rachel.

She looked around her. Her senses were strung out, the adrenalin coursing through her. She stepped to the door and opened it a fraction, peering carefully through the crack. The room beyond was empty. She turned back to look at Rachel. She was staring at his body, fingers in her mouth.

She had never seen anyone dead before, let alone watched it happen. Anna waited until she looked up, then said, 'That's how it is. That's how people die. It's nothing to worry about. He doesn't feel a thing.'

Her words sounded clumsy, inadequate. Rachel was struggling with it. Anna prodded his leg with her foot. He didn't move.

'He's dead,' she said. 'Here one minute, gone the next.' She could feel her heart slowing. 'Let's get out of here,' she said.

TWENTY

The first briefing for the twenty-five-strong squad Alan White had assembled was delayed by over half an hour because White himself disappeared. Bains sat on a corner table by the door to the CID room and rubbed his tired eyes. He needed sleep. He watched the taskless groups of men and women greeting each other, passing rumours, scrutinizing what White had already marked onto whiteboards, laughing, grumbling, muttering and finally settling down into chairs to wait in silence, nothing to say to each other that could take up more than fifteen minutes of banter.

It was his first real break since his shift had started over twenty hours before, but also since Liz had called him, dumping thoughts of Karen into his brain like tiny nuggets of radioactive waste. He had been mercifully occupied since then. There was nothing like a homicide to insert a lead screen between waking consciousness and the rest of life. You threw yourself into a homicide, gave it a hundred per cent of your attention. You did it whether you had wife and family, terminal cancer, half a million pounds worth of debt about to crash about your head, anything. You were given an overriding excuse to forget everything for a while.

But now he had a breather. He looked around the faces of the detectives who were about to be told to cancel their plans for at least the next three days. He could see the excitement slipping the longer they waited, see them gradually remembering whatever little life detail had been worrying them that morning. For himself, he realized the seeds had already been planted when Liz had told him Francis Doyle was looking for Karen Sharpe.

He stood up and walked out into the corridor. He needed to get his mind away from it. He took out his mobile and called Liz's number, realizing only as she answered that his mind had deftly outmanoeuvred him. The first thing she would ask him about would be Karen.

'Have they seen you yet?' she asked, on cue.

'Yes. About an hour ago.'

'So what's going on?'

'I don't know. I didn't ask them.' He began to pace up and down in the corridor.

'Maybe you should have,' she said. 'I'm worried about her.'

'You already said that.'

'You're saying you're not?'

He bit his lip, silent.

'Don't pretend to me, Pete. It's no crime. We loved the woman, for God's sake. We loved both of them. Just because—'

'I'm trying not to think about them,' he said, cutting her off. 'That's the past. We have to ditch the past. Karen used to say that all the time.'

He listened to Liz's silence. 'I'm sorry, Liz,' he said. 'I can't do it any other way.'

'Well, I can,' she said. 'Do you have any contact numbers for her?'

He frowned, confused. 'Why? Why would you want that?'

'So I can try to find out what's going on. She might need our help.'

'She doesn't.'

'But have you?'

'What?'

149

'Any contact numbers? Did she give you anything?'

'She gave me nothing, Liz. You know that. She didn't even leave a fucking note . . .' He caught himself, caught the bitterness too strong to be anything other than a still-raw wound. He took a breath. 'Look. That's not why I called.'

'What then?' She sounded put out.

'I was thinking about tonight.'

She didn't say anything. He was walking outside the offices for the divisional supervision. Alan White was in one, discussing the enquiry with the command team in Wakefield – at least, that's what Jon Hoyle, White's deputy SIO, had told them. Bains could hear White's raised voice as he passed one of the doors. He tried to whisper to Liz. He didn't want to be heard.

'Maybe we should have arranged something,' he said. He heard her sigh.

'It's a bit late now, Pete.'

He paced a bit more, thinking about it. She had offered to spend Millennium Eve with him nearly three months ago and he had refused, insisting he would work instead. As it turned out, he wasn't given an option, but they could still have done something after midnight. People stayed up all night to celebrate 'special' events. He could have given her what was left of it and, for that matter, the hours before he had been due to start.

Christmas and New Year were always difficult for him. The dates alone seemed capable of sinking him into mild despair, as if the burden of striving to ensure smiles and memorableness were itself too much weight. He had been unfortunate enough to have achieved the aim a couple of times and try as he might the memory of those times now infected every attempt at replication. New Year's Eve was particularly effective in bringing out the snivelling, self-pitying idiot. It was incredible that the year before last he had actually managed to put the past behind him. But that had been Karen. Or Mairead. Or the combination of the two. They had come into his life and healed things he had thought would never be cured. He remembered the four of them – Liz as well – running through the fields behind Karen's home in the freezing darkness so that they could get over the crest of the next hill and catch a glimpse of the fireworks lighting up the sky towards Skipton. All drunk except Mairead. At ten she had been just old enough to start appreciating things like that. They had even attempted a few lines of 'Auld Lang Syne'. He cursed out loud, remembering it. They had been planning their lives together and she had simply walked out on him, no reason, no warning.

'What?' Liz asked, hearing him.

'Too late,' he said.

'I asked you, Pete—'

He shook himself from the thoughts. 'I know. I was stupid. I'm sorry. Do you have to go?'

She had already made plans to visit her sister down south later that day.

'I have to now,' she said. 'I can't mess around and change things this late on. I asked you three months ago.'

In front of him he heard the door to White's room beginning to open. He turned to make his way back to the CID room.

'Maybe I don't want to be alone tonight,' he said. It was pathetic, unanswerable. He felt himself cringe as the words slipped out of his mouth. He hadn't even said that he wanted to be with her. Just not alone. It was almost an insult. She didn't reply.

'Can I at least see you before you leave?' he asked.

'I'll be leaving in thirty minutes. This is silly, Pete.'

He walked in front of White's office, glancing through the open door. He was two paces past it, mobile still held to his ear, before he registered what he had seen. He stopped.

'Pete?'

'Sorry, Liz,' he said, whispering. 'I'll call you back.' He put the phone back into his pocket and turned round. White walked out of the room, looked at him then quickly turned away, appearing embarrassed. Three men followed him out. One was DI Hoyle, one he didn't know – a tall military type with a smart suit and handlebar moustache. The third met his eyes immediately. It was Francis Doyle.

TWENTY-ONE

He had even ripped off her wristwatch. She found it on the floor of the storeroom, along with her shoes, socks, underwear (torn, soiled, useless) and outer clothing. She told Rachel to wash her face and hair again while she stepped back into the room, mentally holding her breath, and quickly put on the shoes and T-shirt, then the overalls. Everything else was either too damaged or too soiled. Then she turned her back on the room, allowing herself to think only when she had closed the door on it.

She opened one of the windows in the meeting room and looked out. They were on the first floor with a drop to a ledge a couple of feet wide. It led to a smaller, sloping roof, which dropped into a narrow snicket between the abattoir and a hedge of hawthorn and brambles. She pocketed the mobile Kenny had been using, then turned to Rachel and held her fingers to her lips, whispering, 'We say nothing from now until I tell you, OK?'

Rachel nodded.

Anna passed her out feet first, holding her under the arms and lowering her to the ledge. Then she followed. They walked along to the sloping roof, slid down and landed on cold, hard mud. Anna sucked the fresh air into her lungs, looking around. Behind her, from within the building, she could hear the throb of machinery, the dull wailing of the animals. But no pursuers. She realized she had left the gun behind.

Too late to go back for it. She took hold of Rachel's hand and led her towards the line of poplars at the end of the hedge. There was a tall wire fence between the path and the poplars. Beyond it she could see a slope falling into a bank of mist and, beyond and over the top of that, fields, pylons and the electrified lines for the railway. She looked in vain for a hole in the dense mesh of the fence.

'We will have to climb it,' she said into Rachel's ear. Her breath puffed out in a cloud of condensation. She could feel the cold beginning to grip.

She helped her up, then told her to wait, hanging onto the concrete post, just below a line of rusted barbed wire. She didn't want her dropping down the other side and turning an ankle. She got herself to the top and over without a problem, levering herself off the wall of the building they had just left, pressing the barbs down with one hand and vaulting the top of the fence using the other. Then she helped Rachel down.

'OK,' Anna said. 'We walk quickly, talk to no one.'

They scrambled down a short, overgrown slope leading to the river and looked along it in both directions. The mist was hanging over the surface of the water, a static layer of freezing fog. The water itself was high, running quickly and silently, rubbish caught in the branches and roots of trees leaning over the banks. The liquid looked muddy and sluggish beneath the surface, the distance to the far side about thirty feet. Anna didn't fancy trying to swim it. There was an overgrown dirt trail leading in both directions. She turned left, towards Kirkstall Abbey and the city, dragging Rachel behind her. Beyond the poplars and through the mist she could hear the traffic on Abbey Road.

They moved fast, hand in hand, crossing a little wooden bridge to reach an area of short, neatly cropped grass. They walked across it until they could see the dark shapes of the ruined abbey walls, looming at them through the mist. As the buildings drew nearer they left the fog behind. The grounds were empty, but past the crumbling arches of black stone they could see the road, alive with traffic.

Anna paused, feeling her heart still thumping. A freezing, dull Yorkshire day. Normal life. It had been going on around them all the time. She felt a sensation like dizziness. Everything looked normal. She couldn't understand it. For the first time she became aware of the pain between her legs. She pulled Rachel on, still saying nothing.

The gate onto Abbey Road was open. Anna walked straight out, without pause, hurrying.

'Slow down, Mum!' Rachel was struggling to keep up.

'Not yet.'

'We've done it, Mum. We're out—'

Cars roared past them.

'Not yet.'

She waited for a gap in the traffic then sprinted across the road. Her pulse was still racing. She forced herself not to look back. They walked briskly for a couple of hundred yards, heading east and downhill, towards Leeds, Rachel puffing and complaining. Anna turned up the first street they came to. A short row of back-to-back terraces rising away from the river valley, cars parked up both sides of the road. She scanned them, looking for something not too modern. From the windows of one of the houses she could hear a radio playing a John Lennon song, 'Happy Christmas: War is Over'. There was a smell of bacon and eggs coming from one of the open kitchen windows.

'What are we doing?' Rachel asked. Her voice was high-pitched.

'We're looking for a car.'

'Can't we just go into one of these houses and—'

'No.'

She began to walk up the nearest row of cars, looking

through the driver or passenger window, checking for an unlocked door. They reached the top of the row without luck. She crossed the road and started down the other side. Halfway back down to Abbey Road she pulled open the door to an unlocked L-reg Ford Escort.

'This will do. Get in.'

Rachel sat in the passenger side staring nervously at the windows of the houses. Anna stared at the ignition system, waiting for the knowledge to come to her. Then in less than two minutes she had dragged the steering column casing apart, pulled the ignition barrel out and hot-wired the engine. She pushed it into gear and drove straight out from the line of cars, turning quickly on Abbey Road and driving west, away from the town centre. Out of the corner of her eye she could see Rachel staring at her.

'What?' she said, concentrating on her mirrors and the road. 'What's the matter?'

'What are we doing, Mum?'

'We're getting out of here.' She could feel her teeth beginning to chatter. Rachel too was shivering. She reached forward and turned the car heating to full.

'Where are we going?'

'Don't ask. I don't know. I can't think about it yet. I just need to be clear . . .' Her voice was cracking, a lump caught in her throat. She watched the cars coming in the opposite direction, searching for Stijn's face at the wheel.

'We *are* clear, Mum.' Rachel sounded desperate.

'We're not. Not yet.' She could feel a noise building in her head.

She drove at the edge of the speed limit all the way up through Rawdon, then turned through Nether Yeadon and kept going until she was running back down the long deep slope to the Aire valley, heading towards Woodhouse Lane, the public schools and, in the distance, beneath a low, bruised sky, the mills and chimneys of Bradford. She could feel her limbs trembling now, her face burning red as if determined to mark her with shame. She struggled to find a sense of fear, of being cowed, submissive, wrecked. That was what Anna Hart should have felt. But all she could feel was rage. There was only one way she knew how to deal with this, and it wasn't Anna's way.

She turned off suddenly, down a track leading between tall bare chestnut trees, then stopped, out of sight of the road, engine still ticking over. She leaned over the wheel and began to gasp for breath. She could feel Rachel beside her, arms around her, hugging her, saying things to her urgently, worried. She tried to shut out the roaring in her ears, tried desperately to focus on her daughter's words. When she looked out of the windscreen the trees in front of her were sharp black shapes, hemming her in. The windscreen glass was steaming up, too close to her. She wanted to smash her fist through it, run her arm along the broken glass, *feel* something. She squeezed Rachel in her arms and waited for her heart to stop leaping. There were no coherent thoughts, just a riot of dysfunctional physical reactions. She breathed slowly, conditioned herself to observe it, to stand above it, to watch herself. It would go away.

It was like moving out of her own body. She could see Rachel climbing across the seats, arms around her, crying her heart out. She could see herself holding her daughter and shaking from head to foot. Then beside it all there was calmness, a part of it that didn't touch her. She looked out across the bare brown slopes of the Aire valley, out towards the Bradford winter smog. Bradford. She was coming back to it, back to her past. She had to be prepared.

'We have to find Nick,' she said. She heard her words, saw Rachel move slightly away from her.

'They said he was dead.'

'No. We don't know that. We can't believe that.'

'But the woman on the radio said—'

'That man . . .' She stumbled over his name before she could get it to her lips. 'Stijn. He was asking where Nick was. But he knew about the radio programme. I think that means he's alive.'

She brought the sleeve of the overall up and wiped her eyes. Rachel's expression was widening into something she didn't recognize.

'You heard Stijn asking about him,' Anna said. 'If Nick is alive then there's no one else to help him. The police think he's dead.'

'*Mum!*' She saw the expression now. Rachel was staring at her as if she were mad. 'We have to stop this, Mum. We have to stop it now.'

'We can't stop it,' Anna said. 'Not until we know what has happened to Nick.'

'We *have* to stop it.' Rachel sat back in her seat and began to cry. 'We must go to the police and tell them what has happened.'

'And let the bastard get away with it?' She spoke the words through clenched teeth, feeling the rage slip out. 'I'll fucking kill him for this. I'll kill him!'

Her daughter looked frightened. 'The police will catch him—' Rachel began.

She started to turn the car around. 'We can't assume that. We can't assume anything. Remember everything I've told you.'

'Mum, please! Please.'

Anna slipped the gearstick into neutral and looked over at her daughter, feeling the doubt gnawing at her brain. What was she doing to her? What had she already done? The guilt was a massive lump in her chest. She should never have got her into this. The child had to come first.

'I can't do it any more,' Rachel said, biting her bottom lip, looking at her with wide, black eyes. 'It's not me, Mum. I can't do it.'

Anna leaned over and put her arms around her, pressed her lips against her forehead. She sat still like that until Rachel responded, hugging her back, then sat for even longer, waiting for the tears to stop. She could hear cars passing back up on the road.

'You can,' she whispered to her. 'You can do it for us. You have to trust me on this.'

She gently disentangled herself and looked down at her child. Nearly twelve years old. A voice in her head told her she was wrong. But what else could she do? Unforgivably, she had introduced her daughter to the target. She would pay for that – someday, somehow, they would make her pay. No mistake went unchecked.

But the target had been safe. They had promised her. And it was a simple job. Nick had loved them both, given them a home, a life together. That was *real*. It wasn't part of the script. It wasn't make believe. If Nick was in trouble they had to help him. Perhaps, when they found him, they could get back to the life they had lived together, in happiness. She would not give that up, not until she knew *for certain* that the game was up, her cover blown.

She had to finish what she had started, follow through. Her name was Anna Hart, her daughter was called Rachel. She had been here before, many times. She knew what she was doing. She didn't *feel* like Anna any more, didn't think like her, didn't see things the way she had seen them. But she could *act* like her. That would do.

Where she had kissed Rachel's forehead there was a smudged, bloody mark. She brought her fingertips to her own lips and checked. Her lips were bleeding. They both had split lips. She sighed.

'Please, Rachel,' she said. Her daughter wiped her eyes. 'Trust me.' Rachel nodded.

'The address,' Anna said. 'Stijn gave an address to the other one. He was going there to meet someone.' Rachel frowned at her. 'Can you remember it?' Anna asked, and watched her thinking. 'It was in Pudsey,' she added. 'I just can't recall where.'

'11a, Clifton Lane,' Rachel said, a look like self-disgust pulling at the sides of her mouth.

Anna smiled. 'Good girl. I knew I could count on you.'

TWENTY-TWO

'Listen up!' Alan White stood at the end of the CID room, leaning back against a desk. He was a short man, but solid; the desk shifted slightly beneath his weight, pausing him. He stepped forward. 'Listen!' He waited for the murmur of voices to subside. 'We could spend the next hour doing a standard first briefing, sketching out lines, me asking for your help, trying to involve you. But you all know how it works. The SIO has his own theories and we all get to follow them regardless of how stupid they seem. So we might as well cut straight to that.' He grinned.

It was, Bains thought, one of White's many weaknesses that he thought himself to be more popular than he was.

'You all know already what we're dealing with, so I won't waste time on background. Ask a sergeant if you feel you need more. They were all briefed earlier. All I'll say is we have two deaths and a double kidnapping. That's what we're dealing with. First up: in the early hours of this morning Nicholas Hanley is set on fire and thrown from the ninth-floor balcony of Spencer Tower in Leeds centre. Secondly a taxi driver called . . .' He looked around him in vain for something that would tell him the victim's name. Beside him Jon Hoyle – tall, gaunt and conscientious – leaned forward and whispered it into his ear. '. . . Iftikar Khan,' White said, not even acknowledging Hoyle, 'an Asian mini-cab driver. Shot near the airport. Wounded in the chest, then finished with a head shot. A professional silencing of a potential witness. Two people were kidnapped from his cab. A thirty-nine-year-old woman called Anna Hart, Hanley's partner, and her eleven-year-old daughter, Rachel.' Bains raised his eyebrows. He hoped he wasn't one of the sergeants the detectives were going to ask to fill in the gaps, because he didn't have a clue how White had arrived so quickly at so many conclusions. Less than an hour ago White had at least pretended that he didn't have a clue either. Bains shifted his gaze to the tall, military type with the ridiculous caricature moustache, who was standing to the right of White, his eyes roving across the room. He had been with Francis Doyle earlier. Could he have something to do with the new levels of certainty?

'I know exactly what has happened here,' White continued, 'so there's no point in us trying to mess around and guess any different. This is the line we'll follow: Anna and Rachel Hart were kidnapped at gunpoint. The taxi driver got in the way, so he was shot. Wrong time, wrong place. Tragic, but we don't need to waste hours tracing his past. We find Anna and Rachel and we find his killer. If we do that we also find the people who threw Nicholas Hanley from a nine-storey block this morning. If we do *that* quick enough we might save the lives of an innocent woman and her kid. Got it?'

Nobody said anything. But White wasn't waiting for a response.

'I have four different angles right here in my head right now,' he said, tapping his temple. Bains had a feeling he knew where he'd got them. 'So we're going to work in four teams. Jon Hoyle is my deputy, under him four sergeants. That's it. No fucking around with HOLMES.'

Bains frowned. The Home Office Large Major Enquiry System was meant to help. White stepped up to one of the whiteboards. 'The key to this is not Anna Hart, but Nicholas Hanley.' He began to write. 'This is how it breaks down. One: Hanley's property business. I want a team under Tom Ashton to get into all the offices owned or rented by Hanley and Co., including the one under the flat in Spencer Tower. Seize every item of material you can lay hands on. So far as we are aware there are two other offices – one in Bradford and one in York. Take everything and bring it back here. We'll tell you what to look for once you've got that far. I want all that done by four this afternoon . . .' Hoyle leaned forward again, saying something.

'Yes,' White said. 'His house in Reeth as well. So that's four premises to toss by four p.m. Understood?'

From the front Tom Ashton, an overweight DS from Pontefract, said something signifying assent.

'Good,' White said. 'Somewhere in his business life Nicholas Hanley has crossed someone. That is what is going on here. He fucked something up, or stumbled on something he shouldn't have. I don't know what it was. I don't have the detail . . .' He glanced very quickly at the man with the moustache. 'But I need to have it by four.'

He scribbled another heading onto the board. 'Two: Hanley's last hours. Standard stuff. I want Jane Ferguson to take a team and find out everything Hanley did before he was killed. Work in three-hour chunks. First three hours prior is the priority, then the next three, etcetera. Are you all right with that, Jane?' He smiled at a hard-faced brunette standing in front of Bains. She nodded.

'Speak to Pete Bains, behind you,' White said. 'Before he goes off. Pete worked the Hanley side overnight, before we knew much about it. He can tell you what he's got so far.' All heads turned briefly to look at Bains. He nodded at Jane Ferguson, keeping his face straight. *Before he goes off.* It was the first he knew about that.

'Next: Martyn Cox. You get Imran Akhtar, Hanley's

Asian business partner. He's been in the business less than three years, I'm told. But he came straight in as a partner. What went on there? Why did Hanley need to do that? Before that, Hanley and Co. was an estate agency for white toffs. It sold spreads in northern England and Scotland, usually for double-barrelled families who had so much dosh they wouldn't miss the odd hundred-acre pile needed to raise some readies to keep the Revenue off their backs. A strictly word-of-mouth business. Not the sort of affair you would usually invite an *Asian* into.' He managed to pronounce 'Asian' as if the word were synonymous with 'Paki'. 'So what's Akhtar doing there? As I have it,' another quick glance at the moustache, 'Hanley has continued to run the original business from the York office. Akhtar has started, by contrast, to build up a commercial side from Bradford. Akhtar might or might not be involved here. We just don't know.' He smiled. 'So we're going to assume he is. I want you to toss all his properties, Martyn. Get all his paperwork back here. Pete Bains has already spoken to him as if he were a mere witness, so he should be at ease. I want you to scare him a bit then watch him. That's the plan. Frighten him, then watch where he runs to. Get the Force Tactical Team to help. I've already put in the request. OK?'

Martyn Cox cleared his throat. 'I'll need a warrant to toss his properties,' he said.

White screwed his face up, pushing a finger into his ear and wriggling it around as if there was something in there blocking his hearing. 'Will you?' he asked. 'Accidents happen.' He grinned again.

Beside him Jon Hoyle, the grim counterpoint to his ceaseless clown, spoke up. 'Speak to me afterwards, Martyn. Mr Sutherland and I will get you something.' Hoyle looked at the moustache.

Sutherland – so that was his name. Bains had heard it before. Karen Sharpe had told him about someone called Sutherland, someone she had worked for in her Security Services days. A *spook*. She hadn't trusted him.

'Chop! Chop!' White continued, turning to the white-board. 'Let's not get too intellectual here. We've got lives to save.' He began to write again. 'Last team: Will Price. You have publicity. Get that picture I gave you out everywhere. Look for other photos. Circulate them. Saturate the media with images of Anna Hart and her poor little kid. Do interviews for locals and nationals. Get out and about. Start near the scene, work your way outwards. Do as many streets as you can. Cover public transport, whatever. I haven't thought about it in detail, I don't need to. That's your job.'

'Yes, sir.'

Bains heard the voice from somewhere to the left of him.

'Good. That's it. That's what we're doing. If you work quickly I'm confident we will find this woman and her kid before the next century.' He paused again, scanning faces with an aggressive look, eyebrows raised, daring someone to speak. 'That means today,' he added.

He took a stack of small cards from his jacket pocket and began to hand them out. 'Pass them back,' he said. 'Everyone needs to have at least a couple of these.' Bains waited until the woman in front of him passed him a handful, then looked down at them. They were copies of the photo he had already seen. Anna Hart on a beach somewhere, in a bikini. He heard the detectives beginning to murmur comments as they looked at it.

'Nice, isn't she?' White said. 'A looker. Hands up all the men who do not want to save this woman!' The group stirred uncomfortably. White laughed aloud, alone. When he had stopped he held up a hand, as if silencing applause. 'This is the best photo we have of her right now. I know it's not perfect. I know you can't see her face properly, but it's enough to be working with. Now listen up while I call out the teams.'

Bains listened to confirm what he already knew now. His own name appeared nowhere. As the meeting broke up he tried to push forward to ask White about it. But White made it quickly through the door, muttering *sotto voce* to the man called Sutherland.

'Mr White?' Bains called. 'I need to speak to you—'

White turned to glance at him. 'Sorry, Pete. Someone paging me. I have to take an urgent phone call.'

Bains tugged Jon Hoyle's arm instead. 'Can I have a quick word, sir?'

Hoyle cleared his throat and stepped back into the room. 'What is it, Pete?'

'My name didn't come up. Nor any of three detectives I have down at Milgarth. Are we off the inquiry?'

Hoyle looked confused for a moment. 'I thought you worked last night, Pete?'

'I did, but—'

'Well, that's all it is. You can knock off now. You must be knackered. Tell your people down there good job, well done, get some kip.' He was turning to leave already.

'Mr White said he was going to give me the team looking for Anna Hart.'

Hoyle turned back to him. Alan White could lie without it showing, but not Jon Hoyle. He was an old-style honest detective. He looked embarrassed now. 'I'm sorry he said that, Pete,' he said. 'But you know what Alan's like. We don't even have a team looking for Anna Hart, not specific like that.'

'So that's all it is?'

'What?'

'You decided to rest me?'

'That's right.'

'So when do you want me back on?'

Hoyle cleared his throat again. 'When your normal shift starts, I suppose.'

Bains held his eyes, wanting him to feel uncomfortable. 'That man,' he said. 'The one with the moustache?'

'Yes?'

'Did you say he was called Sutherland?'

'Yes. He's from the Home Office . . .'

'So he says. I've come across him before. His friend was called Doyle?'

'I think so. Why?'

'Doyle was in to see me earlier, asking for Karen Sharpe. If he's told you they were from the Home Office he was lying. They're Box.'

'Box?'

'Box 500. Spooks.'

Hoyle nodded slowly, not looking at him. He didn't ask who Karen Sharpe was, but then the whole Force had at least heard the name. Probably they also knew that Bains had had a relationship with her.

'This has nothing to do with them?' he asked.

Hoyle shrugged. 'I'm not in charge here, Pete,' he said, unable to tell the lie. 'But I imagine these blokes have more than one job on the go. Because they spoke to you about one thing and us about another doesn't link the two.'

TWENTY-THREE

'Anna Hart?'

'Yes? Who is that?' She had asked for the incident room dealing with the shooting of the taxi driver, giving her name. They had asked her to hold, saying they were paging someone for her.

'Chief Superintendent Alan White. I'm the SIO here. Where are you, Miss Hart?'

She faltered. She hadn't expected to get the SIO. She wanted to hang up at once. She felt her stomach tighten. She looked over at Rachel, sitting in the passenger seat, trying to listen in.

'I'm calling about Nicholas Hanley,' she said. She heard the man pause, then an interference, as if he were covering the receiver with his hand. 'Can you hear me?' she asked.

'Yes. Could you hold the line a moment, please?'

She waited. She could hear someone else saying something, just out of intelligible earshot, then the man was back. 'Did you say your name was Anna Hart?'

'Yes.'

'I can't talk to you by phone, Miss Hart. Where are you?'

She felt panicky. 'Why not? Why can't you talk to me?'

There was a long pause. 'Because I can't be sure who you are.'

'Don't be stupid.' She could hear her voice rising. 'Who else could I be?'

'You might be the press – or anybody. Do you understand?'

'No. I don't.'

She heard him whispering to someone.

'You might be the people who kidnapped Anna Hart,' he said, eventually. 'We have to be careful. Do you understand now?'

So they were looking for her. She could feel her pulse picking up. This was dangerous. They could trace the call. She should cut the line now. How did she know who *he* was with? She didn't know what was going on here. She was making assumptions. If her cover was blown then she could assume *nothing*. It had happened twice before and each time someone had blown her from the inside. That was how she had ended up hanging from hooks in a basement in Manchester in 1986. In 1996, the IRA had targeted her because a bent officer had identified her and sold the information.

And then there were 'her own people' – Sutherland and his friends – she knew what they were capable of from long ago. They had been prepared to kill her in 1987, to let her burn rather than watch the operation fold; they were soldiers – all of them – they thought in military terms; a calculus of risk objectives, expendable resources. If it suited them – if it fitted the 'big picture' – they would burn her now. Maybe it was happening already. She could trust no one. Not until she knew exactly what this was about. They were probably trying to pin the call to a cell site even as she was speaking.

She looked quickly out of the car windows, searching for a transmitter aerial. They were parked up on Church Lane, in Pudsey. 'Historic Market Town' the sign off the ring road had announced in nice brown English Heritage lettering. In reality Pudsey was a part of the general suburban sprawl lying between Bradford and Leeds – a depressed area of soot-blackened Victorian civic buildings mixed with ugly sixties fill-ins. Church Lane was one of the main roads. Towards the centre it was littered with charity shops, closed-down banks and travel agencies selling cheap escape routes. Further out, where she was now, it became more residential. Nevertheless, it was still busy with traffic and lunch-time shoppers. She was parked at the corner of Church Lane and Clifton Lane, the engine turning over. She didn't dare switch it off.

She was using the mobile phone she had taken from the dead man. But she wasn't sure what stage the technology was at for tracing mobile calls. Could they trace cell phone calls that quickly? she wondered. Could they triangulate the signal from two transmitter masts?

'Who is there with you?' she asked White. She shouldn't trust him either. Something had happened to get her into this position. This wasn't the time to make naive assumptions about the ordinary police. 'I want to speak to you alone.'

'I am alone.'

'I don't believe you. I heard you speaking to someone.'

'Tell me where you are.'

'Not until you tell me who—'

'If you were Anna Hart you would tell me where you are.'

'*I am Anna Hart!*'

'I can't speak to you on your call. It's standard procedure. Please give me the number where you are.'

She thought again about cutting the line. He was playing some kind of game. She didn't understand it. She tried to think about what the tone of his voice said. He was tense, nervous. Did he know who she was? If so, why not say – or use her original name?

In case she was with the people who had taken her, in case they were forcing her to call, trying to get her handlers to slip up and uncover her. He was right. It *was* standard procedure. Until *he* knew for certain what was going on he would maintain her cover. But that meant Sutherland had told him who she really was. She could hear White listening past her, to the background noise, trying to work out where she was and if anyone else was there.

'Is Nicholas Hanley dead?' she asked. That was all she wanted to know.

He didn't answer.

'Did you hear me?'

'I heard you. If you give me your number or come in to the incident room we could—'

'*Is Nicholas Hanley dead?*' She caught herself starting to shout, seeing Rachel's eyes filling with tears. 'I need to know,' she said, controlling it. 'I need you to tell me.'

She heard someone else saying something, louder now, almost audible. The voice sounded familiar. Maybe he didn't know who she was. Maybe he really was a policeman, looking for her, frightened only that she was being held, forced to make this call.

'Is Nicholas Hanley dead?' she asked again.

'Yes,' White said. 'I'm sorry. He died this morning.'

She took a deep breath. Rachel looked down at her feet. She had heard.

'How did he die?'

'I can't tell you that kind of thing unless . . .' She didn't get the chance to interrupt him. Whoever was in the background said something to him, cutting him off. There was a short pause, then White said, 'He was murdered. He was thrown off the balcony of his flat in Leeds. He died very quickly.'

Detail. It didn't sound like White was inventing it. But her mind refused to react. Even the detail could be a lie.

White himself might not know what lies they had fed him. They *could* be burying her. It was possible. That was what they called it in London. Erasing her original identity, because they had made an error somewhere, something she wasn't even aware of. Or because it suited them for other purposes. You never knew. Never. *Assume the worst: they had blown her themselves, then pulled her original ID. Karen Sharpe didn't exist any more.*

'Who says it is him?' she asked. 'Who identified the body?' She wanted more, but she was frightened now, unsure of who was there, of what they could do.

'Are you in danger, Miss Hart? If you are in danger—'

'Who has identified him?'

A pause again, then she clearly heard the man in the background say, 'Tell her the truth.' The voice *was* familiar. Her heart began to race. 'Who is there with you?' she asked at once.

White ignored her. 'Mr Hanley's sister has identified the body—'

'Why? What is *she* doing here? She doesn't even—'

'Also Imran Akhtar, Mr Hanley's business associate.'

'His sister doesn't even live here. When did she arrive? Did you ask her to come here?'

'That's not important.'

'She hardly speaks to him. I don't understand.'

'She was here already. On business.'

'Where? What business? Tell me where she is, so I can speak to her.'

'I can't tell you that.' The line went blank for a moment, as if he had cut the connection.

'Hello?' She could hear movement of some sort, a scraping noise. 'Hello? Are you still—'

'Yes. I'm here.'

'There is someone there with you,' she said. She felt her

head pounding. It was all too confusing. Too many possibilities. 'I don't trust you,' she hissed. 'You're lying to me.' She felt her breath catching. 'You're playing some kind of game . . .' Again she heard the voice behind him. 'Tell me who is there with you and I will agree to meet you.' She shouted the words, but he didn't react. She waited. This time he must have learned how to use the mute button because she heard nothing. He was checking. She could tell. He might have been the SIO in name, but he wasn't in charge.

'Miss Hart?'

'Yes?'

'Is Rachel safe?'

She looked quickly at he daughter, who was looking at her as if she had a screw loose. Maybe she did.

'Tell me who is there,' she said.

'A man called Mr Sutherland,' White said. 'One of my sergeants.' He said the words carefully, as if he had been told exactly what to say.

So he was there. She moved her hand from the steering wheel and wiped it on the leg of the overalls she was wearing. Suddenly she was sweating – her palms, down her back, under her arms, in her hair. She could feel it breaking out all over her. She cut the line.

She put the phone in the left breast pocket of the overalls, looked at Rachel. 'His sister says it's him,' she said.

Rachel chewed her lip, tears still in her eyes. Anna could see her thinking it through.

'Why did they get *her*?' Rachel asked at last. 'Nick hardly speaks to her.'

Anna shrugged. 'I don't know. I don't trust it though. She lives in Portugal. What's she doing over here suddenly? Would she even recognize him?'

'You think it isn't him?'

'I don't know. They say Imran Akhtar has been there as well. But I don't trust either of them. We should speak to her. Find out why she's here. Why would Stijn have asked me where Nick was if he was dead?'

'Did they tell you where Diana was?'

'No. But I know where she'll be. They said she was here on business. If she wasn't staying with us that must mean she was at the stables.'

'Who was in there with him?'

Anna looked at her, wondering whether she should say. It had started to rain outside and the windows were steaming up. She wound hers down a little and looked out through the crack. The air was thick with water now, but she could still see the entrance to 11a, Clifton Lane, an ordinary terrace house with a blue door. Presumably the house was split into two flats. She could see a doorbell with more than one button. There were dark curtains at all the windows. Parked up outside the place was a black BMW SUV, which Rachel had told her had been parked outside the abattoir.

'Mum?' Rachel asked again. 'Who was in there with him?'

Anna didn't look at her. 'No one we can trust,' she said.

TWENTY-FOUR

Bains went to the gents' toilets, walked into a cubicle, closed it behind him and sat down on the seat. For a while he stared at the back of the toilet door, forcing his mind to observe the scrawled graffiti, trying to slow the torrent of thoughts coming at him.

The graffiti was uninspiring; mainly football jokes – or were they comments? He knew little about football, so it was hard to say: 'Man U Bell Ends do it again – 12/5/98'. What did that refer to? He was surprised the comment had not been erased in over a year, assuming the date was when it had been put there.

He took a long, deep breath. A 39-year-old woman, an eleven-year-old kid. A man called Doyle looking for Karen Sharpe. Doyle and Sutherland in with Alan White, assisting the search for Anna Hart. What had Jon Hoyle said? *Because they spoke to you about one thing and spoke to us about another doesn't link the two*. He reached into his pocket and took out the photo of Anna Hart.

She looked happy, he thought. The realization brought something like a sharp pain to his chest, a slight constriction to his breathing. He looked away from her. Instead, he tried to look more closely at the background. His mind wanted to scrutinize her, to take in the physical details and think about them, but he forced his eyes to look elsewhere.

She was on a beach somewhere. The photo must have been taken with a camera which allowed adjustment to depth of field, because although she was clearly in focus, little else was. There were the vague outlines of beach huts, possibly made of reeds or thatch – so probably not somewhere in the UK. The sea had no waves that were noticeable, so perhaps the Mediterranean. There were shapes which could have been five or six other people, in the distance. The light was bright, the sun not quite behind her, but not behind the camera either. Consequently, she was ever so slightly over-exposed. She was moving forward, one arm outstretched as if about to catch something, wearing a bikini he had never seen before, thin and plain coloured. A holiday snap.

He held his breath and let his eyes settle on the face. Almost a complete profile with the head angled up slightly. The hair was short, cropped, very, very blonde – almost a bleached white – and looked as though she had just got out of bed. He noticed his palms were sweating. He could see now how he could look at that face, at that hair, and somehow not see the resemblance. The face was different, subtly, but perceptibly different. It might not be her. He put the picture back in his pocket, stood up and opened the cubicle door.

In the CID room he asked aloud whether anyone had a magnifying glass. There were a handful of detectives in there. The question brought a snigger and a round of Sherlock Holmes jokes, but a DC called Gates had one. He was almost embarrassed to admit it.

Bains sat down at an empty desk and took out the photo again. He looked at the legs, carefully. They were long, slender, but with a firm muscle structure. They were attractive. He focused the magnifying glass on the right thigh, immediately saw what he had been looking for, quickly put the glass down and sat back.

It was like something had struck him in the chest. He looked around the room at the others, continuing as normal. No one was looking at him. He could feel the sweat down his back now. He picked the glass up again, looked again, set it down once more. The detail was so obvious he did not see how he could have missed it the very first time he had looked at this photo. A bubble of scarring, about five inches above the knee, about two inches from the midline, to the left. She had taken a bullet there in June 1997. He had met her for the first time a couple of days before that.

He looked again at the face and felt a hard lump form in his throat. This time he saw that it was her straight away. She had dyed her hair, there was something different about her, but it was definitely Karen Sharpe.

TWENTY-FIVE

'*Someone is coming.*' Rachel whispered the words, voice full of panic. '*Mum! I said, someone is coming!*'

Anna had already seen the door of 11a, Clifton Lane beginning to open. 'I see it, Rachel,' she said, looking over. 'There's no need to whisper, no need to worry. He can't see you at this distance and he certainly can't hear. Just keep still if he comes out . . .' She felt her heart picking up beats. She took a breath, keeping her eyes on the doorway, but turning her mind away from it. You had to let the fear be in you, but not take over. That was the trick. You had to use it. Could she teach her daughter this?

'If *we* can see *him* . . .' Rachel began. She started to shrink down in her seat.

'It doesn't mean he can see us,' Anna finished. 'Trust me. The glass reflects at this distance. And refracts too – it's covered in rain. Also, he probably won't be looking.' She watched, head back, eyes sideways. They were far enough away, and the day was rainy and grey, visibility poor. Nevertheless, if Stijn was checking, Rachel was right – he would see them. He wouldn't be able to recognize them, not at that distance through the rain-streaked windows, but he might see the smoke coming out of the exhaust, see that *someone* was there. If he was careful he would want to be sure who it was.

A figure stepped out of the door. It wasn't Stijn. Some-one shorter, darker. She recognized him at exactly the same time as Rachel spoke:

'Is that Imran Akhtar?'

Anna nodded. Nick's business partner. They had met him three times at Black Carr Hall. Nick had invited him for dinner. Neither of them had liked him. On all three occasions there had been something suspicious and watchful about him, poorly cloaked beneath a veneer of obsequiousness. Neither had been able to understand why Nick had brought him in to the business.

He was wearing a suit and a raincoat, and had some kind of glove – or was it a bandage? – on his right hand. Aside from that, he looked the same as the last time they had seen him – smart, well groomed, with a very neatly shaved beard and moustache, probably dressed in expensive clothes, with choice items of very gold jewellery on his fingers and wrists, a small, black briefcase – every inch the successful, legitimate businessman. What was he doing at a grotty terrace in Pudsey?

He stepped out from the doorway and looked up at the rain, then turned back and spoke to someone out of sight, still inside the house.

'*Is* that Imran Akhtar?' Rachel asked again. She sounded as though she couldn't bring herself to believe it.

'It is,' Anna replied, without taking her eyes off him. 'It doesn't surprise me.'

Akhtar produced an umbrella, raised it, then stepped away from the door. A taller person followed him out – Stijn, unmistakable at any distance. He was carrying a plastic carrier bag containing something. Anna heard Rachel take a deep breath.

'I see him,' Anna said. She thought her voice sounded calm. She didn't feel it. The *idea* of looking at him, of seeing him again, of placing herself in his vicinity, had been merely theoretical. The fear it produced had been easy to control. But seeing him in reality was different. She felt a flood of disgust, a welter of unpleasant memories flashing through her mind before settling on the raw stink of his sweat, the slightly sweet odour of his saliva and breath. He had sweated so much that beads of it had dropped off his head onto her face. His mouth had been inches from her eyes and face, breathing onto her. She saw a repeat image of him pulling his fist back to strike her, from above her, on top of her. She closed her eyes on it, every muscle in her body tense now, but even so aware that already her mind was protecting her. What she was remembering was not the worst of it.

He didn't look in her direction, but stepped out and around Akhtar and walked straight towards the BMW. She let out a breath, slowly, then glanced at Rachel. Her eyes were fixed on him, her mouth tightly shut. She was holding her breath.

'You can breathe, Rachel,' Anna said quietly.

Stijn got into the BMW; Akhtar pulled the door shut. Stijn started to turn his vehicle, which meant he was going to drive out past them, right in front of them.

'I'm going to duck down,' Anna said. 'You stay up and watch him. Don't look directly at him. Tell me when he's turned past us. Watch where that bastard Akhtar goes, too.' She moved her head and shoulders so that they were below the line of the door frame, her head leaning sideways and touching Rachel's leg.

'Mum!'

'Be calm, Rachel. It's OK. He won't see you. He probably didn't even notice what you looked like.'

'Mum!' Her voice was shaking.

'What's Akhtar doing?'

'I can't do this, Mum. I'm frightened.'

'What's Akhtar doing?'

'He's driving past us . . . oh my God . . . not Akhtar . . . the other . . .'

Anna waited. 'Is he gone yet?'

She heard Rachel sigh. 'He's gone. Akhtar is going the other way.' Her voice was almost inaudible.

Anna straightened up. 'Good girl.' She looked for Akhtar's car. 'Is that his – the Merc?'

'Yes.'

Anna noted the registration as it turned out of sight at the end of Clifton Lane.

'We should go to the police now, Mum. We should tell them what we've seen—'

'No. I'm going in there to have a look.'

'Mum, please! We can't.'

'You don't have to come. In fact, I need you to stay here and watch the outside for me.'

Rachel moved quickly across the seats and pressed her face against her arm. She was crying again, shaking with fear. Anna put an arm round her and held her tightly. 'Just let me do this, Rach,' she said. 'Just hang on for me. Please.'

'Why? Why, Mum, why?'

'Do you remember when all this started, Rachel?'

Rachel said nothing. She was pressing her face into her mother's chest now, sobbing.

'Do you remember when we first met Nick?'

Anna felt her nod slightly, still sobbing.

'It's been good, hasn't it? We've had a nice life with Nick. We've had fun.'

She could feel her thinking about it, hanging on tightly, thinking about it.

'We've probably had the best time you and I have ever had. We've got along well. We've done things together.' Rachel began to move away from her. 'And Nick has loved us. He has really loved us, Rachel. He took us into his home and made it our home.'

181

She paused. Rachel wiped her sleeve across her eyes, looking up at her.

'You like him, don't you?' she asked, speaking gently. 'You like Nick as much as he likes you.'

Rachel nodded slowly.

'So do I,' Anna said. 'And I think he's in trouble. Maybe we have got him into trouble. I don't know. Maybe he's already dead.' She faltered, feeling a rush of emotion struggling to get out. 'I hope not . . . I hope to God . . .' Her vision blurred, her eyes prickling with tears. She swallowed the lump in her throat, took a breath. 'I hope he's alive,' she said. 'And if he is then we have to try to find him before that man does. If that man thought he was dead he wouldn't be looking for him. Do you understand?'

Rachel frowned at her. 'I understand that. But I don't see why we can't go to the police.'

'Because we don't know enough. We don't know what's going on. Think back to what I told you back then, when we met Nick. Do you remember I said there was only one rule?'

'Three. You said there were three rules.'

'OK. But do you remember the first – the golden rule?'

'The third rule is the golden rule.'

'OK. The third. Do you remember it?'

Rachel nodded.

'We know nothing, Rachel. All we know is that something is fucked up. Until we know more you follow the golden rule. For all we know everything that is happening is a calculated attempt to get us to forget that rule. And if that happens – and Nick is alive – then it might mean we really have let him down when he needed us.' She pulled Rachel to her again. 'I don't want to do this if we don't have to, Rachel. But we have to.'

She waited until Rachel had stopped crying and was breathing normally.

'OK,' she said. 'Wait here. If you see anything suspicious – anyone approaching the door, anyone going down that alley that leads to the back of the house, anything at all – you lie flat across the seats and sound the horn three times. I'll leave the engine on. Can you do that?'

Rachel was staring at her. 'You know I can, Mum. But can *you* do this?'

Anna frowned.

'I was there, Mum,' Rachel said. 'I heard what happened to you.' She was worrying about her. 'Are you sure you're OK?'

Anna bit her lip. She didn't want to think about it. If she thought about it she would get upset again. 'I can do it,' she said. 'I need to do it, Rachel. I need to stay angry. If I'm not angry I'll just collapse.'

She walked quickly down Clifton Lane, eyes ahead. When she got to the short path leading to number 11a she turned through the gate immediately, walked up to the door and looked at the bells. There were two: flat 11a and flat 11b. From the positions 11a was the ground-floor flat. She pressed both buzzers. She had a story in her head, ready. She was Akhtar's assistant (the overalls might just help – they weren't standard secretarial clothing, but they did have Arabic writing on the breast pocket). He had forgotten something. She was here to retrieve it, but had forgotten her keys. However, no one answered the bell. She tried the door. It was locked.

She walked back up the street, winking at Rachel in the car, then round to the access alley leading to the rear of the house. She counted down to number 11 then turned into a small, high-walled yard. There was one back door to the premises, alongside it a kitchen window. The door was locked, the window closed.

She examined the lock. It was pickable, but not without proper tools. She had nothing. She looked around her for a suitable stone, found a loose brick on top of the yard wall, then scanned the back windows of the opposite and adjacent houses. Through those that didn't feature net curtains she could see no one watching, but that didn't mean some nosy neighbour wasn't out there, ready and willing to do their civic duty. There was nothing she could do about that. She stepped up to the kitchen window and gently tapped the brick against it until the pane broke.

She removed the pieces carefully, between finger and thumb, taking her time and concentrating on the task. Maybe, if anyone was interested, they would notice the overalls and think she was someone from the council, repairing the place. When she had all the pieces out she reached in, unhooked the catch and swung the window open. She listened briefly to the silence beyond, then climbed in.

The kitchen looked ordinary enough. There was a kettle, some plates on the draining board, a few cups and spoons. No cooker, no fridge. She walked through one of two doors out of the place. It led straight into what would have been a living room, if this had been someone's home. It wasn't though. On a table in the centre of the room was a mountain of loose papers. Against the walls were three filing cabinets, a small photocopier/fax machine and a shredder. Akhtar must have been using the place as an office.

What was she looking for? The paperwork scattered across the table looked as if it had just been rifled from the buff file jackets lying on the floor around the table. There were a few bank statements, but mainly she was looking at details of properties. She took time to check them.

One side of the table – looking less disturbed – contained piles of copied details of sales and purchases carried out by Hanley and Co. She saw properties in Scotland, Lancashire, Northumberland, Yorkshire and Wales. The other side of the table was strewn with about thirty pages of standard estate agent's sheets on less well-appointed properties, most of them in Yorkshire. She hadn't even been aware that Nick dealt in that kind of place.

There was an abandoned coffee mug beside these sheets, still half full of tepid liquid. Either Akhtar or Stijn had just been going through the details. She read through them, looking for something she recognized, or which might mean something. Nothing came to mind. She was considering whether she should take copies of them all when she quite clearly heard three loud blasts of a car horn from the street outside.

She gathered all the sheets up, folded them into her back pocket then stepped up to the window to view the street. She could see nothing. She moved back to the kitchen. Nothing happening to the rear. She stood still, listening. She could hear nothing. Suddenly it occurred to her that Stijn or Akhtar might have returned and discovered Rachel, sitting there waiting. Quickly she slid the bolt on the back door, turned the key in the lock, pulled the door open and stepped outside. As she did so she heard the horn again.

185

TWENTY-SIX

'You're working with some people who say they're from the Home Office,' Bains said. He waited for White to deny it, to shut him up, but he just sat across the other side of the desk staring at him. White had looked hostile from the moment Bains had knocked and entered his office.

'Jon Hoyle told me that,' Bains continued. 'He also told me that the fact they were working on your inquiry had nothing to do with the fact that they visited me early this morning asking for Karen Sharpe.'

White stirred a little, fiddling with a fat gold fountain pen, but still looking at Bains. The expression on his face was one of mild irritation.

'I don't think that was true,' Bains said. 'I suppose you were told to say that and I don't blame either of you for doing what you've been told to do. I know how these things work. I also know a little about one of the men you're working for. Enough to know he's not from the Home Office.'

White looked away from him, brow creased. 'Did I tell you to knock off, Pete?'

Bains thought about it. 'No,' he said. 'I don't think you did.'

'Well, I am now. Go home, Pete. You're tired, I'm busy. I don't think ruminating about where people come from or who they work for is helping anything.'

'I don't know what they told you about me,' Bains cut in. 'But I imagine it included information that I had been in a relationship with Karen Sharpe. I don't know how much they've told you about her,' White took a noisy, sharp breath, sucked between his teeth, 'but I can't see how me having had a relationship with her should mean I can't be trusted on this inquiry.'

'Nor can I, Pete.' White looked at him again. 'I can't see that it could have anything to do with it. After all, we're not looking for Karen Sharpe, are we?'

Bains nodded, then took the photo from his pocket and placed it on the desk between them. 'This may sound crazy,' he said, 'given the lack of connection between your Home Office friends and this inquiry,' White scowled at him, 'but I think I might have noticed something about this photo.'

White rubbed his hands across his face. 'Yes?' He sounded angry now.

'If you have a look at this photo with a magnifying glass,' White smirked, 'you will see a small, distinctive mark on her right thigh.'

White pulled the photo over to him and looked at it. 'So?'

'It's a bullet wound – an old one.'

'You're a doctor now?'

'No. I've seen the injury before. It's very distinctive.'

White nodded, a look of disgust on his features. 'I knew this was where you were going—' he started.

Bains cut him off. 'I've seen it on Karen, sir. This photo is of Karen Sharpe.'

White stood up. 'You're sure about that, are you?'

'Yes. I'm certain. I was there when she took that bullet.'

'Karen fucking Sharpe. So that's who we're looking for? That's your theory, is it?' He walked over to the door and opened it, peered out into the corridor, closed it again, then walked back to his desk and picked up the phone.

'I believe so. I assumed you knew already. I was—'

'Sherlock fucking Holmes.'

Bains closed his mouth and looked at him.

'Your problem, Pete,' White said, 'is you don't know how to take a hint.'

Bains waited as he dialled a number and paused for a response.

'I thought you had more sense,' White said, looking out of the window. Bains wasn't sure who he was speaking to. 'I thought you could be trusted to be discreet.'

'Are you talking to me?'

'Is there anyone else in here?' White replaced the phone. 'He's engaged.'

'I only want to know what's going on,' Bains said. 'I think I should be told—'

'Why?' White stared at him. There was a pinched look to the sides of his mouth. 'Why should you be told anything? Why *you*?'

'Because I—'

'Because you had a fucking relationship with Karen Sharpe?'

Bains opened his mouth, then thought better of it.

Suddenly White looked tired. 'I can't tell you anything,' he said. He ran his hands through his hair. 'I need to ask.' He sat down again.

'Ask Sutherland?' Bains said.

White turned his head sideways and moved his mouth. He looked like he was about to spit on the floor. 'That's right,' he said. 'Ask Sutherland. Meanwhile you get out of here and you say nothing about your theory to anyone. You understand that?'

'Of course—'

'Of course? Why of course? Do you have any idea what's going on?'

'Not for sure.'

'You don't have the faintest idea. We're looking for Anna Hart. That's what you know. You talk to no one, Pete. Is that really, really clear?'

Bains stood up. 'It is.' He turned to leave.

'I'll call you,' White said, 'when I know what to do about you. Keep your phone on.'

Bains turned back to him. 'What to *do* about me? What does that mean?'

White leaned back in his chair. 'I think you're straight, Pete,' he said. 'That's what I've told anyone who asked me. But others are not so sure about you. They think you might be harbouring grudges. It would have been best for you if you had just kept out of all this.'

'Harbouring grudges? What the fuck does that mean? And who the fuck are you talking about?'

White smiled. 'You have a temper, too. That doesn't help.'

Bains swallowed. 'I'm sorry.'

'Doesn't matter to me.' He waved a hand. 'But just think about what might be going on.' He looked up at him, expectantly.

Bains frowned. 'I *have* thought about it.'

'Just say Anna Hart was in danger because her *cover* was gone,' White continued, voice lower. 'Just say that was what was going on here. You would have to suspect, wouldn't you, if that had happened, that her *cover* had been blown from the inside?'

Bains frowned.

'From the inside,' White repeated. 'From in here. Right here. By someone who knew her well.'

Bains took a breath. 'Are you accusing me?'

'I'm not accusing anyone. But someone has fucked her good and proper. And everyone has to be suspected. You

189

know that. There are people running this thing now who would happily accuse you, Pete.'

'*Are* they accusing me?'

White sighed. 'Of course they fucking are. Why do you think I'm telling you this?'

'That's ridiculous. I haven't seen her—'

'I know. That's what I've said. But until we know what we're doing I would advise you to keep a low profile and your mouth shut.'

Bains looked at him for a while, saying nothing, holding his temper in check.

'Just tell me one thing,' he said finally. 'Does this mean that Rachel Hart is Mairead?'

TWENTY-SEVEN

There was nothing wrong. No police sirens, no police cars, no nosy neighbours, no suspicious males, no Stijn, Akhtar or anything else that would warrant her sitting on the horn for so long. She was still pressing it as Anna got back to the car.

'What? What's up?' Anna asked, breathless.

But there was nothing. She was worried Anna had been too long, worried something had happened to her. She tried to hug her as she got in, but Anna pushed her off. Her heart was thundering in her chest. She had run all the way back to the car, terrified of what she would find. 'You have to stop this,' she shouted. 'You panic too much. You have to toughen up, Rachel.'

She drove furiously for five minutes, taking the car out of Pudsey and back to the Stanningly by-pass, saying nothing more. She was frightened if she opened her mouth she would shout at her again. But the damage was already done. She had upset her. And the kid had been nothing but concerned about her. It was totally unforgivable.

At the roundabout for the ring road she turned back and pulled into the car park for the new Marks & Spencer. She parked in amongst other cars and stalled the engine, cursing. Rachel wasn't looking at her.

'I'm sorry,' she said, after a while. 'I'm really sorry. I got a real fright back there. I heard the horn and thought something must be happening to you.'

'Well, *I* heard nothing and thought something must be happening to *you*.' Rachel's eyes flashed at her, full of anger.

'I know. You're right. I'm sorry. I should not have shouted. I'm really sorry.'

They sat in silence for a moment.

'Are we finished now?' Rachel demanded. The apology hadn't worked. 'Can we go to the police?' Her voice was loaded with resentment.

'No. We're going to see Diana Hanley. We have to—'

'You promised me.'

'I did not.'

'You said that would be it. You said after the last thing . . . you said . . .'

'I still don't know what's going on,' Anna said. 'I didn't promise anything.'

'You said we would stop this.' Rachel's voice was going up. '*You said we could STOP!*'

Anna ignored her, fiddling with the wires beneath the wheel, trying to get the car started again.

'I can't do this any more!' Rachel said. She was going to cry again, but she was angry, too.

'You can.'

'*I can't! I'm hungry!*'

Anna straightened up and looked at her. She had almost stamped her foot. 'You're hungry?'

'Yes. You've given me nothing to eat.' It was true.

'You're right,' Anna said. 'What am I thinking of? I'm sorry. You must be starved. I'll go and get you something to eat.'

'We've got no money.'

'I'll borrow something.'

'You mean steal.'

'I mean borrow.'

'*She* wouldn't do that.'

'Stop it.'

'It's true. Anna Hart would *never* do that.'

'Remember what I told you! We can't let this drop. Not now.'

'I am remembering! You're the one who has for-gotten.'

Anna bent over again, trying to ignore her. The car started.

'You know she wouldn't do this,' Rachel said. She was pleading with her now. Not shouting.

'She's learning,' Anna said, starting to reverse out. 'She has to learn.'

'To start cars without keys? How would Anna Hart know how to do that? How would she learn?'

'She just has.'

'She wouldn't do any of this. She wouldn't stab a man. She wouldn't steal a car. She wouldn't break into a house—'

'Stop it. Stop it now.'

Anna pulled the car out, heading back to the by-pass.

'You said you would get me food,' Rachel said. Her voice was subdued now. She was trying not to cry.

'Not here. I'll stop somewhere else. After we've spoken to his sister.'

'You're being horrible to me.'

'And you're being a little bitch.'

She drove to the ring road. Her heart was beating furiously, her mind full of confused thoughts. She *was* being horrible to her. She knew it. She was doing every-thing she shouldn't be doing, everything Anna Hart wouldn't have dreamed of doing. She was losing control.

'Anna wouldn't speak to me like that,' Rachel said, very quietly.

She kept driving, not looking at her. *Welcome back to the real world*, she thought.

'I wish Nick was here,' Rachel whispered.

'It's because of Nick that I'm doing this.'

'No, it's not. It's because of you.'

TWENTY-EIGHT

Suddenly Bains didn't feel tired at all. He walked to the Weetwood canteen and ordered a tea. He needed to slow his brain. Everything was coming at him too fast. He stood at the window and sipped the liquid, not tasting it or looking at the view. How long before White got through to Sutherland? He needed to know now what was going on. He put the paper cup down and cracked his fingers, methodically, one by one. His heart was racing. Already he knew too much. He needed to distract himself.

He found Jane Ferguson and forced himself to explain to her what they had been doing down at Milgarth. 'I'm going to stay on,' he said. 'At least until we get the video footage bottomed.'

'I'll give you two of the team now,' she volunteered. 'You can take them back to Milgarth with you.' Obviously she wasn't in the loop.

He drove back to Milgarth with two female detectives called Kerr and Walsh, concentrating on the road. The women were meant to replace the team he had worked with through the night. They were very young. He filled them in and asked them if they had ever processed video material before. They knew the basics.

Back at Milgarth Paul North, predictably, opted to knock off straight away, yawning his disapproval of any suggestion that they might work longer than their allotted shift, which was already long past. Hayward said she would do a few more hours. Chris Greenwood wouldn't hear of quitting until he had covered all the CCTV and video angles.

Bains asked Hayward to pick up the two tasks he had left with North – chasing photos of Hanley to compare to the video footage, and tracking down his medical records – then he took the two new detectives into Greenwood's video cave and they sat down to watch what Greenwood had unearthed while Bains was at Weetwood. It would keep his mind occupied, at least. He checked his mobile for a signal as he entered the room. White still hadn't called.

'This bloke,' Greenwood said, placing his finger on the image. 'This bloke is interesting.' He had managed to scrounge a better TV monitor. The image was larger, but more blurred. Greenwood had frozen the feed. Bains leaned forward and looked. He was viewing the vestibule camera from Spencer Tower. The time at the bottom read '10.25: 30.12.99' – the morning of the day before. 'The time lapse is four seconds,' Greenwood said. 'It takes at least fifteen seconds to cross through the path of the vestibule camera so it should catch everyone. This man is entering the building here. Ten twenty-five yesterday morning. Watch him.' He played the film.

'He's distinctive,' Bains said. The figure Greenwood had pointed out looked to be easily over six feet and strongly built, with a bald or shaved head. He was wearing a short leather jacket.

'That's why I noticed him,' Greenwood said.

'Wouldn't someone so obvious take more care with cameras if they were about to kill someone?'

The DC called Kerr asked the question. Greenwood shrugged, as if the query were irrelevant. 'He's looking at the board which lists the companies in the building,' he said. The man stood in front of the board for the time it took the recording machine to switch twice to the vestibule camera, then disappeared in the direction of the security desk.

'Did he sign in?' Bains asked.

'As you can see,' Greenwood said, 'there were several people in and out at that time. We seized the reception logs this morning and four people signed in around ten-thirty. I rang and asked the security company how accurate the timings were. They said not very, so it's hard to pinpoint which might be him, if he signed. So four possibles, I think. They're meant to be getting the guy who was on duty to call me, to see if he remembers this man.'

'Did he come out again?' Bains asked.

'Two hours later,' Greenwood skipped the tape forward. He had noted all the timings on his pad. They watched the same man re-appear from the direction of the security desks. There was a good shot of his face, peering directly up at the camera. Greenwood paused it.

'He knows he's being watched,' he said. 'He's quite happy to be on camera.'

'Why shouldn't he be?' Bains asked. 'For all we know he's a nobody.'

'Just wait,' Greenwood replied, winking at him.

'He's an ugly fucker,' said the DC called Walsh. 'Is that acne on his skin?'

'Acne scars,' Greenwood said. 'Plus some other scarring here . . .' He pointed to above the eyebrows. 'He looks battered – like a rugby player, or a boxer.'

'That image is good enough for a still,' Bains said.

'I'll try to get one when we're done here,' Greenwood said. 'If you change your mind about him being nobody.'

'Do we know whereabouts he went in the building?' Bains asked.

'Like I said, if he signed in he could be one of four people. As they sign in they are expected to note where they are going. But security doesn't ring up to check.'

'Did any of them sign to go up to Hanley and Co.?'

'No.'

Bains pushed his chair back slightly. 'That's it?'

'No.'

Greenwood bent towards the floor and changed tapes. He fast-forwarded the next tape to the early hours of that morning.

'This is the underground car park camera,' he said.

The numbers at the bottom of the screen read '03.27: 31.12.99'. Bains watched as three figures passed quickly through the camera's field of view. Greenwood rewound the tape, then paused it.

'Where's their car?' Walsh asked.

'They can't have come in one. If you enter this car park in a car you must pass straight across the camera. The camera is mounted behind the entrance, pointing away from it into the garage, so you can't see the doors themselves, but it's my guess that these three must have come in via the doors to the underground garage on foot.'

'How?' Bains asked.

'The security company say users are issued with infra-red devices to trigger the doors from outside. They must have used one of those.'

'So they knew someone on the inside,' Walsh said.

Bains looked more closely at the paused image. 'Is that your rugby player again?'

'I think so.' Greenwood smiled.

The image was very poor, but it certainly looked like one of the three was tall, muscular and bald, wearing a dark jacket similar in length and cut to the one they had observed previously.

'This man is Asian, I think,' Greenwood said, pointing to a shorter male, three-quarters in view, in profile.

Bains squinted, looking at him. 'It could be Akhtar,' he said, surprised.

'Akhtar?'

'Hanley's business partner. I spoke to him earlier. Do you have any other images of him?'

Greenwood smiled again. 'I do.'

He changed the tapes.

'None of those three leave Spencer Tower via the main vestibule or garage. But this is from the junction of the Headrow and Albion Street. If you were to leave Spencer Tower via one of the side doors – the doors covered by the broken CCTV links – and walk straight to the Headrow you would be there in less than five minutes.' He messed around with it, fast-forwarding then rewinding until he had it where he wanted it. The tape was a very rapid time lapse, which Greenwood appeared to have spliced into one tape. The delays made the figures passing across the junction appear stilted, like something from an old movie. The image was black and white.

'Right there,' Greenwood said, playing a passage again, stopping it, rewinding it, then playing it yet again. The movement was so fast he had to point out what he wanted them to see. 'Two figures crossing the Headrow here. Note the group of youths coming in the other direction, already watching what is going on up ahead. My guess is the first firefighters were arriving. This is timed at just after four-twenty.'

Bains focused on the two Greenwood had pointed out.

'Yes. You're right,' he said. 'That's them.' The same bulky, bald individual, crossing quickly, head down. Beside him the same Asian man. 'Three in, two out,' he added. 'Probably at around the right time to have been involved.'

'That the third is missing means nothing,' Greenwood

said. 'He might have turned north on Albion Street. I haven't covered everything yet, but the third guy wasn't very distinctive.'

'What happens when they get across?' Bains asked him.

Greenwood played it again. 'They reach the other side and split up. The Asian heads off to cross Albion Street, the tall one follows it down towards the railway station. But . . .'

He switched on a machine lying on the floor beside the video machine. The image on the screen was replaced by a much clearer still.

'This is from the cameras pointing down East Parade. They're run by a private company and recorded digitally onto CD. The image is good. This is our man here.' He ran the image and pointed him out. 'My guess is he's gone down Albion Street, then cut across to Park Row, down Greek Street and onto East Parade. Watch. He disappears down the snicket that leads through Park Cross into Park Square. The timings would match and this is definitely him entering East Parade at four twenty-seven. Notice the car keys.'

Bains nodded. The man was clearly visible pulling something out of his pocket, then swinging it from his fingers. He walked off camera.

'We lose him?'

'Yes. Half the cameras in Park Square are down for repair. He's not on the images I have. It's a one-way system out of Park Square and other cameras might just cover one of the exit points, but I haven't got that far yet.'

'But how would you know what car to look for?'

Greenwood raised his eyebrows. 'Because I *do* have him in Park Square from earlier on in the day.' He changed video tapes again. 'Back to video – the usual crap quality from Park Square. But here he is, I think.'

They watched a grainy black and white image of a tall man getting into a dark-coloured BMW SUV and pulling off. Greenwood paused it.

'That was at twelve twenty-three yesterday afternoon. He left Spencer Tower just after eleven-thirty.'

'The image is useless,' Bains said. 'We can't get anything from—'

'Not from that,' Greenwood said. 'But he turns onto St Paul's Street. The same digital system at East Parade picks you up as you come out of there.' He paused childishly, looking over at Bains.

'And?' Bains said.

'If it's him then I got a nice shot of him at the wheel and I got the plate: HTZ 1342. It's registered to Hertz rent-a-car.'

'Did you call them?'

'I did.' He looked down his pad of notes. 'It was rented ten days ago, in person, from their offices at Manchester Airport. The customer produced a South African passport and driving licence to verify ID and paid with a credit card. They gave me the number.'

'His name?'

'Josef Stijn.'

TWENTY-NINE

Nick had told her that his sister Diana had lived in Portugal for nearly ten years. She had a business over there, breeding Lusitanian stallions. She had a husband, but rarely saw him. He lived in Chelsea; her children went to a public school in Yorkshire. They had a place in Cornwall where they occasionally got together as a family, but Diana had other, more absorbing interests in Portugal including, Nick said, a man much younger than herself.

Nick's relationship with his sister had seemed peculiar and she asked him little about it. He had a habit of changing the subject whenever Diana was mentioned. She had visited Nick once during the time they had been with him, but had pointedly refused to stay at Black Carr Hall, so Anna had never met her. Nick had seemed relieved by this, though it had been difficult to work out why. It was tempting to think that he was slightly frightened of his sister. When they spoke by phone the conversations were always short and to the point (and usually about money). Nick usually came away looking distracted and confused. Nevertheless, he wasn't openly critical of her.

Off a small country lane running round the back of Woodhall Hills golf course, Diana's stables occupied about thirty acres of good fenced grazing land, on the slopes of a valley between Leeds and Bradford. Nick said his sister visited the place about once a year, and she had insisted on staying there the one time she had visited Nick during the last eighteen months. If she were here now on business, as White had suggested, then she would be staying in that cottage.

Calverley was a small village about midway between Leeds and Bradford, to the north-west of Pudsey. The land Diana Hanley's stables occupied was prime development area, a shrinking oasis of countryside sandwiched between the county's two major cities. It took nearly twenty minutes to get there from Pudsey. By the time Anna was leaving the ring road it was nearly two o'clock and her daughter had said nothing to her throughout the entire journey.

She drove at a careful speed up Priesthorpe Road – in fact nothing more than a narrow lane with an intermittent surface – and quickly checked the long lane that led to the stables as they passed it. There were no police cars in sight – no cars at all, no sign of anything suspicious. She parked further up Priesthorpe Road, between a waterworks ditch and the lane to the stables. She didn't want Diana Hanley to have any warning. Outside it had stopped raining and the temperature was quickly dropping. She thought it might snow soon. The cloud cover was dirty, indistinct and low.

Her daughter was staring out of her window, arms crossed. Ahead of them three workmen were sitting around the van parked up on the verge by the waterworks ditch (the sign on the van said 'Yorkshire Water') eating from packed lunchboxes, drinking from a thermos, talking amongst themselves. The hedges were steep to either side, though bare of leaves.

'Look, Rachel—' she started.

'My name's not Rachel.'

She swallowed. 'I have to call you that,' she said.

'It's not my name.'

'I'm sorry about everything,' Anna said. 'I really am.'

Rachel ignored her, didn't even look at her.

'I didn't promise anything before,' she continued. That

got a response. Her daughter turned on her, ready with accusations. She held up a hand to silence her. 'But I am promising you now. This will be the last of it. If I go in there and she says she has seen Nick and he is . . .' She looked away from the child. 'If she says her brother is dead, then I'll go with it. We will drive up to Eccleshill and go to the police. OK?'

Rachel stared at her, as if she were trying to work out whether she could trust her.

'I promise you,' Anna said.

Reluctantly, Rachel nodded.

'Can I have a hug now?' Anna asked. 'Before I get out?'

Rachel put her arms around her and squeezed, but Anna could tell her heart wasn't in it. She was angry. Anna knew how it was. It would take time before she calmed down. She was like her mother.

'I'll leave the engine on,' she said. 'For the heating. If anything bothers you, even if you think I've been in there too long, you can get out and go to those workmen.' She pointed up to them. 'Tell them you need the police. OK?'

She leaned down and kissed her quickly, then opened her door. She stepped out onto the verge, feeling the cold grip her beneath the overalls, then leaned back in.

'We had a better time before,' she said, 'when Nick was around. At least we didn't argue then. We have to try to get back to that, to find him and get on with our lives. Just as we were. That is what is going to happen, Rachel. I promise you that.'

Rachel nodded, unsmiling. 'Meanwhile, it's back to normal,' she muttered.

Anna closed the door and set off.

The lane to the stables turned between two hawthorn bushes, then ran between long hedges to a yard enclosed on three sides by farm buildings. Through an archway

Anna could see horses in the fields beyond, blankets on their backs, motionless, breath coming out of their noses and mouths like steam. There was a single car parked up in the yard. She didn't know it. She could see no sign of life from the other cottage, occupied by Lisa Beadle, Diana's farm manager.

She paused and let the familiar surroundings sink into her, remembering. The last time she had been here was perhaps the happiest time of her life. Nick had brought that to her. The place was different now, in winter, but the memories were still hers. She knocked on the door of Cleveland Cottage, a low seventeenth-century stone dwelling, originally built to house poor farm labourers.

She recognized the woman who came to the door from photos Nick had shown her and from the resemblance of certain facial features. She was dressed in what looked like riding gear, with boots and a body-warmer, her hair untidy, her shirt sleeves rolled up. She looked as though she had been interrupted, pulled away from something urgent. On seeing a stranger at the door she brought her attention to focus, with innocent puzzlement at first, then alarm. Her eyes found the injuries on Anna's face, saw the blood clotting in her nostrils, but the concern didn't last long. The expression changed quickly as she recognized the person beneath the bruises. From some source or other Diana Hanley had seen Anna Hart before.

'Yes?'

'Diana Hanley?'

'Yes.'

'I'm Anna Hart. Can I come in?'

She watched the woman struggle to find the right facial expression.

'You're Anna Hart?'

'That's right. I live with—'

'Of course. I think I recognize you from photos Nick sent.' She risked a smile, but it wasn't very warm. Then she glanced back into the interior, as if there was something – or someone – there. Anna very much doubted Nick had sent her anything.

'What on earth has happened to you?' Hanley asked, focusing again on her face, but still blocking the entrance. 'Are you OK?' She had a strong public school accent.

Anna wondered how bad she looked. She could feel the swelling around one of her eyes throbbing, but not with pain. More than anything, if she allowed herself to attend to it, she felt hot, almost feverish. By contrast, the temperature outside felt severe. If she was kept at the door for much longer her teeth would begin to chatter.

'I'm alive,' she said. 'But it's cold out here. Can I come in?'

Hanley moved aside, still trying to smile. Anna could see her thinking frantically.

'Of course. Please come in. I was just about to . . .' She stopped, in the process of turning to walk into the gloomy interior. Anna stepped inside. 'But what happened . . . have you . . . what happened to your face?'

Anna waved her hand dismissively. 'It's not important.'

Hanley didn't look convinced. Then her face dropped. 'Oh my God,' she said. 'Perhaps you don't know. Have you . . . do you know about . . . have you . . . ?' She looked genuinely at a loss. Behind her Anna could hear a newscaster's voice coming from a TV set.

'Have I heard about Nick?' she asked.

'Yes.'

'I've heard what the police have said. That's why I'm here.'

'You've been to the police?' Hanley glanced at her wristwatch.

'Yes. They told me you had identified Nick's body.'

Anna heard the newscaster say something about Nicholas Hanley. She saw that his sister heard it, too. They paused, both looking at each other, but both listening for what would come next.

'*Police have issued this photo of Anna Hart and seek help from anyone who may have seen her.*'

There was silence, presumably as the photo appeared on the TV screen. A silence grew between the two women as well. Anna stared at Hanley, waiting for her to break it.

'I thought you said you had been to the police?' Hanley said, at last. She was trying to control her voice, but she sounded suspicious and a little frightened. She looked again at her watch.

'Only just. They probably put the appeal out before I saw them. Did you identify Nick's body?'

Hanley looked at the floor, biting her lip. 'Where have you been, Anna?' she asked, as if they were sisters, or friends. Again she couldn't prevent a nervous glance back into the interior of the cottage.

Anna closed the front door. 'Did you identify his body?' she asked again.

'Everyone has been worried about you—'

'Did you identify his body?'

Hanley nodded, then brought a hand up to her face, still looking at the floor. She looked as though she wanted to cry, but there were no tears in her eyes. Anna began to walk into the cottage, but Hanley looked up quickly and stepped sideways, barring her way. Anna frowned, staring at her. Hanley remained where she was.

'What did he look like?' Anna asked, deliberately not looking past her through the open living-room door. There was something there Hanley didn't want her to see.

'Look like? What do you mean?' There was a trace of panic in her tone.

'Where was he? Where was the body?'

'I thought you had been to the police. Didn't they tell you?'

'I didn't ask. Where was he?'

'On the ground. In Leeds. That's where it happened. I don't know . . .'

'Who was there?'

Hanley shrugged. 'Does it matter?'

'Were the police with you?'

'Obviously. They were—'

'How many?' She glanced past her into the living room. There were boxes and bags strewn across the floor, papers in piles. She was packing. Why? Anna looked back to her, face impassive.

'I don't know,' Hanley said. 'It was upsetting. I wasn't—'

'Are you going somewhere?'

'Going somewhere?'

'You're packing.'

'Well, yes . . . I mean . . . no . . . I'm looking for things.'

'What things?'

'Paperwork. I need to sort things out for the lawyers. The police told me to—'

'I should be doing that. I was his partner.'

Hanley looked up at her, mouth firmly shut. Her eyes met Anna's then averted. She took a breath. 'Perhaps you should be. But you weren't here . . .' The words were forced.

'I'm here now. Can I come through – see what you've been doing?'

208

Hanley shifted slightly, uncomfortable. Anna watched her thoughts forming.

'Where have you been, Anna?' she repeated, looking again at her watch. Her mind was elsewhere.

'Are you expecting somebody?' Anna said.

'No . . . I'm not . . . I was just . . . it's just that . . .'

'I hope I'm not interrupting anything.'

'It's not that . . .' She looked at the front door behind Anna, then back at her face. Her expression hardened. 'The police are looking for you.'

'I know that.'

'Where were you?'

'Don't you know already?'

Hanley frowned. 'No. How would I know? The police told me nothing.' On the TV, Anna heard the announcement again – her own name, then Rachel's, followed by the number to call.

'Look. There's no point in pretending,' Hanley said. 'We were never best of friends – you and I—'

'We never met,' Anna said.

'No. I mean . . . that's not what—' Her lips compressed, her eyes looking anywhere but towards Anna. 'That's what I meant,' she said eventually. 'We have never got on, because we have never spoken. That isn't going to change now. I've just lost my brother. I'm not at my best. My head is full of . . . things . . . I'm not sure what I'm meant to be doing.' She began to move sideways, towards a small table and a telephone. 'They are still asking for you on the news,' she said. Her hand closed over the handset. 'I think I should tell the police you're here.'

Anna stepped over and placed her hand on top of Hanley's, gripping it firmly, holding the handset down on the cradle.

'Not just yet,' she said. She was standing close to her

now. She felt Hanley freeze, then move to pull her hand away. She held on.

The woman was lying. She knew it. She forced control upon herself, shutting her eyes, but she could feel the anger rising. *I am Anna Hart*. She heard the words, repeated like a mantra. *I am Anna Hart*. Was she speaking aloud?

Hanley was raising her voice, pulling at her hand, trying to free it. Anna wanted to squeeze the fingers, break them. She resisted. Eyes still closed, she placed her free hand flat against Hanley's shoulder and pushed until she was back against the wall by the table, her left hand still pinned to the phone. Hanley tried to resist, but she was off balance. She was saying, 'You're hurting me. Please stop it. You're hurting me . . .' Over and over again. Anna held her against the wall, counting to herself, ignoring the noise, then slowly eased the pressure on her fingers. She opened her eyes. 'You're lying,' she said, voice flat. 'There's something you're not telling me.'

Hanley shook her head vigorously. Anna let her hand move from the phone, then took a deep breath. 'But let's not do it like this,' she said. She stepped closer still, and saw the alarm in Hanley's eyes deepen. She was rubbing the hand Anna had grasped as if the bones were broken. Anna looked down at it. The fingers were white, bloodless.

'You'll be fine,' she said. 'It takes more than that to do damage. You must have got worse nips from your horses.'

'What do you want?' Hanley asked, voice shaking. She was still pressed flat against the wall. 'Are you mad? Coming in here and doing this to me? Have you taken leave of your senses?'

Anna moved her hand from her shoulder and leaned it

against the wall, inches from her head, blocking her in. She looked into her eyes.

'What do you want here?' Hanley asked again.

'I want to know what's going on.'

'You know as much as me.'

'I doubt it. Why are you here?'

'This is my property.'

'Not here. England. Yorkshire. Why are you over here?'

'For the stables.'

'When did you get here?'

'What is this? Why are you questioning me like this?' She pushed forward suddenly, slipping under Anna's arm. Anna let her go. She could walk straight into the main room now.

'My brother has killed himself. I am not in the mood to—'

'Let's see what you've been up to,' Anna said, silencing her. She stepped into the main room and stooped down to look at the nearest pile of paperwork. She could see the images on the TV out of the corner of her eye. Hanley was objecting. Anna ignored her, letting her eyes take in the detail of what she was looking at. Property details, copy deeds, bank records. The place was the same as the place Akhtar had in Pudsey. She looked over to the huge fireplace. There were logs, paper and firelighters placed in the grate, a box of matches on the hearth. She stood up.

'Planning a fire?' she asked. Hanley was standing by the entrance to the next room, jaw working furiously, still rubbing her sore hand. She was caught between fear, the need to express outrage and the struggle to look as if she were grieving for a lost brother. None of her reactions were natural.

'When did you get to Yorkshire?' Anna asked her again.

'I've been here weeks.'

'Weeks? And we didn't know?'

'I told Nick. I've spoken to him nearly every day.'

Anna nodded, searching her eyes. Could that little bit be true?

'You said he killed himself. Who told you that?'

'The police. I don't know anything about these things.' She looked at the floor.

'How? What did he do?'

'He set himself on fire and jumped from his apartment in Spencer Tower.' She said the words in a rush, as if they genuinely would hurt, were she to think about them.

Anna knew his business had property there. She hadn't known it was an apartment. It confirmed what White had told her.

'Why was he there?'

Hanley shrugged. 'I have no idea.'

'Did you speak to him yesterday?'

'Yes. In the afternoon.'

'At home? At Black Carr Hall?'

'No. He was on his mobile.'

'Did you know what he was meant to be doing this morning?'

Hanley looked up at her, a different expression in her eyes. 'Of course. He was meant to be with you.'

'Where?'

'Where? What do you mean? He had planned for you three to go away somewhere.'

'Where?'

'I don't know. How would I—'

'He didn't tell you?'

'No. Why would he? I didn't ask.'

The phone began to ring from the hallway. They both

stepped towards it, Hanley almost running. At the last moment Anna paused and let her pick it up. Hanley turned from her, frightened she would snatch the thing. Instead Anna just watched her.

'Hello. Yes?' Hanley turned to look at her as she listened. 'Yes. Who are you?' Anna could hear a voice speaking on the other end. It had an official tone. She reached her hand to the cradle and cut the connection. Hanley spun on her, for a moment looking as if she would lash out. Then she remembered her fingers. She stepped back and looked at them again. There were tears in her eyes. Anna took the phone off her and replaced it on the cradle.

'Who was it?' she asked.

'The police.'

The phone rang again. Anna picked it up this time, holding a finger to her lips to indicate that Hanley should be quiet.

'Hello? Who am I speaking to?' A male voice at the other end, official, vaguely familiar. Was it White – the one she had already spoken to? Sutherland? No. Someone else. 'This is West Yorkshire Police. Is there anyone there?' Hanley was opening her mouth to shout something when Anna cut the line again.

'You were going to say?' Anna said.

Hanley looked at the floor.

'You were going to shout something, weren't you?' Anna said. She could feel a tension building behind her forehead. 'That would have been silly.' She looked for the line connecting the phone.

'They will know something is wrong,' Hanley said. 'They will come here now.'

Anna found the connection and jerked the line from the wall. She looked around her. Maybe there was more than one line in, or more than one connector cable. 'You're fucking with me,' she said between gritted teeth.

She didn't know how to handle the woman. She wasn't telling her the truth. But what could she do about it? She could feel the anger rattling around inside her, with nowhere to go. She wanted to ask the woman more questions but didn't dare to now. If she didn't get out of there soon she was going to go too far. She leaned against the wall and kicked at the phone connection box until it was unusable, concentrating her anger into her foot, making each blow deliberate, excessive, loud. Hanley stood back a few paces, watching her, lips trembling.

'I know you're up to something,' Anna said. 'I know something is going on.'

Hanley was right. The police would be sending someone round. She had to get back to Rachel. She moved over to the door, carefully walking around Hanley, keeping her hands to herself. She opened the door a crack and peered out. The stable yard looked the same. She stepped out, closing the door without looking back.

THIRTY

Greenwood had more footage to trail through, but he didn't need help. So Bains took the two new DCs back up to the CID room and asked them to work their way through two lines, as quickly as possible: firstly, check all hotels in the area for registrations for Stijn; secondly, try to get detailed recent history for his credit card from the credit card company.

'I thought we were supposed to be concentrating on finding Anna Hart.' It was Kerr who raised the objection. She was an angular, bleached-blonde woman, probably not more than twenty-two years old.

'And I thought we were meant to be working to Sergeant Ferguson,' Walsh added. She looked to be of similar age, though in the car on the way down she had done nothing but speak of her two kids.

'Jane gave you to me,' Bains said. 'And sometimes, to find something, you have to go around the houses a bit.'

He left them to it and walked to the canteen. It was past midday. White still hadn't called. Bains had neither slept, nor fed himself since before midnight. He felt wide awake, filled with nervous energy. It wasn't just Karen they were looking for, it was Mairead, too. All his emotional control had vanished the moment he realized that. He felt like he had when they had been together; he felt like the kid's father.

He had no hunger, but decided to force himself. He had to preserve energy, and for that he needed food. He stood in line behind about twenty uniforms and selected the vegetarian option from the trays of frozen produce listed under 'Today's Menu'. He ate meat, but didn't like the look of the roast pork; slices of tired, grey meat swimming in puddles of grease. The veggy option was bad enough – overcooked cheese and tomato pizza with soggy chips and processed peas. The woman serving him made cheerful jokes about the pitiful quality of the food. She slopped a brown gravy all over his chips – without asking – which he suspected was made with the juices of the pork.

He sat down by himself, near a window, and for a while contemplated the traffic. His eyes were jumpy, shifting focus, stinging around the edges. He couldn't concentrate on anything for long. Finally his gaze settled on his own reflection. A head streaked with grey hair, deep lines cut into his forehead and around his eyes. He was forty years old, but thought he looked ten years older. Every morning there were new grey hairs appearing. His goatee was shot through with white. Years ago a therapist had encouraged him to look at himself in the mirror, to consider how he appeared to others. His most common expression had been a frown – intense, black eyes, full of anger, staring out of an unsmiling face. Nothing much had changed.

He looked away. These days he tried not to think about things like that, about his life and where it was going. The therapy hadn't solved anything. He had started it in 1989 – after the death of his daughter – but it had done nothing to suppress the grief, the sense of helplessness, the guilt. For years he had walked around with a headache so bad most people would have been hospitalized. It was instructive what you could get used to. He had persisted with the shrink because a Federation lawyer had said it would look good for the disciplinary proceedings. He had crossed many lines during the last self-destructive months of 1989, but only a couple of errors had blown up in his face, and in the end nothing had come of them either. The Force protected its own.

He tried not to think about it, but the truth was he had been treading water until Karen Sharpe appeared. Karen and Mairead. They had pulled him back from something, given him something to care about. Then they had dropped him right back into it. He caught sight of his eyes again. There wasn't any sense to what he was doing – filling his waking hours with activity, keeping himself occupied. He didn't care about crime, didn't worry about victims, didn't give a shit whether he got a result or not. Not really. Not like some of the people he worked with. The bit of him that kept going was like some automated survival machine. Karen had taken the rest away with her.

Best not to think about it. He forced himself to think about Alan White's game plan instead. White had rostered nobody to cover the work Bains was getting Greenwood, Kerr, Walsh and Hayward to do, yet those lines were crucial. He thought that was because White had listened to what this Sutherland wanted. They needed to find Karen, fair enough, but they weren't necessarily adept at putting investigative lines together. Chris Greenwood, just by doing everything they would ordinarily do with this kind of death, had unearthed someone who might be responsible. If that was so, and Stijn really was suspicious, then finding him was the best chance they had of getting to Karen and Mairead, provided the death of Hanley was indeed connected to their disappearance. But what possible sense did it make to kill Nicholas Hanley and then, two hours later, to kidnap Karen and Mairead? Was it about Karen's false identity being blown, as White had hinted? What had she been doing? Bains had left it to Chris Greenwood to call Jane Ferguson with the information about Stijn. But would she do anything with it?

He checked his mobile as he watched Jodi Hayward enter the canteen, look for him and walk over. No missed calls, no messages. Liz would be on her way now, travelling south. He tried to imagine the two of them together for the New Year. What would they have done? He liked Liz. She had helped him. But she wasn't Karen.

'I've found his doctor,' Hayward said, sitting down opposite him.

'You're too clever by half,' he said, picking up his fork. She frowned. 'Sorry,' he said. 'It was a joke.' He put a chip into his mouth. It was tasteless. He chewed it, swallowed, then put the fork down again and pushed the plate away.

'You not going to eat that?' she asked. 'I'm starving.'

'Help yourself.' He slid the plate towards her.

'I love these pizzas,' she said. She began to cut it up and eat it, chewing with enthusiasm. He watched with detached interest, wondering how she managed to look as though she never ate anything.

'You must burn a lot of nervous energy,' he said.

'Yeah? Why is that?' She spoke with her mouth full of food, little bits of it spitting out and landing on the table between then. He looked away.

'What have you found out about his doctor?'

She finished chewing. 'He has a normal GP, up in Reeth, near his home. I only had to make a few calls to find him.'

'That's not what his sister said.'

She shrugged. 'What did you think of her?'

'Not my type.'

'Nor mine. Stuck-up bitch. What's his wife like? Chris says you've got photos.'

'She's not his wife.' He dug in his jacket pocket and passed her the photo of Karen/Anna. 'She's been living

218

with him just over a year, according to the sister.' He felt something pulling at him as he spoke.

'But the sister also said his doctor was in London,' Hayward said. 'Which was certainly untrue. Maybe she's lying to us. Is there a will?' She was looking at the photo, holding it less than six inches from her face. She clearly needed glasses.

'Yes. According to his business partner. We haven't found it yet,' he said.

'Did you think that the sister might have something to gain?'

His turn to shrug. Akhtar had told him Hanley had left everything to his sister, but he didn't really care. That wasn't what all this was about. He was sure of that. 'It's not my inquiry,' he said. 'There's thirty detectives up at Weetwood to think about that sort of thing.'

'She looks like Karen,' Hayward said, still looking at the photo.

He frowned at her, his heart beginning to thump. 'Karen?'

'Karen Sharpe. Your ex.'

He took the photo off her and pretended to look at it.

'Don't you think?' Hayward asked him, smiling.

'Maybe,' he said. He looked up at her, face bright red. 'But so what?'

Hayward held up her hands. 'So nothing. Just a comment. That's all.'

He put the photo away, wanting her to get up and go now, so he could be left alone to think about it. Why hadn't he recognized her the first time he had looked at the picture? 'Good work on the doctor,' he said. 'But what about the photos of Hanley? I asked you to—'

'North Yorks have got some from the house. They are biking them down.'

'Good. In that case you can probably knock off if you—'

'The doctor is also giving all his medical records to North Yorks. So we should get those at the same time. I got the blood type though – to speed things up. He's type O.'

'Who is type O?'

'Hanley.'

'Did you tell the inquiry that?'

'Is it important?' She looked reluctant to tell Alan White anything.

'I already got the type from the stains we found at the flat,' Bains said. 'The SOCO sent them off immediately. The type from those on the balcony is O, but the stains on the inside are AB. You need to tell them so they can expedite the DNA. Two different types. It might mean the perpetrator left blood.'

His phone started to ring. He almost upset his chair as he stood to pull it from his pocket. He saw Hayward staring at him as he answered it. 'Yes?'

'Bains?'

'Yes.'

'Alan White. Where are you?'

'Milgarth. I'm with—'

'Sutherland is there now. He's waiting for you at reception. You need to speak to him, urgently.'

THIRTY-ONE

Even before she got to the car she was thinking to herself that it was too late, that she could do it no longer. The need to react, to do something, not to be passive, was too much. There was too much to hold down. She couldn't be Anna Hart – not in this kind of situation. Rachel was right.

Rachel. Why couldn't she see her? She had a clear view to the car as she came out onto the lane. She had two hundred yards to cover, but as soon as she stepped from the lane and focused her eyes on the rear windscreen she realized she could not see Rachel's head in the front passenger seat. She caught her breath and controlled her first impulse – to run to the vehicle, to panic. Probably Rachel was lying down. She quickened her pace. In front of the car the workmen were in their hole now, digging. The car looked the same . . . or did it? What was it she was noticing? The doors were closed, the windows slightly steamed up. But the engine was off. No fumes coming from the exhaust. She had left it on for the heating.

She began to run. There was probably no need to worry, but she needed to know quickly. She reached the car out of breath, sprinting the last few yards, then pulled the driver's door open.

Empty. She stood back and looked up and down the road. Her mind was a total blank, like the space in front of her, staring at her, jumping into her eyes. She bent into the vehicle and looked at it again. Where Rachel had been sitting there was nothing. She felt something struggling to escape from her throat. A scream. She swallowed it.

She popped the boot and walked around to it, adrenalin rushing at her neck. It was empty. She ran to the front passenger door and opened it, expecting to see Rachel somehow sitting there, alive and well. The empty space rose up towards her like something tangible; a noxious, visible thing, laced with ugly premonition. She dipped her head inside it and looked ridiculously behind the seats. She could *feel* the pure, empty, vacant space where her daughter should have been – it was suffocating her.

She stood back and sucked at the freezing air, scanning the fields around her. Nothing. Small flakes of wetness settled on her cheeks. It was snowing. She ran to the waterworks ditch. There were two men in the hole, one at the side of it. Two Asians, one white, all middle-aged. They stopped working as she ran to them, watching her, the one with the spade leaning on it. The hole was awash with ankle-deep freezing water, the ditch itself waist height. She could see the snow curling down towards it. Where the flakes landed they were lying, not melting.

She could hear herself shouting questions: *Where is she? What have you done with her?* The one by the side of the ditch began to move towards her as she strode to their van and opened the doors. Tools. Nothing else. She turned quickly to face him. He was speaking to her. She took a breath again and tried to listen. He was saying something about a car.

'What?' she demanded. 'What are you saying?'

'We thought it must be the kid's dad,' he said. 'Do you want us to call the police?'

From the hole the white one shouted over, 'It was a dark blue Volvo. One of the new models.'

'What?' she said again. She could hear the words but they weren't registering. 'Tell me again,' she said. 'Tell me it all again. From the beginning.'

'Are you the kid's mother?' The one in front of her was asking the question.

'Yes.'

'Well, she didn't look bothered.'

'She looked like she knew him.' The one from the hole again. She stared at him, then looked back to the one beside her. Her ears were filled with a thumping noise.

'You tell me it,' she said, placing her finger in the centre of his chest. 'Just you, first. Tell me what happened. Quickly. From the beginning.'

'Do you want me to call the police?' he asked again.

She bit her lip, controlling herself. 'I am the fucking police,' she said. 'Now tell me what happened.'

He told her. She rehearsed the detail to herself as she ran back to the car, as she sat within the interior and struggled frantically to get the thing started again. Only five minutes ago, maximum, a dark blue Volvo saloon had pulled up in front of her car. A man had got out, walked straight to her car, opened the door and said something. Rachel had got out, running to the man, wrapping her arms around him and hugging him. The man had spoken to her, kissed her, gestured to his own car. Rachel had pointed to the lane Anna had walked down. They had discussed something. Then Rachel had run to the man's car and got in. He had not carried her, he had not threatened her. She had walked – no, run to it, of her own free will. The man had got into her car and stalled it. Then he got out, looked over to them, walked back to his own car and drove off, over the crest of the hill and down towards Bradford. Half a minute later she had emerged from the lane.

She needed to find them. Her fingers were freezing now, making the task of starting the car more difficult. She cursed and split two nails, one so badly it started bleeding. There was no pain. Her whole body had been numb since the morning. The car started. She drove at full speed up the lane towards Bradford, bumping the suspension through the potholes without even noticing.

They had described the man as of average height – shorter than herself. He had been wearing a Barbour jacket, thigh-length, 'ordinary' trousers and dark shoes. He had average-length brown hair, walked normally, nothing unusual about what they could hear of his voice. His face looked 'normal'. Average, normal, average, brown, ordinary. The description was useless. She had to find the car. They had at least a two-minute lead on her.

She turned left on Woodhall Lane – a proper two-lane surfaced road – without thinking about it, overtook three slower vehicles, accelerating on the downhill stretch until she saw the junction with a larger road drawing closer. Leeds Road. She screeched to a halt at the junction. Which direction would they go? Right to Bradford, or left to Leeds? She had no idea. She forced herself to stop the vehicle, to stay at the junction, to think about it. She could take a chance, take any direction and follow it to a conclusion. But when would that come – and what *was* the conclusion, if she didn't catch up with them? She felt the panic wriggling inside her as though it were alive, forcing its way out. The alternative was to try to piece together what she knew, try to make the choice intelligent. Who would Mairead have willingly got into a car with?

Suddenly she was crying. A car sounded a horn behind her and she tried to pull quickly towards the verge, to let it past, but the tears flooded her eyes, blinding her. She hit the curb and a road sign before she could recover. She braked and stalled. She felt the reality of the situation swamping her. They now had more than three minutes on her and there were innumerable possible directions they could have taken. Three minutes in the opposite direction – back towards Calverley from the junction of Woodhall Lane – would place them on the way to Leeds by now. She could not find them by herself. She could not do it.

She banged her fists off the steering wheel and stared out at the swirling snowflakes, the cars streaming in front of her on Leeds Road, the slush already turning black beneath their wheels. Everybody going about their business, oblivious. She began to sob uncontrollably. *Mairead*. She had thought it without realizing. That was her real name. Not Rachel. The whole thing was over. Within the space of twelve hours everything had spun out of control.

She pushed a fist into her mouth, leaning forward over the wheel, feeling the sobs heaving up within her chest. She didn't know what to do. The tears ran over her hand, down the sleeves of the overalls. She bit down onto her knuckles, stifling the strangled scream that was pushing up against her throat. She could hardly breathe.

Chasing around hoping to find them by chance was useless. Mairead had got into the car of her own free will. Why? That was the heart of it. The workmen had said they had thought the man must be her father. *Her father*.

This had all started, over twenty months ago, because her father had sent a letter. Was it possible that he was here? Was it possible that James Martin had somehow found them, despite everything?

James Martin. There wasn't anybody else it could be. There was nobody else Mairead would hug, nobody else she would run to and kiss. She brought a sleeve across her eyes, soaking the tears away. She had to get control of things. There had to be a way she could find out if Martin was here. She reached beneath the steering column and tried to start the car again.

It wouldn't work. She tried for nearly five minutes, her

frustration and anger mounting. It was useless. The hopelessness was crushing her, interfering with her breathing, clouding her vision, making her fingers shake. She didn't know what to do. There was nothing she could do.

There had to be another way. She needed a vehicle with keys. But there was nothing parked up near her. She wiped her eyes again and tried to think. She was being foolish. It wasn't just James Martin she had to consider. There *were* others.

Mairead would go with Pete Bains. But the description didn't match. Pete was a Sikh. The workmen would have seen that. But Pete could have got someone else to go to her, someone to help him. But then she wouldn't have hugged that person. Mairead would hug Liz Hodges, but she was *very* distinctive – tall, black, female. No mistaking her. Who did that leave? She felt her heart leaping and racing.

Nicholas Hanley. Boring, normal, average, ordinary Nick. He fitted the description.

She opened the car door, stepped out and let the cold strike her face. A car swerved past her and the open car door. She saw an angry face behind the wheel. Why hadn't she thought it at once? Nick. It had to be him. Even the Barbour jacket the workman had mentioned. She looked back up the road she had driven down, squinting into the thickening snowfall. She needed to get back up there, to Diana Hanley. Quickly.

THIRTY-TWO

Francis Doyle stood directly beneath the no smoking sign in the interview room and lit a Marlboro.

'It says no smoking,' Kirk said, right on cue.

'If you don't like it you can leave,' Doyle replied, not looking at him.

'I can't leave. Mr Sutherland told me to speak to his man—'

'So put up with it.'

He took a drag, inhaled, savoured the stench, exhaled into the corner above Pete Bains's head. Bains was sitting behind the interview table. Doyle thought he looked very confused.

'I was told Sutherland was coming here,' Bains said to him, squinting through the smoke.

'He changed his mind,' Kirk said. It was true. Sutherland was behaving strangely. He had taken a call on their way and left the car immediately to catch a cab going back in the other direction. Doyle had no idea why. Worse still, as Kirk had pointed out, he had instructed Kirk to question Bains. But Doyle had no intention of letting him do that alone.

'Your name is Kuldeep Bains?' Kirk asked Bains. The room was hot and stuffy, so much so that Doyle had taken off his jacket. Kirk, leaning across the table so that he was only a foot or so from Bains's face, still had his on. He was a big man and there were beads of sweat running down his forehead. Doyle could smell him.

'That's right,' Bains said. He was still trying to work out why he felt like a prisoner.

'So why call yourself Pete?' Kirk asked.

Bains shrugged. 'It's a long story, but—'

'To disguise your ethnicity?'

Doyle was surprised Kirk could come out with a word like that.

'White people gave me the name,' Bains said, face hardening. 'They couldn't pronounce Kuldeep.'

Doyle thought that was enough already. He stepped behind Kirk and pulled out the chair opposite Bains, forcing Kirk back. He sat down on the chair.

'I'm sorry about this, Mr Bains,' he said. 'But things are difficult at the moment.' Behind him Kirk started to splutter something. 'Can you get us some coffees, Kirk?' Doyle asked him, without looking back.

'Mr Sutherland said that—'

'But he's not here, is he?'

'He told me that—'

'Who is in charge here, Kirk?' He turned slightly in his seat until he was looking at him. 'Who is in charge, right now, in this room?'

Kirk chewed his lips. Doyle turned back to Bains. 'Until recently we employed Mr Kirk as a driver. I'm sorry if he offended you.'

Bains frowned, unsure what to say. Behind him Doyle heard Kirk slam the door as he left. He smiled at Bains. 'I don't suspect you of anything, Pete,' he said. 'All right if I call you Pete?'

Bains stared at him.

'However, I would like to know why you didn't let on you knew Anna Hart was Karen Sharpe as soon as you saw her photo.'

Bains groaned. 'Is that what this is about? Because I didn't recognize her?'

'Didn't you?'

'No! I don't know why. I don't know how it could have happened.'

'I do. I saw Ms Sharpe in the flesh when she was Anna Hart. She was good at it. Not just a matter of changing her hair. More like changing her whole personality.' He tapped ash onto the floor.

'So why suspect me of anything?'

'I don't. Mr Sutherland is the one who is suspicious. You let Imran Akhtar walk this morning. He was worried about that, too.'

Bains threw his hands up. 'I had nothing on Akhtar. He was a witness. What was I meant to do? Is he involved in this?'

'We'd certainly like to speak to him.'

'I took details off him. You should—'

'We've tried. He's AWOL. Disappeared as soon as you let him walk. You also let Hanley's sister go – tell me about her.'

'Hanley's sister?'

'Yes. Diana Hanley—'

'She's his fucking sister, for Christ's sake. What could she have to do with his death?'

Doyle shrugged. He wasn't about to tell Bains too much.

'I took her details, too,' Bains said. 'Ring her. Get her back in—'

'We tried her phone already. She hangs up on us. We've sent someone round to retrieve her.'

'Sutherland thinks I blew Karen's cover because I let two witnesses walk? Is that what's going on here?'

Doyle stood up, taking a last suck at the cigarette before dropping it to the floor and grinding his shoe into it. 'I don't know what Sutherland thinks,' he said. 'But *I* believe what you told me this morning – that you haven't seen or heard from her since the twenty-eighth of March nineteen-ninety-eight.'

'The twenty-*fourth* of March.'

'Exactly.' He tried to smile at the man, but all he got back was a deep-cut frown. 'I can usually tell when people are lying to me,' he added. 'I don't think you're lying, Bains. Besides, you gave us Gatz. You wouldn't have done that if you were behind all this.'

'Gatz?'

'Jan Gatz. You know him as Josef Stijn. There are other names, too. He's a contractor . . .' He felt a ripple of fear just talking about the man.

'What kind of contractor?'

Doyle looked at the worry etched across Bains's face. Bains definitely needed to know as little as possible. But he also needed to know enough to keep him quiet. That would mean frightening him.

'Stijn is a Rhodesian, originally, domiciled in South Africa. He worked for the police there in the eighties, then he vanished. There are warrants out for him in three African countries and two European.'

'Warrants? What for?'

'At least one for murder.'

'What kind of contractor?'

Doyle found another cigarette. 'A high-level contractor,' he said, lighting it. He noticed his hands were shaking slightly. It had been that way ever since Bains's team had told them about Stijn. 'He served time as a mercenary at one point.'

'What kind of contracts?' Bains's voice was wobbling now.

'Anything that earns well. At the moment he's attached to two brothers from Pakistan – "investment bankers". They have their own banks, offshore havens. That sort of thing. Ahmed and Mohammed Rouf.' He blew out the smoke and watched Bains for a reaction to the names. There was none, but then the names were quite common. 'Have you heard of them?' he asked. Bains shook his head.

'They're big. Property all over the place, English public school education, Oxbridge, the polo circuit, high society . . . They wouldn't spit on the likes of you and me.'

'So why do they need a contractor?'

'They have a couple of sensitive businesses.'

'Banking scams? That's what this is about?'

'No. It's a bit worse than that. I said they own banks, but there's no money in banking . . .' He smiled at Bains again. Still no response. 'Not real money. They deal in brown powder. Heroin. It's produced mostly in Afghanistan. You have to pay to have powder factories in Afghanistan. That's why you need to own a bank.'

'You have to pay the Afghan government?'

'Yes. You could call it that. You have to pay the Taliban. Or others. Fundamentalist Arab interests.'

He saw Bains thinking about it, still not there, still not grasping the size of it.

'So what was Karen doing? What has this got to do with her? Was she dealing with these two?'

'We wish. She was dealing with Nicholas Hanley.'

'The dead guy?'

'Yes.'

'He was her target?'

'Yes.'

'How is he connected to Stijn and the Rouf brothers?'

Doyle sat down again. 'We're not sure. That's why we put her in.'

'But he *is* connected to them?'

'Yes.'

231

'So is Karen in danger from this guy Stijn?'

Doyle looked at the desk.

'Has *he* kidnapped them?' Bains demanded. 'Has he taken Karen and Mairead?'

'All we knew was that her cover was in danger.'

'Has this guy got Karen and Mairead?'

'We tried to pull her yesterday. We sent coded priority messages all day. She didn't respond.'

'Did you put her up for this? Did you send her on this *with an eleven-year-old kid*?' Bains's voice was rising.

Doyle frowned at him. 'She did that herself, without authority. She also moved in with Hanley, without authority. You know what she's like, Bains. Don't shout at me.'

'So has he kidnapped them?'

'Kidnapped?' Doyle looked away again, wishing now that Kirk would hurry back with the coffee. 'Yes. At least, we hope so . . .'

'You *hope* so?'

'Yes. Instead of doing what he has done to Hanley.'

The blood drained from Bains's face. He stood up and paced to the end of the room, agitated.

'Assuming the scene Alan White is working is genuine,' Doyle said, 'then they weren't killed with the taxi driver. That's a good sign.'

Bains started chewing at his fingernails, still pacing back and forth. 'Why?' he asked, thinking aloud. 'Why the need to kill them?'

'If the cover was gone that would be enough.'

'Just that?'

'Just that. I fear you haven't understood the size of it yet. There are very determined interests at work behind the Roufs. They need very considerable wealth to operate. They don't hesitate when it comes to protecting that wealth. They don't think like us. They're Fundamental-ists. Do you understand?'

Bains was only half listening. The other half was trying to work out the connections for himself. 'Why kill Hanley?' he asked.

'We don't know. A sterilization exercise?' Doyle shrugged.

'Sterilization?' Bains looked shocked.

'Yes. They discover a leak, so they clean up *everything*, just in case. That's why the priority now is to find Stijn. He may be the cleaner.'

Bains sat down again. 'I want to be on that team,' he said. 'I want to help.'

Doyle shook his head at him. 'Too dangerous. You could let something slip.'

'Let what slip? That she's Karen Sharpe, a police officer? What harm would that do? We should be broadcasting it through every available—'

'That Stijn doesn't know who she is might be the only thing that's keeping her alive. We have to assume he is questioning her about it. If we go public with her ID we blow her only chance. We have to be extremely careful.' He considered telling him about the phone call she had made to Alan White, but that seemed too complicated. 'There is some hope,' he said, instead. 'Two traffic officers think they may have seen her on Abbey Road this morn-ing. They got the make of vehicle and we're doing area searches down there now. They saw a woman driving a car. There were two rear-seat passengers, one a child. The woman had a bloody nose.'

'And they let her go? Fucking idiots!'

'They didn't know about the alerts.'

Bains sat back in his seat. He started drumming his legs against the floor, eyes roving across the ceiling and walls, full of frightened energy. Doyle looked up into the pall of smoke gathering above them, then reached back and opened the interview room door a crack. He knew what Bains would be thinking, what the next question would be. He had been through the same process himself.

'It doesn't work,' Bains said finally. 'Why would they kill Hanley if they didn't know for sure who she was?'

'Because they didn't mean to kill him. Because he died during a . . . process.' He saw Bains's facial muscles freeze. 'We have to assume they were questioning him.'

'Like they are questioning Karen?'

'And Mairead.'

THIRTY-THREE

Karen began to run. At first the snowflakes stuck in her hair and on the sleeves and chest of the overalls, but very quickly she became so hot they melted as they landed on her. Her shoes weren't made for wet weather, still less for running or running through slush. On a stretch of slippery pavement at the junction of Woodhall Lane and Rockwood Road she almost fell. She cursed Anna Hart and her expensive tastes, ignored the pain in her legs and chest, climbed a fence bordering the golf course and started to cut across the fairways. Very quickly she reached the fields at the other side. The ground became more treacherous – wet with new snow, but with hard furrows in the soil beneath. She slowed down. It had taken her just over five minutes to drive the distance she was covering. If she was careful she guessed she could get back on foot in about fifteen minutes.

The route led sharply uphill to a line of trees to the rear of the stables. She had a view through the falling snow nearly all the way back to the road where she had originally parked, leaving Mairead to her fate. The thought broke her pace, flooding her mind with guilt. Despite everything she had been taught, despite everything she knew, she had left Mairead alone in a stolen car. She should never have done that. Even Mairead had known better. If she had listened to the child this wouldn't have happened. The whole idea of going to Diana Hanley had been senseless. She was involved, *Karen* knew that already; all it had achieved was to warn her.

She had perhaps a mile to cover. Athletes could run a mile in under four minutes, she remembered, but within five minutes she was gasping and slowing. She hadn't run so hard in over eighteen months. The muscle in her right leg was weak. She could feel it pulling and tightening under the mass of scar tissue, threatening to lock into a cramp. Just short of the trees she stumbled and fell headlong, rolling through the thin covering of snow. She paused and tried to catch her breath. Through the trees she could see the dark outline of the farm buildings. Already the daylight was fading. She pushed herself up and began to run again.

The trees gave onto hedges and fences. She was about to take the shortest route to Hanley's cottage when she saw a shift in the pattern of light ahead of her. She stopped, dropping to one knee behind a crumbling stone wall. As her breathing slowed she could hear something. She got up and ran in a low crouch to the end of the wall. From the other side of the wall she heard animal movement. She looked quickly. There were three or four horses, penned in a small enclosure, blankets on their backs. They looked nervous, uneasy.

She ducked back down, crossed the gateway into the enclosure and came up behind Lisa Beadle's cottage. She passed windows opening onto a kitchen and a dining room – all empty – then stopped again. From the other side of the building, from the yard, she could hear the sound of police radio sets. She backed out past the enclosure again, then came around the side of the main stable block, walking quickly. As she approached the rear entrance to the stable she saw blue bands of light stroking the snow in front of her.

Inside the stable block the air was warm and close, rich with the odours of dung, horse sweat and tanned leather.

She moved in front of a row of stalls, hearing the horses react to her presence, a ripple of movement running along them as she passed. Mairead's horse was here somewhere. One of the animals began to neigh and snort. She found a ladder leading to the upper level and climbed it as quietly as she could, still trying to get her breathing back to normal.

Lying flat on her stomach, she edged forward until she could see through the main barn doorway straight into the yard beyond. There was a single parked police car. Its emergency lights were spinning silently on the roof, and a uniformed officer was leaning against it, talking into a radio set clipped to his shoulder. She tried to listen, but he was facing away from her. Almost immediately another one joined him and pointed back towards the entrance to Hanley's cottage. They both looked around them, then got back into the car and reversed out of the yard.

She came down carefully, then left the barn the way she had entered and walked quickly around the block to the rear of Hanley's cottage. She peered through windows at the scene she had so recently left, searching in vain for a sign of life. There was none. She found the back door and tried it. It was bolted. She kicked and it gave way at once. Without pausing she stepped in and listened. The place was empty. Hanley was already gone. She moved quickly through the three or four rooms, checking everything she could see. Everything was exactly as it had been fifteen minutes before. Diana Hanley must have left the place the second she had walked out.

She stood in the front room and looked at the piles of paperwork on the floor. The emptiness closed about her. Mairead was gone. There was nothing in here that could help. She sat down on the floor, face quivering. She didn't know what to do.

She could have stepped out, spoken to the police. She buried her face in her hands and rocked backwards and forwards. Why hadn't she spoken to them, asked them for help? A low-pitched moaning noise began to come out of her mouth. She could hear it in her throat, feel the air escaping through her lips. She *couldn't* go to the police. Not yet. She didn't know what was happening; she didn't know who had her daughter, whether Hanley was alive or dead, whether her cover was gone. She knew nothing.

If she went to the police she would be delivered straight back to Sutherland. Sutherland had been there when she had spoken to White. There in the background, behind it all. Sutherland couldn't be trusted. If it suited his purposes he would burn her, happily. Maybe he had already done that. If her cover was gone then it was because someone had *chosen* that; it had to be someone on the inside. She had seen it happen before. She knew things about powerful interests. Maybe someone had been bought, maybe she knew something damaging, maybe it just suited them for other purposes. She had no idea. She felt a dull aching pain growing in her chest. She slipped over sideways onto the floor and curled into a tight foetal ball. She wanted it all to go away.

If she went to the police it would all be out of her hands. At best. But at worst she would be stepping into range. She had to do this alone.

She had encouraged Mairead to trust Nick Hanley. She had lied to her, implicitly, never telling her Nick was a target. If he *had* pulled up in a car, she *would* have run to him, kissed him. Anna Hart – the name brought bile to her throat – had *loved* the man. It was too fucked up to think about, what she, Anna Hart, had done with him. That wasn't *her*. She had not been there when that had happened.

She began to gasp, her face flush with blood, pinpricks of light dancing behind her eyelids. She was having some sort of panic attack. It was doubling her up, filling her with blind physical fear. She had to ignore it, she had to *think* . . .

The police thought Nick was dead. But Diana Hanley had been lying – she knew that from the evidence of her own eyes – and Stijn had wanted to know where Nick was. He *could* be alive. Mairead *could* be with him. But if Nick knew the truth about her . . . *what would he do?* She rolled to her knees and clutched the top of her head. It was too much. She couldn't think properly. There were too many things unexplained.

She opened her eyes. She was crying and rolling around on the floor. It was ridiculous. She stood up, steadying herself against the wall, trying to stop it.

Nicholas Hanley. Mairead would think he was safe, harmless. Lovable, caring Nick. Anna Hart had told her daughter nothing of him, or of the world he was a part of. For all she knew he could be in it *with* Stijn. They could be together, the whole thing put together to get her to break cover. If that was so then Mairead was with Stijn now.

'*Fucking Anna Hart.*' She hissed the words to herself, banging her forehead off the wall in front of her. She had to find them before Mairead let anything slip. She had tried to train her, but at the end of the day her daughter was just a kid.

THIRTY-FOUR

In the incident room they were struggling with quantity. Bains stood at the door watching them. Doyle had given in, but would only allow him to assist with the paperwork. He didn't want him out on the street or anywhere near the press; didn't want his help locating Stijn. Bains had to find a way to get round him.

The searches were bringing in more material than they had bargained for. At least, that was how it looked. The room was gradually sinking under a mountain of records and papers seized from Hanley and Akhtar's various business or home addresses. There were four detectives coming in and out with boxes and exhibit bags, another four trying to organize it all. Tom Ashton was lumbering about in the middle of them, sweating profusely, looking very irritable.

Behind him Bains could see a young, clean-shaven man in a smart black suit who must have been one of Doyle's lot, talking quietly into a mobile phone, head turned away from the activity. The detectives had been briefed by Sutherland and were meant to be searching urgently through the material for certain items. Bains wasn't even sure what Sutherland was trying to find. Not necessarily anything that would lead them to Karen. Maybe, he thought, Sutherland was only interested in what they could find against the Roufs. So far the squad hadn't got much further than stage one – sorting it all into piles.

'Did you discover anything yet?' Bains asked the nearest detective. She was sitting at a desk piled to head height with brown file jackets. He didn't know her.

'Are you here to help?' she asked, not even looking at him. She was methodically going through the files, writing a description of their contents in a notebook.

'No,' he lied. 'Just to get an update.'

'You on the squad?' Still not looking at him.

'Yes. I'm Pete Bains.' She looked up as if he might be holding out a hand for her to shake. He wasn't.

'So *you're* Pete Bains,' she said, voice heavy with sarcasm. She turned her attention back to her notebook. 'Well, so far all we have come across is evidence of high activity across various bank accounts during the last few weeks. And we were told where to look for that by our minder over there.' She nodded her head towards the man on the mobile.

'Moving money between accounts, or out of the country?'

'Some of it into Diana Hanley's accounts. A lot of it into offshore accounts. There seems to have been a lot of money moved.'

'What was in the office in Spencer Tower – the one they tried to burn?'

'All sorts of stuff. Hard to say what's relevant at the moment.'

'So what are you looking for?'

She paused, turning a page of her book. 'Properties which were actually bought by the business or bought on behalf of another company or person. Identify that company or person. Those are the instructions.'

Bains frowned. 'That's it?'

'To start with.'

'How will that help locate Anna and Rachel Hart?'

She shrugged. 'I do what I'm told. I can't see how it would help find Nicholas Hanley's killer either. But I don't get told the big picture. I'm not a sergeant.' She smiled at him.

He suppressed an urge to ask more questions. Karen had feared Sutherland. It was possible Sutherland didn't give a shit about locating Karen, had decided she was dispensable. But it was unwise to jump to conclusions based on Karen's paranoia. This whole thing was personal now. It was eating away at him, twisting his insides with acid. It wasn't personal for either Sutherland or Doyle. But Doyle had seemed genuinely to want to find her. Maybe there *was* a point to looking for bank transfer details, but he couldn't see it.

From Chris Greenwood – still on, but working now for Will Price and the team looking for Stijn – he discovered that DC Kerr had tracked down the hotel Stijn had used. It was the Hilton in Bramley. Within easy reach of the airport, it was also only a ten-minute drive from Weetwood. A detective was still at the place with a SOCO team. Bains decided there was no way he could sit in the incident room looking through paperwork. There was too much at stake.

He drove to Bramley on roads full of dirty slush. It had snowed and melted already, but the sky seemed to have more to give. The detective Will Price had sent out was called Gary Clark. Bains found him in the bathroom of Stijn's hotel room, crouched over and staring at the plug hole of the shower cubicle. The SOCO Bains had already spoken to about Spencer Tower – Elaine Merrington – was on her hands and knees in the bedroom. Bains didn't dare disturb her.

'You lost something?' he asked Clark.

The detective stood up. 'Just trying to help the SOCO.'

'Don't,' Bains said. 'You'll fuck it up. Has he checked out yet?'

'Who?'

'Stijn.'

'He checked out yesterday.'

'How long was he here?'

'Ten days. I've lined up interviews with some staff members who might have come across him. I asked for help with that, but so far—'

'Do they have CCTV here?'

'In the lobby and bar. I've got the last five days. They wiped the rest.'

'Good. What have you found in here?'

Clark gave him a summary. It didn't take long. There had been nothing left in the room and housekeeping had already cleaned it by the time they got there. The SOCO had found some good lifts, but they already had Stijn's prints from INTERPOL.

'Did you go through the rubbish?'

Clark nodded. 'That was all I could do, really. But since I didn't know what might have come from here it wasn't much use. I've bagged the lot, but there was nothing obvious.'

'Did you check what calls he made?'

Clark took out a notebook and read a series of numbers to Bains. 'That last one,' he added, 'also appears as a vague impression on the notepad we found on the bureau.'

'*His* pad?'

'It's a standard hotel one. I didn't find any crumpled sheets from it in the rubbish. But there was a faint impression of that number on the top sheet. Visible – like he had written it on the sheet above and torn it off. We could put it up for an ESDA test if—'

'Not much point since you already have the number from hotel records.'

'But it might show other things that I can't see.'

'True. What was the number again?'

Clark read it again. 'I checked it already,' he said. 'He's called it three times in ten days. The last time was at eight thirty-five yesterday morning. They were all very short calls. It's in Calverley. I even rang it, just to see. Whoever was there hung up on me twice. I've told Jon Hoyle about it. We should have HOLMES running on this really. Then they could have sent someone to go round there. We're getting confused already – no one knowing what everyone else is doing. I thought you were meant to be knocking off, for example.'

Bains nodded, distracted. The number sounded familiar. He wrote it on the back of his hand using Clark's pen, then stepped out into the corridor and called Chris Greenwood again.

'What was the number Diana Hanley gave me for her place in Calverley?'

Greenwood found it and read it out to him. It was the same. The last number Stijn had called from his hotel was Diana Hanley's stables in Calverley. And he had done this *before* Nicholas Hanley had fallen to his death. Bains tried to think about that. Doyle had hinted there was a connection to the sister. It could mean that, or that she was in danger. Either way, she needed to be asked about it quickly. He tried the number himself. It seemed to ring, but nobody answered.

Pacing the corridor, he called Greenwood again and got Diana Hanley's mobile number. He punched in the numbers and waited. No answer. Behind him he heard Clark coming out into the corridor.

'The number is the stables where Diana Hanley was staying,' he told him. 'She gave me that number this morning.'

'Diana Hanley? Is that the victim's mother?'

Bains shook his head. Clark had been right about the lack of co-ordination. 'His sister,' he said. 'She's not answering. I'm going over there now.'

THIRTY-FIVE

Lisa Beadle, Diana Hanley's farm manager, had a Range Rover, of course. That and at least one other vehicle, because the Range Rover was in her garage and she was out. Karen didn't even have to force a door to find the keys. She could see them hanging on a hook just inside the porch. She broke a window and took them.

The snow had stopped by the time she made it back to the Leeds Road. As she started the long descent down into Bradford she could feel her heart slowing, her breath gaining regularity. She knew what to do now.

It was the last day of the Millennium, the day Rachel and Anna Hart were meant to be jetting out of the country on a specially chartered flight. A tiny snigger escaped her lips and she felt a knot of bitterness twist inside her. There were no early flights from Leeds/Bradford. Nicholas Hanley had set them up. She had been so lost in it all she had missed the obvious. She had trusted him – in some perverse way – but he had betrayed her.

In front of her, the snow had turned to a black slush. The traffic out of town was heavy, the fumes from the bus exhausts staining the air a dirty brown. She had the Range Rover heating on full blast but her limbs were still shaking as if she were freezing. The clock in the dash said it was nearly three o'clock. Time was running out.

The cloud cover was low and brooding, quickly growing dark ahead of her. It would be night soon. Everything had happened so quickly. 'Please, Mairead, please,' she whispered. 'Please just hang in there. I will come.'

The tower to Lister's Mill came into view, up in

Manningham. Below it the city fell in rows of mill terraces and Victorian slums into a narrow basin of converging streets and seventies concrete blocks – the city centre. She could see the clock tower of the town hall in the middle of it all – a decaying nineteenth-century reproduction of something from fourteenth-century Sienna, the stonework long ago turned black by decades of mill smoke and smog – and beside that the roof of Bradford Central police station – the Tyrls. She had not been here for over eighteen months. She was coming back. The thought brought an acid taste to her mouth.

She had only one lead. Akhtar. She had memorized a lot of information about Imran Akhtar during the last year and a half. Not because they had told her to, but because she had been suspicious of him from the moment they met. What Hanley had told her had confirmed her fears. She knew where Akhtar lived. She knew several of his bank account numbers. She even knew the names of his wife and kids, his sisters, his uncles. She had seen photos of them. Now was the time to use that information. Akhtar would lead her to Stijn, Stijn would lead her to Hanley and Mairead would be with Hanley. Then Hanley would learn about loyalty.

Karen had learned about loyalty at an early age. When she was little they had thrown stones at her in the street. Kids her own age. She could remember a half-brick hitting her kneecap one day – the initial blow, the numbness and then, as she tried to walk, the realization that, even though there was no pain and no blood, she was hurt quite badly. She had required an operation and had limped for a year after that.

On her thirteenth birthday – the first time she was allowed home from Victoria College, where she had started that same year – a boy two years older than her had thrown a metal ballbearing the size of a golf ball from no more than ten feet away. She had walked around a corner in the village and he had been waiting. The object hit her right in the middle of the forehead, and had produced a concussion requiring a three-day stay in hospital.

In those days they didn't do scans for such things and hadn't even X-rayed her. Her father made light of it in the way that only doctors can, because he had seen too much trauma in his life to be able to see pain as anything other than an 'indication', even when the sufferer was his own child. For David Young, anything that wasn't immediately life-threatening was negligible.

Helen Young. That had been her name then, the name with which she had been christened. Later she had agreed with James Martin, Mairead's father, to change it to Sinead Collins. 'Young' could be either a Catholic or a Protestant name in Northern Ireland, but usually it was Protestant. The kids who had thrown stones at her were Catholics.

She had picked her new name because of Sara Collins. Much later, in a psychiatric hospital, when she could remember very little *except* her early childhood (and couldn't speak about that without crying uncontrollably), another doctor had told her that she had 'fallen in love' with Sara at a very early age. That might have been true. Certainly she had hero-worshipped her from almost the first day they had agreed to become friends. 'Agreeing' to become friends was something only boys did back then, but Sara would have flattened anyone who called her a girl.

At nine years old Sara was fiery, intense, taller than anyone else their age and graced with blazing red hair and skin so dense with freckles she looked permanently sunburned across her cheeks. She was feared by children throughout Cross, not only because it was rumoured her father was the local 'provo', but because she could fight. As she got older they started calling her a tomboy, but only behind her back.

Unpredictably, in a way only possible with children, Helen Young and Sara Collins became inseparable. The relationship wasn't very balanced – Helen was the new girl and didn't know how to look after herself; Sara knew the ropes and protected her – but it had a profound effect on Helen. It made Karen cringe to remember it. She had been so weak. Within weeks she was copying everything Sara did, speaking like her (the foul South Down accent), intensely proud that she was her best friend. She had assumed Sara felt the same about her.

Cross was a village of no more than sixty households on the outskirts of Newry. From the outside it looked idyllic. There was a church, a village hall, a post office, two pubs, a chippy and narrow streets of cottages dating back to the sixteenth century. The place was so small you were never far from a landscape overrun with copses, hedges and tiny, intricate green fields.

But of those sixty families, only eight were Protestant, and they all lived in exactly the same area, a small hill to the northern edge of the village. 'The Castle' Sara used to call it, not for any similarities to Dublin Castle (she used to fall asleep during history lessons), but because the last house up the lane was a rambling ruin with collapsing gable ends. There were eight detached houses on Newton's Lane and the second from the end – a converted farmhouse – belonged to the Youngs. Sara lived on the tiny, run-down council estate hidden between the centre of Cross and the main Newry road. Like everywhere else in Northern Ireland, what was on the surface in Cross was only the beginning of the story.

Helen's mother, Jane Nesbitt, was a house-proud, neurotic Free Presbyterian. Jane's father had been a labourer on an estate in North Belfast. All her family ties remained in the city, even after David Young saw in her something worth rescuing. He was from considerable inherited wealth, but his own misguided version of *My Fair Lady* was doomed to fail. Jane bitterly resented the move south upon which he insisted. She gave in and tagged along reluctantly, but she brought herself with her. A little bit of the Upper Ardoyne in rural Down.

The move meant her daughter would have to attend the 'mixed' school where she was to meet Sara Collins. Even before there was any real sectarian violence in Northern Ireland Jane did not approve of her only child speaking to 'taig brats from the estate'. She made sure her daughter knew it, but by then Helen Young was too far under Sara Collins's spell to listen. She learned to hide her loyalties.

In 1970 a neighbour and friend of her mother's from Newton's Lane – a buildings contractor who had been working on Long Kesh prison – was shot dead in Belfast. Almost overnight, the 'Troubles' arrived in Cross. By that time, through Sara, all little Helen Young's friends were Catholics. One by one they were either told by their parents to keep away or Helen's mother found out about them and banned contact. Jane had unsubtle methods of persuasion. In later years she even managed to mix it with gin, to give Helen the true feel of Loyalist authority. As the friends disappeared she didn't replace them.

But she persisted with Sara. Even after she was packed

off to boarding school in Belfast. At school it was Sara she missed, not her parents. By that time her mother couldn't look at her father without picking a fight with him. Already she was at the bottle before midday. So her absence was a relief, even for a thirteen-year-old. But Karen could remember many a night when stupid little Helen Young had cried herself to sleep because Sara Collins was no longer with her.

The pain lasted until her third visit home, in the summer of 1975. She had written many times to Sara, since leaving Cross, but never had a single response. Too needy to read the signs, her plan was to simply turn up at Sara's house, as she always had, looking for her. On her first night back, though, her mother sent her to the chip shop. There was no food in the house and her father was on call in Newry. Jane was drunk.

Waiting in the chip shop queue Helen Young was surrounded by a group of jeering teenagers, some older than her, some younger, most of them female, all of them Catholic. One of them wanted to fight her. She refused and tried to ignore them. Ahead of her in the queue, adults looked back with a mixture of amusement and approval. In the end she had to fight them all. Or rather, she had to lie on the ground in a sobbing huddle, as they stamped, kicked, punched and spat at her. One of them finally broke a pop bottle on her head, bringing the ordeal to a bloody end.

An ambulance came from Newry. It took a long time. Meanwhile, she sat dizzily on the chippy steps, bleeding profusely from a scalp wound, three teeth broken, covered in cuts and bruises and trying not to throw up. The only adult who was nice to her, who called and waited for the ambulance, was Mrs Kelly, who owned the chip shop.

Mrs Kelly was a Catholic and there was a lesson in that, but not so memorable a lesson as the one given by Sara Collins, who had broken the bottle on her.

THIRTY-SIX

Akhtar lived in Heaton, not far from the house where Pete Bains had lived, probably still lived. Karen stopped the car at the edge of Lister Park and walked quickly uphill until she found the turn-off for Wilmer Crescent. Pete Bains was another no-go area. She waited at the corner for a few moments, scrutinizing the parked vehicles.

It took her less than a minute to spot the plain clothes officer in the blue Astra. It wasn't hard – she recognized him. A DC from Holbeck called Fred Coe, one of those who had been around too long and was just waiting to get his years in. What was he doing here?

She took a detour through the streets below Wilmer Crescent and came up through a snicket behind the Astra. Coe was placed near the entrance to the close where Akhtar had a small detached house. He would be able to see Akhtar – or anyone else – leaving or arriving by the front gates, but not if they were more careful. He wasn't making much of an effort to be covert either. She watched him reading a newspaper. He was inattentive, bored.

She cut down the drive of a property behind Coe's car, made her way through rear gardens and came up to Akhtar's house from behind trees. As she stepped onto his rear lawn she could see his wife at the kitchen sink. Naheed Akhtar. The kids were Zaf and Yas, six and ten respectively. They went to Ashdowne Lodge and Brontë House, both private schools.

Naheed didn't notice her until she was almost at the kitchen window. Karen stood there – not three feet in front of her – and waited. Around her the thin covering of snow was melting. She watched Naheed catch sight of her, register surprise, then frown. She didn't have a clue who she was. That was good.

Karen mouthed, 'Can we speak?' She watched Naheed take off an apron and step to the back door.

'Who are you?' She stood in the door, wary, but not afraid. She took in the bruising on Karen's face, the blood, then the overalls and the lettering on the breast pocket. She was wearing ordinary black jeans and a pale blue shirt. She was about five years younger than Karen, with long black hair and a pretty face, but she looked harassed, like a mother of two with too much to do. Karen stepped towards her.

'I'm Anna Hart.' The words were clumsy in her mouth – transparent lies already. 'We haven't met. But I know you're Naheed.' She held out a hand. Naheed Akhtar looked at it, then looked back into Karen's face, perplexed.

'Anna Hart? I've never heard of you. What are you doing here? How do you know who I am?' She looked back into the house. Karen could hear children shouting, playing. But the response seemed truthful, which was also good. If Imran Akhtar had not told his wife who Anna Hart was then she had a chance of co-operation. 'Is your husband in?' she asked, moving her hand away.

'No. What do you want? Are you from the police?'

The question was interesting. Karen frowned, trying to feign confusion. 'No. I'm not. Is he in?'

'No. I don't know where he is. Who are you? Why are you wearing those clothes? Has something happened to you? You have blood on your face.'

Karen sighed and looked sideways, unsure what to say. 'Yes,' she said finally. 'Something *has* happened to me. I was raped this morning.' She said the words dispassionately, then felt them tug at her. Her lower lip quivered, despite herself. She tried to get her thoughts away from it. She saw Naheed Akhtar read her reactions and stop herself from saying something glib. Instead she cleared her throat and took a step backwards.

'Raped?' she said, as if she didn't know what the word meant.

'Yes. Can I come in? I have only these clothes. It's cold.'

Naheed was caught between sympathy and uncertainty. 'You were raped? I don't know what to say. Why are you telling me that? I asked you who you are.'

'I'm Nicholas Hanley's partner.' The name meant something to her, but Karen wasn't sure what. 'Do you know who Nicholas is?'

'Someone Imran works with. You are a business partner? He has never mentioned you. How do I know who—'

'Do I look like I'm lying?'

'I don't know what you look like.'

'I'm not a business partner. I was Nicholas Hanley's girlfriend. Nicholas Hanley and Imran are business partners. That's how I know who you are.'

'It doesn't matter. If you were raped you should go to the police. What has all this to do with me?'

There was too much information for her to deal with. Her voice was going up in pitch.

Karen stepped forwards, into the door frame. 'Your husband knows who did it to me, Naheed.' She spoke the words clearly, deliberately. 'That's why I'm here. I need to find him so that I can find this person. You have to help me.'

Naheed took another step backwards, frightened now, unsure what to do. Karen followed her into the building,

255

then paused. She had to get her sympathy. 'I'm sorry,' she said. 'I should not be . . .' She brought her hands up and covered her face. 'Nick is dead. The police have told me Nick is dead . . .' She sank into a crouch, resting her head in her hands. 'I'm so sorry. I don't know what I'm doing . . .' She dragged the words out in a whispered stutter, cracked with emotion. She began to sob, faking it at first, then realizing with shame that there were real tears running through her fingers. The emotions were something alien, swelling inside her. She let them come. Raped woman snaps under pressure. She could see herself doing it. Breathing in big gasps, tears flowing freely, huddled on the kitchen floor, uncontrollable, devastated.

She waited until she felt Naheed's hand on her shoulder before she began to stop. When she finally looked up her vision was so blurred she had to draw the sleeve of the overalls across her eyes to be able to see her. She could just imagine how bad she looked. Blood, tears, face contorted with grief and confusion. She could see it all reflected in the woman's expression. She was crouching on the floor beside her, face lined with anxiety and pain, trying to soothe her.

'You should stop crying,' she was saying. 'What has happened is over. You cannot be hurt in here.' She was speaking to her as if she were a little child. Karen tried to smile gratefully, struggling with a sudden feeling of contempt for the woman and her pity, though that had been precisely what she had sought to evoke.

She followed Naheed Akhtar into a large kitchen, full of the smell of freshly baked bread. The trite domesticity made her nauseous. Or maybe it was what Anna Hart had been through, finally getting to her. She began to retch, and Naheed ran to her with a glass of water. She took it off her and gulped at it like a thirsty dog. Naheed closed the back door, then the door into the main part of the house – the door leading to the children. She offered Karen a seat at a narrow breakfast bar. Karen sat shakily.

'I don't know what has happened to you,' Naheed said. Her voice was wavering, frightened. 'Imran told me nothing of this. He did not tell me about Nicholas . . . he did not . . .'

'Did you ever meet Nicholas?'

She shook her head firmly. 'I have nothing to do with his business. Nothing.' There was a trace of determination to it, as if his business were something dirty. 'But if this man is dead then I am sorry for you.'

'They are saying he committed suicide, that he jumped off a building in Leeds.' Karen looked up, making sure she had her full attention. 'He was on fire,' she said, dropping her voice to a terrified whisper. 'He had set himself on fire.'

Naheed covered her mouth in horror.

'Things are happening,' Karen said. 'Bad things. I don't think he killed himself. I think he was murdered. By the same people who did this to me. I have to find them. You have to tell me where Imran is.'

'I don't know where Imran is. Imran tells me nothing. The police were already here this morning, looking for him . . .' She stopped herself, almost biting her tongue off.

'I'm not from the police, though,' Karen said. 'I want to find him so he can help me. Do you know where he might be?'

Naheed shook her head, glanced at her, then looked away. 'I don't have a clue,' she said. 'He doesn't tell me anything. His business is no concern of mine.'

She sounded angry about it, but she was nevertheless lying for him. Karen was sure of it.

257

'Did he leave for work this morning? You must have some idea where he is.'

'What has this to do with him?' She turned on her, almost shouting. 'If you were raped that has nothing to do with him. You are confusing me, coming into my home like this . . .'

The door opened, silencing her. A small boy with deep, brown eyes and untidy hair walked in, glancing momentarily at Karen before crossing straight to his mother. Naheed started to ask him to go away, to go and play with his sister, but he wasn't listening. He started to say something in Urdu.

'No. You cannot. It's too early.' She answered him in English, but he kept repeating himself in Urdu. He stood at her side, holding onto her leg, looking up at her. Through the open door Karen could hear the sound of a TV.

'He is hungry,' Naheed explained to her. She was getting flustered.

'The man who did this to me—'

'Not in front of the child. Please!'

'He was not your husband. But your—'

'Please. He is only six years old!'

'Your husband knew him. He was with him. I saw them together afterwards.'

Naheed picked up the boy and held him, shielding his head from Karen. But her attention was divided. She couldn't cope. The boy struggled free and started to shout at her, stamping his feet.

'That's why I have to find him,' Karen said. She got down off the stool. The noise was irritating her. She thought about grabbing hold of the kid and screaming at him. If she shook him hard enough the mother would react. Would that get the information out of her? She had to do it some way. She wasn't leaving without knowing Imran Akhtar's whereabouts. She stepped towards them, flexing her fingers.

'I don't know where he is. Please . . . leave us . . . please, leave us . . .' Naheed was saying. The child noticed something was going on and fell silent.

Karen stood in front of them both. 'What did the police want?' she asked. She looked from the child to the mother, then placed her hands behind her back, out of the way.

'The same as you. They wanted to find him . . .' There were tears in her eyes now.

'Is he in trouble of some sort? Why would the police want him?'

'I don't know. I don't know.' She began to cry. 'I haven't seen him for weeks. He is not the same. Something is happening to him. I think he is dealing with men he shouldn't be dealing with.'

'Have you seen any of them?'

She shook her head. The little boy buried his face into the back of her legs and began to cry as well. Behind her Karen could sense that the ten-year-old girl had appeared, too. She glanced towards the door and saw her standing there, staring.

'I have seen no one,' Naheed said. She leaned over the kitchen counter and buried her face in her hands. 'He tells me nothing. He is like a stranger to me.'

'But he *is* in trouble?'

'The police said I should call them, if he came. Call about my own husband! I cannot do that. I cannot . . .'

'Has he called you?'

'No.'

'But you did see him this morning?'

There was no denial.

'Listen, Naheed,' Karen said, 'you are a good woman. I can see that. You are not involved in any of this.' She reached out and placed a hand on the woman's shoulder. 'I don't care about being raped,' she said. 'That is over with. But I am a mother, too. I have a child, the same age as yours.' She pointed back to the girl. 'These people . . . the people who are doing this . . . they have taken my child . . .' Her voice broke suddenly, genuinely. She took a breath. 'Please help me. I don't know what they will do with her. I don't know what is happening. But I have to find her. I am desperate. She is my only child. Your husband is with these people. He knows where she is. You have to help me. You have to tell me where he is.'

Naheed stared at her. 'They have taken your child?'

Karen nodded. She could feel her cheeks quivering, the lump massive in her throat. 'Rachel.'

'And Imran knew about this?'

'He was there when it happened.' She looked straight into her eyes as she told the lie. 'We were both kidnapped this morning. They raped me. I managed to get away. But they took her elsewhere. Afterwards I saw Imran talking to the one who took her. I think it might be something to do with their business – with Nick and Imran's business.'

'And why can't you go to the police?'

'I have been to the police. They are looking. If you watch TV you will hear the appeal they are putting out. But I cannot sit around waiting. I have to do something.'

'He is at his uncle's.' She spoke the words with sudden decision. 'He must be in trouble, because that is the only reason he ever goes there. To get "advice". I have warned him about this. I have told him we will leave him if it goes on. He has gone too far.'

'Did you see him today?'

'Yes. He was out all night and came back this morning.

His arm was bandaged. He had blood-stained clothes. He has been doing something . . .' There was disgust in her voice. 'I know what he is capable of.' She bit her lip and pulled the little boy towards her, protectively. 'He does not think of us. He does not think of his family.' Below her, the boy started to sob.

'Does he keep any paperwork about the business here, in the house?'

'Nothing. He would not want me knowing what he does.'

'Which uncle is he with?'

'Mohammed Hussain. He has a car business. They will be there.'

'On Frizinghall Road?'

'Yes. How did you know?'

'That doesn't matter. When I am gone will you call him? Will you warn him that I am coming?' She waited for Naheed Akhtar to shake her head.

Karen could not believe her, but the premises owned by the uncle were only a three-minute drive away. She could pull the phones out and search for Naheed's mobile, if she had one, or she could trust her and hope that made a difference. She began to walk towards the back door.

'You've done the right thing,' she said, opening it.

Naheed Akhtar nodded, her hand on her little boy's head. 'He doesn't mean to do these things,' she said. 'He is a stupid man. He has always been like that. He does what others tell him to do. You won't hurt him, will you?'

Karen smiled at her. 'I promise,' she said.

THIRTY-SEVEN

Stijn was already stopping the car at the Hartshead Moor services on the M62 when he heard the radio announcement start. At first he didn't register who they were describing – '*a conspicuously tall male, very well built, either shaved head or bald*' – then he heard the car registration number. It was the hire car he was driving.

He switched the engine off and looked carefully around him. The car park was moderately full. Most vehicles were parked up and empty, but there was a steady stream coming in and leaving. One car passed right in front of him as the announcement was made. He glanced at the driver – middle-aged, uninterested – then looked away. Not that one, but it was inconceivable that there was *nobody* here listening to the same radio station. It was Radio Leeds, one of the main local stations.

He heard the cop making the announcement give a police website address. There was a picture of the man they were looking for there, he said, and encouraged listeners to look at it and remain alert: '*The man we are looking for goes under several names, including Jan Gatz, Josef Stijn, Michael Steinmayer, Michael Getz, Jan Josefs and Michael Kruger.*' All his names. They had all his names. '. . . *Anyone with any suspicion that they are dealing with this man should contact us.*' A contact number was given. '*Under no circumstances should the man be approached or challenged. He may be dangerous.*' Then followed the appeal for Anna and Rachel Hart that he had already heard several times. He switched the radio off.

So they had still not found the woman and the kid. He

opened the car and stepped out onto the tarmac, noticing how he towered above the roof of the vehicle, clearly visible from all directions. The air was bitterly cold. Above him the sky was prematurely dark. The few inches of snow beneath his feet had frosted over already. He started to walk towards the service buildings, head down, shoulders hunched. It was all he could do – duck his head against the cold, but move normally.

The images had to come from some CCTV camera he hadn't seen. Hopefully they would be poor quality. But poor quality or not, he needed to be out of this shit hole and far away. Nicholas Hanley had fucked up his exit plan. He had fucked up everything, in fact; plan A, plan B and plan C.

The police had his image and his names, and they knew he was connected to the deaths. He didn't know how that had happened so fast, but it had. The most obvious source of information would have been the woman or her kid, but he knew now it couldn't have been them.

The woman had been quicker and cleverer than he had allowed for. Or Michael Kenny had been more stupid. The phone call telling him about Kenny's death at the abattoir had come just as he was approaching the place. Someone had contacted Mohammed Rouf direct, then Rouf had called Stijn. Stijn had endured his anger, but left the arrangements to him. It was not his responsibility to ensure that everything worked as he had been promised it would. Kenny's name had come from Rouf's people, not his own contacts.

Hart and the kid hadn't gone to the police because they were with Hanley. He had guessed that long before Rouf told him Hanley had called and tried to dictate terms. It hadn't surprised Stijn. Rouf had expected Hanley to set up two people he had lived with and loved, one of them a child. Stijn had known Hanley would not do that. Hanley had even told him how much he loved the pair of them. Stijn had felt nothing comparable in his life – he noted the fact dispassionately – but he knew from vicarious experience how much grit that kind of emotion could drop into the works.

He pushed open the doors to the main vestibule and looked for the restaurant. People passed him, glancing at him, but no double-takes. He turned away from the restaurant into the shop and found a black woolly hat. He paid for it and pulled it over his head. At least that was one part of the description struck out – 'bald or shaved'.

From the entrance to the restaurant he picked out Diana Hanley across the other side of the room, noted her position and walked slowly back to his car. She was easy to spot. There was no one else around her, no one within earshot. She was sitting alone at a corner table in the window, smoking. Had she watched him pull up and park? He knew it was her because Rouf had provided him with a picture of her, not so long ago. Diana Hanley had been important, in the past. There had been something intimate between Ahmed Rouf and her. But she wouldn't know what he looked like, unless she had been listening to the radio. He dialled her mobile number.

'Yes?' She sounded anxious. From the car window he could just see her, inside the restaurant, ear pressed to the phone.

'Diana Hanley?'

'Yes. Where are you?'

'I'm here. Looking at you.' He let the words sink in. He watched her scanning the faces on the inside of the restaurant. 'Not inside,' he said. 'Outside. I can't come in.'

'Why not?'

264

'Haven't you listened to the radio recently? The police have put my description out. We can't meet in a public place.'

'We have to.' A hint of desperation.

'We can't. There's a cheap hotel attached to this place. Go there and rent a room. Call me when you're in.'

Silence as she thought about this.

'I don't want to do that,' she said finally. She was frightened of him. Something her brother had told her, no doubt.

'Well, that's the way it has to be. If I get caught by the police, you get caught – remember that. You identified his body. And I'd have to tell them the rest of it to save my skin. Besides, you called me for this meeting. I didn't want it. I can start my car, turn around and drive away right now.'

'No. OK. I'll do it. Stay there.' She cut the line.

As he waited he thought about Ahmed Rouf and Diana Hanley, copulating. Rutting like rabbits. The idea amused him, like all miscegenation. He had met Ahmed Rouf only once, in Zurich, at a club there. Rouf had been as friendly and normal as you could imagine. No pretensions, no swagger. Imran Akhtar – the idiot they had made him use here – was meant to be related to Ahmed Rouf in some way, but he was cut from a different cloth. Rouf had been a well-groomed, clipped individual, tall and fit, with light skin, a finely trimmed beard and clever eyes. He had offered Stijn a cigarette, a normal Marlboro, but Stijn didn't smoke. He would have fitted well with the English upper classes. He had the voice, the clothing (expensive, understated, casual), the manners. It was easy for him, of course. He had been to some expensive private school over here, and knew the codes. But Stijn knew where his money came from. At the end of the day the polo-playing playboy thing was just a diversion. Diana Hanley was about to discover that. Her credit with Ahmed Rouf had run out in one quick blast, over twelve short hours.

It took her about ten minutes to ring with the room number. He walked slowly over to the motel part of the area, entered the lobby, nodded in a friendly way at the receptionist and carried straight on through, as if he were checked in. Hanley herself opened the door to him. She had a mobile phone pressed to her ear and was talking. He stepped inside and watched her, listening.

'Of course,' she said. 'If you want me to come down I will. But are you sure it's necessary?'

She sounded like she was talking to someone official. He drew his hand across his neck to signal that she should cut the call. She moved her hand over the microphone and mouthed, *It's the police.*

He frowned.

'Thank you, Mr Bains,' she said. 'I'll see you then.' She ended the call.

'Mr Bains?' he asked.

'A policeman. He wants me to go to Weetwood police station.'

'What did you say?'

'I said I would, of course.'

He smiled. 'But you won't?'

'Naturally not. You must be Stijn?'

She held out her hand to him, trying to conceal her unease, to take charge of the situation. He looked down at it, but made no move to take it. She reached into a pocket, found a packet of cigarettes and lit one. Her eyes were bloodshot and strained. She moved her hand away, left the door and walked back into the room, turning her back to him. Very brave, he thought.

266

'How did you know who I was?' she asked. She stood by the bed. There was a black leather bag there. He closed the door and locked it, then walked over to the bed. He saw her looking anxiously back at the door.

'I've seen a photo of you,' he said. 'Playing polo with my boss.' He saw her relax slightly. Perhaps feeling a little safer.

'What do you want to tell me?' he asked, though he knew already. She walked over to the bedside table and stubbed out the cigarette she had just lit.

'I don't want to tell you anything. I've been asked to give you something – as a gesture of good faith. So Ahmed will know we are honourable in this business.' She began to reach into the bag. Stijn reached a hand across the table and closed it around her arm, gently.

'I don't know anyone called Ahmed,' he said.

'I think you do,' she said, face set. She shook her arm free.

He smiled at her. 'What do you want?' he asked.

'That's not your business.' Her voice was stuffed with contempt for him. Or maybe it was just the accent. 'My brother has already called your boss—'

'Yes. I know that already. But humour me. Tell me what you hope to get from this?'

'I don't have to speak to you. I'd rather not. My brother—'

'That's not the way to negotiate,' he said, interrupting her. He thought the situation was almost funny. 'You should know better than that.'

'Don't presume to teach me anything.'

'There has to be give and take in a good negotiation.'

'This isn't a negotiation. I want nothing from you. I have brought this for Ahmed, not for you – to prove that we want nothing from him. You have only to take it to

267

him.' She took a brown parcel from the bag – A4 size – and threw it onto the bed in front of him. He smiled at her again, then sat down on the edge of the bed. He heard the springs creaking beneath his weight.

He tore the seal on the parcel as she watched. He glanced at the contents. There was no way of telling if it was genuine, not here. But it looked like a high-value bearer bond.

'Your brother seems to think this is a negotiation,' he said, looking up at her.

'No. There can be no discussion. The rest of these will be returned when we have guarantees for our safety and when we are out of the country.'

'I said your brother seems to think this *is* a negotiation.'

'And I'm telling you that he doesn't. Can you understand that? When we have left England—'

'We? Who would that be?'

She frowned. 'My brother and I.'

'Not Anna and Rachel Hart?'

She made a little tutting noise and even looked as if she would smile at the thought. 'I rather doubt it,' she said.

'But your brother has asked for their safety. That is why I didn't kill them this morning.'

She opened her mouth to say something, then closed it. He watched her frantically thinking it through, completely wrong-footed with surprise, seeing suddenly that it might be true, that her brother really might feel enough for the pair to try to save them, without telling his sister. Something like panic crossed her features.

'You didn't know?' he asked. 'Think about it. There was no need for your brother to steal the bonds to guarantee his own safety. The people I work for had already given those assurances. We went to all that trouble this morning to make sure your brother would be safe. We found a

268

replacement, we killed him, you identified the body. All your brother had to do was get on the plane and leave . . .'

'No. He didn't trust you . . .'

'That may be.' He was right not to. Stijn had told Rouf from the start that it would be easier to just kill Hanley. 'But it wasn't his own life he asked for when he called my employer . . .'

'That is nonsense. I do not believe it. Please take the package and go now.' Her voice was wavering. 'You have to leave. If you do not leave I will call the police . . .'

'What would you tell them?'

She stepped over to the phone and placed her hand on the receiver. She was uncertain now, thrown by what he had told her. She wanted rid of him quickly – no doubt so she could call her brother to check his story. 'I have already told the police where I am,' she said. 'I told that officer I was speaking to when you came in.'

'So what? Is he coming?'

'He will come if I ring.'

'You're not going to ring,' he said quietly. 'And I doubt you have told anyone where you are.'

'Get out, Mr Stijn. Leave me now. I *will* do this if I have to. There are police cars stationed at these very services. They could be here in moments.'

He rolled lazily across the bed, reached out and closed his hand around hers, crushing it against the phone. He squeezed until he saw pain flashing in her eyes, then stood up and closed his big, flat hand across her mouth, just as she started to shout. She was still trying to shout as he bent his head forward and whispered into her ear, '*I will kill you if you don't be quiet.*' He tightened his grip on her hand until he felt something crack inside it. Her face contorted with pain, her eyes big white circles, staring up at him. He let go of her hand and waited for her to catch her breath, then took his hand from her mouth. She fell back against the window.

'Let's get down to business,' he said, stepping towards her. 'Did you really think you could just bring me here and walk out?'

She held her damaged hand and stared at him in sheer fright. He heard her mutter something about Ahmed Rouf, but it was too unclear. He reached over and curled a hand through her tired, brown hair, pulling her head back. She gasped, her face trembling.

'Your brother has property that belongs to others,' he said. 'I need to know where he is.'

THIRTY-EIGHT

Diana Hanley had told Bains she was having a business meeting with a horse trainer, at the services on the M62, at Hartshead. He didn't believe her. She was probably at Hartshead, he thought, but not for a business meeting. Her excuse for the location was that it was on her way back home – to London. He could get to Hartshead in thirty minutes, if he used the light and horn, forty if he didn't. But would she still be there?

Was she there at all? Either she had been lying to him about that or about something else. Perhaps something was wrong. It hadn't seemed as if she had been lying about the location. Her responses had been too quick. And if you were inventing a location, why choose a motorway service area? It was too silly.

Bains stood in the main room of Diana Hanley's house and tried to ignore a mounting feeling of panic. He was clutching at straws, trying to do something when there was nothing he could do. He felt strung out – not just because he was tired – but because he had been living on adrenalin ever since he had found out that Karen Sharpe and Anna Hart were the same person. He surveyed the mess left by Diana Hanley and wondered if anyone would notice if he put his fist through something. He put his knuckles in his mouth instead. He had thought Hanley had been burgled – the back door had been forced and left open and it looked as if someone had turned the place over – but no, she had told him she had left the cottage like that, and there was nothing for him to worry about. He hadn't believed that either.

What was it? Something he had picked up in her voice? He sat down on a small chair in the hallway and stared at the telephone socket, his legs moving compulsively to some frantic, inaudible adrenalin beat. He had only noticed the socket after he had called her. The phone line had been ripped out and the socket crushed. That was why all his calls into the place had appeared to ring without answer.

He could call in the problem, ask Alan White to get the traffic sergeant at Hartshead Moor to look for her. There would probably be two or three traffic officers nearby who were sitting around doing nothing. He could even call through to them himself, without going through White. That would be preferable, because White was just going to be annoyed that he wasn't doing paperwork at Weetwood. But he could imagine their reactions if he called through with nothing other than a vague description and a hunch that she was lying. She wasn't after all, a suspect in the case. Not officially. She was a victim. And he didn't even know what kind of car she was driving, let alone the registration plate.

He looked at his watch. It was nearly four o'clock. Outside it was dark, with small flurries of snow falling through the air. The darkness made him want to shout out with fear. He was frightened for Karen, but more for Mairead. He had already tried the cottage opposite, hoping they would know what kind of car Hanley drove, but they weren't in and there were signs that they too had suffered a forced entry – a broken porch window. He would have to call that in, whatever he did.

He stood up and walked back out to his car. Diana Hanley had promised to go to Weetwood police station immediately. He could always go back there and wait to see whether she did that. But that might be to let things slip. The man they were looking for – Stijn, Gatz, Kruger, whatever name he was using – had probably killed her brother. Why had he called her? Bains had not told her of the evidence of Stijn's call to her – a part of him suspected her of something. Whatever it was, the line had to be hunted down before it vanished. There was a connection between Stijn and Hanley, and there wasn't time to take it back to White, run it through the inquiry and wait to see what happened.

He got into the car, started it and reversed so that he could turn. The back of the car hit the wooden fence bordering the yard with a loud splintering noise.

He got out and looked at the damage, running his hand over his face. The fence was knocked down, the car was scratched and dented. He had known the fence was there. He was dog-tired. If it wasn't for the adrenalin he would sleep on his feet, right now.

He looked up into the sky. The clouds were too dark to see anything. He had to do something. Drive over to Hartshead, check if she was there, then knock off and get a few hours sleep? It wasn't on his way, but it was more in the direction of his home than a drive back to Weetwood, where he should have been. Even if she was no longer there he could look at the CCTV there and probably find out what car she was in. If she did turn sour on them that would be useful later.

He started to disentangle the broken fence from the rear bumper of the car, pulling at the cold wood with his bare hands. A piece was stuck there and wouldn't move. He kicked out at it. 'Fuck you, Karen,' he shouted suddenly. 'Fuck you for doing this!'

THIRTY-NINE

Some time ago they had given her a number to call, an intelligence clerk in Northern Ireland who would know about James Martin. That was after Martin had contacted her, telling her he was coming for his daughter as soon as he got out. Martin had spent the better part of the last three years in jail, for terrorist offences. She had been living with Pete Bains when he sent the letters, but it wasn't the first time he had tracked her down. The time before that he had been sent to kill her. Looking back on it now, it seemed like it had happened twenty years ago.

But it hadn't. The consequences were still with her, in tangible form. She had a child and Martin was the father. Thinking about him brought on powerful and conflicting emotions. Only living with Pete Bains had started to stop all that.

Using the dead man's phone she dialled the number of the clerk. Part of his task was to collate information on known suspects, tracking when they crossed to mainland Britain and back. She had used the 'facility' twice before, so the man would know her. The question was whether he would know more. Would Sutherland already have warned him that she was AWOL? Given the inefficiency she had become used to, it was unlikely, but possible.

'Len Freeman. Can I help you?' The heavy Northern Ireland accent sent a little shiver down her spine. Once upon a time she had spoken like that.

'Mr Freeman. It's Karen Sharpe. I need an update on James Martin.'

'Anything wrong?'

'No. Just the usual.'

'Of course. Just hold a moment, please.'

The 'usual' was shorthand for Karen and James's complicated and unhappy history. They had met when she was a stupid 24-year-old, in Belfast. The stupidity had not been falling for him – she had been tasked to do that – but falling for the myths woven by the officer controlling her. Back then, that had been Harry Singleton, Sutherland's predecessor. Nearly three years later in London the lies had come home to roost. In 1988 she managed to delight Singleton, make a life-long enemy of the Provisional IRA and slip straight off the edge of a psychiatric precipice. But not before she had fallen pregnant to Martin and given birth to Mairead.

She could recall little of that time. She had been ill for many months afterwards and too many memories had dropped out of existence while she was in hospital. She could not even remember Mairead's birth. But she knew that she had loved James Martin – really loved him.

The thought of it made her cringe. She'd just gone through the same process with Nicholas Hanley. The same thing all over again. She felt sickened, disgusted. The last eighteen months had the quality of a dream, as if someone else had been involved, but it had been her. She had been there, doing all that with him. She was like some kind of slut.

'James Martin,' Freeman said, cutting into her thoughts. 'Yes. I remember the last time you called. He was living in Newcastle, County Down. Is that right?'

'Yes.'

'I haven't heard much about him since then.'

'I just need to know whether he's still there.'

'I understand. Let me try to find out for you.'

She waited as he clicked away at a keyboard, looking for

information – or sending a message to Sutherland? Whichever it was going to be, she had to ride with it now. She needed to know where Martin was.

In front of her, in a solitary industrial lot off the bottom of Frizinghall Road, she could see the office lights of the car parts business Akhtar's uncle owned. Occasionally she could even see figures moving about inside. The place was closed, according to the sign on the door, but Akhtar's conspicuous Merc, along with his memorable personal plates, was parked up outside. The street lighting was poor, but all the same, she didn't dare leave the engine on. She had been waiting nearly fifteen minutes so far. It had stopped snowing outside, but the air inside the vehicle was beginning to chill.

'Was he early release?' Freeman asked.

'I think so.'

'He was just out, I think, when you last called.'

'I think so. Yes.' She tried to keep her voice normal, unexcited.

They had sent her coded text messages all yesterday, warning her to get out, telling her that it was compromised. Yet she had remained in place. Why?

She had been confused. She had lived a normal, happy life with her daughter and Hanley. She had let that get to her, forgotten who she was and why she was there. When she had lived with Pete Bains it had been different. She had argued with Mairead the whole time. Mostly, she had let Pete look after her. But then, with Pete, she had been Karen Sharpe. That was reality. Anna Hart had lived a normal life with Nicholas Hanley. Anna Hart had got on with her daughter like a house on fire. But Anna Hart didn't exist. Karen Sharpe was who she was. There was something wrong with her. She could live a normal, happy life if she wasn't Karen Sharpe, but when it happened in reality, as it had with Pete, she couldn't bear it.

'I've found him,' Freeman said.

'Yes?' In front of her the side door to the building opened and a man stepped out.

'He's in prison,' Freeman said.

She eased the breath silently between her lips. The man began to walk carefully towards her, watching where he was placing his feet.

'He's on remand,' he added.

'I didn't know,' she said. It was Akhtar. She turned her head from him and tried to act like she was just someone taking a call on a mobile.

'He assaulted a policeman.'

'Assault? That's not like him.' Akhtar turned at the end of the lot and moved towards a car in front of her, a Ford Focus.

'It's definitely him. I thought you'd be glad.'

'Thanks for the help,' she said. She cut the line but kept the phone to her ear.

So it wasn't James Martin who had taken Mairead. That left Hanley. He had to be alive. Her head began to fill with anger. It could only mean one thing. He knew who she was. The thoughts squirmed malignantly. *He had known about her and said nothing. Nothing had been as it seemed between them. He had been living a lie.* But for how long? She felt an irrational, primal sense of betrayal.

In front of her the Ford Focus pulled into the road. She would find Hanley. She was sure of it now. All she needed was thirty minutes with Akhtar, alone.

FORTY

Stijn sat down on the bed, resting his thighs. They were trembling and he didn't know why. He looked around him, seeing the room for the first time. The place was tiny, barely enough space to set the single high-backed chair between the double bed and the television. The television was flickering in his peripheral vision. He didn't care what programme was on, couldn't even focus on what they were saying. He just wanted the background noise. He had drawn thick drapes, designed to dull the constant hiss of the motorway, on a view of the rear of the service area and the steadily falling snow. It was night outside already, too easy for anyone passing to see straight through.

He felt confused, something that rarely happened, so it was hard to work out why. His thighs – and now his arms – were really trembling, his breathing rapid, as if he had just completed some strenuous physical effort. But he had done nothing.

He worked hard at being fit. As a child he had been tall and big-boned, but not well built. His size had been a liability – he was clumsy and uncoordinated with it, all bones, joints and angles. The image he had of himself was of someone defective, a simpleton. He saw himself bumbling around their farm just outside Salisbury, always breaking things and being beaten for it. Deep inside he registered a small internal flinch at the memory. His father had been a drunken bum who had blacked his mother's eyes, held knives to her throat, screamed at them all.

He looked over to where Diana Hanley was bound to

the chair. Her head was flopped forward and her whole body was shivering. Below the neck almost every part of her was streaked with blood. From some of the wounds he could still see it pulsing out of her, running down her naked flesh onto the cheap hotel carpet. He had held a knife to *her* throat. He had blacked her eyes. He had only not screamed because it would be heard.

He tried to think about it. What had he done to her? The same things he had seen done to his mother? But this was different. This was business.

So why was he sweating? He looked down at his legs and could see the stuff staining through the fabric of his trousers. There was so much he thought he had wet himself. It had been the same with the woman at the abattoir. So much sweat, his heartbeat racing. He had thought he was going to pass out, that he wasn't going to make it.

If he walked over to Diana Hanley and pulled her head up he would see that look in her eyes again. That was what had stopped him. It had been there with the man they had burned this morning as well. It was there with all of them. He felt sick thinking about it. He eased himself backwards onto the bed slowly, as if he might pass out if he moved too quickly. He began to breathe in short, staccato bursts. His hands covered his face. Everything was confusing him now.

He could hear Hanley trying to scream; a tired, cracked, old woman's scream. But she was so weakened she couldn't even hold her head up to shout. And the gag was very tight, covering her whole mouth, suffocating her slowly. All that came out was a muffled, low-level noise, not enough to drown out the TV. Still, somebody would hear, if they passed the door. He should do something about it. Shut her up. Or get out of here.

He raised his head a little and watched her. Soon she would put so much effort into it she wouldn't be able to get enough air through her nose. She would stop then. Why was she doing it anyway? She couldn't be in pain. Her body would be in shock now. There would have been pain at first, but even so, not too much. He knew the scientific facts. The incisions were too deep for pain, the blade went in underneath the densest concentration of nerves. Eventually a feeling *like* pain would swamp her senses. But it wasn't real. He had been there, he knew. Living things – animals, humans, whatever – always screamed if you subjected them to this kind of thing. Animals were worse. They bucked and kicked, convulsed. He had seen it happen so many times. Too many times.

He let his head fall back onto the bed and groaned. His head was filling with it now. All those images. He tried to massage the thing that was in his throat, blocking it. He could hear the groan coming out of him still, like the noise of a buffalo at night. He had been taught animal noises. *His stepfather* . . . His thoughts faltered. *His stepfather . . . long after his father had left . . . his stepfather . . .* The thought wouldn't come.

What? His stepfather what? He rolled onto his side, moving his hands to his temples now. A pain was building up there.

His stepfather had been good to his mother. He had not hit her. And he had tried to make something of the scrappy bit of land they rented. But it hadn't stopped his mother walking out on them. That had been *his* fault, presumably, because he was so ugly and clumsy.

Dolf. That was his stepfather's name. He had been a strong man. Shorter than his father, but stronger, in every way. It was his stepfather who had made him watch as he killed the roebuck after he took them from the traps. He had held his head from behind, gripped tightly, his hands so huge he could close one of them over his whole head, holding it like a ball, squeezing so tightly that the blood supply was constricted, so that even as he watched he became light-headed and dizzy.

The animal would kick and convulse, the blood welling, the eyes looking up at him. What had he seen in their eyes? Blankness? Were they blank, like people always said of animal eyes? Why had the animals looked at him at all? Watching him watching them, his stepfather's voice gentle in his ear: '*Tell me when the light has gone. Tell me when the light has gone . . .*'

That had been the point to it all – to look into their panicked eyes and be able to tell his stepfather when they were gone, when they were dead, when the 'light' had finally left their eyes, like an electrical charge shorting to earth. Though nothing changed physically, though the eyes would still be looking at you, the body twitching slower and slower, the terror changing into acceptance, you could still see the moment when they were looking but no longer seeing. To get there – to make that moment obvious – the animal had to die slowly. So his stepfather had arranged that for him.

He rolled suddenly off the bed, breathing heavily. He liked most animals. The only things he would happily kill were cats. Cats made his skin crawl.

He didn't want to think about it. His stepfather had been good to him. He had taught him how to fight, how to train, to build up muscle, how to look after himself. It had been hard because those things were hard. He stood up and moved towards the woman. She had known, he thought. That was why she had held out for so long. She had known how it had to work. Perhaps, as a child, she had even been through the same things he had. Because she knew that even when she told him where her brother was, he would still have to go further. The only possible proof of her truthfulness was that she would die with it. And even that wasn't proof.

You had to get the pain level up to where it interrupted all other allegiances. That took time and care. What he had done to her would do it, but not immediately, not for the first twenty minutes or so. He had seen it before. The body went into shock if the injuries were severe enough. It took time for it to communicate the harm to the brain. Meanwhile she was screaming and crying only because she was conscious, because she knew what was going to happen, because she had known from the start that he would not walk out of here and leave her.

He picked the blade up again and moved behind her. He would do something about her eyes. There was no harm in it, no complication. All the movements were very simple. He pulled her head back and looked down at her from behind. He saw her eyes find his face. He watched her chest heaving as she went again into a blind terrified panic, her limbs stretching against the plastic ties, her head tossing from side to side, a shout of some sort in her throat, begging him to do something. It was hard to distinguish the words. He would need to get her to the point where this struggling was impossible, then remove the gag and see what she had to say. She had already given him the address, but he had to be sure of it.

He took hold of her head at the base of the neck and held it firm. The eyes were looking right at him. That look. Was it fear, or helplessness? What was it? Blankness. Underneath it all a blankness. As if there was really nothing there behind it. He placed the blade against her cheek, readying himself. This was hard to do. But it was something necessary. You had to remember that the struggling was automatic, that there was no real conception of death. No one could visualize their own death. Not that clearly.

'We haven't long,' he told her. The words sounded thick in his mouth because he had taken out his teeth. He moved the blade a little and felt as giddy as the silly, awkward teenager he had once been. His legs felt weak, like they would give way. 'I'm sorry,' he said. 'But I have to be sure I can do this.'

FORTY-ONE

In the car park of the Hartshead Moor services Bains drove slowly through the lines of cars, looking for signs of Diana Hanley. Since he had no idea what car she drove he looked only for faces at the wheels of the cars, not the cars themselves. She wasn't there.

He parked some distance from the main building and sat for a few minutes behind the wheel, watching the snow curling out of the sky. Probably Diana Hanley was totally innocent of anything. He needed to remember that. The car park contained about seventy cars and only a dozen or so drivers had been inside their vehicles, so it was possible she was inside the place.

He got out and walked across a thin covering of snow to the entrance. As he was walking through the main doors he saw a traffic car shoot down the slip to the motorway, lights already flashing. He stepped back out and hurried quickly through the snow to the small police building attached to the back of the place, housing the motorway traffic team. There were no cars left in the yard. He slipped his pass through the door and stepped in. The place was empty. It was fortunate he hadn't called. He walked quickly back to the main building.

First he scanned the faces of the people in the shop, then stepped into the restaurant area. A dirty trail of water led from the hall towards the self-service counters and the place had an air of neglect. Behind the counters the staff stood around aimlessly, looking as though it would be a chore to serve anyone. There was a soap playing on some widescreen TVs hanging from the pillars and the ceiling, the noise of Australian family life vying with the pop music piped out of separate speakers at an uncomfortable volume. The eating areas were divided into sections, but the place was nearly empty. It took him about a minute to confirm she wasn't there. He stood looking at the shabby fixed furniture, feeling his anxiety growing.

He took out his phone and dialled her number again. She didn't answer. Probably by now she was halfway to London. He walked through the main doors and stepped outside, wondering whether it was worth going to the manager of the place and seizing the tapes from the CCTV. He only had her word for it that she had ever been here. He was relieved now that he hadn't bothered Alan White with this.

The snow was coming down steadily, probably because they were at a higher altitude here. To the left of him, hidden behind a high embankment, he could hear the motorway traffic, a constant background growl. In the beams of the tall lights spanning the carriageway the air was thick with a dense spray, thrown up by the wheels, like the mist that hangs over waterfalls. He let the snow fall on his head, noticing the damp, icy touch of each snowflake as it stuck gently to his skin, then slid off. The flakes were very large. Mairead would have liked it. Where was she? He bit his lip and let his eyes stray over the cars again, methodically checking each one.

The Christmas before – the one he had spent with them – had been clear, cold and sunny. Ditto the last one, though he had been working then. Usually it didn't snow at New Year either. If snow came it was normally way beyond the festive period, in late January or February. English people were brought up to expect snow at Christmas. He didn't know why. He could only rarely remember a Christmas or New Year that had been white. Even the stuff that had fallen today was melting in Leeds and Bradford. It wouldn't last until midnight. Maybe up here, where the altitude was different, on England's highest motorway. That was what the sign said on the M62.

His eyes stopped. What had he seen? He stepped forward, looking at the car they had settled on – a silver Mondeo. No. Not that one. He moved back two cars and felt his heart jump. A black BMW SUV. He read the registration again. It was Stijn's hire car.

He ran over to it and looked through the windows. It was empty. He looked back towards the service buildings, a feeling of exposure coming to him. Maybe he was being watched, right now. If Stijn were in there eating, or drinking, he would probably be alert for people approaching his car. Bains's eyes passed across each window, searching, but finding nothing. A shiver followed an icy drop of water from the nape of his neck to the middle of his back.

He was moving back to the restaurant before he realized he had forgotten the toilets. He started to run and knocked into a truck driver as he went through the doors. The man threw back some kind of racial insult.

The two middle-aged women in the ladies turned from the sinks and watched as he moved along each cubicle in turn, pushing doors in. He was in and out before they could say anything. The gents was a larger area, but also nearly empty. He moved back into the restaurant. Had Stijn been here the first time he had looked? He had not been looking specifically for Stijn. He could have missed him, but it seemed unlikely, given the description. He took a breath and moved carefully through the floor space, checking faces. No one there looked even vaguely like the man. Walking over to the windows he placed his face against them, shielding his eyes from the reflections.

Stijn's car was still there and still empty. He stepped back, frustrated. Had Stijn abandoned it?

He walked quickly back through the entrance hall, intending to go for the CCTV at least. On the way he took out his mobile and tried the incident room. The line was busy. He tried to remember Alan White's personal mobile number. It was in his organizer, but that was in his car. He looked back towards it and then his eyes saw the Days Inn motel sign at the far end of the building.

His heart began to quicken. He sprinted towards the place, trying the incident room number again as he ran. The line was still ringing as he slammed through the motel doors and pulled up in front of a teenage receptionist.

'A big guy,' he said, out of breath. 'Shaved head. Have you seen him?'

She looked at him as if he were mad and stepped back a pace, away from him.

'I'm police,' he said. The line was still ringing in his ear. He grappled with his left hand to extract his ID and flipped it at her. 'It's urgent. Have you seen a big guy pass through here?'

She frowned. 'Yes. About half an hour ago. Why?'

'Where? Where did he go?' His heart was thumping now. 'Is he still here?'

'I think so. He went through there.' She pointed to a set of double doors. 'I thought he was checked in.'

He cut the line on the phone and turned to run through them, then stopped, spinning back to her. 'Do you have anyone staying here called Stijn or Gatz?'

She frowned and started to look at a computer screen.

'Quick,' he said. 'Do you remember?'

'I only started a few hours ago. I don't know . . .' She was getting flustered. 'No,' she said, finally. 'No one by that name.'

'What about Hanley? Diana Hanley?'

'Yes. I remember her. She only came a few—'

'What room?'

'Number one-four-five. It's on the left at the end—'

'Call the police,' he said. 'Do you understand.' He looked at his mobile. There was no time to try the incident room again. 'You call nine-nine-nine now. Say a police officer is in danger. You got that?'

'But—'

'Now! Do it!'

He started to run, his mind emptying. The doors flashed past him, the numbers moving quickly up. He tucked the phone into his pocket, turned a corner and could hear it straight away, a muffled scream, suddenly cut off. He felt his insides lurch and sprinted the last few yards.

When he got to the door he could hear a TV on the other side, but no other noise. He felt his head reeling with adrenalin and tried to get the mobile into his pocket, but dropped it. He stood back from the door and began to shout a warning, at the same time kicking at it with all the force he could summon. The lock gave at once, splintering. He shouted again, 'This is the police. I am coming in.' The second kick sent the door slamming against the wall. He stepped forward into the room and took in the scene in front of him.

He was looking down a short passage, leading past the bathroom and toilet, to a main room. There was a TV on the cabinet in front of a double bed, a big wooden chair knocked over and on its side by the windows. A woman was sprawled on the floor at the foot of the bed, a man bent over her.

Bains's legs carried him forward. He couldn't tell if the woman was Hanley. There was blood all over her. He couldn't see her face. The man was almost kneeling by her. He was a huge, lumbering shape. It was Stijn. Unmistakably. He had a hand reached out and was touching her neck, gently, as if he were feeling for a pulse. As Bains came in he didn't react at all. Then he looked up, unsurprised. He straightened.

'Too late,' he said. 'She's gone.' He spoke the words sensitively, as if he were a doctor who had just finished an examination. 'There's nothing we can do for her now.'

Bains stopped and began to dig in his pocket for his ID. Stijn started to stand.

'Stay there!' Bains shouted. 'I know who you are.' Suddenly he felt afraid. The man reached full height. He was too big to handle. Bains saw a long filleting knife on the floor by the woman. 'Do as I say!' he shouted. 'Get down on the floor.' There was blood all over the floor, but Stijn looked spotless. He was wearing some kind of thin business suit, a pale shirt, a tie. He began to walk towards Bains.

Bains got the ID out just as he was closing on him. 'I'm police!' he screamed, then dropped the ID and lashed out at the man, both fists flying. His blows struck his face and chest, but Stijn walked straight through them, not even pausing. His hand caught hold of Bains's throat, thrusting him back against the wall of the room. He said nothing. Immediately Bains started to thrash at him – kicking, punching, pulling at the hand, clawing at his face. Stijn leaned back, out of range. Holding Bains's head against the wall he began to squeeze his windpipe. Bains started to choke.

It happened quicker than he thought it would. He could keep up the kicking and punches for only seconds before his strength was sapping, his vision blurring. There was no pain. Just the feeling of constriction, of mounting

289

pressure in his head. His sight went first, then his hearing. Moments before he blacked out he could feel his body banging off the wall, trying to twist from it, still fighting.

FORTY-TWO

She had been injured many times, over the years. So many bones broken, so many little scars. Most recently, in June 1997, she had taken a bullet in the thigh. She still limped from that, especially when she got tired. She was tired now. She had told Nicholas Hanley the scarring was from a car crash.

The same incident had given her a blood clot on the brain, requiring surgery – she had a small plate in her skull where they had opened it up – and a broken nose. But that was the third time someone had broken her nose. The first had been when Sara Collins had attacked her outside Mrs Kelly's chippy.

There had been many months in hospitals over the years. The physical stuff healed fast, the mental effects lagged. She had known a lot of psychiatrists, psychiatric nurses, therapists and quacks. She had spent so much time trying to piece together her personality that she had lost track of what the original looked like – if there had ever been one.

The pain caused by Sara Collins was still there though. She was the first. Her loss left a hole, a gaping, gnawing gap. If she concentrated she could still find it now, somewhere deep within her chest. The incident at the chippy cost her months off school. Not because of the injuries, but because she swallowed a couple of bottles of her mother's pills afterwards. A cry for help, they said. Swallowing her mother's pills was one of the few ways to get her mother's undivided attention.

Sara Collins had taught her to be patient with revenge.

That kind of patience was a civic virtue in Northern Ireland. When older boys picked on Sara she just took it. But she got them afterwards, no matter how long it took. She could bear grudges for years.

For a long time Helen Young wasn't strong enough. She planned all the others carefully, found out who they were (most admitted it to her face). She watched them, thought about it, took her time. But not Sara. It was another six years before she could think about taking her pound of flesh from Sara Collins.

The ringleader at the chippy had been Paddy Carroll, a boy two years older than her, a bit fat and a bit stupid. Helen waited for him with a half-brick, behind a hedge he passed on his way back from school. He went down with the first blow. She turned him over and flattened his nose, then left him.

She went through five others with the same kind of care. She identified them, traced their routes, waited until she had each of them alone. She was fourteen and some were older than her, so she made sure she had a weapon. It was small, childish stuff compared to what the adults were doing in 1976.

She was twenty before she grew out of Sara and her lessons. By then she was copying someone else – someone with more power. Sara Collins, Harry Singleton, James Martin: all her life she had copied other people, modelling herself on them, looking up to them, wishing she *were* them.

Being fiery, attractive and independent at the age of thirteen didn't stop Sara Collins from reverting to type. When Helen – now Sinead Collins – found her in 1982 she had two kids, a drunk, unemployed husband and lived on one of the worst estates in North Belfast. She was a threat to Sinead Collins, someone who knew her real identity, so there was a legitimate excuse. Sinead had someone torch their semi one weekend, while they were all back in Cross visiting relatives. She had wanted to do something more physical. She consoled herself with the fact that none of Sara Collins's possessions were recovered from the blaze. Sara moved back to Cross after that, into the same estate where she had grown up. Probably she was still there now.

As a child Sara had been interesting. It was easy to see how a weaker child might fall under her spell. She had been able to keep her emotions under control, pay out the anger slowly, using it. Helen had picked that up and passed it in turn to Sinead, and then to Karen. Karen knew all about the uses of anger.

She waited five minutes after Imran Akhtar entered the house before leaving her car and walking up the front path. He had driven straight here, making no attempts to watch for people following, taking no deviations. He wasn't used to this. As she politely knocked on the door she hoped that would make him sensible. The plan, at least to begin with, was just to talk to him.

The house was at the end of a cul-de-sac in Undercliffe, off Killinghall Drive, a lower-class mixed area. The entrance was screened from the semi next door by a huge leylandii hedge. She looked behind her as she waited for him to answer. Because the house was tucked back off the road there was no line of sight to the other houses in the street. She didn't know the address and hadn't seen it during her daily trawls through Nicholas Hanley's paperwork. The lights had been off when Akhtar had arrived; he had switched them on when he entered. His car was parked up right outside the short driveway, blocking it. She guessed his uncles might consider this place somewhere safe that he could go while they made the relevant phone calls and tried to find out what to do. Nick Hanley had told her Akhtar's uncles were from the same family as Ahmed and Mohammed Rouf. They were the poor, dirty cousins in Bradford. But they were still cousins.

Akhtar opened the door cautiously. There was a small porch above it, blocking his view from the upstairs windows, but she was sure he had tried to find out who it was before answering. He opened it stupidly, an inch at a time, waiting until there was enough room to see her face. He kept the light in the hallway off, making it more difficult to see anything in the darkness. He had his face almost flat against the wood and there was no chain. She moved her head sideways, looking downwards, forcing him to inch it open even further. She waited until she could see enough to know that the eyes in the crack were his. They widened as he recognized her. Immediately he tried to close the door. She put her shoulder to it.

The door slammed into him, knocking him back. She pushed it open and stepped through. He was staggering to his knees, moving back into the hallway, hand to his nose. There was blood running between his fingers. So far so good. Nice and easy. She got in and got the door closed behind her. But as he came back to his feet she saw him pull something from the back of his trousers. Before she could get halfway to him he was pointing it at her – a gun. She felt a shock like electricity, running through her. He was already trying to pull the trigger.

She closed the distance quickly, kicking his legs away whilst he was still pointing it at her. He collapsed to the floor, rolled, but held on to the weapon. He hit a small table with a telephone, knocking it over. Beside the table there was a wrought-iron lampstand, with no bulb or light shade. She picked it up with both hands, inverting it and swinging it over her head. The first try caught his legs and he shouted out. He was up, trying to get away from her, but at the same time trying to raise the gun. She swung a second time.

This one caught his head. In the darkness she couldn't see where. He went straight down again, arms and legs splayed. She stepped above him and swung it once more, bringing it into the middle of his chest. She heard something snap, but the blow brought him back to life immediately. He began to twist sideways, more clumsily now, without co-ordination. The gun dropped out of his fingers. She changed grip on the lampstand and swiped it sideways, striking him in the back of the head. His limbs jerked, but he was still trying to pull himself along the floor. She kicked the gun away and stepped closer.

'Lie still, Imran. Lie fucking still.' She looked into his eyes. They were shocked, unfocused, and there were flecks of spit and blood all over his face. His mouth was wide open, a rasping noise coming from the throat. She hit him again, then crouched over him and checked. His eyes were closed now; he was out of it.

FORTY-THREE

It felt like a split second of time. One moment Bains was wriggling against the wall, the blood supply to his brain cut off, the next he was gone. A moment later he was spluttering and choking on the floor, his eyes filled with stars. He had no consciousness of the gap between.

He concentrated on trying to get air through his throat. Even when he realized it was working, that he was breathing, that there was no need to panic about it, it was as though someone had pushed a dry tennis ball into his larynx. He began to retch.

He had eaten too little all day. Bile dribbled from his mouth to the carpet. He waited until he could see and hear again, then tried to turn his head. The headache was immediate, from one temple to the other, like someone driving a nail into his skull. He groaned and collapsed to the floor. Then he remembered what had happened. Where was Stijn?

He had to wait for minutes before he could move. This time he went slower. He pushed himself against the wall by the bathroom and let his eyes focus. The woman's body was still there, silent, immobile, naked, covered in blood. He looked towards the door of the hotel room. It was open. Through it, a long way away, he could hear someone shouting.

There was a breeze on his face. He found the source. The curtains were blowing and billowing. The window behind them was open. Stijn had gone. He had no idea how long ago. His ears picked out the words being shouted. It was the receptionist, or some other woman, shouting for him, asking if he was safe. He began to pull himself towards the door.

He got to it on hands and knees and looked along the corridor. She was standing with her hands to her mouth at the door into the corridor, staring at him. He held up a hand to her, feebly. He didn't want her to see the woman's body. 'Stay there,' he tried to say, but instead he began to cough.

He crawled into the corridor and pushed himself back against the wall. She took a few steps towards him, shaking.

'Have you called the police?' he asked her, but the words came out broken and twisted. She didn't understand. 'The police?' He had to shout to achieve a whisper.

She got it this time. She nodded.

'Good. Just wait.'

He let his head sink back against the wall and closed his eyes.

Things started to happen quickly. First a uniformed officer running up to him, checking him, stepping into the room. Then more of them, followed by the ambulance crews and detectives from the squad. By the time Bains could stand and move about the place was full of uniforms and panic.

Jon Hoyle arrived and started organizing everyone. The place was a crime scene and anyone who wasn't essential was contaminating it. He cleared everyone from the hotel except witnesses, medics and the two detectives he had brought with him. The exodus included all the guests from the hotel. They formed a small, sorry crowd, just outside the entrance. Bains stood inside reception and watched the snow falling onto them.

He spoke slowly to a medic, his voice a pained whisper.

297

His throat was sore, his head pounding with pain, but his breathing had returned to normal. The medic gave him an injection of some kind – a painkiller, an anti-inflammatory – he wasn't sure what.

Stijn had nipped the blood supply to his brain, blacking him out. You had to know how to do it – how to squeeze the veins instead of the windpipe. Constricting the windpipe took longer. The medic explained it all to Bains. He listened with half an ear, knowing already what had happened.

They wanted him to go to hospital, to check his brain, to do scans. He wouldn't let them. He could walk, he could talk, he could see and hear normally. The only problems he had were a splitting headache and a sore throat.

Jon Hoyle stood in front of him and asked him questions about it. Bains answered truthfully, his voice getting stronger as he went along, the shaking in his legs easing. The medic put that down to shock.

'You should have called, Pete,' Hoyle said. 'You shouldn't have gone in there alone.' His voice was low, serious. They still hadn't brought the body out of the room.

'Is it Diana Hanley?'

'Yes. She's in a bad way.' Hoyle was speaking quietly. 'He's done some nasty things to her.'

'She's alive?'

'For now. They can't get her out of there yet though. I'm not sure she'll last.'

'What did he do?'

Hoyle shook his head. 'Not sure. It's a mess.' He looked away. 'We'll wait for the report.'

'I think he went out through the window.'

'I see that. There are some prints out there, in the snow.

They head back to the car park. We've got people going through the whole service station now, getting everyone to check their car is still there. He either took a vehicle or ran on foot. His hire car is still out there.'

Outside, Bains could hear the beating of rotors in the distance.

'We've got the chopper up with infra-red,' Hoyle said. 'If he ran they'll find him. He can't go far.'

'But what do we do when we find him? He's not just going to tell us where they are.'

'We'll question him. We can't do anything else.'

Bains nodded. Hoyle put a hand on his shoulder.

'Are you OK, Pete? Can you breathe?'

'My throat feels swollen.'

'Your voice is funny. You need to go with the ambulance.'

'It's just bruising. He cut off the blood to incapacitate me.'

'He tried to kill you.'

'I don't think so. He could have done that, if he wanted.'

'The girl on reception was quick. Maybe he was disturbed by her. She remembered your name from your ID. If she hadn't given it God knows how long it would have taken to get here. She called then shouted for you from the corridor outside the room. She might have saved your life.'

Bains nodded. 'I'll thank her.' Hoyle was too easy with the conclusions. Bains didn't want to think Stijn had tried to kill him. He didn't want to think he had been that helpless or that it had been that close.

'You really should go with the ambulance,' Hoyle said again.

'I don't want to. I need to keep working. Karen is—'

'Karen? That's still a dirty word, Pete. We can find Anna Hart without you. Get in the ambulance. Do as you're told.' He walked off to talk to one of the other sergeants.

Bains stood by the main entrance to the hotel. The snowfall was thickening and he heard one of the uniforms say they were thinking of closing the M62. Whatever the medic had jabbed him with was taking effect, but not the way he wanted. His eyes were closing on him, forcing him to suck at the cold air to stay awake.

He watched them taping off the scene. A pleasant sensation was stealing through his limbs, relaxing him. The headache drew into the distance, then vanished. Jon Hoyle was still busy inside. Alan White hadn't arrived. He heard a sergeant report to Hoyle that no cars were stolen and X-Ray 99 – the air unit – had found nothing. He waited until Diana Hanley was brought out, surrounded by tubes and drips, and put straight into the back of the ambulance, then he walked back to his car.

He sat dreamily at the wheel. It must have been some kind of opiate they had given him. He hadn't asked for that. There was a bottle of water behind his seat. He drank thirstily, then waited for his head to clear so that he could drive. He would have to go home now. The medic had finished him.

FORTY-FOUR

Karen went through the house quickly. It was sparsely furnished, unoccupied. A sofa and chairs stood in the living room, but there was neither TV nor radio. When she took the telephone from the hallway and plugged it in the line was dead. In the kitchen she found that the electricity and water were on, but that the fridge was unplugged and open.

She took his gun – a Glock, modern, with fifteen rounds in the clip and the safety still on – and went upstairs. There were three bedrooms, only one of which had a bed in it, but no sheets. In the bathroom she found toilet paper, a tube of toothpaste, and an old bar of soap. That was it.

There were a number of ways she could do this. She had to think of the fastest.

The light in the hallway was poor. She dragged Akhtar into the lounge, then knelt down beside him and felt for his vital signs. He was breathing, his pulse slow. When she peeled back the eyelids his pupils dilated in response to the light. His heartbeat seemed strong enough, but there was already a swelling spreading across the right half of his face and head. His right eye was closed up. She checked his scalp for wounds and found large contusions in two places, but no cuts. She had split his lip, broken some teeth and gashed his jaw, just beneath his left ear. The blood was coming out in a sluggish trickle. The cut was about an inch and a half long. It wouldn't kill him.

She pulled the belt from his trousers and wrapped it around his wrists multiple times, pulling it tight and tying it off. Then she pushed him onto his back and slapped his face. His eyelids flickered for a moment, but there was no other response. She tried kicking him gently, in the side, then on his legs. When she bent down to shout into his ear his mouth closed slightly and she saw a trickle of blood run away from it. What was the matter with him?

She used the mug from the kitchen to throw cold water over his face. She went to the kitchen and back three times, but it didn't work. She squatted down beside him on the carpet. His breathing was now very shallow. She had been moving within a rarefied bubble since this started, too much adrenalin, but the bubble began to pop now. She began to get nervous.

She felt through his trousers for his testicles and twisted them sharply. His chest moved slightly, but not the eyes. She tried nipping his nose with her fingers, closing his lower jaw with her other hand. Even after a minute without air there was no response. She leaned forward quickly and placed her ear to his chest. The heartbeat was still there, but it was faint, stuttering. She panicked.

He was the only link she had to Hanley and Mairead. She had not hit him that hard. She had not even badly cut him. This couldn't be happening.

There was some blood-staining on his chest, just showing through the sweater he was wearing. She remembered the blow to the chest. She took the sweater off and saw more blood running away beneath it. She unbuttoned his shirt and stared in astonishment at the injury. The edge of the lampstand had caved in two or three ribs, right over his heart. There was a wound where it had struck, then a deep concave injury. The broken pieces of rib would be buried in his lungs, or worse, his heart. She quickly felt his neck with the tips of her fingers. There was no pulse at all. She couldn't believe it. She opened his mouth and placed her ear to it. She could feel nothing. He wasn't breathing. She could see his face beginning to turn blue.

She started to give him mouth to mouth, working shakily, trying to move her hands gently on his chest as she compressed it. After a few minutes she placed her ear against his chest, just above the wound. She pulled her face back quickly, stunned, blood all over the side of her cheek. His heart had stopped.

She tried resuscitation, over and over again, frantically trying to recall everything she had been taught ten years ago. She tried it for so long her mouth began to feel dirty and her wrists ached. But still he didn't respond.

She stood up, not knowing what to do, the panic really racing through her now. She should call an ambulance. She had to try to save his life. She looked down at him and for the first time could see it. He was inert, already inanimate. Moments ago he had been breathing. She crouched down and began to shout at him, picking the chest up by the ends of the shirt and shaking him. His body was completely flaccid. She stood back and began to cry.

FORTY-FIVE

'It's like a game,' her mother had told her. 'A kiddies' game. You just pretend to be someone you're not. After a while you get to like it.'

For a while it *had* been simple and easy, just like playing a game. Mairead had liked it. But all that had changed now. She felt miserable and frightened.

They were in a house in the middle of nowhere. She had no idea where she was. On the way she had tried to see street signs or place names through the windows, but for most of the journey it had been snowing and the windows were steamed up.

'Where are we?' she had asked, as soon as he had turned off the road and started bumping the Volvo down the dirt track.

'Somewhere safe,' he had replied. But he hadn't looked at her. There was something different about Nick. She didn't know what it was. She had been so relieved to see him she hadn't noticed it at first.

He had pulled his car in front of theirs, got out and run to her. She had almost cried when she realized who it was. She had wanted to hug him, to kiss him. They had thought he was dead. She had started to tell him about that, but he interrupted her.

'We've got to rush,' he said. 'Let's go. We're going in my car. Your mum's coming later.'

She had felt doubt right then. His tone of voice had given something away. She had told him where her mum was, objecting, but he said he already knew. He had already spoken to her, he said, on the mobile. 'She's with

Diana. She'll meet us in half an hour.' He smiled at her, hands in the air. 'What can I say?' he said. 'I'm doing what she has told me to do. She says get you out of this car, warm you up and we'll meet up later. You coming?'

It wasn't unusual for her mum to change plans, to leave Nick to pick her up or drop her off. So she had got out of the car and run to his. It was almost automatic. They had been living with him for over a year. They knew each other. But halfway down the road, as he locked the car doors, she had felt the doubt again.

'What's going on, Nick?' she had asked.

'Nothing, Rach. You're safe now.'

And again he hadn't looked at her as he spoke.

She had tried not to think about it, to trust him, but the euphoria at seeing him hadn't lasted long. Her mouth was sore, her front teeth loose and wobbly, her nose throbbing and bleeding. She had a headache and she was hungry and cold. The clothes she was wearing felt damp and awkward. And behind all this there were the things that had happened to them. She didn't want to think about them, but she wanted to know what was going on.

She had started to tell him about it all, speaking quickly, excitedly. She had got as far as them escaping through the abbey grounds when she realized he was shaking his head furiously, hands pressing into the steering wheel so that his knuckles were white.

'I can't listen to it,' he had whispered. 'Please, Rachel, I can't listen to it.'

So she had shut up.

Her mother had said there were only three rules. The first was 'You are not lying'.

'If you think of yourself as lying, pretending, making it up, then you won't be good at it,' she had said. 'You have to think all the time that you are not lying, that this is who you are.' The rule worked well. When, for instance, kids at school asked her about her eighth birthday party (she had said they spent it with Nick, but hadn't thought to work out how that could have happened) instead of becoming flustered and trying to make more things up she had just said she couldn't remember more than that. People forgot things. That was their problem, not hers.

Rule two appeared confusing, alongside rule one: 'If you have to lie, keep as close as possible to the truth'. Never completely make it up, never pretend you know something you don't. Mairead understood that well enough. She had only got into difficulty about her eighth birthday because she had made up something completely false about it.

Rule three – the golden rule – was an absolute: 'Never ever stop unless I tell you it is safe'. She had asked how her mum would know whether it was safe or not, but that had been more complicated. 'It's a trust thing, Mairead,' she had said. 'You have to trust me on this. Sometimes people might try to trick you. Remember the rule. *Never ever stop.*'

So she was doing that now. Nick had called her Rachel, her mum wasn't here to tell her to stop, so she was Rachel again.

Acting like Rachel wasn't hard. As far as she was aware there was no difference between Rachel and Mairead except the names. For her mum it was different. When her mum had changed her name she had become completely different.

She looked out of the window onto a landscape steadily sinking under snow and felt the tears starting again. She had spent nearly the whole day in tears and her eyes were red and sore. He had said her mum would join them in half an hour, but it had taken them half an hour to get here. That was at least two hours ago. She was upstairs, in the room where he had said she should wait. Downstairs she could hear him making calls on a mobile phone. Sometimes he raised his voice and she could make out a few words clearly, but mostly it was just a mumble. She couldn't tell who he was talking to.

They had travelled, she knew, by the motorway, the M62. She had even seen the sign at the top of the pass – 'England's Highest Motorway'. That meant they were somewhere in Lancashire, she thought. He had turned off at the other side of the hills and taken roads she hadn't recognized, finally ending up on a twisting single-lane road. The snow had thickened as they got higher. Before they reached the turn-off to the dirt track leading to this place the going had become very slow. Once or twice the wheels had got stuck and slipped. He had told her that the road ahead was closed, because of snow. So wherever they were, it was isolated, cut off.

At the turn-off she had looked back through the rear window and seen the snow gathering in growing drifts jutting into the road. She had wondered how her mum was going to get there, but said nothing. By then she had known something was wrong. She was trying not to ask him questions. If she asked him questions he might start asking her questions, or get annoyed with her. She had never seen him angry, and wondered if he *could* be, but she didn't want to risk it.

She was so hungry her head felt dizzy. The pains in her stomach had gone away, but she was thirsty all the time, even though he had given her a drink of water when she asked for one – about an hour ago. She looked around the room. He had not locked the door. It looked no different to the rest of the place – shabby, worn, falling to pieces.

There were large patches in the ceiling where the plaster had come off. The floor looked as though it had not been cleaned in months. There was an old iron bed frame, but no mattress. The window she was sitting at had a deep sill, so she could tuck herself right into it. The pane of glass was cold against her arm, but she didn't mind that.

The place was probably an old farm. There had been three or four buildings beside the one they had run to. She guessed it was a long time since anyone had lived here, but there was still electricity and water. She tried to think what Rachel Hart would do in this kind of situation.

Not just sit around. She got off the sill, walked over to the door and opened it. She was at the top of the building and there were two flights of stairs leading back down, one at the end of a long, narrow corridor. She started to walk down the nearest flight. The stairs were uncarpeted and creaked immediately, but she ignored that. She was Rachel Hart, she had done nothing wrong – there was no need for her to skulk around. As she reached the landing on the second floor she could hear his voice more clearly. She shouted out for him.

He came moments later, looking flustered and slightly annoyed.

'I asked you to stay up there, Rachel. I have to make calls. This is important.'

She held her ground, staring at him. 'You told me Mummy would be here.'

He stood in front of her, the mobile in his hand, obviously wanting to get back to it. She watched him struggling with something in his head – running his free hand through his hair, a pained expression on his face – then he sighed.

'OK,' he said. 'Let's go downstairs and talk about it.'

308

The place was freezing downstairs. The snow had already piled so high against one of the windows that she could see it. The room would have been a kind of living room, when people were living there. There was an old table with four chairs, one of them with a broken leg, and, in front of a huge old hearth and chimney breast, a threadbare green sofa. There was wood and paper piled up in the fireplace. She asked him to light it. He looked unsure.

'Is that a good idea? There's electric radiators in every room. I've switched them on. It will just take time to heat through. The fire will make smoke. People will be able to see the smoke.'

'What people, Nick?'

He sucked at his teeth. 'You know already, Rachel. There are some nasty people out there. You know what's going on.'

She looked away from him, biting her lip. 'I don't know,' she said. 'I only know what happened to us. Where is Mummy?'

He sat down at one of the chairs by the table. 'Sit down, Rachel. We have to talk about this.'

'I need some food.'

He looked panicky for a moment.

'I haven't eaten all day,' she added.

'You'll be OK,' he said. 'You won't die.'

'Is there any food?'

'I don't know. I haven't looked.'

'What is this place?'

'Somewhere safe. I told you.'

'Is Mummy coming?'

He said nothing.

'You told me she was coming,' she said.

'I hope she is. Eventually. I don't know what to say,

Rachel. I don't really know what's happening. Everything is very confusing.'

'We were meant to be getting a flight out of here.'

He looked away from her, guilt written all over his face.

'You were going to meet us,' she said. 'Instead . . . instead we had a crash . . .' She sat down on the sofa. She didn't know how much to tell him. 'Why do we need to hide?' she asked, instead.

He sighed again. 'We've screwed some things up, Rach. Me *and* your mum. That's why we need to hide. We're all in danger. I'm trying to work things out. That's why I need to make the phone calls, why you have to let me do that. I'm trying to solve things, to get us all back together.' He looked at the floor as he spoke.

'Mum as well?'

'Yes. If I can. But you know there are problems, Rachel.' He looked up at her.

He was fifty years old, about three inches shorter than her mum and slightly fatter, with grey hair that he dyed dark brown. Ordinarily he shaved every day except Saturdays and Sundays. Today she could see a thick stubble on his chin. In places the stubble was grey or white. His face looked tired, stressed and slightly greasy, with dark rims under his eyes. She hadn't seen him like that before. Usually he was relaxed, always ready to make a joke and tactile. He had hardly touched her since she had got into his car. He had only ever been generous, caring and affectionate with her, had never shouted at her or told her off. He left that to her mum. She was sometimes quite poor at judging what adults were feeling, sometimes spot on. Right now she thought he looked hurt. She felt as if she must have hurt him but didn't know how.

'I don't know what problems there are, Nick,' she said.

'But I'm glad to see you. I'm frightened as well though. I want to see Mum.'

'Well, your mum should have thought of that, shouldn't she?'

He sounded bitter. She wondered what he knew about them. Would it matter if he knew they had changed their names?

'Is she coming or not?'

'I don't know.'

She started to cry. She didn't know what to say to him, didn't know what he knew, didn't know what she should do for the best. There was nothing she could do but cry.

He came over to her and hugged her, but as she cried into his shoulder she could feel that he was hugging her differently. 'I love you, Rachel,' he whispered into her ear. 'You know that, don't you?'

She nodded, still crying.

'If I ask you a question will you promise to tell me the truth?'

She nodded again, without changing position, her mind alive with danger signals. He was sitting alongside her on the sofa now. He pushed her away from him gently, so that he could look into her eyes. She looked straight back at him, wiping the tears away.

'Do you know what is going on?' he asked her.

She frowned. The question was unclear.

He rephrased it. 'Do you know who you are? Do you know who you really are?'

She frowned again, her heart beating faster. Rule number three. The golden rule.

'You know what I mean, don't you?' he said. He was speaking very slowly, very gently. 'If you tell me the truth nothing will happen to you. I will still love you, Rachel. You are not to blame for any of this. What is between you and me will always be there.' He was staring into her eyes. 'Can you tell me who you really are?'

She let the tears start again, still keeping her eyes locked on his. 'You're frightening me, Nick. What do you mean? You know who I am.'

She held his gaze as he chewed his bottom lip, frowning deeply.

'Tell me who you are,' he said finally.

'You know who I am.'

'Tell me.'

She really began to cry. 'I'm Rachel Hart, Nick. You know that.'

He gave in and let her hug him, but she could feel that he was still thinking about it, disturbed.

They sat like that until she became aware of a scratching noise from the door. Probably it had been going on for some time. She moved away from him.

'What's that?' she asked, glad of the distraction. She could hear a mewing now, a pathetic plaintive noise. 'There's a cat somewhere.'

They walked to the door together and opened it. A cloud of fine snowflakes blew into their faces on the back of an icy blast of wind. A small, black and white cat ran past them and jumped onto the sofa. She ran to it immediately. It was freezing and looked half starved, but it pushed itself against her, arching its back, purring.

'You have to find some food for it, Nick,' she cried out. 'Even if you don't feed me, you can't let an animal die.'

He stood at the door watching her. He looked sad and confused.

'I'll feed you both,' he said.

FORTY-SIX

Bains felt dead on his feet as he opened the door to his home. He stepped inside warily, expecting the place to have been turned upside down by the spooks, but there was no sign that they had been in. He switched the lights on in each room and looked around. Everything was as it should have been.

Downstairs, he switched the lights off and sat down in the chair in the back room. There were too many thoughts flying through his head. He couldn't make sense of it all. He needed to eat something, check the time, maybe let himself sleep a little. After that he could think.

Through the patio doors he could see straight down his lawn to the bottom of the garden, to where the swimming pool had been. He had got contractors to fill it in nearly a year ago. There was a rockery there now, looking bleak and brown, like the pile of earth on a fresh grave.

His daughter had drowned in the pool. Millie. She had been three years old and nearly three and a half feet tall. That was 30 July 1989. A month later, to the day, his wife – staying with her parents at the time – had taken an overdose. They hadn't discovered her until it was too late. Ten years ago.

Only meeting Karen and Mairead had given him enough strength to get the pool filled in. He had even started to think about moving out of this place. The house – a massive detached mansion in Heaton, still partly owned by his father's company – was far too big for him. But there was a cord fixing him to it, a chain of guilt. He needed to have the memories pushed into his face, each and every day. Otherwise he would forget about them, forget what he had done and get on with his life. But he didn't want that. It was bad enough that they were dead.

He ran his hands through his hair. He needed to wash it, he needed to shave. He let his head sink back. Within moments he was sleeping.

He awoke because he could hear somebody crying. For a few seconds he didn't know where he was. Not in his bedroom. His eyes picked out the detail. He was in the armchair in the back room, the patio doors were open and there was a cold breeze on his face. He squinted into the gloom, turned his head slightly and she was standing there, right in front of him.

He didn't react. He thought it was a dream. She was dressed in some kind of overalls, her hair cut short like it had been in the photo of Anna Hart. Just standing there, her hands at her sides, weeping.

He stood up. 'Karen?'

She didn't reply. He stepped quickly towards her, frightened she would vanish, then all at once realized he was awake, that it was real.

'Jesus! Karen!' He stopped in his tracks, his whole body flooded with relief.

'I need your help, Pete,' she said, whispering. 'Please. I need help.' She was trying to control herself, but it was like something had broken inside her. She couldn't stop crying.

He closed his arms around her. 'It's OK, Karen,' he whispered.

'I've fucked everything up,' she managed. 'All my life. I've screwed up everything. But it's worse now.'

314

He didn't say anything. He held her tightly, pressing his hands into her back. She pushed her head into his neck and let it come out. She couldn't stop it.

'I've lost Mairead,' she gasped. 'They've taken her. I don't know what I can do.'

He pushed back from her, feeling the fear grip him. 'You've lost her?' he heard himself repeat it. But she was really sobbing now, pulling herself towards him and crying her heart out.

There was a big white sofa in the room where they used to sit to watch DVDs – all three of them. She let him place her on it and switch the lights on. He sucked his breath in as he looked at her. He told her she was thinner and she could see him trying to control his reactions. She knew how she looked; too thin, with dirty hair and a face covered with bruises and cuts. There was caked blood up her nostrils. As she cried she could feel it running in streaks down her face.

'What happened to you, Karen? What happened?' His voice sounded hoarse. He sat on the edge of the sofa, a hand on her leg. She could see him inspecting her face and body, his eyes narrowing.

'It doesn't matter,' she said. 'It wasn't me. All this . . .' She gestured with her hand to her injured face and body. 'All this happened to someone else. Mairead is all that matters. You have to help me.'

'I will. But you need to tell me what happened.'

She started to tell him, crying still, wiping her eyes on her sleeve. She had to stop every second sentence and catch her breath. She told him she had been working undercover, for over eighteen months. Mairead had been with her.

'I know that,' he said.

'I was this stupid, upper-class bitch called Anna Hart,' she said. 'Mairead was Rachel Hart.'

'I know.'

She stopped. 'How do you know?'

'I was on the squad looking for you. The SIO told me.'

'They knew it was me?'

'Just the SIO. He told me when I found out. We had a photo from your luggage. You were on a beach somewhere. It took me a while to realize it was you.'

'Who told the SIO?'

'He has Sutherland up there with him.'

She wiped her eyes. 'If I tell you more, Pete,' she said, 'you have to promise me you will not go to Sutherland with it.'

'Don't be stupid.' He reached his hand over and took hold of hers. He sounded offended. 'You know I wouldn't do that. We'll do what you think is best.'

She told him about Nicholas Hanley, the trip they had planned, the taxi drive from the hotel, the gunman, the abattoir, the rape, the visit to Diana Hanley's, and Mairead's disappearance. She gave him the whole tale, trying to tell it dispassionately, looking at her knees as she spoke, not at him. The only thing she left out was Akhtar. She didn't know what to do about that.

When she stopped he looked stunned.

'You have to help,' she said again. She closed her hand over his.

He couldn't speak. She could see he was struggling with his emotions.

'You have to forget the detail, Pete. We haven't time for it. If you are on the squad there are things you can do.'

He nodded, swallowing hard.

'I've tried everything I know,' she said. 'I've run out of ideas. Maybe if you take the name of this man to your inquiry – Stijn – maybe you will be able to get something from that.'

He shook his head grimly. 'We already know about him.'

'You know about Stijn?'

'Yes. His real name is Jan Gatz.' He stood up and rubbed his throat. 'I ran in to him earlier,' he said. 'I was trying to trace Diana Hanley. There's a connection between them. They agreed to meet at Hartshead Moor services, I think. I walked in on their meeting.'

He told her what had happened, pacing up and down as he spoke. 'He must have been trying to get information from Diana Hanley,' he said finally. 'They wouldn't tell me what he had done to her.'

'Is she alive?'

'She was when I left. But she was in a bad way. Stijn left her for dead.'

'You should have gone to the hospital.'

He dismissed the idea. 'I'm fine. It's nothing. Not compared to what . . .' He broke off, unable to voice it. 'We have to work out who has Mairead,' he said. 'That's the first priority.'

'I told you who has her. Nicholas Hanley. That's why I went for his sister.'

'He's dead, Karen. I've had a preliminary autopsy on him.'

'Only his sister identified him. She was lying.'

He frowned. 'You're guessing that,' he said. 'He has a business partner called Imran Akhtar. He identified him as well.'

'I know. I tried to find Akhtar. I spoke to his wife . . .'

'The inquiry wants him, too. We've lost him.'

'Yes.' She paused. She didn't want to lie to him. 'I've lost him as well.' It wasn't completely false. 'Akhtar was dirty,' she continued. 'He was with Stijn in Pudsey. They were connected.'

'You think Akhtar might be dead?'

'Dead? Why?' She tried not to sound edgy.

'You said he *was* dirty.'

She looked away. 'You know what I mean.'

'Why do you think Hanley is alive?'

'Because Stijn heard the radio coverage about him being dead but was still prepared to do that to me in order to find out where Hanley was. He didn't do it for pleasure.' She almost spat the words.

Bains walked over to the patio doors, thrusting his hands in his pockets. 'I feel sick,' he said. 'I can't think about it.'

'It's not important.'

'It is.' He leaned his hands against the door frame. She waited for him to control it. 'I have Stijn on CCTV from Spencer Tower,' he said, turning to face her. 'He torched the place. That's almost certain. Akhtar might have been with him. There were images of someone who looked like Akhtar as well. Why would Stijn be looking for Hanley if he thought he had just killed him?'

'Because he knew it wasn't Hanley. He *must* have known it wasn't Hanley.'

'So who was thrown from Spencer Tower?'

'I don't know. Does it matter? Someone else. You only think it's Hanley because of Akhtar and his sister.'

'And you think his sister is in on it. But Stijn almost killed her. That doesn't make sense to me. None of it makes sense. They told me it was all about drugs money. Is that true? Why were you attached to Hanley?'

'He was laundering funds. They wanted me to identify the beneficiaries of high-value property transactions which they thought were laundering operations. They told me it would be easy, no risk.' She laughed bitterly. 'No risk. *An easy job*. I must be fucking mad.'

'Did you find out?'

'Yes. He was layering funds for two brothers from Pakistan: Ahmed and Mohammed Rouf.'

'Deliberately?'

She shrugged. 'Maybe he didn't realize at first. He knew in the end though.'

'Stijn is connected to the Roufs. They told me that.'

'Obviously.'

'And that's what this is about?' he asked. 'That's why people are dying?'

'People die for less.'

'Less than what?'

'The Roufs are big. The funds Hanley was moving are only a small proportion of it. But it's not just the quantities, it's what they do with it. They have bigger people leaning over them, people who don't give a shit what they do. I should have got out when I found out it was them.' She held her head in her hands. 'Some of the money was funding terrorism. Extreme Arab stuff. They should have told me that before they put me in. Sutherland should have said . . .'

'Could Stijn have been sent to kill all of you? One of Sutherland's men said he might be a "cleaner".'

She looked confused. 'I don't know. If they wanted to kill Hanley, why stage his death and set fire to the body? It sounds to me like they were trying to fool you it was him.'

'With his sister in on it?'

'Yes.'

'That doesn't work. If she was in on it, why would Stijn then try to kill her?'

'Nothing works. If her brother was in on it, why would Stijn be trying to find him? I don't know the answers.

319

That's why I'm here. Because I'm desperate.' She was close to tears again.

He sat down on the sofa, a little further away from her. 'But even if Hanley is alive,' he said. 'Why kidnap Mairead?'

'I don't know that either,' she said. 'But we're wasting time thinking about it. You have to believe me. Mairead can *only* be with Nicholas Hanley. At first, when the workmen told me about it, I thought she must have gone off with James. But then—'

'James?'

'James Martin.'

Bains nodded. He knew who he was.

'But I've checked that. He's in prison in Northern Ireland. Then I thought it must be you.' A sob caught in her throat. 'You, her dad and Hanley are the only people she would run to like that.'

'She was close to Hanley?'

She nodded, unable to look at him. 'I shouldn't have taken her. I know that . . .'

'You shouldn't have gone at all.'

'I know.' She was silent, eyes downcast, her limbs trembling.

'So Mairead trusts him? Is that it?'

She nodded. 'They got on like you two used to . . . they got on great. She didn't know he was the target. She thought he was just someone I met at the gallery. She treated him like he was her father.'

'And you? Were you close to him?' His lips twisted as he asked the question.

She shook her head. 'Please. I feel like a slut . . .' The tears were coming again. 'I don't know what's wrong with me. You were right. I need help for it.'

He cleared his throat. 'I don't understand it,' he said. 'I

don't get any of it. But I know what we have to do. You have to go to Sutherland. That's the only thing you can do.'

She stood up at once. 'You promised me—'

'I didn't say—'

'I will leave here now, right now. I came because you were the only person I could trust.' She was shouting at him.

He stood up next to her, placing a hand on her shoulder. 'I'm not going to do anything,' he said. 'I love you, Karen. I wouldn't do anything to hurt you. Not ever.'

He touched her again, on the arm. 'I won't do anything you don't want me to,' he said. 'You must know that. But you tell me what options we have.'

FORTY-SEVEN

The kitchen was as ramshackle as the rest of the farm. The gas supply was a canister, which was empty. There was no kettle or pans. There were cupboards with broken doors, in one of which they found rusting crockery, a tin opener, old plates and three tins of food: Fray Bentos steak chunks; 'value' baked beans; and Del Monte pineapple rings in syrup.

'It's a whole meal,' Nick said. 'Beans and steak followed by pineapple chunks.'

She felt sick thinking about it. 'How do we heat it?'

'That's a good point.' He searched around. 'We could put them on plates in the oven. The oven runs on electricity, I think.

'Give the meat to the cat,' she said. 'I'll eat the pineapple rings.'

The cat's fur was thick and clean, but there was little fat beneath it, and they could see an indentation around the neck, where a collar had once been.

'The poor thing must have belonged to the people who lived here,' she said, as he opened the cans. 'They must have abandoned it.'

'It looks healthy enough.'

'It's too thin, Nick. Open your eyes.'

'There haven't been people living here for months. It hasn't starved to death. It must be living on something.'

'Cats are survivors,' she said, quoting her mum. 'They know how to adapt.' She started missing her then, and looked over to where Nick was forking smelly chunks of steak in gravy onto a plate. At her feet the cat

322

was going crazy, rubbing up against her, purring. She stroked it.

'Why did they move out of here?' she asked. She had to get him to talk more. She had to find out where they were.

'I don't know,' he said. 'They sold up. Probably it was difficult to make a living up here.'

'Did you buy the place off them?'

'The company did.'

'Are you trying to sell it?'

'No. We own it.'

'Why?'

He turned round and looked down at her. 'Shall we feed the cat?' he asked.

The animal was excited about the food. It ran to the plate, sniffed, tasted – but it wouldn't eat the stuff.

'It knows it's shit,' she said.

'There's nothing wrong with it. Food keeps for years in cans.'

'It was shit when it went into the can.'

'Stop swearing.'

She laughed. '*Shit* isn't a swear word, Nick. *Fuck* is a swear word.'

'You know what I mean.'

He passed her a plate with a few slices of pineapple on it, then washed a fork for her. There was no table in the kitchen so she sat on the floor by the cat, which was still inspecting the meat.

'They get used to eating mice,' Nick said. He leaned against the wall. 'If you let them get wild, they learn to fend for themselves, then they stop trusting the food you give them.'

'It doesn't seem like a good survival technique,' she said.

323

'Sometimes it is, sometimes it isn't. Depends on the mouse population.'

'Out here she won't have any problems.' She forked a ring of pineapple into her mouth. It tasted sugary and soft, but not very much like pineapple.

Nick watched her, a faint smile playing at the corners of his mouth. He liked her, she knew that. Normally she could get whatever she wanted out of him.

'Are you going to tell me what's going on?' she asked.

'I don't know what's going on,' he said. 'If I knew I would tell you.'

'We're not staying in this place tonight, are we?'

He looked around. 'No.' He seemed vague. 'I hope not.'

'Can they find us here?'

'They?'

'The people you're worried about.'

His face darkened. 'No. No one knows about this. Except Diana.'

'Is she coming over?'

He frowned at her. 'You are your mother's daughter,' he said. 'I know what you're trying to do.'

'Do you?'

Her front teeth were sore when she chewed. She opened her mouth and pointed to them. 'That man hit me this morning,' she said, calmly. 'Right here. Not the one who died, but the big one. I've never been hit so hard.'

He shifted position uncomfortably. His expression was full of guilt. 'I'm sorry, Rachel,' he said. 'I haven't been thinking straight . . .'

'It was interesting,' she continued. 'There was a lot of pain and blood at first, from the split lip and the loose teeth—'

'Your teeth are loose?'

'Yes. Do you want to see?'

He turned away from her, as if squeamish. She knew he was blaming himself, but couldn't work out why.

He paced over to the kitchen window and gazed into the darkness. 'I should take you to a doctor,' he said. 'This is all ridiculous.'

'After a while I got used to the pain,' she went on. 'I started to think about it, instead of just reacting to it, and then it wasn't so bad.'

He squatted beside her. 'Show me.'

She opened her mouth. 'Don't touch them,' she warned.

'Do they still hurt or feel loose?'

'Yes. But it's not important. They tighten up. Nadine Clough at school fell off her bike last month and almost knocked hers out. She could move them around like pegs. Mrs Ashton said they would tighten up within days and they did. Mine will be OK.'

He stood up. 'You sound like your mother,' he said. She stopped eating. His voice sounded sad again. 'I really loved your mum, Rachel. You know that?'

She nodded, wondering about the past tense.

'I thought she and I were in love with each other. That's why I brought you both into my home. I've never felt for anyone what I felt for your mum. My life was a waste of time before she came.' He looked like he was going to start crying.

'She's not gone, Nick. She was looking for you. That's what we were doing. She thought you must be in danger. She was trying to help.'

He turned away from her and stood by the cooker, breathing heavily. 'She is gone,' he said, after a while. His voice sounded faint.

'I know the name of the one who hit me,' she said. 'He was called Stijn. I heard the other one call him that.'

He brought a hand across his eyes, trying to hide the action, then looked back at her. Behind him, through the kitchen window, she saw a pattern of light flicker across the ceiling.

'I know,' he said. 'I know who it was.'

How did he know? She heard alarm bells in her head. The light outside turned into a beam. 'I think there's a car on the road,' she said quickly, standing up. He looked behind, out through the window.

'You're right. Quick. Let's get upstairs. We need to know who it is.'

They ran through the front room and up to the first floor. There was a window from what would have been one of the bedrooms, facing out towards the track into the place. They rubbed the condensation from it and stared through, so close their faces were almost touching.

They saw a car bumping up the road, turning slowly through the snowdrifts.

'It can't be going straight on,' Nick said. He sounded worried. 'The road ahead is closed.'

It turned onto their track.

'It could be Diana,' she said. 'Or Mum.'

He glanced at her. 'It won't be your mum,' he said. 'It could be Diana.'

Why not? Why not her mum? She moved away from him slightly. They watched the headlights pick out their own car.

'It's a Land Rover,' Nick said.

It pulled up behind his own car and stopped.

'I think it is Diana's car, the one she hired.' He was squinting, trying to read the registration plate.

The headlights went off, the engine stopped and the

driver's door opened. Someone got out. Without the headlights it was difficult to see. The figure switched on a torch and shone it at the ground, then walked slowly towards the house, stepping carefully through the snow. Too big to be his sister. Mairead heard him catch his breath.

'Shit!'

She watched the figure walk into the light from the house. She felt very cold and very frightened. 'It's the man who hit me,' she said. The man who had hurt her mum. The man who had thrown the bucket of blood over her. She pulled away from the window. She couldn't even bear to look at him.

Nick was rigid, silent. Suddenly he too moved away from the window. 'How can he have found us? Shit! Shit! Shit!'

He knew who the man was. He was frightened of him. She watched him walk quickly to the room door, then back again, hands flat against his face. He was shaking from head to foot. Downstairs the man started to knock at the door.

'I don't know what to do,' he whimpered. 'I don't know what to do.' He was panicking, face full of fear.

She started to cry. 'We have to run,' she said.

'We can't run! We're in the middle of nowhere. He'll catch us immediately. I'll have to speak to him. I'll have to.' He turned to her. 'I don't know whether I can control this, Rachel. If anything happens you will have to run. I'll try to hold him up. We're in a place called High Top. The nearest village is called Delph. It's in Lancashire.'

'We have to call the police, Nick. You have to . . .'

'No. We can't do that.' He looked at her, face quivering. 'You don't understand, Rachel. We can't call the police. Not yet . . .'

He walked out of the room, leaving her. She followed him to the stairs and crouched there, listening, waiting to see what happened. She heard him cross the room and drag the front door open.

'Hello, Nick.' The same accent, the same high-pitched voice. She heard him step in. 'I'm not disturbing you, am I?'

'How did you . . . why are you . . . how . . . ?'

'How did I find you? Your sister told me. Shut the door. It's going to be a cold night.'

The door closed.

'My sister? Where is she? Is that her car you're in?'

'Yes. I'm returning it. I thought she'd be here with you by now. Wasn't that the plan?'

'How did you get her car?'

'I think I should be the one asking questions, Nick.'

'What do you want?'

'That's not very welcoming. It took me quite an effort to find this place. You're a clever man. To a point.'

'What do you want?' Nick sounded desperate, his voice wavering.

'Are they here?'

'They?'

'Don't fuck with me—'

'Rachel is here.'

'Rachel? You mean Sharpe?'

'Yes.'

She felt her heart jump into her mouth.

'You don't even know her first name, do you?'

'Her name is Rachel.'

'Her real name.'

'No.'

She looked behind her, along the passageway leading to the other side of the house. Could she run now, open a

328

window, get out? They were high up in the moors. She had seen no houses on the way. How far down the valley to the nearest house?

'Where's the other one – her fucking mother?'

'I don't know.'

'Don't lie.'

'I'm not. She's not here. You need to call your boss, Stijn. You don't know what's going on here.'

She heard some rapid movement, a scuffle of feet on the floor, then suddenly the cat appeared, bolting up the stairs towards her.

'Fucking cats. I hate cats.'

The animal ran straight past her, along the passageway.

'What was the plan then?' The chairs by the table scraped on the floor. One of them was sitting down. 'Just let me know, out of interest.'

'You need to call Ahmed Rouf, Stijn. This is out of your hands now.'

'Is that right?'

There was a long silence.

'Yes,' Nick said finally. 'We've been speaking to him.'

'We?'

'Diana and myself.'

Stijn laughed. 'Is that a fact?'

'Yes. We have an arrangement.'

'I've heard about it. So where are the bonds?'

'Not here.'

'No?'

'No.'

'Where then?'

'You don't need to know that.'

'I do actually. That's why I'm here.'

Another silence.

'They're with Diana. Are you going to call Rouf?'

'I don't think so. Not until I've some positive news for him.'

'What do you mean?'

'Not until I know where they are.'

'They're not here.' Nick's voice was rising.

'So you say.'

'They're with my sister.'

'If that's true then it will be a great pity.'

'Why do you say that?'

The chair moved again.

'You're well out of your depth, Hanley. You say the bitch isn't here?'

'No.'

'And the kid's upstairs?'

'Yes. Leave her out of it. I'm warning you.'

Another laugh from Stijn. 'You brought her into it, not me.'

'Where are you going?'

'To check. You stay here.'

FORTY-EIGHT

'You have to get my mobile. I lost it in the taxi, but Hanley won't know that. He will try to call me on it.'

Bains stood by the side of the bathtub and watched her.

'You have to get my mobile,' she said again. 'Do you know where it is?'

She was showering, the door to the shower wide open, as if she lived there with him, as if the last eighteen months hadn't happened.

'I know where it is,' he replied. 'It was taken from the rear of the taxi. Unless it's already gone to technical services, it's in a box in the incident room at Weetwood. But that's not the right way to go about this.'

He watched her hand movements, rubbing the soap in, spreading the hot water over her bruised skin. She was moving urgently, concentrating, but unconcerned about his presence. He had been about to shut the door on her and leave her to it, but she insisted there was no time for that. So they were arguing about it still, as she cleaned herself.

'You are washing evidence,' he said. 'You shouldn't be doing this, Karen.'

She laughed, the water running into her eyes and down her chest. 'Evidence? This will never get to court.'

'You don't know that.'

'I do. Even if we caught up with him, even if we took him alive, I would never give evidence against him. You know how it works. Rape victims get mugged in court.'

'There's no other way to do it. If you do nothing you

let him get away with it. You have to report it. You have to—'

'You want me to behave like some fucking moaning wash-out, weeping on a rape liaison officer's shoulder? You want me to place my faith and confidence in the forces of law and order? You're making me laugh, Pete. We know how that works. I'll deal with it myself.'

'You're a police officer. You can't—'

'*You're* a police officer. I used to be. And all that means is we know how it works. Spare me, Pete. I couldn't give a shit about the world's rape victims, I couldn't give a shit about justice. I'm thinking of me. I wouldn't give him the pleasure. Anna Hart is going to have to live with this one.'

She spoke about Hart as if she were someone else entirely.

'We *are* going to catch him,' Bains said. 'He's distinctive.'

'He might not want to walk into custody.'

He recognized the way she was thinking. 'We are going to take him *alive*,' he said. 'We are going to arrest him.'

She didn't reply, busy soaping between her legs. 'You have to get my mobile,' she said again. 'Hanley will call me. He could be trying to call me now. He won't know I don't have a mobile with me.' She had already tried calling Hanley's mobile number. The line was dead. Bains thought that, if Hanley were alive, pretending he were dead, he wouldn't be so stupid as to have kept his own mobile. He would get another.

'That's all guesswork, Karen,' he said. 'Maybe he knows about the taxi, and the kidnap. Maybe he was in on it. You're making assumptions . . .'

'No, I know this man. He wouldn't hurt Mairead. He loves her. If he has taken her it must be because he wants something from me. If he has found out who I am then maybe he thinks I am a threat – because of what I know about him. Maybe he thinks he has to do a deal with me. I don't think he would try to hurt me. He will call me. We have to get my mobile back.'

'He is already hurting Mairead – if he has taken her from her mother and is thinking of using her to get something. That's not how you act towards people you love. You're not thinking clearly, Karen. This man is wrapped up in money-laundering for terrorists.'

'I am thinking clearly.' She switched the water off and stepped out, dripping. He passed her a towel. 'You don't know him like I do. He's a harmless idiot with more money than sense. He can't even lie properly. He has a moral objection to lying.' She smirked at the idea. 'He got pulled into all this by his sister. She was with one of the Roufs for a while. They met at a polo match in Bahrain. Rouf asked favours and she persuaded Hanley to handle property transfers for them. She didn't know what was behind it all. When it got too big they moved in Imran Akhtar to watch over Hanley. Akhtar is related to the Roufs. It was a nice set-up. Akhtar made sure Nick handled all the Roufs' deals. Who would suspect a middle-aged, upper-class white idiot of having his fingers in the terrorist pot?'

'They could have got all that information by searching his premises. There's boxes of documents at Weetwood now showing suspicious deals. There was no need to put you in there.'

'The documents won't show anything. The deals are all layered. The paper chase leads back to anonymous IBCs or offshore banks. They didn't have a clue who was behind it until I went in.'

'So how did you find out?'

'Nick told me everything about it – the Roufs, his

sister, the lot. He couldn't *wait* to tell me. The thing must have been like a lead weight for him. He needed to trust someone with it, share the burden. I was willing.' She stood forward, closed her eyes and towelled her hair dry. 'He's not dangerous, Pete. He's doing their washing for them, that's all. He couldn't hurt Mairead if his life depended on it. He wanted to *marry* me, for God's sake.' She stopped, realizing what she had said. Bains felt the look in his eyes – felt the hurt there – and looked away from her.

'I'm sorry,' she said. 'I shouldn't talk to you like this.'

'Why not? We're not together. We're colleagues now. That's it.'

She stepped towards him. 'I don't feel like that about you,' she said. 'I never stopped feeling what I felt for you. That was someone else in there with him. It was Anna Hart, not me. You have to understand that.'

He sighed. She wanted him to touch her, to say something reassuring, but he couldn't. 'That *was* you, Karen,' he said. 'Your psychological theories about it are totally screwed up.'

She looked at the ground, still standing right in front of him, naked, within reach.

'Dry yourself,' he said. 'Then we can get you some clothes.'

'I didn't know what I was doing, Pete. I'm sorry for it.'

He stepped away from her. 'So am I.'

She started to dry herself again. There were so many bruises on her body that he had to stop looking at her.

'Have you had anything to eat?' he asked.

She shook her head. 'I don't need anything.'

'You look skinny, Karen. You should eat something.'

'I've lost weight,' she said. 'I lost a lot of weight when we left here.' She looked around the bathroom and smiled. 'Everything is still familiar,' she said. 'Even the smells.'

'I lost weight, too,' he said. He felt uncomfortable. He was trying to keep his eyes off her. She looked at him and waited. 'Why did you leave me, Karen?'

She shook her head slowly. 'I don't know, Pete,' she said. 'I shouldn't have.'

'It's been hard without you.' He felt stupid saying it.

They walked through to his bedroom. It was unchanged from when it had been 'their' bedroom. He pointed out her clothes, in drawers inside the wardrobe. He had moved them, but not far.

'I have Mairead's stuff, too,' he said. 'All the things you left. It's still here.'

She picked out some plain underwear, jeans, a T-shirt, a fleece.

'I left you to do a job,' she said. 'Because they asked me to.'

'Is that how it happened? They asked you?'

'Yes.' She started putting on the underwear.

'Look at me and say that. Tell me the truth.'

She didn't look at him. 'OK,' she said. 'No.'

'You asked them?'

'Yes.'

'Why?'

She straightened the bra and pulled the T-shirt over her head. Her own clothes. She put the fabric to her nose and smelled it. 'I did it because I thought James Martin was coming after us. If he found Mairead he would take her off me. I had to disappear. It was the best way.'

He took hold of her arm, gently turning her towards him. 'Look at me, Karen. You never used to lie to me. That wasn't the reason. You know it wasn't.'

She faced him, in the T-shirt. He was standing very

close to her. 'No. That wasn't the reason,' she said. She put her face in her hands. She was breathing quickly. 'I don't know why I did it, Pete. That's the truth.'

'What was wrong with us? We were happy, Karen. We were perfectly happy. What was wrong with it?'

'There was nothing wrong with it.' She started to shake. 'I just couldn't stand it. I don't know why, Pete. It wasn't you. You were the person I've been most happy with, *as me*. But that's just it. *I don't want to be me.*'

He hugged her again, giving in. He squeezed her until the shaking slowed and she was able to look up at him. It felt like he was sliding into some kind of pit, but he couldn't get himself to stop. 'You will do it to me again,' he said. 'If we were to get through this, if we were to start again – you would do it to me again, wouldn't you?'

She shook her head, then looked confused and sat down on the edge of the bed. 'I don't know,' she said. 'The truth is I don't know. But I don't want to, and what I said I felt about you is what I still feel.'

'What?'

'You know what.'

She started to pull the jeans on. He took a deep breath. 'Assuming he's alive,' he asked, 'do you have any idea where Nick Hanley would be?'

'There are so many places.'

'Abroad? Why not out of the country?'

'I don't think so. Apart from the holiday cottage, he has no property abroad, no connections. His world is here. If he is in trouble, he will be hiding somewhere near. He will call me.'

'To say what? What could he want from you?'

'I don't know.'

'We need to take it to the inquiry. There's so much new information. We have to tell them what's going on. If we can't go to Sutherland then we have to go to Alan White.'

'Sutherland is running Alan White. You told me that yourself.'

'Or even to Sutherland. Why not to Sutherland? You work for him, Karen.'

'I *worked* for him. I'm out. The whole thing is fucked up. I should never have gone near him again. Stijn is here because someone blew my cover. For all I know that could have been Sutherland.'

'That's crazy, Karen. He works for the government.'

'You don't know what they're capable of.'

'For what reason? For what purpose?'

'I don't know.' She began to raise her voice, face turning red. 'But they've fucked me in the past and would do it again. I can't trust him.'

He took a breath. He wasn't going to get anywhere pushing against it. She was being irrational, paranoid. 'OK,' he said. 'So someone on the inside might have betrayed you. That was then. Right now they have a forty-man team looking for you and Mairead. We have to use it. We can't do this alone. How can they harm you if we go to them now?'

'They could give my cover away and put Mairead in danger. I don't know anything yet. I'm praying she's with Hanley, but what if Hanley, somehow, is with Stijn – or ends up with Stijn – what if Stijn tortured Hanley's sister to find out where her brother was and succeeded? He will be there now, with them. Mairead's only chance will be to deny everything, to act the part. If we take it back to the inquiry and someone blows her cover then she's fucked.'

'I know what you're saying, Karen, but they could do that *now*. They know who you are *now*. Why would you

337

coming in make a difference? They could blow your cover right now, if they were dirty.'

She had no answer to it. She frowned and started pulling on the socks and shoes. 'I don't know. You're confusing me, Pete. But that's just one reason. We can't trust them anyway.'

'Why?'

'Because they'll fuck it up. They'll find out where she is and put a helicopter over, or a convoy of cars around the place. They'll put snipers up, they'll bring in too many people, they'll fuck it up. They always do. They'll advertise it like a football match. Nick will find out – or Stijn – they'll panic and accidents will happen. You can't trust them, Pete – not Five, not Six, not the fucking police, not Special Branch, none of them.'

She stood up, fully dressed. 'Are you going to get my mobile or not?'

338

FORTY-NINE

He saw the kid running from him as he started to climb the stairs. He had gone halfway before he realized Hanley was coming up behind him. He stopped, took the gun out of the shoulder holster, turned and pointed it at him.

'You wait down there,' he said.

'I can't,' Hanley said. He was trembling like a leaf. 'I can't let you hurt her.'

'I'm not going to hurt her. I'm going to check her mother isn't here.'

'I've told you she's not. I don't lie.'

'No?' He stepped back down the stairs, waving Hanley in front of him until they were both back in the main room. 'So why is the kid here?'

'I was going to pick my sister up. They were there – outside her place. She'd left Rachel in the car. Until then I thought you still had both of them.'

Stijn smirked. 'You wouldn't have had to steal from your friends if you'd known they'd got away.' He watched a drop of sweat run away from Hanley's hairline. 'You're a weak little fuck, Hanley. I knew you wouldn't be able to go through with it. I knew the moment you didn't show that you were going to try to save the bitch and her brat. You should have known better.'

'I've spoken to Ahmed. I've spoken to him already—'

'Ahmed Rouf won't bargain for his own money. The bonds are his already. You think about that while I'm checking the kid.'

He turned to go, but Hanley actually reached out a hand, as if to stop him.

Stijn paused and looked at it, poised above his arm. 'What are you going to do?' he asked. 'Go ahead. Touch me. Let's see what happens.'

Hanley took his hand away. 'I won't let you hurt Rachel.' His voice sounded like a squeak.

Stijn laughed. 'Does "Rachel" know where we are?'

'I don't know.'

'Have you told her?'

Hanley looked at the floor.

'Have you told her where this place is?'

'Yes.'

'Good. I'm going up now. If you follow me I'll shoot her through the legs. Do you understand that?'

'You can't be serious.' Hanley's face was bloodless, staring at him in horror.

'I can do worse than that,' Stijn said. 'You know what I can do. She'll still do what I want if she's bleeding to death. Do you understand? You stay here and do nothing and she stays healthy. You come up and I fuck her. Got it?'

He nodded feverishly. He was a small, pathetic man; he would have been bullied all his life if he hadn't had money.

'Where's your mobile?'

Hanley took it out for him. 'It's a new one. I got a new one, like you told me . . .'

'Is there a land-line into here?'

Hanley shook his head. Stijn grabbed the phone, turned his back and stepped onto the first stair. Hanley was still standing there, rooted to the spot, as he closed the door to the stairwell.

The kid was in a room on the top floor, cowering in a corner behind a bed frame. He put the gun back in the holster when he saw that she was alone. No need to check the rest of the building. Her mother wouldn't have left her. He closed the door.

'Is your mother here?' he asked, to be sure. She shook her head, eyes wide with fright.

'Come over here,' he said. He sat on the wide window sill. 'I'm not going to hurt you or anyone if you do what I tell you to do.'

She stood up hesitantly, bottom lip in her mouth, hands at her side. She was wearing the same clothes. He could still see the stains where he had thrown the blood over her.

'Come here,' he said again.

She walked slowly up to him, stealing a furtive glance at the door.

'Don't think to run,' he said. 'You know what I can do to you. There's been a lot of mistakes made today.' He could twist it out of her, but it would take time. Maybe she was frightened enough already. He had never seen a kid sweat like that before. 'What I did this morning was a mistake,' he said. 'I'm sorry for that. For what I did to your mum and you. But it's done now. We need to move on and make sure it doesn't happen again. Do you want to do that?'

She didn't say anything, just stared at him like he was some species of wild animal.

'I need to talk to your mother,' he said. 'Face to face. If I can do that everything will work out. Do you know where she is?'

She shook her head.

'How did you end up here then? Tell me how you . . .' What were the words he was looking for? 'Tell me how you "lost" your mother.'

'Nick came and took me.' Her voice was thin, slight,

barely audible. A smell came to his nostrils and he realized she had wet herself already. He looked at the stain spreading down her trousers.

'You should have said if you wanted the toilet,' he said. He tried to smile at her, but he wasn't very good at smiling. She didn't react.

'Where did Nick take you from?' He heard a scratching noise at the door. He glanced towards it and watched her do the same. 'Where did Nick take you from?' he asked again.

'From outside his sister's.'

'And where was your mother?' The scratching was the cat trying to get in. He could even hear it mewing.

'Inside.'

'Inside Diana Hanley's?'

'Yes.'

'And you?'

She looked at the door. The noise began to irritate him. The animal had tried to rub up against his leg downstairs. He had kicked at it, but obviously it didn't learn.

'And you? Where were you?'

'In the car,' she said. 'Waiting.'

'Good.' Diana Hanley had told him all about Sharpe's visit to her. So far it sounded like the truth. Diana Hanley had also told him Sharpe wasn't with her brother. Past that she didn't know any more, because her brother hadn't told her that he was trying to use the stolen bearer bonds to get Sharpe and the kid released.

'Did your mother speak to Nicholas Hanley this morning? After you left the abattoir?'

'No. She didn't have a phone.'

He stood up. She backed away from him quickly. He could feel his skin crawling just thinking about the cat. He strode to the door and pulled it open. The animal ran past

342

him, straight to the girl. She tried to shoo it away – she could sense the danger to it – but the animal was too stupid. He stood for a moment watching her, then walked over to them, taking out his mobile phone.

'Do you know where we are?' he asked her. He tried not to look at the cat, still pushing itself against her legs.

She shook her head.

'Is that no?' he asked.

'No. I don't know.' Her face didn't alter at all. So she *could* lie.

'Hanley told you where we are,' he said.

She stared at him, face straight. 'I don't remember.'

'Is your mother a policewoman?'

She frowned, then shook her head.

'What's your mother's name?'

'Anna Hart.'

He nodded grimly. She was terrified of him, but she was still lying. He sat on the window sill again.

'Sit down,' he said, and pointed to the floor.

She crouched next to the cat, but didn't stroke it. When it rubbed up against her she pushed it away. She kept her eyes on him.

'Would you like to speak to your mother?'

She nodded, biting her lip. Tears came into her eyes.

'Do you know how we can contact her?'

'No.'

'Who would she go to, if you were missing?'

'The police. They are probably looking for me.'

He had heard another of the radio broadcasts not ten minutes ago, as he had driven up the road. Sharpe hadn't gone to the police. He didn't know why. They were still appealing for both of them under the names of Anna and Rachel Hart.

343

'She could have gone to the police this morning,' he said. 'When you escaped. Did she go to the police?'

'No.'

He put his mobile on the window sill and held his hand out for the cat.

'Why didn't she?'

'I don't know. She did call them.' She coloured at once, realizing her mistake. 'From a phone box,' she added quickly. 'She called them from a phone box.'

'Is that right?'

The cat walked over to him. He took his eyes off her and forced himself to look at the thing. It seemed to have no idea of its effect on him. He could feel his stomach moving, his mouth filling with bile. He opened his mouth and took a deep breath. It was trying to get affection off him. It wasn't very different to the cat they had when he was little. He could see the kid watching him.

'Cats make me ill,' he said, still looking at it. 'Physically ill. They make my skin creep.' He had to speak through gritted teeth. The thing was slithering around him, leaving its hairs all over, purring. 'Watch this and think,' he said.

He waited until it was between his legs then bent down and closed his hand around its throat. Twisting it upwards, he tightened his fingers quickly, bringing his other hand up to hold its body. He could hear it trying to hiss and squeal. He could hear the girl gasping, but he had to close his eyes. He couldn't even look at the thing as he did it.

He twisted its neck like it was a chicken. He heard the spinal column go, then the bones crunching as he rotated the head, pulling and twisting at the same time. When he had it through 360 degrees he let the thing drop to the floor.

He opened his eyes. The girl was still sitting there, rigid, both hands in her hair, face stricken, her mouth gaping. He looked down at the cat. Its back legs were kicking slightly, the head rolling around the floor, but the tongue was already protruding and the eyes were glazed. The same as chickens; it would be dead many seconds before the heart actually caught up and stopped beating.

He wiped his hands on his trousers. They were bleeding where the thing had scratched him. He felt sick from touching it. He cleared his throat and spat on the animal. The girl flinched.

'Does your mother have a mobile?' he asked. She closed her mouth but couldn't take her eyes off the animal. He could see its chest moving still. He waited for it to stop and her to look up at him. There were tears running down her cheeks, but no noise.

'Does your mother have a mobile?'

She nodded.

'Do you know the number?'

'No.' She looked again at the cat.

'Ignore the fucking cat,' he said. 'If you don't answer me correctly I'll do the same to you.'

He had her attention.

'Where did she get the mobile?'

'From the dead man.'

'Of course.' He picked up his mobile and pulled up Michael Kenny's number. 'You call her and you say exactly this – are you listening?'

She nodded. Her whole body was trembling and shaking.

'You say where we are – you know where we are, right?'

'Yes.'

'You say where we are then tell her to come alone or you die. Say, "Come alone or I die." Got that?'

'Yes.'

He pressed call and listened. The tone rang for twenty to thirty times before cutting off. Was the kid lying to him again? He tried again. The same thing.

'Have you lied to me?' he asked.

She shook her head, frantically.

'Come over here.'

'I don't want to.'

'Come here, so I can touch you.'

'I don't want to.'

He stepped towards her and placed a hand on her head. She was so light he could probably lift her off the floor by the hair. He eased himself to the floor, sitting down so close to her his thighs were touching hers. She went as stiff as a plank of wood.

'Think of another number,' he said. She was shivering. 'Where would your mother go? We have to contact her.' He pulled on the hair a little, rotating her head sideways and back so that her face was tilted back towards his. She was so close he could have leaned forward and kissed her, if he had wanted. She was making a bubbling noise in her mouth. 'Concentrate,' he said. 'Where would she go?'

She said something, but she was sobbing so much he couldn't make it out.

'Speak clearly,' he said.

'To Pete Bains.'

'Pete Bains?' Where had he heard that name before? Was it another trick. 'Who is he?'

'We were living with him, before we met Nick.'

'You think she would go back to him?'

She tried to nod.

He released her hair. 'OK. Number two. Let's try Pete Bains. If he answers you don't speak to him. You only

346

speak to her. Do you know his number? Do you remember it?'

'I think so.'

'Tell me it.'

347

There was something wrong with her. It took him time to sense it. At first she had been so distraught he had seen only that. The emotions hitting her were so extreme there was nothing she could do but tremble and cry. He had tried his best to console her, holding her, reassuring her. She had seemed like Karen then – a broken, stricken Karen – but still the woman he knew. It had been difficult, beneath all that panic and grief, to see the changes. But then she had wanted to wash herself.

He could understand it from a simple level – she had been raped, she felt soiled, damaged – but that left out the urgency. He felt a dense, black anger looking at her injuries, thinking about what had happened to her. But that was nothing compared to the urgency. His heart was racing with fright every second they were standing there, doing nothing. Mairead was out there somewhere, they didn't have a clue who with. She was in danger. Every minute that passed the chances of her being harmed increased. There wasn't time to chat idly in the shower about Nicholas Hanley, or consider what had happened between them eighteen months ago. There wasn't time to wash, to change clothes, to talk. They had information. They had to get it in, quickly. They had to get to the inquiry.

She wanted him to recover Anna Hart's mobile phone, as if sitting around waiting for a phone to ring on the basis of some guessed theory would help at all. She was worried about Sutherland, about things getting screwed up – that was a part of her and always had been – but this was at another level. This was paranoia, something clinical. She had no idea how to find Mairead. No idea at all. There was nothing they *could* do but go to Alan White.

'This phone has been ringing,' she said. She handed him a mobile. 'It belonged to the guy I knifed – Kenny. He's tampered with it, I think, so it doesn't store any numbers. Someone just called twice, while we were in the bathroom.'

The guy I knifed. She said it with no emotion. He felt terrified thinking about it. What was he doing here speaking to her? There were bodies all over the city. This 'Kenny' was probably still rotting on some abattoir floor where she had left him. She had done nothing about it. There would be clues from that body which would point back to the conspirators. They had to recover them and use them, link them in to the rest of this. Even the phone – he dropped it suddenly on the table, as if it would burn his fingers – was full of forensic traces. And she was handling it as if it were a toy.

'Karen,' he started, 'we have to talk about this.'

'There's nothing to talk about. We go to Weetwood. You get Anna Hart's phone and copies of anything else that might help. We have to dig in and work it out. Even if he doesn't call, there will be links we can follow, just you and I. We will be able to find her. We've done this sort of thing before.' She sounded insane.

'There's forty men waiting to do that,' he said. He felt helpless. There was no rationality to her thoughts. But to call it in would betray her.

She had been crying her eyes out minutes ago. Her mood had swung from grief to coldness; fixated on the phone, she was moving around him as if all this were normal. She turned from him and opened the patio doors.

'The car is out the front,' he said.

'We can't go out the front. There's an eye watching your place.'

'An eye?'

'One of Sutherland's lot. Waiting for me. I saw him when I got here. We will have to go out this way.'

'But my car is out the front—'

'We can take another one. It will be safer that way.'

'I don't have another one.'

'I didn't mean one of yours.'

His phone started to ring. Did she mean *steal* a car? He took his phone out, held it to his ear. He had to get her in to Weetwood. This had to stop.

'Hello?'

He froze. A child's voice.

'Mairead?'

She was over to him in a split second, pulling the phone from him. She took it so quickly he thought she'd broken his fingers. He watched her face blanch. She staggered, reached out a hand to the table. He could hear her gasping for breath.

'Mairead?' she shouted. Her voice cracked and she spun towards him.

'She's gone.' She looked at the phone desperately. 'How do I call back? How do I recover the number?'

'What did she say?'

'*Help me!*' she screamed at him. '*I need to call back!*'

He took the phone off her and searched for the number. 'It's withheld,' he said.

'No. No. No.' She sank to the floor, shaking. 'I could hear him,' she said. 'I could hear him shouting at her . . .'

He stooped beside her, trying to understand. 'Who? Who could you hear?'

She began to pull her hair with both hands. 'That man. I could hear that man. Stijn . . .'

He caught his breath. 'What did she say, Karen? Where is she?'

'She said she loved me . . . Shit . . . I called her "Mairead". He could have heard . . .'

'Did she say where she was?'

'High Top. Delph. In Lancashire.'

Delph. He knew it from walks on Saddleworth Moor. 'OK,' he said. 'I have maps from walking there. We'll find High Top and call it in. The Lancashire Force can be there in minutes.'

'No.' She stood up too quickly and fell back against the table. He put out a hand to help her, but she knocked it away. 'No. We can't,' she said.

'Karen—'

'We can't. He said for me to come alone. I could hear him shouting. She was crying, Pete. She was crying. She sounded terrified. He said he would kill her if I didn't come alone.'

FIFTY-ONE

Mairead barely had time to say the things he had told her to say before he was grabbing the phone off her and shouting into it. She started to cry, sobbing things out to her mum, hoping she would hear. But Stijn was laughing. He threw the phone away and pulled her head back by the hair. She felt him pressing his face up against hers and didn't know what he was doing. She tried to pull away from him. His hands were holding her head against him, twisting her face towards his. She started to blubber and scream.

The door opened suddenly, swinging back on its hinges. Stijn released her, turning towards it. She saw Nick standing there. He had a gun in both hands – a long rifle with a telescopic sight. It was the same gun she had seen him use when they went target shooting. He held it up to his shoulder, aiming. There was a flat, percussive bang. The gun jerked backwards and Stijn rolled across the floor, a hiss of air coming out of his lips. She scrambled away from him. Nick worked the bolt to get another round into the breech.

His hands were jumping around, shaking, sweat running down his face. He was too nervous. Stijn started to pull himself to his feet.

'Run, Rach!' Nick shouted at her. 'Get out of here!' He turned the gun around and swung the butt at Stijn. It struck him across the side of the head with a cracking noise. Stijn's feet slipped beneath him. She forced herself up and ran to the wall by the door. Nick shouted again: 'Get out. Get out of here.'

There was blood coming out of Stijn's left leg, at the top, near the groin. He slid down the wall until he was flat out on the floor, in front of Nick. Nick swung the gun into his back. A low-pitched, grating noise started to come out of Stijn's mouth. Nick took a step away and tried again with the bolt. She wanted to turn her eyes away from it. His hands were too unsteady, too slippery with sweat. She couldn't bear to watch but couldn't turn away. She stood by the door with the breath rushing out of her, transfixed.

Stijn began to move. He was like a massive bear, all his movements ponderous, slow. He began to pull himself along the floor, towards Nick, leaving a trail of blood behind him. His eyes were popping out of his face with the effort. Nick kept taking a step away from him, still trying to get the gun to work. When Nick's back was pressed against the wall Stijn stretched out an arm and grabbed his ankle. Nick turned the gun to hit him again, but Stijn pulled his leg away so suddenly and with so much force that Nick spun backwards, head banging off the wall. His body hit the wooden floor like a sack of cement. The gun slipped from his fingers.

Stijn got both hands on his legs and began to pull the body towards him. There was blood on Nick's head and his eyes were opening and closing rapidly. Stijn twisted his fingers through his shirt, hauling at him with both hands.

She started to scream. Nick wasn't moving. His head was twisted to the side like something was broken. Stijn was dragging himself up his body, grinding his teeth with the effort. When he had his face above Nick's, his chest leaning on him, he pulled his head back then drove it down into Nick's face. She heard bones breaking. Stijn twisted to look at her, face bright with blood. She turned from the wall and ran.

She could hear him headbutting as she ran. Over and over again. He began to shout as he was doing it. She got to the end of the long passageway and tripped down the bare wooden stairs, almost falling, sobbing to herself the whole way. Even when she got past the next landing and down the next set of stairs, back into the main room, she could hear him shouting above her, and the thudding noise as he smashed his head into Nick's face.

She opened the front door onto a freezing blast of wind and pitch blackness. For a moment she faltered. Stijn was still cursing at the top of his voice. Then she heard a loud crash, as if he had thrown something across the room. She took a breath and stepped into the night.

FIFTY-TWO

The M62 was closed. Karen banged her fists off the steering wheel in frustration. The signs were up at Chain Bar junction – snow and ice in the hills, blocking it from Ainley Top. She let the car glide through the slush onto the slip road, then stopped on the hard shoulder.

'Give me the map.'

In the front passenger seat, Pete was still worried. 'We need to call it in, Karen. They could be there ahead of us.'

'They won't be anywhere ahead of us in this weather.'

'They could get a helicopter up there.'

It was a fixation with him. Call the thing in, get help. He didn't understand because he had never been here before. He had led a life littered with grief and loss, but he hadn't lived with sociopaths, psychopaths and killers. He hadn't watched how they worked, how they reacted to threats. If Stijn even caught a whiff of rotor blades or blue striped vans he'd go off the edge.

'A helicopter is the last thing we need,' she said. 'Give me the map.'

He passed her the map. It hadn't taken them long to find High Top because she had seen the name twice before – on one of the documents she had taken from Akhtar's place at Pudsey and in the paperwork at Diana Hanley's stables. Akhtar's documents were in the abandoned car, where she had left them, but she could recall the photo of the place.

She remembered the whole address when she saw it on the map: *High Top, Brun Clough, Delph*. Brun Clough was a feature at the head of a narrow valley running from

355

Delph into the Pennines. On Bains's walking map there were a group of buildings there called High Top Farm. Above them was Standedge – the highest ridge of the moors, the watershed between Lancashire on one side and West Yorkshire on the other.

The place was isolated. The road over the tops to Marsden, Slaithwaite and Huddersfield ran near to it, but it was minor and twisting. If they had closed the M62 there was no chance a smaller route would be passable. The M62 was the quickest way over, but there were others. She scrutinized the map.

'We can get to it from this side,' she said. 'From the road leading up from Marsden.'

'That's the A62. It will be closed.' Cars crawled past them on the slip road, wary of the slush.

'I know that. But we can get as far up as we can, then walk. High Top is just over the summit. We can get to these buildings here, hopefully.' She pointed them out to him. 'Then leave the car and walk. There's no other way.'

'If we call Alan White—'

'He will do nothing. If we can't get there, he can't. It's as simple as that. And they would never put a helicopter up in this muck.'

She pulled onto the motorway and drove to Ainley Top. There were barriers across all the lanes, flashing multi-coloured lights, two traffic cars. Past them the road looked clear of snow, but the highest stretch was still ten miles away. She pulled off and started threading her way through the back roads in the valleys between the M62 and Marsden. The night was dirty and dark, the sky full of cloud, but it wasn't snowing.

There was no traffic crossing the valleys to Slaithwaite, and no snow in the fields around them, but it started to hail as they came down the long bank towards the A62, big pellets of ice that bounced off the windscreen like stones. She drove quickly through Slaithwaite and almost immediately passed a flashing sign at the road side: 'Snow and ice – A62 closed at Standedge'. She said nothing. Bains sat beside her, mute, looking away from her.

Marsden looked bleak, hemmed in by the dark mass of the moors, with tight rows of terraces on steep cobbled lanes, high mill walls and a bridge over a fast-flowing, swollen torrent – the River Colne. The hail was coming down thick, whipped across the road in sheets by the wind coming off the moors. The few people they passed were scurrying around under umbrellas. They hit another illuminated sign at the other side of the village, as the road began to climb: 'Standedge – snow and ice – road closed when lights flashing'. The lights were flashing.

'We'll get there,' she said. Bains looked over to her, opening his mouth to speak, then closing it again.

'Say it,' she said. 'Say what's on your mind.'

He sighed and ran a hand through his hair. 'I'm frightened, Karen,' he said. 'I'm really frightened.'

'That's normal,' she said.

The hail stopped suddenly, as if it had been switched off. She tried to see the hills around the car, but it was too dark. As the road turned and the headlights passed across a field, she could see fresh snow, higher up the slopes. The air in front of her looked crisp, frozen, with patches of ice shining on the road surface.

'*You* don't seem frightened,' he said.

'I'm not thinking about it.'

'I can't help thinking about it. Why would he want her to call you? Why give you the address?'

'Because he wants to get me there.'

'Why?'

She shrugged. 'To kill me.'

He nodded, the crease in his brow a dark, deep line. 'That's what I thought,' he said.

'That doesn't worry me.'

'It doesn't worry me either. We can deal with it. But if he wants you there to kill you . . . and he has Mairead . . . then there's no reason . . .' He stopped.

She had been pushing this thought from her brain since leaving Heaton. 'Why keep Mairead alive?' she said, voicing it.

Pete stared out through the windscreen.

'I can't think about that,' she said. 'She is alive.' She had to swallow her breath to keep it from sticking.

She drove in silence, struggling with the tension. The road was beginning to climb steeply now. At the side of it drifts were beginning to appear.

'I'm afraid of what we might find,' he said. His voice was hoarse, holding back the emotion. 'I'm really frightened, Karen.'

'I can leave you here,' she said. 'You don't have to come.'

'That doesn't solve anything.'

'At least you won't have to look.'

He glared at her. She kept her eyes on the road. Snowflakes began to float in the headlight beams.

'Snow,' she said.

'I've done this before,' he said. 'You know that.'

She didn't answer him. She didn't want him to start talking about it, to put images in her head.

'I found Millie,' he went on. 'I found her dead, floating on her face.'

Millie. His dead daughter. She tried to think of something else.

'I haven't told you this,' he said. 'But I was on the phone at the time . . .'

She thought about Anna Hart's art gallery in York, rented for her by the government because Nicholas Hanley had been displaying his amateur paintings there for years. It was an easy way to meet him. She thought about the weeks spent learning about modern art.

'. . . I was talking to someone when I should have been looking after her . . .'

The snow was quickly getting thicker. She slowed down. The road surface was still clear, but to either side of it the drifts were tall slush-stained piles thrown up in the headlamps.

'. . . I was talking to a woman . . . I was on the phone when I should have been watching her . . .'

It was no good. She had to silence him. 'Be quiet, Pete, please,' she said. She spoke gently. 'You *have* told me this. You've told me it all before.'

'I have never told anyone this before. I was talking to a woman. I was seeing someone else. That's why I was distracted . . .'

She stopped the car. 'You have to shut up, Pete. This isn't helping.'

He looked at her, eyes grey and tired. 'It was my fault,' he said. 'I didn't realize she had been shouting until I hung up. I ran down to her . . . she was floating there in the middle of the pool. My daughter.'

She rested her head on her hand, propped against the door frame. She started counting, mentally, waiting for him to stop.

But he had already stopped. She looked over to him. 'Can we get on now?'

'I don't know whether I can go through that again,' he said.

She drove on. She felt angry with him. 'You won't have to,' she said. 'Mairead isn't your daughter.'

The wheels began to slip. 'Ice,' she said. 'There's ice on the road surface. How much further do we have to go?'

He looked gloomily at her, as if she had heard nothing he had said. 'There's a pub about a mile further on,' he said. 'It's just before the pass over the tops. It will be closed for winter. If you make it there then we haven't far to the top.'

The car was an old Renault not made for dealing with ice. It had been the first unlocked vehicle she could find. It took her nearly ten minutes of stubborn coaxing to get it up to the pub he had spoken of. By then she couldn't see the road surface for snow. The pub was a big place, but completely lightless and closed up. There was a rope across the entrance to its car park. She pulled straight through it and stopped.

'We won't get any further,' she said. 'We will have to walk from here. How far to the top?'

'Not far. In summer it wouldn't take you twenty minutes. In this weather we might not even be able to find it.'

She opened her door. 'I'll find it. Are you coming?'

He reached behind the seat and passed her a head torch he had brought. He fitted one over his own head.

'You know I am.'

FIFTY-THREE

Mairead ran through the snow, trying to get away from the noise, thinking she would just keep going, however deep the snow, however far it was. She ran past the cars and up the lane, but before she reached the end of it the cold gripped her chest in a vice, stopping her. She wasn't sure what happened if you froze to death, but she knew it was possible. There would be no cars on the road – unless Stijn came after her – no one to rescue her. She would never make it down the valley without a torch and proper clothes.

She turned back. She climbed the stone wall flanking the lane and dropped into the field alongside, remembering that you could see right up the lane from the windows of the room Stijn was in. But the field was full of snow, almost to waist height. She sank into it, twisted her ankle and staggered forwards, falling full length. Wet through, she ignored the pain in her ankle and headed for the lights from the building. There was a wind blowing across the field, so icy it made her face and hands sting as though they were burning. She couldn't feel the pain in her ankle, couldn't feel her fingers or her toes. She climbed another wall, further behind the house. In the distance, up at the house, she could still hear a noise, carried to her on the wind. It sounded like a dog moaning.

The farmhouse was surrounded by buildings, too many of them to count or be properly aware of in the darkness. She picked the biggest, an old barn with a high, vaulted roof. There were huge padlocked doors at the front and a smaller, wooden, sliding door at the back, also padlocked.

She kicked the snow away from the bottom of the door and found a small gap where some planks were missing. She got onto her belly and crawled in.

Inside, it took her eyes a while to adjust. There was light shining in from the house, through a cobwebbed, begrimed window, high up in the roof vault. She had expected the place to be empty, but as soon as she got to her feet massive, glinting shapes jumped out at her. She held her breath and forced herself to stand still. The shapes became clearer. It was farm machinery, stacked around the walls and into the roof space, the kind of machines you hooked onto the back of a tractor. At the furthest end, almost buried beneath bales of hay, there was a tractor with both its big wheels removed, standing on chocks. The smell was stale and damp, a mixture of engine smells and wet, rotting hay. But it was out of the wind, and quiet. She began to look for a place to hide.

There was a gallery running around the place about twenty feet above the floor, with two ladders up to it. At the furthest end of the barn the light was so poor she couldn't make out what was there. She walked into the darkness and felt with her fingers. There were sharp spikes protruding from something – a ploughing or raking machine, leaning back against a stepped mound of soggy bales. She squeezed past the machine and started to climb up. Her feet sank into some of the bales as though they were mud, and cobwebs stuck to her face, but she didn't care. She didn't care if there were spiders, rats or mice. She just needed to get away from Stijn.

The hay was piled almost to the roof rafters. The gallery broke off either side of the pile. She rested on a level with the gallery and searched with her fingers until she found a gap in the bales. She squeezed through and pulled a bale down to cover the gap, leaving a hole at the top to let air in. She let herself sink back into the hole, let her breathing slow. Then she really began to shiver.

She could hear nothing, not even the wind outside. It wasn't like she had read in books. The hay did nothing to warm her. She had never been so cold in her life. The clothes she was wearing were drenched from where she had fallen into the drift. Now the water in them was freezing, so they were as stiff as cardboard.

She wasn't good at judging time without her watch, which she had lost somewhere that day, but guessed it was over half an hour since she had spoken to her mum. Her mum would come, she knew that, but would she be quick enough? She didn't know whether she could stand this for much longer.

The cold seeped into her like a drug. The shivering stopped at the same time as the pain in her limbs. Everything became numb. She began to feel really tired. She tried desperately to keep her eyes open, to listen, but it was so difficult. She knew what was happening, she knew that this was what happened when people got hypothermia. She forced her mind to think of nothing but staying awake.

She hoped that if Stijn were not dead he would never know she was there. If she kept very quiet and very still he wouldn't see her even if he opened the big doors and came in. She guessed she only had to keep awake for half an hour more, at most. Then her mum would come.

She did what her mother had taught her to do when she was panicking. She started to count to herself. She concentrated only on the numbers and pushed all the other thoughts from her mind. The picture of Nick, lying there, his head horribly twisted, kept trying to jump before her eyes, but she wouldn't let it. If she thought about what had happened she would start to shake and cry. She didn't have the strength for that.

She had reached 2,747 when she heard a splintering noise coming from the doors. Someone was breaking the lock. She began to breathe quickly, trying to hold her breath and yet breathe faster all at once. She tried to bring her hand up, to cover her mouth, but her arm wouldn't move.

She saw a shaft of dim light pierce the darkness above her and heard a heavy sliding noise. He was opening the door. She tried to move her body forward a little, to be able to see through the crack between the bales. Her body wouldn't move. She wanted to scream. None of her limbs would work.

She closed her eyes and concentrated, flexing her fingers in her mind. She tried again to move her legs. They moved suddenly and sharp pains shot up her thighs. She brought her hand up to her mouth and clamped it over her lips. Her fingers were like blocks of ice. She placed a hand behind her and inched herself forward, controlling her breathing, going very slowly.

The crack was tiny. She flattened her face against it and let her eye adjust. The door was in front of her, wide open, but she couldn't see the space immediately below her. The machinery leaning against the hay was in her way. She could see the spikes sticking out of it. She tried to move slightly, to see around them.

He was leaning against the wall of the barn, right by the door, resting heavily on a piece of wood or metal, clutched beneath his arm like a crutch. He had a gun in one hand but he wasn't looking around. His head was sunk forward and he was panting heavily. She could see blood all over his face, all down his trouser legs. She could even see the light reflected in little puddles of it, leading away from him, back into the snow. He had tied something tightly around the top of his leg, where Nick had shot him.

She saw him move his head slightly and realized what he was doing. He was listening for her. She stopped the breath in her throat and froze. Her heart was beating so loud she was sure he would pick it up.

'I know you're here,' he said suddenly. His voice was thick, the words coming between gasped breaths. 'I know you're here. I know you're watching me. I can feel it.'

She thought her heart would burst with fear. A tiny strangled sob started to wriggle up her throat. She sank back into the hay and clamped both hands over her mouth.

Please, Mummy, please. Come now.

FIFTY-FOUR

Karen could see the line of the road snaking through snow drifts for about a hundred yards. After that everything was black. She set off almost at a run, trying to follow the road. Bains kept about ten paces behind her.

Within minutes they were in the middle of a blizzard. She switched the head torch on and looked for a fence, a line in the snow – anything that would show where the road was. She could see nothing. All around her there was nothing but snow and darkness. She stepped into it, heading uphill. After a few steps she sank up to her thighs.

Bains came up beside her, took her arm and shouted into her ear. 'Over there.' He pointed into the night. 'We walk over there and then look for the next one.' The wind was so strong he had to shout. She took a few paces after him. There was a shadow in the torch beam, deep behind the flurries of snow. Bains was already moving towards it, getting ahead of her. She chased after him, stumbling across uneven ground, praying she wouldn't turn her ankle.

It was a short, squat stone tower, about fifteen feet high. The snow had drifted into it, almost burying it at one side. Bains made his way around it until he found a set of steps leading up to a doorway. They stood on the steps, sheltered from the wind, bodies pressed against the tower. Bains struggled to get out the map.

'It's a ventilation shaft,' he said. 'There's a line of them running right over the top, and there's one near High Top Farm, on the other side.' He showed her on the map.

'Ventilation for what?'

'There's a three-hundred-year-old disused canal that runs under these hills. Railway tunnels, too. The main cross-country line to Liverpool runs right beneath us.' He banged his hand off the dirty stonework then pointed through the gaping doorway. She looked in.

The place was ruined, covered in graffiti, stinking of fungi and urine. There was an opening no bigger than a manhole to one side with a thin grey vapour rising through it. She looked over the edge into a cavernous black shaft.

'I should have brought a compass,' Bains said, behind her.

They stepped back into the gale and walked around the tower, looking for the contours of the land. At the far side there were the broken remains of a shute, leading from inside the tower back out onto the hillside.

Bains shouted, 'When they were excavating the tunnel they brought the rock up through these shafts.' He pointed to a steep slope down to the moor, a slag heap. Then he showed her it on his map. 'We go that way,' he said, pointing uphill.

They skirted the slag heap and made fast progress. The snow began to thin, revealing stiff, long blades of grass. Within ten minutes she was covered in sweat and breathing furiously. She kept behind Bains, following the beam from his head torch. The next tower was smaller, round rather than square, capped and unused. They couldn't get into it.

'We're getting to the top,' Bains said to her. 'Not far now.' The wind was so strong now that he had to place his mouth right against her ear to be heard.

By the time the ground began to flatten she was out of breath. Then, as her feet started to move downhill, the snow stopped and the wind dropped off. No more than three hundred feet above her the clouds were racing past in long, broken trails, like mist. Between them she could see stars and moonlight. Ahead of her on the downhill slope was a series of dry-stone walls. She could hear her breath, gasping, her feet crunching through the snow, her heart. At the first wall she stopped, waiting for Bains to catch up.

'I can't see anything,' she said to him. 'Where is it?'

'We're over the edge now,' he said, panting. 'It should be straight ahead.'

She set off again, going so fast she almost collided with the next wall. She saw a diffuse pattern of light in the darkness ahead of her and headed directly towards it. Within seconds she realized she was looking at a building, with lights on. She watched as currents of air broke the cloud above it. It was a farm complex.

'That's it,' Bains said from behind her.

But already she was beginning to sprint.

FIFTY-FIVE

He stood for so long, head cocked, listening, that Mairead thought she would faint. Then he began to move. She watched him lift his head and squint into the darkness, turning to search from one end of the barn to the other. She saw him sniff the air. He took a step forward, uncertainly, still leaning on the crutch, then brought up the pistol and swung it in an arc, from one end of the barn to the other. Her legs began to shake.

'I can smell you,' she heard him murmur. 'I can smell your frightened body.' Then suddenly he lifted his head and screamed at the top of his voice: 'COME OUT!'

She jumped back, unable to stop herself. The bale she had been leaning against moved, widening the gap. She could see him walking towards her now, dragging the wounded leg, waving the gun in front of him. Then he stopped and did something to the gun. She heard a click, followed by a sliding noise. He stepped forward again, limping. She pushed herself back into the hole, wanting the bales to bury her. But she could still see him. The gap in front of her was wide open. He pointed the gun at the base of the hay bales. He was standing right beneath the upturned machine.

The first shot sent her heart into her mouth. The noise was a terrific, deafening crack. She moved her hands to her ears. He fired a second, then a third. He was moving the gun around, pointing it at different parts of the haystack. A scream began to slip through her throat. She saw him look up, directly at her. Their eyes met and she lost control.

Her brain reacted automatically, catapulting her forward. She was shrieking at the top of her voice. It was one step to the edge of the bales and another to the cast-iron framework of the machine. She threw herself at it, leaping into the open, landing with both feet on the thick metal bar, then kicking off. She felt it move under her feet, saw another shot explode beneath her, then she was flying through the darkness.

She landed on her chest, the air driven out of her, then rolled, forcing herself to keep moving. She had crossed from one pile of hay to the next. She fell sideways, falling onto the front of the tractor, then down onto the ground. Her head banged off something hard, she saw stars, heard a crashing noise behind her. She pushed herself to her feet and scrambled towards the doorway. She looked back only when her feet were out into the yard.

The noise had been the machine falling. At first all she could see was the machine, flat on the floor where Stijn had been standing. Then she saw him. He was on his back, underneath it. His head was twisted and staring at her, a howling noise coming from his open mouth. The gun had been knocked from his hand and there was blood spreading out beneath him. One of the machine's spikes was pushed straight through his body, at the top, near the arm. It was pinning him to the ground. She stepped forward, unsure, thinking she should either pick the gun up now, while he was down, or turn and run. Behind her she could hear someone shouting.

As his hand reached out to retrieve the pistol she realized it was her mother.

FIFTY-SIX

Three quick reports, one after the other, a gap, another one, then a little girl's scream, high-pitched and terrified. Bains saw Karen break her pace in the snow, lose her footing and fall. As she came to her feet a man began to howl in the darkness.

They had two walls to cross before they could get to the place. Karen began to shout as she was running, calling out Mairead's name. She was about twenty paces ahead of him. He saw her go over the first wall, then glimpsed a child running across the front of the main building. He stopped and yelled at the top of his voice, cupping his hands around his mouth, 'Lie down, Mairead! Take cover!'

He could see her clearly now – taller than when he had last seen her. He wanted her flat on the ground, out of sight, immobile. He scanned the windows of the buildings frantically. Where had the shots come from? He called out again, the same instruction: 'Get down!'

She turned towards him, then Karen shouted something else. She was clambering over the last wall. Mairead began to run towards her. He took his mobile out. No signal. He reached up, switched off the head torch and started to sprint.

He fell over the first wall, stumbled through a field of snow-covered rocks and made it over the second wall in time to see Karen in a crouch, pulling Mairead with her to the safety of a ditch. The torch on her head was still on, flashing its beam all over, advertising their position. He threw himself to the ground and began to pull himself towards them on his belly.

'Switch the torch off!' he yelled. He got to his knees and ran in a half crouch, zigzagging, his blood bursting in his ears. He went past them and straight on, throwing himself into a snowdrift behind a parked Volvo.

He crawled forward under the wheels and looked along the line of land between the buildings. He saw movement from within a tall barn and looked back to where Karen and Mairead were. He could hear Mairead crying, but couldn't see them.

A man came into view, bent over, staggering – Stijn, a gun in his hand.

'Keep down!' Bains shouted back to them. 'Keep your heads down!' The man heard and twisted towards him, pointing the gun towards the car. He saw a puff of smoke from the barrel, a whiplash of sound, then something shattered above him. He flattened himself out.

He counted to ten then looked up again, quickly. Stijn was moving away, between the two buildings and out into the darkness behind them, limping, a hand held up to his chest. Bains waited until he was out of sight then crawled back to Karen.

She was holding Mairead to her chest, trying to stop her sobbing. He lay down on his back beside them and waited to catch his breath.

'It's Stijn,' he said. 'He's run, I think. He took a shot at me. He has a pistol. Is Hanley here, Mairead?'

'He's in the house,' Karen said. 'Stijn has hurt him. He shot Stijn in the leg. Stijn is wounded badly. Which direction did he go?'

'Out the back, past the buildings. He's running, I think.'

Karen prised Mairead away from her. 'We've got to keep on him.'

'He's armed, Karen. We can't.'

She moved into a crouch and looked towards the house. 'Does your phone work?'

'No. No signal.'

'Shit.'

'We should get in one of the cars, try to get away.'

'I'm going into the house. Nick is in there. Mairead says he had a gun. I can't let Stijn get away. You stay here with Mairead.'

'No, Karen—'

She was up already though, running across the space between the ditch and the open front door. He looked at Mairead, wiping her eyes, shivering. She looked so terrified he wasn't even sure she had recognized him. He reached out and took her hand.

'It's OK, Mairead,' he said. She stifled a sob.

FIFTY-SEVEN

Karen went straight through the open front door and rolled across the floor, fearful Stijn would have doubled back and re-entered through the back. The torch came off her head. She took it in her hand, looked at the empty room then moved through to the kitchen. A plate of uneaten meat on the floor, the rear door closed. She crouched down and went up to it. It was locked.

She searched the rest of the house quickly. On the third floor she found Hanley. He was dead. She didn't even have to touch him to know it. She felt nothing looking at him. All she could think of was Stijn. Hanley's hunting rifle – a big 7.62-calibre Parker-Hale with telescopic sights – was on the floor beside him. The bolt was stiff. She eased it carefully, ejecting a spent cartridge. There was one left. She shouldered the rifle and moved back downstairs.

She kicked the lock off the back door, opened it and stepped again into the freezing night. Beyond the pool of light thrown out by the house lights she could see nothing. She listened. The wind was blowing into her, but there was no noise. She fitted the torch around her head again and walked quickly past a shed, into the space between the big open barn and the house. There was a clear trail of blood in the snow, mixed with large, unclear footprints. Her eyes traced it from the barn out into the darkness. She switched the head torch off and followed it, squatting low until her eyes adjusted.

She had gone only twenty paces before another building started to come into view, the same construction as the ventilation towers they had followed from the other side of the moor. She went down onto her belly and crawled through his footprints until she reached it. The footprints ended, but she could see no doorway. She raised herself cautiously and immediately heard a faint clanging noise, from somewhere above her. She climbed the stones and peered over the edge.

The tower had no roof. Below her a large, circular ventilation shaft was wide open, plummeting down into a lightless void. Two caged ladders were attached to the inner walls, alongside each other. The noise she could hear was footsteps on the rungs. He was down there, climbing down the ladder. She switched the head torch on and shone it down the smooth, wet sides of the shaft. She could see to about fifty feet down each ladder, but he was further than that, lost already in the blackness.

She pulled back and took a breath. Heights had never bothered her, nor darkness. She wasn't Anna Hart now. She would have to go after him. She looked back towards the house and saw Pete Bains crouching at the back door, Mairead behind him. They were looking for her. Pete had his phone held to his ear and was speaking into it. She stood up and ran over to them.

'He's gone down a ventilation shaft,' she said. 'I'm going after him.' She stooped and pulled Mairead to her, kissing her. Pete was saying something, objecting, telling her he had got a signal, that the local police were on their way. But she cut in, interrupting him.

'Get her warm,' she said. 'Keep her inside. Do you know how many tunnels there are down there?'

Pete started to shout at her. Mairead started to cry. She brought her hands up, covered her ears and repeated the question. He told her there were two train tunnels and a canal tunnel, all interconnected, all nearly three miles long.

'But not from here,' she said. She remembered the line of the tunnels from his map. 'If he gets to the bottom it's less than a mile to the exit on this side of the moor. He will be out the other end before we can get a car through this snow. I have to stop him.'

She turned without looking at Mairead and ran back to the tower, shouldering the rifle as she went. This time, as she leaned over, she could no longer hear Stijn. He was strong, built like a bull, but wounded. Maybe he had lost his grip, fallen. If not he would have a head start on her, but he would be slow. She climbed the stones to the ladder, lowered herself down to the first rungs and began to descend. As her head disappeared below the lip she could still hear Mairead crying.

FIFTY-EIGHT

It was like a wind tunnel, the air rushing into the shaft from outside. The metal rungs were ice-cold and slippery, covered with freezing moisture. When she turned her head to look down, the beam lit up about fifty feet of the stonework below her, then lost itself in a suspension of tiny water droplets rushing downwards and past her in dense, shifting layers, like rain.

She hung on tightly and moved slowly, methodically. The ladder was narrow, no more than a foot across. She tried to count the rungs. The motion of stepping down them became quickly repetitive. She had to concentrate to keep her limbs co-ordinated. The head torch only confused her – reflecting off the stones with every movement of her head – so she reached up and switched it off. She allowed the darkness to swallow her. Every fifty rungs she stood with both feet on the same rung and listened to her own breathing. She allowed her left arm to hang loosely, resting it, then did the same for the right.

By the time she was a hundred feet down the draught was roaring around her ears like a gale. The further she went the stronger it became. The currents were funnelling around the bore in a vortex. She squinted into it and tried to see the light from the sky above her. The opening was almost invisible. A pale disc of light, shifting and blurred through the rain.

Somewhere past three hundred the rungs disappeared beneath her. She rested her legs, then felt around in the space beneath, reaching her feet out to the sides while hanging on with her arms. There was nothing. The ladder had either stopped or broken off. She reached up and switched on the head torch. Above her she could see nothing but a hail of water falling into her face. She turned the beam downwards and tracked it along the edges of the shaft. There was an opening built into it directly beneath her, a wide archway of massive stones, about eight feet below the end of the ladder. She could just make out a solid surface beneath her. She put the torch back onto her head, lowered herself to the last of the rungs and let go.

She landed awkwardly. The bottom of the shaft was strewn with broken rocks and deep puddles of water. Picking herself up, she tore the torch from her head and circled it quickly around her. He wasn't there, he hadn't fallen. She looked for blood, but there was so much water coming down the shaft it would have been quickly washed away. She took the rifle from her back and stepped down through the archway.

She was in an arched tunnel, about twenty feet high. The water vapour falling down the shaft behind her was billowing into it in a thick mist. There was a wind coming through it that was strong but not as powerful as in the shaft. To the left, in the direction she guessed to have been east, back towards the house, the darkness became impenetrable within feet. In the other direction she could see a faint, diffuse light, far into the distance. There was no sign of Stijn.

She guessed she was in a railway tunnel, long disused. Along the middle, running past her feet, there was a fast-flowing shallow stream of water. She could see the remains of sleepers piled along the sides. The iron railings had been removed. The construction was stone, the same stone that had walled the shaft, but the place was like a pin cushion. Everywhere she shone the torch there were tiny jets of water forcing through the stones, coursing off the sides and running into the stream. In places the stonework had crumbled and collapsed into the shaft. She shone the torch around her and listened to the wind rushing past her, the water trickling and dripping into the darkness. There were no other sounds.

The stream was flowing west, downhill. It took her a while to realize that there was an incline. She began to feel her way towards the light she could see in that direction. In the murk it had looked no more than a slight shift in the texture of the darkness, but it was a narrow opening in the tunnel wall. She turned into it and walked through a shaft not much higher than her head. She came out into another tunnel, running parallel to the one she had left.

It was the main-line railway tunnel, still in use. The light she had seen was artificial. There were cables running along the walls and bright yellow lights on both sides, spaced at about fifty-yard intervals. Wider and higher than the previous tunnel it was well drained and maintained. Along the middle were two parallel sets of rails, the light reflecting off the gleaming iron surface. She was enveloped in silence. There was no wind, no water. A dim yellow glow was spreading out through a thin, gently stirring mist, brightest at the points where the bulbs were, but quickly fading in the spaces between. Behind the dank mist she could smell soot and engine grease. The walls of the tunnel were thick with it, a deep black deposit layered across everything she touched.

She switched off the torch and listened.

A long way further along she could hear someone panting, footsteps stumbling across the sleepers. She peered into the gloom but the mist was too thick.

She began to run. As she did so she became aware of a background humming, growing slowly in intensity –

either an extractor fan, a generator, or the combined buzzing of the light bulbs. It was impossible to tell. It was too faint and too low to be a train. She stepped between the first set of rails onto an even surface of black gravel chippings and began to sprint.

She took it in short bursts, each time stopping to regain her breath and listen. The footsteps became louder. She was gaining on him.

She passed a connecting shaft back down into the older tunnels, then another, and worked out that they were evenly spaced. Still she could hear the panting ahead of her, still the mist was too thick to see more than the distance to the next light. From the noise she could tell that Stijn was walking, not running. She would catch him.

She missed her footing on the sleepers, stumbled and fell. When she looked up she saw the mist stirring around her, disturbed by her motion. The noise ahead of her had stopped. As she watched she saw the mist around the next light part slightly. A human silhouette formed out of the darkness, the light behind it. He was standing in the middle of the tunnel, motionless.

She placed her hand on the rail next to her and could feel it buzzing. She held her breath. The humming noise was mounting rapidly in intensity. Beneath her she could feel the ground beginning to shake. A train. She stood up and looked for a shaft down into the lower tunnel. The space between the rails and the tunnel wall wasn't wide enough. She would have to find a way out quickly. She began to step forwards, towards the noise.

The humming turned into a deep rumble. The ground began to vibrate violently. The mist began to sink and move. She could see Stijn clearly now. There was a cold draught on her face. Within seconds it had become so strong that the mist was being swept away beneath it. She stepped out into the middle to look for a gap. A wall of wind hit her with a force so strong that she almost lost her balance. She saw a light, becoming quickly brighter, then the yellow lights in the distance were suddenly obscured by a huge, swelling black shape that seemed to completely fill the tunnel.

As it rose to meet them on the incline the single headlight split the darkness with a brilliant, blinding beam. She stumbled towards the wall, and brought her hands up to cover her eyes. Then, in the brightness she saw an opening in the tunnel, not ten feet away from her. She began to run towards it. By the time she got to it the sound in her ears was deafening. She looked along the tunnel to see Stijn framed brightly in the beam, the train rapidly bearing down on him. The light behind him was so intense his silhouette was engulfed by it. She scrambled frantically for the opening in the tunnel wall. She had just enough time to see Stijn move to the side before her feet found the connecting shaft and she fell to her knees.

The locomotive passed within inches, it seemed. She flattened herself against the flagstones as a thundering blur of metal and light crashed past her in the darkness above. Behind the engine came the carriages, a massive flashing chain of indistinct images. She watched the wheels rattling and squealing along the rails, saw the windows streaming into a long band of light and covered her head with her hands. Behind the train came a sucking backdraught of air so polluted with coiling black smoke she had to hold her breath. She waited until the darkness had closed about her again before standing up. Her legs were trembling.

She stepped out into the tunnel.

Stijn had not come back out. Turning back to the connecting shaft, she ran quickly down to the lower tunnel, switching on her flashlight. Stepping into it she was just in time to see a figure crossing it ahead of her. He was moving straight over, towards an opening in the opposite wall of the tunnel. She dropped to one knee automatically, without thinking, steadying the gun against her leg, trying to see through the telescopic sight. The lighting was ridiculous, the target so small there was no room for precision. She saw movement through the cross hairs and pulled the trigger.

The noise was loud, reverberating and echoing in the enclosed space. The flash from the muzzle was so blinding that for seconds afterwards she could see and hear nothing. She remained in position with her eyes closed and the gun held out in front of her. As the blast faded she could hear a slow cracking noise running through the roof of the tunnel above her. The rocks were shifting, groaning, splitting. Millions of tons of earth, not thirty feet from her head. Holding her breath, she looked up at the stonework. There was no visible cracking. She looked back to the opening where Stijn had been. There was nothing. One shot and she had missed.

She threw the gun to the ground, stood up and began to sprint again. Where he had disappeared the torch beam picked out another shaft, narrow and suffocating, so low that she would have to crouch double to pass through it. It ran sharply downwards. Instead of smooth flags there were steep steps. The stream running through the first tunnel was coursing steadily down them. She took them two at a time, trying not to slip in the water. At the bottom, she passed through a massive subsidence in the roof of the shaft, clambered over a pile of rocks and almost fell face first into a long pool of still black water. She shone the torch onto it. It stretched into another tunnel, deeper than the other two, completely filled with stagnant water. The canal. The oldest tunnel. A profound, subterranean silence closed around her.

The surface was smooth, unruffled. Stijn had not gone into it. She shone the torch across it and picked out the far wall. The water was at a level about three feet below the roof, and it was impossible to see whether there had ever been a towpath. She leaned forward and peered along the surface of the water. The tunnel was dead straight, inundated. She could see nothing beneath the surface, couldn't tell how deep it was. The atmosphere was oppressive. She felt her pulse quickening, the panic rising within her gut.

All around her the roof of the connecting shaft had caved in. She shone her torch upwards and saw that the landslip had created a cavern about thirty feet high. The water was dripping off the bare, exposed rock. She was in an unstable cave, more than five hundred feet below light and air. She needed to get out of it quickly.

Shooting had been stupid. It had almost brought the roof in and it had obscured her view. It was clear that Stijn hadn't come down here, which meant he was still in the tunnel above.

She manoeuvred herself cautiously up the pile of riven, jagged rock that had come out of the ceiling. It was only when she got to the top that she saw the blood on the stones at her feet. At exactly the same time she sensed movement to the right. She spun quickly, trying to get the beam of light into the darkness. He came at her as she realized her error, launching himself forwards in a blind, clumsy tackle. She was still turning as he hit her.

She fell backwards, her body hitting the ground with a tearing jolt, her head banging back against the rock. The head torch went out. He handed on top of her, his weight against her chest, driving the air from her lungs. She could feel his hand trying to find her windpipe, the breath hissing out of his face. He was pinning her to the rock, trying to strangle her.

She began to writhe and struggle, knocking the hand from her throat and lashing out at his face. Her fingers caught hold of his neck but slipped away immediately. His skin was wet, covered in blood or sweat.

Pushing against his face with one hand, she began to feel around the ground with her fingertips. Her fingers closed around a loose rock and she brought it against the side of his head. She felt his strength falter. She managed to knock him sideways, enough to turn onto her side and begin to crawl away. Within moments he was back. She struggled to twist and felt something hard being pushed against her ribs.

A gun. She brought her left hand down and caught hold of it, forcing it away. She could hear her voice screaming at him. If he fired in here they would both die; the ceiling would come down and they would be crushed.

It became a desperate struggle to control the gun. He managed to get on top of her again, one hand around her throat, the other trying to bring the gun into her face. She tried to twist sideways but was being held fast by his weight. He started to shout at her, the words in a foreign language. The effort of pushing the gun away made her pant and gasp for breath. Her arms quickly began to tire. The gun was moving closer to her face, Stijn screaming at her through clenched teeth.

She couldn't do it. The gun was already against her body. He could pull the trigger at any time. She began to yell and shout, trying to squirm away from the barrel. She managed to get her hand over his mouth and lock it under his chin. But he was still too strong. She couldn't push his head away. She shifted her attention to his eyes and tried to get her fingers into them, her other hand still fighting with the hand that held the gun. She could hear her own voice, shouting in the darkness, begging him to stop. She was weaker. Even wounded he was stronger and heavier. She was going to lose. Even as she got her fingers to close over one of the eyes and began to dig in she felt the barrel of the pistol pushing against her neck. Her head began to cloud. Within seconds the thing would be against her face.

Abruptly, something gave way. The change came suddenly, his body collapsing onto her. She turned the gun away from her face. Where her hand was pressed against him she could feel his eyes closing, the head dropping forward. His breath began to come out in short gasps.

He had lost too much blood. He was slipping into unconsciousness. She moved her hand around the gun until she could feel his finger, where it lay across the trigger. She began to twist the thing away from him, trying to loosen his grasp. She had to be quick. He was fading now, but he might recover. She pushed her own finger under his, right on the trigger. Above her his whole body was leaning towards her, the head lolling forward. Suddenly, he began to convulse. Even as it started she knew what was going to happen. She felt his finger tightening against the trigger. There was nothing she could do.

The flash was like a starburst, the noise searing her ears. The report crashed into the space above them, the single explosion swelling rapidly into a deafening, percussive echo. Mounting in intensity, it filled the cavern, bouncing off the rock, shaking everything. The ground beneath her began to shudder.

She pushed Stijn sideways and rolled from under him. She began to crawl quickly back towards the tunnel entrance. Even as she found the first step she could hear the rock giving way. In a rush of dust and debris the roof came in. The noise was like an earthquake. She lay in a tight ball, hands protecting her head, waiting for something to hit her.

FIFTY-NINE

When silence returned she moved her hands away from her head and felt into the darkness with the tips of her fingers. She could see nothing. Debris had fallen close, but not a single rock had hit her. She checked her body for injuries. The blood running down her neck was from the back of her scalp, where she had hit it on the ground. Feeling for the wound she found that the head torch was still strapped around her head. She pulled it off and examined it with shaking hands. The battery had become disconnected. She struggled to link the wires and held her breath as she turned the switch. It worked.

All around her the air was thick with dust. She shone the beam through it and saw that the steps out of the place were intact. She walked carefully back up them until the entrance to the main tunnel appeared through the murk. She was not trapped. Carefully, she retraced her steps to the cavern below and began to look for him.

He was buried. She could see his limbs protruding from beneath a pile of stones at the edge of a larger fall. She started to clear the rocks away from him. It took a while. One rock was so large she had to walk back into the railway tunnel and find a length of wood to use as a lever. She worked quickly, throwing the loose stones down the slope to the canal.

The body she unearthed was shattered. One of the legs was twisted back beneath it. She straightened it out. The bone in the thigh had come clean through the flesh and was protruding through a tear in the trousers. There was no reaction as she moved it. It looked like the bone

387

of a cow, or a pig – a big, thick length of splintered bone.

The legs were soaked with blood, great pools of it gleaming in the light of the torch. She could see it pumping from beneath the trousers. She realized that if blood was still pumping the heart was still beating.

She pulled the chest round so that the body was lying face up and looked into the eyes. They were wide open and staring straight at her. The face was black with soot, the eyes two bulging white circles. Not expressionless, but living, focusing. The pupils were dilated in shock, the expression glazed, but he was alive.

'I can't feel anything,' he whispered. The voice was startling, faint but clear in the silence, the same high-pitched South African accent. 'I'm cold and I can't feel anything . . .' The words trembled as they crossed his lips. The unknown was with him now, reaching up to drown him. He was afraid.

'That's because you're dying,' she said. Her voice was flat, without emotion.

'You have to help me. I can't get out of here if you don't help me.'

She laughed. The noise echoed around her. It sounded cracked, insane. 'It's too late for that.'

She reached down to where the bone was sticking through the leg and moved it slightly, watching his face. He didn't react.

'Your spine is broken,' she said.

He tried to cry, whimpering in his throat. But nothing came out of his eyes. She stood back and watched him. He looked like a clown, blubbering through a mask.

'. . . You have to help me . . . if you help me I can live . . .' The words were coming in short bursts, breath snatched between them.

'Tell me who put you on to me and I'll help you.'

'Ahmed Rouf.' He answered at once.

'I know that. Tell me how they found out about me.'

'. . . Akhtar . . . the *kaffir* . . . he recognized you from Bradford . . .'

She sighed. So Imran Akhtar had started it all. Not Sutherland, not someone inside.

'What was your contract?'

'You.'

'Just me?'

'You and the kid.'

'For what? To do what?'

'To kill you both.'

She ran her hands across her face, thinking about it, imagining it. He started to gasp for breath. She leaned closer to him. 'Was Hanley in on it? Did Hanley want me dead?'

'. . . He tried . . . Hanley tried to save you . . .' His voice broke up and he began to choke. She watched, wondering whether that would be it, whether he would die then and there. She felt frozen. She reached into his mouth and prised the false teeth away from his gums. She threw them backwards, over her shoulder, into the canal. He started to breathe again, but there was frothy, pink blood in his mouth, from his lungs. She wiped her fingers on his clothing.

'Did he want me dead?'

'. . . He tried to save you . . . he stole bearer bonds from Rouf, to bargain with him . . .'

'But he knew what was happening?'

He didn't answer. His eyes were rolling, the lids closing. He no longer looked like the man who had raped Anna Hart. He looked broken, pathetic.

'What was meant to happen to Hanley?'

389

'. . . Get him out . . . fake his death . . . get him out. Because you knew about him. Because he was loyal. They were to give him a new identity. They should have just killed him. They gave him a chance, but he couldn't do it . . . he couldn't let the kid die . . . After the fire I lost him . . . he took the bonds, made contact with Rouf to try to save you . . . I had to find him, get the bonds back . . . I thought you would know where he was . . .'

'Who was the man you burned – the one you threw from the tower?'

He tried to move his head, eyes closed. '. . . Nobody . . . a nobody . . . he owed them money . . . that's all . . . a drug dealer . . .'

The eyes snapped open and he stared up at her. He began to plead again, his voice so faint she could hardly hear it. She crouched down and looked at him.

Nothing was how it seemed. She had been to zoos when she was little. She could remember looking into the eyes of tigers. There was nothing in the eyes of a tiger. A tiger's eyes would reflect the same thing whether the beast was pacing in a cage or pulling flesh from your bones. But the eyes staring up at her now were not like that. They were normal human eyes. The eyes of someone frightened and helpless. At some point he had even soiled himself. She could smell it. She looked at the blood gathering in a dirty puddle on the ground around him and felt so disgusted she began to retch.

She stood up. He started whimpering. She thought for a moment that she would simply walk out and leave him there. Leave him to die.

But she couldn't do it. She took hold of him under the arms and began to drag. The body was a dead weight and it was difficult. She could hear him trying to form words, trying to thank her. The ground fell downhill to the start of the canal. The surface was uneven, strewn with rocks. It was a struggle to get him to the water's edge.

She could still hear him trying to thank her as she heaved him into it. She got his head and shoulders in, then bent down and pushed the rest. The head went under quickly, then the whole body found its level and floated back up. She stood back and watched. He was belly down, face turned into the water, the limbs hanging uselessly, frantic bubbles of air boiling around his head.

She began to count. She had reached fifty before he began to tip, slowly, the feet and legs sinking first, the chest following. As the chest dipped under the head came up above the surface, gasping for breath, still alive. He was starting to scream as he went under. Shouting for his mother. The water closed over him, silencing it.

A stream of bubbles rose to the surface. She shone the heat torch there, trying to see movement below. The beam bounced back at her. She waited. He didn't reappear. The ripples spread out in a wide circle, lapping against the stonework.

It was as though he had never been there.

SIXTY

As she turned to leave, the heat torch began to flicker. She could feel the shock of it all. Her chest was heaving, her heart pounding. She staggered back through the tunnels like she was drugged, banging off the walls and tripping up. There were no thoughts in her mind. Just confusion.

She found the freezing tunnel of air plummeting out of the ventilation shaft and, looking up, didn't know whether she would have the energy to make it.

The climb seemed endless. Very quickly her arms and legs grew so stiff she had to pause and rest every ten steps. Her feet slipped off, her hands missed the rungs. Halfway up the torch fell off her head and went crashing into the darkness below. From the beginning she could hear shouting from above her. She knew it was Mairead's voice, but couldn't make out what she was saying.

As she neared the top she saw their faces leaning over, watching for her. She pulled herself onto the stonework slowly. Pete held Mairead away from her until she was clear of the ladder. Then they collapsed in a heap, Mairead hugging her, crying again, Pete talking incessantly. It felt as if every bone in her body had been beaten. She felt no relief.

They walked her to the house where Hanley's body was. In the darkness, down the valley, they could see blue flashing lights, but nothing had so far made it up the road. They closed the doors on the cold and sat at the table in the main room, silent. The body was above them, stifling everything. Pete said there were still four hours until midnight. Mairead was pushed up against her, Pete had his arm around both of them.

'Is it over now?' Mairead asked her.

She nodded, staring into space.